·C·H·R·I·S·T·O·F·E·R·U·S·

or
Tom Kyd's Revenge

·C·H·R·I·S·T·O·F·E·R·U·S·

or

Tom Kyd's Revenge

ROBIN CHAPMAN

SINCLAIR-STEVENSON

To Joan Littlewood

First published in Great Britain 1993
by Sinclair-Stevenson
an imprint of Reed Consumer Books Ltd
Michelin House, 81 Fulham Road, London SW3 6RB
and Auckland, Melbourne, Singapore and Toronto

A CIP catalogue record for this book
is available at the British Library

ISBN 185619 241 5

Typeset by CentraCet, Cambridge
Printed and bound in Great Britain by
Butler & Tanner Ltd, Frome and London

'O world, no world but mass of public wrongs
Confus'd and fill'd with murder and misdeeds'

Tom Kyd

·P·R·O·L·O·G·U·S·

TAMBURLAINE:	Who's this?
THERIDAMAS:	The governor of Babylon.
TAMBURLAINE:	Go bind the villain. Hang him in chains
	Upon the ruins of this conquered town
	And let our soldiers shoot at him.
ME:	Do all that's worst. Nor death nor Tamburlaine
	Torture or pain can daunt my dreadless mind.

The day I played the governor of Babylon was that very day our auxiliary soldiers overshot and killed the woman suckling her child. At first no one could believe it. Oh, people's eyes saw, their ears heard, but minds in a theatre are seldom ready for real hurt. Were these screechings part of the action? Was this another attempt to provide spectacular horror? Why not? The author of the play was renowned for excess. But no. This was no actor. This woman was one of the audience. Her breasts were real and spouting blood. Not our property pig's blood either bought fresh each morning at Smithfield but her own heart's blood, her life's blood. The redness fountained out of her as she flung her baby at our painted heavens. The tightly swaddled lump, more chrysalis than creature, soared towards the fixed stars, turned over and fell to be caught by Tamburlaine himself.

In the pandemonium that followed I was quite forgotten, left to hang on my mock-marble pillar. We had two to uphold our world. That afternoon the prompt-side one was doing duty for Babylon's battered walls. Despite theatrical appearances to the contrary I felt very comfortable up there on my hook.

Let me explain. Under my governor's costume (slashed apricot velvet) I wore a leather harness with a brass horse-ring poking out at the back. As I was hauled up, festooned in chains for execution, this ring slipped over a hook on the pillar and the unseen harness distributed my weight quite evenly. The chains were purely decorative, of course. All I was then required to do was to plead for my life, fail to deflect the Scythian tyrant from his purpose, mime terror, and finally, as our soldiers fired their volley of blanks to one side of me, simply groan and writhe before becoming dead meat. Oh, and I too spouted blood. But mine came from bladders concealed in my sleeves which I pummelled and squeezed in my death throes. I was rather proud of my performance on the pillar. I'd rehearsed it three times that morning under Christofer's direction and he'd said I was far more effective than our usual governor (he'd lost his voice in a Thames fog) who was much older than I. It made a death all the more dreadful, Christofer thought, to see a beautiful young man, such as me, so ruthlessly destroyed. I agreed and put my heart and soul into it. But in the event I was ignored.

As they carried the dying woman outside I had time to realise my own good fortune. Why, I could've been her! My luck had held against the odds. As ever. As – to hell with hubris – it always would. And at this thought I began to laugh. And laugh again. Part of me said, stop this, stop it, how can you? But at this self-injunction my laughter redoubled, became a bloated monster, a bellowing hippogriff with a heaving life all its own inside my stomach, solar plexus, chest. To control it was agony. I was sure I'd burst and in my squirmings wrench out the hook that held me so high above the stage. The hanging corpse had, as is said in the theatre, corpsed. It often happens, especially in tragedy. Enacting a solemn scene the player finds something funny – a look in the eye, a misjudged piece of business, a property not planted. And starts to laugh. At once he tries to repress this inappropriate response. But at this the damage is done! For as firmly as you try to quell your amusement so the pressure builds inside you to release it. You become a plugged volcano until the top blows off and the torrent of red-hot laughter spews everywhere. It's a thing every actor fears and – dare I say it? – surreptitiously enjoys. At least in the telling afterwards. How we boast of such subversive moments, what legends we make of them – a week later.

But then as suddenly as it had begun my laughter left me. Perhaps because I had no one to share it with? And was replaced by the oddest sensation I've ever felt. Where before I'd imitated the impact of those eight bullets, now, as if in the grip of some hideous magic, my body seemed to feel them pierce my skin and explode on bone. And I jerked and bucked accordingly. This was beyond pretence. This was like some mysterious fleshly commiseration with that woman's dreadful fate? Or was it? No. Let me be honest. This was also a kind of cowardice. Yes. Wild funk. And next, yes, next I felt my bowels melt. And not with compassion either. No, this was liquid fright. It was running down my legs. Yes, I was shitting myself most shamefully. For all to see. Though no one did, I think. Well, not at first, not at that precise moment of liquefaction. Everyone was too busy pushing and shoving to get out. The galleries resounded with thudding feet.

Half an hour later, when the woman had died, all our extras had been arrested and my fellow actors came to get me down, their noses wrinkled. Tom's running bowels became a running joke however much I protested the narrowness of my escape from death that November afternoon.

We never discovered who'd placed the bullets in our carbines. Our company armourer (a most trustworthy ex-militia man) denied all culpability; he had loaded them himself with blanks in the presence of several reliable witnesses. Our extras swore their innocence under duress and were eventually released. Christofer insisted an agent of the Lord Mayor had done it to provoke a riot to get the theatre closed; others supposed that the Privy Council itself had ordered it. I said I couldn't believe in such conspiracies against us. Why, we were favourites at Court and had already been booked to present four plays at Christmas. As always I was wrong.

Nor – naturally enough – could I recognise this incident for what it was: a fateful rehearsal for my future.

Oh, yes, I've hung once again on such a pillar. But not in a theatre, not so comfortably and not to be shot at with bullets blank or otherwise. No, this second time was at Her Majesty's pleasure. The pillar was stone, there was no hook and no convenient harness. My own weight was arranged to supply my own discomfort. To relieve it all I had to do was to betray my friend to Eliza's intelligencers.

Eventually I did. Whereupon I was congratulated. I asked what time it was. My interrogators smiled out of the sun at me. I'd been placed so I might be dazzled by the windows' slanting light while they spoke from inside their own shadows. One said, 'It's five o'clock, sir.' Another, 'Listen and you'll hear St Mary strike.'

As the clock nearby resounded amid an outcry of gulls I began. I heard myself say, my voice a decrepit whisper, 'I'll tell you everything, gentlemen. Everything you need to know. Everything.' They smiled again. They nodded. They agreed I had agreed to do so. My new world, new condition, three days in the making in their forcing house as they call it, was now kind and softly spoken.

It's from this moment that I measure my broken times. From that five o'clock of that fifteenth of May. I won't say in this year of Christ. This year's beyond redemption. A fallen angel of a year, God help us. Not that I've ever entirely believed in Him but I do allow He may help those of sounder faith. Indeed He should if He can. If. The issue's doubtful. Where's the health in any of us now? This age is rotten, the state worse, our sufferings deserved.

I've devised a calendar. In it days are years. It begins, exactly at the moment I've just described – last May – the clock striking, seabirds screaming, me saving my skin, well, some of it. According to this crackpot calendar I am today one hundred and four. I certainly feel it. A sprig Methuselah! Though God forbid I should ever come to rival our venerable ancestor's final count of nine hundred and sixty nine. Too many. Far too many for poor Tom. I couldn't bear them. Each one a log to my bent back. And me with only one good leg to support such a load of day-years. Oh, no! I'd rather hobble straight to hell. Christofer would say I'm there already. 'Why, this is Hell, nor am I out of it.' He's right. Look! I can see four devils at its mouth. I can hear 'em cry, 'Here comes another customer. See his knee? Look at his hands. The fellow can hardly hold a pen let alone walk. Welcome, sir, dear sir. You know how to squeal, don't you? Or so we've heard? You're a by-word for betrayal.' And I'll say, 'Aye, gentlemen, do your worst. It'll be as nothing to what Eliza's demons have already done.'

Oh, my mind! As crippled as my body. No thought in it is straight. Even as I think one thing another nags to be considered. And then another. So many. A howling pack of thoughts tearing at each other while baiting me. No! Be off with you! Get away from here! Let the place be cleared. Let *me* be clear. Give me plain thoughts in due order. Yes. Think one thing at a time. Let me start where I am. This place first. Describe it. Then time – but measured by a less fanciful way than heretofore. And finally let me recount what I've done. Yes. Confession must be my task. I've nothing else. Take thought. And start. Confess. Confess everything.

·T·E·X·T·U·S·

·I·

I am in Sussex. I inhabit a black and white summer house. It would be pretty if the weather was. This has been a most unseasonable August. Such winds, such rain, such unremitting dullness. The harvest faces ruin. The farmers predict famine and for once I think we may believe them. But meanwhile I'm cosseted here – swaddled in luxury. Crippled I may be but I live in perfect comfort. My bed is soft, my diet good, my clothes clean. And here I'm welcome to remain as long as I wish. Quite hidden from the world. Lost to view. Gone to earth. I'm as if I'd never been.

Who's disappeared, did you say? Who? Tom Kyd? Kyd? Would you say we've heard of him? Remind us. Oh, that fellow? Yes, I seem to remember the name. Yes. Didn't he write a rather well-thought-of play? I'm sure we saw it at the Red Lion? We didn't? Not at Newington Butts? No? Very well if you say so. At the Rose then? Right. Yes. What was it called? *Don Horatio*? No, it was more like *Spain's Tragedy* or – or, yes, it's coming back to me now – *Hieronymo's Mad Again*. Oh, heavens, yes! Such fun, so macabre. Hugely effective. Buckets of blood. Especially when the old dad finds his murdered son's body hanging from the trellis. And the boy playing the girl was a peach, wasn't he? So luscious. One could've eaten that one whole. And you knew the author? Fancy, lucky you.

There! I've broken my own rule. I wander out of all bounds the very minute I resolve to be simple and straightforward. Mind you, I've known a dozen theatregoers who talk just like that and as a playwright I've always been the first to take refuge inside other people. But no longer. This time I'm determined to be myself. So back to here. To where I am.

This ornamental shepherd's cottage stands on a knoll with a view of the South Downs. Its position immediately proclaims it a rich man's toy; a place built for amusement. Cottages for the lowly lie low. Sometimes when the wind is southerly you can hear the sea. The crest of the hill directly in line with my window is crowned with a dark knot of oak, ash and thorn. Chancton Ring it's called. The folk here say it's old and full of magic. They may be right. I've visited the spot several times, limping my way up the hill, and have found it strangely consoling. There's a magpie mystery about it. Your heart takes ease there.

I have an occupation of a kind. I'm neglecting it now to write this. My benefactress, whom for a number of reasons I prefer not to name, has encouraged me to translate a play from the French. It's a dull thing. The tragedy of Cornelia, wife of Pompey the Great. I suspect she's set me this schoolboy task as part of a regime for my regeneration. She's an active woman hating idleness in herself and others. Noble, dark, contemptuous. Her wit's sharper than a dragon's tooth. But offered a fire hot enough I suspect she might melt. In my former, sporting days I might've relished the challenge. I call her Pandora. Not to her face, oh no. To myself. To identify her, to secure her within this hidden away world of mine. To her face I say *madam* or *your ladyship*.

My meals – breakfast, dinner, supper – all arrive punctually from the great house that stands beyond a grove of mossy oaks where fallow deer graze at will. I too am at liberty to wander where I want. Pandora insists I continually exercise my knee. That way, she says, my limping will become a brisk soldier's motion suggesting past heroism.

My nights could be shared if I chose. I have only to say the word. Last week, for instance, Pandora offered me the pick of four of her girls. She assured me that whoever I selected would be thoroughly examined by her own doctor and then delivered to my bed scrubbed to pink perfection.

At my refusal she frowned. She said, 'I hope the attentions of our Blessed Virgin Eliza spared your manhood?' Pandora hates the Queen. Perhaps they're too alike? Except Pandora is much younger, of course. And far more handsome. The Queen's beauty is in the eyes of her beholders and the hands of her hairdresser – not to mention her dressmakers.

I said, 'Yes, my lady. Mr Topcliffe spared those particular parts of me.'

'I daresay he was hoping to remove them officially on the scaffold?'

'I expect he was.'

'Then for that at least you may be thankful, Thomas.'

When Pandora calls me by my full name there always seems to be irony in it. When I'm plain Tom I feel she simply likes me. Both impressions may be false however. She's not a transparent person. She glitters yet is opaque. Like an opal set about with diamonds. But to tell the truth, despite the comparative mercies of the Queen's favourite torturer, I've felt little or nothing stir below my belt since this new age of mine began. So here I sit, still entire but quite unstirrable, aged one hundred and four.

Days, I mean of course. Days of the real world. Today, this day in the turning world of the corrupt, the crawling, the so-called chivalrous, it's the twenty seventh of August. A hundred and four days – fancy *adieu* – since, since, since – no, I can't say it. I can't! No. Oh, God! Having named this day as my day of all days, the day of my confession, I find – I'm panting with the effort of evasion – I find I cannot do it! It's too terrible a secret. And too like that other document I put my hand to. I mean the one I signed last May. And yet I yearn to admit it. I know I must. But how? How?

Perhaps I can come at my crime like a crab? Seize it sideways – as though it were a shrimp? There. Already I belittle it in search of false comfort. It's no shrimp at all; rather a leviathan. In the scales of sin my crime weighs among the heaviest. It's cardinal not venal. I shall join those thousands fixed in ice up to their necks whose tears freeze even as they fall. I once aspired to translate the sweet Tuscan poet but his nimble threefold rhymings quite defeated me. As much as the fearsome matter of his hell's ninth circle haunts me. There, worshipful reader, down in that profundity, you may find all those who betrayed their own flesh and blood. Oh, yes, I count Christofer akin to me. He was my spirit's son, my heart's brother, my friend, my lover, my pupil, my better. I taught him everything I knew. He took it as of right and like a runner with a torch outstripped his rivals. Left us all behind. Gasping for breath that wasn't there. Was I jealous? Of course I was. We all were. Every man-jack scribbler in London was jealous of Christofer. But only I betrayed him.

And I'd been closest to him. Oh, yes, I shared his glory. And had enough of my own to make me feel, on occasion, his equal, his co-mate. We lived together, worked together. We named ourselves Castor and Pollux, those heavenly twins begot by Zeus upon a minor river-god's wife. Sporting Zeus posing as a cockswan to get between the legs of our silly simpering mother, Leda! How we laughed at that. It suited us in our violent success to see ourselves as the fruits of an ingenious, curiously exciting rape. Christofer and Tom – the prize poets of the town, free to attempt anything, to astonish all, to offend most. We were licensed fools more quick-witted than our masters. Or so we thought. Never conceiving in our vainglory that others, hidden from us, managed the machinery of state, dictated life itself, manipulated our very existence each and every day, with more dexterity, more cunning than we had ever dreamed of. Oh, we boasted we knew everything about the world and presumed that this was true. To listen to us was to pierce through all corruption, all connivance, all human wickedness. Life, we said, was a child's story of cruelty and greed so obvious it was laughable. We were the children.

Oh, my hand! How it disgusts me. I mean my writing – my script. I used to boast the most accomplished hand in Gray's Inn. I began as a lawyer's scribe, a scrivener like my father except he also dealt in bonds. And became wealthy. He's still alive as is my mother. Their shame in me is measureless. I wrote from prison imploring them to visit me. I wished they would, I wished that they would wish it, too. They didn't. They came nowhere near me. Didn't even reply. Perhaps they burned my letter without reading it? The plague was increasing at the time so perhaps my parents were understandably concerned for their health?

The reason my handwriting is a meandering snail trail is crudely simple. What happened happened like this. After I'd told my interrogators all they required to know concerning Christofer, and after I had appeared before the Privy Council where I was again congratulated upon my cooperation with the state, I was restored once more to Topcliffe's custody. He'd been instructed, I supposed, to deliver me straight to prison where I would be held at Her Majesty's pleasure. But foolishly I hadn't allowed for the Queen's executioner's pleasure. I'd assumed in the flood of relief at my torments being at last at a stop that Topcliffe's cruelties had been part of a purely professional practice quite devoid of personal animus. Wise child was wrong. Topcliffe at once completed my education, my introduction, at the late age of thirty-five into the ways of the world as it really is; and not as I and Christofer had poetically imagined it. Oh, we'd portrayed beastly tortures and cruel deaths galore upon our stages and convinced ourselves we mirrored life. We did. Except that at the close, our victims and our dead rose smiling to receive applause. Topcliffe's play was different.

First he broke my left knee with a pistol held at no range at all. Point blank except it wasn't blank. Then he smashed the fingers of both my hands with a blacksmith's hammer. Only then was I transported to prison. The Queen, Pandora tells me, publicly deplores such usages while insisting her chief interrogator enjoys her complete confidence. She calls him 'our unfortunate necessity' or, with reference to his diminutive size, 'our exiguous instrument'. And then giggles. With age and absolute power she has become a great giggler, Pandora says.

My broken knee is Topcliffe's signature. It marks me at once in public. Were I to walk again from my lodgings in Bucklersbury into Poultry and Cheapside all the market men, like my conjured demons, would know me at once for what I am: Top's man. I dare swear I'd meet a dozen of me in a morning. We left-leg hobblers are a common sight in the city. We serve as a powerful warning to others to love Eliza Regina and to hate the Whore of Rome.

Can I teach myself to like this scrawl? Make myself prefer it to my former hand? Convince myself it reflects a poignant history whereas the others I professed were mere form, as pretty as they were professional? Our minds, it is said, can accommodate anything.

My scrivener's script were all Italianate in style. I bevelled my broad pens to an extreme angle. So acute that the downward strokes could be thick and strong while the upward or lateral ones flew like birds. For this handiwork I could soon charge double that of any other copyist in the Inns of Court. I was famous from Oldbourne, as my father still calls Holborn, to the river. And what's more I was ambidextrous. Not that I ever used my left hand professionally – it was never as accomplished as my right. But given wine and company I could be persuaded to demonstrate my double-handed skill. My finest party piece was to extemporise a sonnet with my right hand while inscribing the old ballad *Timor Mortis Conturbat Me* with my left. It was on one of these occasions that I hit on the line 'Come live with me and be my love' which Christofer promptly filched and beat out into finest, thinnest, prettiest gold.

No, say what I will, I can't admire this dithering scribble. I know manner isn't matter but I was bred to love a proper hand. Besides the whole business brings Christofer back to me, into my mind's eye, hunched over his work, writing like a drunken spider, never caring a jot or blot what his scripts looked like. Oh, the times I've had to transcribe him just so the actors could read and learn their words, his words, his inimitable, illegible words. And that last time, too. That fatal last time. No, don't let me think of it! Not any more. No. Banish that thought! It presupposes a trick too vile to contemplate. Oh, I can, I mean I could, perhaps, guess at how it was achieved but not why, not why. There seems no reason in it. None! And yet there must be. That's one thing I have learnt: the state has reasons for everything though reasonable men may not discern them. Nor are they intended to. What makes the thing worse is that that last time was my fault. Oh, yes, the fault's all mine.

Forgive me. These flaccid effusions are beside the point, except as a way of avoiding the horrors of last May. I shall be severer with myself in future, I promise.

So back to my first resolve. I've said something of where I'm placed. In Sussex. Immured within an estate belonging to Lord Fitzwalter who's never at home. I am not his guest. I doubt he even knows I'm here. No, I'm his sister's acquisition. Pandora happily despises her younger brother. Robert is twenty-four years to her thirty. And that's another quirk of hers: she's quite open about her age. Indeed she's the most outspoken person I've ever met except for Christofer when sober and myself when drunk. Pandora says Bobby's not fit to be the Earl when their father dies which will be soon apparently; he's already blown to three times his former size by the dropsy. Meanwhile his son mortgages the estate in return for clothes and horses. He loves to play the noble knight at Court. At this moment he's in London being measured for his armour for the Queen's tournament in November; he's determined to have ostrich plumes sprouting from a helmet of beaten gold. Not plate. Suppose his opponent were to scratch it with his lance and it was suddenly revealed as less than genuine? As mere gilding? What shame would redound upon the family name! No, pure gold it must be. The vast ostrich plumes are intended, Pandora says, to distract the spectator from the extraordinary disparity between his great body and his pin head. Her derision is merciless. From time to time he aspires to be a patron of the theatre. Most young nobles do. I've met him once or twice. We actors used to call him Bobby Spend-All.

So much for my condition. Now nothing's left for me but to delineate what I do here. Well, I chivvy myself to obey my noble hostess's command and translate *Cornelia*. But my heart's not in it. I call it my rent-play. Otherwise I invite myself for walks, telling myself this too will please imperious Pandora. Didn't she say only last week, 'I can see how beautiful you once were, Tom. You can be again if you try.' Perhaps she's right? I used to take pleasure in my looks. I prided myself upon them as if I'd invented them myself. Blond hair, cornflower eyes that worked wonders upon the chilliest of girls or the warmest of boys, a fine frame only a hair's-breadth under six feet. Sporting Tom I was known as. Compared with me Christofer was a dwarf. But then again true beauty comes from within, doesn't it? Working from the inside to the out? And within me now all is sick. My head, my heart, my liver all gobbled up by guilt. Can exercise cure guilt? No. So working on my contrariwise principle that having sworn one thing I invariably do its opposite I shall go for a walk. Yes. Up to Chancton Ring. I'll let the ash trees talk to me. There's usually a breeze up there. My broken heart can make their leaves say anything I want to hear. When I was last there they told me. jokes and laughed. I could almost fancy Christofer was with me Perched somewhere in a crook between trunk and bough, chewing an apple. He loved apples. He thought they would preserve his teeth which were white and small and sharp like a ferret's. Yes. I shall go.

Only I didn't. Well, not till later. Because after struggling into my boots – I have a special method of descending from a chair into my left boot since the knee refuses to bend more than a fraction – and having mislaid my favourite walking stick, an Irish thorn of polished barbarity, only to find it where it couldn't have been but was, I made my stiff-legged approach to the door just as someone knocked even as I opened it. I was surprised, Pandora wasn't. Doors invariably open quickly for Pandora. She had jumped down from her horse and was smiling, almost laughing. She seemed to be nursing a secret pleasure. She shone with energy. Her companion remained in the saddle.

'Tom! I've brought someone who knows you.'

I stared past her at the man. Did I recognise him? If so from where and when? My past life is like a far-off country I lived in long ago. Even the events of last year seem lost in purple distance. This man? Thick set, broad cheeks, small eyes, sudden smiles out of no expression at all? Yes, he was familiar. But where had I known him?

'My dear Thomas,' he said. And I knew. That voice like muscat wine running over gravel – I'd heard it often – yes, in conference with Lord Strange. 'No need to gawp, old son. I'm still me. Dick Baines at your service.' And he swung off his horse more nimbly than you might've expected given such bulk. He advanced on me, his meaty, mottled hand thrust forward.

I took it carefully. I said, 'I try not to shake hands.'

He let go, noticed my left was equally deformed and winced expressively. 'Ouch. Mm. Her ladyship's told me. Says you had a bout or two with Rick Topcliffe? Last May, was it? What a bastard that man is. Rumour has it his father was a bull mastiff, his mum a twelve-stone fishwife.' He laughed. In his mouth my disgrace suddenly sounded as nothing – a minor defeat at fisticuffs to a stronger opponent. It was kind of him. And I was grateful. I smiled, remembering I'd always liked Dick Baines. He had a texture that made you laugh. Well, me anyway.

Pandora said, 'I can see you remember him now.'

'Oh yes. You used to come to Lord Strange's house in Whitefriars.'

'Quite so. But his lordship's taken himself off to Lancashire. Can't say I blame him. He doesn't need the plague on top of all his other infirmities, does he? Poor old Ferdinando. He's wasting away. All skin and bones. And he shakes, too. I tell him it's Eliza's curse on him for being a Stanley. She's got some of her wizards at work on him. That's my theory.' Another all-encompassing laugh.

Baines, I now remembered, had been one of Lord Strange's many brokers. 'I play about with Ferdy's loose change,' he used to say with a lewd wink. Dick can imbue anything with innuendo. I sincerely believe he could even make the litany sound fruitily obscene.

'You'd come from Gray's Inn, I seem to recall?'

'Yes. Lord Strange liked my work as a copyist. He gave me a job as a secretary.'

'He's had plenty of those in his time. Each one prettier than the last. Did your unfortunate friend Christofer ever work for him?'

I'd forgotten that trick of his: the bland observation, then the routine joke followed without pause by the pointed question. 'No,' I said. 'Not in that way. Though he did become part of his lordship's theatre company.'

'Ah, yes. As did you, did you not?'

'Yes.'

'A man of many parts, my dear.' Dick had turned to Pandora. 'Wouldn't you agree?'

'Whom do you mean, Dick? Tom or his friend?'

'Tom, of course. His friend's dead, or so I thought?'

'You know perfectly well he is,' said Pandora.

'I'm sorry,' Dick turned to me. 'It was a sad business.' How much had Pandora told him? This concern must have shown in my eyes because he grinned and said, 'Oh, no cause for alarm, cherry pie, her ladyship has told me all. She's confided your entire history to me.' More grin. 'And I shall wear it in my heart's heart, never fear.' Open laugh. 'It's a grievous tale. You must feel pretty sore. In your shoes I'd be hopping mad. What'll you do about it? I'd want redress. The bloodier the better. Like the character in your play.'

'Which play was that?'

'Whichever you please,' he said, still laughing. 'You wrote several, didn't you? But two especially – on the same theme if I recall aright? But do correct me if I'm wrong. One where the son must revenge his dad and the other where the dad must revenge his son? Both excellent. Tremendous fun. Nearly fell off the stage laughing. So did my lady here, too.'

'He's teasing, Tom. We didn't laugh, I promise.'

'Quite so. No, a joke, sweetheart. We were transfixed with pity and terror.'

But tease or no tease here was a new thought for me. Had I in my fictions unwittingly presaged my own destiny? Christofer always maintained he became his own heroes when at work on his plays. He was Tamburlaine, he was Faustus, the Duke of Guise, Barabas the Jew. Each one a monster. But afterwards he reverted to his everyday self – sharp-tongued, quick of temper but also generous to a fault and slightly hypochondriacal. Had I

·18·

done the opposite? Remained who I was, opinionated, carefree, cocky, only to be required now to impersonate my sad heroes? Must I like them proceed reluctantly, doubtingly to my revenge? Was this my fate?

Pandora said, 'You mustn't encourage Tom to do anything, Dick. He's got to recover first. He improves every day. You should've seen him when he first arrived here. The man was a wreck, a ghost.' She turned to me. 'How's your knee this morning?'

'Better, madam.' This wasn't true. It was the same as yesterday. But Pandora's the kind of woman who demands you be positive. Not falsely or unjustifiably – she isn't a fool, quite the reverse – but she does believe life exists to be moulded into shapes that will please and divert her. I sometimes think she regards me as a lump of human marzipan – her marzipan guest.

'I'm glad. And there's colour in your cheek, too.'

'As there is in yours, madam.'

Pandora laughed. 'Dick and I amuse each other. We're old, old friends. I like to have him in my bed occasionally.' She smiled. 'We galloped here to see you.'

This seemed a *non sequitur* but her eyes danced, embracing Baines and then, briefly, me – as if – or was this fantasy? – as if she were considering me as a prospective equal to this occasional lover standing beside he. Was that her meaning? And had Baines frowned? That big flat face so quick to crease into forceful laughter (the laughter you often hear at Court which has more volume than mirth within it), that face could also reflect subtler, fleeter things. But he, Dick Baines, would be too wise in the world surely to show jealousy of so haughty a mistress? I decided I'd been mistaken. Pandora hadn't weighed me in the scales of her favour and Dick hadn't frowned.

'I'm honoured by your visit, madam,' I said.

Dick said, 'Am I to understand Ferdinando's cast you off, Thomas?'

'I appealed to him for help but he didn't reply. I wrote three times.'

'When would that have been?'

'Last June, while I was in prison.'

'Ah so. I was abroad. Muscovy. Buying furs. I expect Ferdy's chaplain intercepted your letters. He reads everything, you know? And he never cared for you. Told me so himself. Saw you as an interloper.'

'Father Ignatius read them?'

'Bound to have done. Ferdy's eyesight's worse than ever.'

'But wouldn't he have read my letters aloud to Lord Strange?'

'Only if it suited him. But as I say I rather doubt it did, old son. I don't suppose Ferdy knows anything of your plight.'

I was shocked. How could Father Ignatius have disliked me? I'd been so negligible; he so remote, so austere, so established. I said, 'I never realised.'

'I'm sure you didn't. Iggy's quite a politician. Masterminds the whole household, finger in every pie, rules on all matters temporal and spiritual. At the moment he's not only badgering Ferdy to return to the old faith – he renounced Rome last year, you know – but he's also nagging him to give up the theatre. Wants him to withdraw his patronage. Hand over his company to anyone who'll take it, lock, stock and barrel.' He laughed as if I ought to be delighted at this news.

'The company owns my plays,' I said.

'Well, they'll be sold on, too, I daresay. Quite a capital asset, I should've thought. Don't suppose you'll see a penny from the deal either.'

'No – I won't.'

'But then you poets live on air, don't you?' Glinting smile.

'I wish we could.'

'If wishes were horses, dear boy, beggars would ride.'

'I am a beggar now.'

'No, you aren't, Tom. You're my guest. I don't entertain beggars.' Pandora spoke so sharply I was embarrassed. Then she turned to Dick. 'And I didn't bring you here to tease him either.'

'I was merely establishing the facts, my dear. In the hope I might be of some assistance. Put in a word, possibly? Help restore Tom to his former employment, perhaps? As favourite secretary, admired poet, actor and playwright? No wonder

Ignatius blocked his letters. Jealous as hell, that's Iggy. Subsists on green bile and self-abuse.'

We laughed but Dick's laughter was the loudest – it sloshed all round us like milk in a churn. I still felt obliged to apologise to Pandora. 'I didn't mean,' I said, then rearranged my words. 'I mean I wasn't belittling your hospitality, madam, when I said I was a beggar.' Was I blushing? It felt like it. Me? At thirty-five? Red as a beetroot? Like a boy actor being measured for his first pair of sponge breasts?

Pandora regarded me coolly. 'No, you belittled yourself, Thomas.'

'Forgive me.'

'Don't apologise either. I won't have you cringe. Do that and I'll turn you out of doors.' And there was little or no joke in her voice.

Dick slapped me on the back. 'Don't you believe a word of it, Tom. Her ladyship has great plans for you. That's more than clear. I recognise the signs, sweetheart. First she babies you then slaps you. So watch out.' More hearty laughter.

'You're wrong, Dick. Tom doesn't need indulgence. He needs practical encouragement.

'Still busy blaming yourself for what happened, is that the trouble?'

Pandora answered for me. 'Yes, he does. I've told him time and time again he can't be the only one to blame. These things don't happen like that, do they?'

'It would seem unlikely, I agree. There always tend to be other players in the game. But of course the vital, indeed, only question is: why were you and your friend Morley . . . ?'

'Marlowe.'

'Sorry – hopeless with names. Why were the pair of you singled out for attention in the first place? After all, we've got dozens of uppity young poets – every one of 'em aiming to offend authority – just asking to be arrested for treason or blasphemy or shooting the moon. So why pick on you two?'

'They thought Christofer was an agent of Rome.'

'Ah? Is that so? Really? Then, of course, one understands. Mm. And who would you say were *they* exactly? Can you give names?'

'A few.' I was surprised by this sudden close questioning. Surely Pandora would've named my persecutors to him? Hadn't Dick said she'd told him everything?

Pandora must have read my look. She said, 'I mentioned Sir Thomas Heneage. And Burghley's son – Robert.'

'Her ladyship believes it's only the precious apex of the pyramid that matters. But we lesser people know better, don't we, Tom? We have to become familiar with the lower slopes. Our very lives depend on such considerations, do they not? So who else was there at your interrogation? Can you recall?'

'Robert Poley.'

'Good Lord above! Bob Poley? Never knew he worked for Heneage. Would you credit it? It only shows how careful we must be these days. Anyone else?'

'Then there was Topcliffe, as you said.'

'With his loyal apprentice Roger?'

'Yes, that was his name. Yes, he had help.' Tears sprang to my eyes. I couldn't continue. I said I was sorry, strangled a sob and felt even more ashamed.

'Anyone else?'

'No.'

'Doesn't matter. Bob Poley's enough of a shock to be going on with. So they really imagined Morley – sorry Marlowe – was working for the Pope?'

'Yes.'

'And you were arrested first? Before your friend?'

'Yes.'

'So you could inform upon him? Was that the idea?'

This time my agreement was more nod than word. How could I speak? How could I tell this bluff and breezy man what I'd said about Christofer that afternoon, that evening, that night last May? When I became the Father of Lies himself? I'd held out for three days. I'd resisted for seventy-two hours. At Her Majesty's most secret centre. At that other place that is worse than Bridewell, worse than the Tower. Eliza's privy intelligence house at Chelsea. There Mr Vice holds sway. Heneage is known to all his cockroach acolytes as Mr Vice or even Mr V. The title derives from his other more public function as the Queen's Vice-Chamberlain. Some say it is a privilege to be questioned at Chelsea. It proves your importance to the state.

As I stared dumbly at Pandora and Baines, like a heifer that's received the slaughterer's fatal blow but is yet to acknowledge its effect, I felt tears slide down my cheeks. I had no will to stop them.

'Oh, God. Now look what you've done, Dick.'

Why was she so indignant? Did she really suppose I could slough off my crime like a winter snake its skin? For God's sake, she knew what I'd done. Hadn't I told her? And hadn't she said it was true cause for grief?

I found my tears drying on my cheeks. And that I was staring at her with an anger akin to hatred. How dare she patronise me thus? I tried to speak but couldn't. Because of the pillar. I could see it in my mind's eye: Topcliffe's pillar.

It's in the main interrogation room at Chelsea. And it was in order to escape another return to it that I told all those lies about Christofer. They'd said, without rancour, as a statement of fact, 'Next time, Mr Kyd, you'll hang there till you rot.' I knew I could believe them. Hadn't they trained me to believe them?

You're suspended from Top's pillar by steel manacles. Very soon your stomach is raked by fiery cramps. Your feet begin to dance. Your hands swell until blood oozes out at your fingers' ends. You cry out for a stool to be placed under you but your interrogators are deaf. They watch you patiently and sometimes confer among themselves. They know they need do nothing further since you with your own weight are supplying the torment they require. When at last you faint the stool comes. But only so you may recover your senses and thus allow the Queen's agents to remove the stool again. It's a lengthy, solemn process in which you appear stark naked before your richly dressed superiors. Some say the pillar's better than the rack. A counsel of imperfection if ever I heard one. Word has it Topcliffe invented this method at Eliza's own request. She'd received complaints from the Lord Mayor of London that the rack left men unfit for service as nightsoil removers – an ordinary occupation of the politically or religiously unsound in these troubled days. That – or the collecting of the dead from plague houses; diseased Protestants are commonly carted to the quicklime trenches by brutally reformed Catholics. And so it is that Gloriana's state is secured against Rome's agents of darkness. Defended by living ghosts or raven-ravaged heads on poles stuck up at every city gate. It's treason to say so, of course. With this page alone my life is forfeit. The truth is treason now.

What I said about Christofer was, however, enough to ensure him a fate worse than anything I have so far suffered. That it did not happen – at least not so elaborately, so painstakingly (if you'll forgive the hangman's pun) is no thanks to me. Even so his death remains a puzzle. Not least because, despite my false witness, it seems to have been gratuitous, offering advantage to no one. Certainly it was that sinister thing, a covert killing. What we may call a *subfusc* murder. I've cudgelled my brains but still I can see no reason in it. After all, Heneage could have used my evidence against Christofer to procure the state a salutary trial of a notorious atheist followed by a magnificent public execution. He could have made an almighty show of it. A spectacle fearsome enough to subdue the most rebellious spirits in the land. Whatever their persuasion. And if he still thought Christofer had been a secret sympathiser with Rome or Vatican agent, well, all decapitated men on a stick are much the same, aren't they? Like toffee apples. Not that Christofer would've been allowed the privilege of the block. Not noble enough. Oh, no, he'd have been tokenly hanged, then disembowelled alive, then dismembered. That's what my lies laid him open to.

But no, Mr Vice in his wisdom preferred a hugger-mugger assassination at Deptford Strand. And then had it put about that Christofer died in a quarrel. Said he'd refused to pay his share of the cost for supper! That, for me, proves it a lie by those who didn't know him. Christofer was the most generous of men. Absurdly so. Quite reckless with money. He used to spend like a sailor back from the Indies. And he always grabbed the bill in company. He'd never let anyone pay. The only way such a tussle might've ended in murder is if they *hadn't* let him pay.

Pandora said, 'There. You've tied the poor man's tongue with your questions, Dick.'

'*Mea culpa*,' he said with a cheerful shrug.

I said, 'You needn't fear, madam. I shan't shed any more tears.'

'Oh, you may, Tom. But not of self-pity. It's only self-pity I detest.'

I'd hoped for a more gracious acceptance of my resolve but Pandora's demands are as precise as they are exacting. I replied with care, saying, 'Everything I told them about Christofer was a lie.'

'Ah? Is that so?' said Dick.

'I told terrible lies.'

'Don't we all, dear heart?'

'To save myself.'

'Quite understandable. Who wouldn't?' He turned to Pandora. 'He should spend a spell at Court, shouldn't he, my dear? That'd put him in the way of it.'

Pandora caught Dick's smile and returned it. They really were comfortable together. 'I'm not sure Tom would be entirely *persona grata* just now.' We all laughed at the patent truth of this.

'What kind of lies did you tell, Tom? Did you say your pal was a secret seminarist over from France to hear mass in private – or what?'

'Oh, no. They did try to make me say that but I told them that was quite ridiculous.'

'Ah? Brave of you. Most stout-hearted. So what *did* you tell Heneage and Poley! Bob Poley! I still can't get over that bundle of news.' He laughed. 'Brainless Bob, intelligencer to the Queen, extraordinary.' More laughter, 'Do continue, dear boy.'

'I said Christofer held some unconventional views on certain subjects.'

'Such as religion, I daresay?'

'Yes.'

'And of course when he was hauled up before the Privy Council it was on a charge of atheism, was it not?'

'And blasphemy.'

'They're one and the same thing these days, aren't they? Both capital offences.'

'Yes.' I had to force myself to speak. I said, 'As her ladyship knows I told the authorities at Chelsea – but only out of extreme pain – you must understand that – I told them Christofer hated God and his Son. And that he thought the Jews had done well to crucify Him. Also that the Virgin Mary was a Levantine whore and her Son a bastard who'd sodomised his disciple John.'

'But in truth he'd never said such things?'

'No. Or only when he was drunk.'

'Ah. When he was drunk?'

'And only then for fun. Out of bravado. He didn't mean them.'

'No question of *in vino veritas*?'

'No. Christofer loved to shock.'

'Quite. You poets do, don't you? Look at Ovid. Not to mention Aretino. Filthy stuff. Wonderful. Luscious. Yum-yum. Yes?'

'Well, that's all, really. I mean, it's enough to give you an idea of what I said, isn't it? Christofer was always joking. Lots of his jokes were fabulously rude. They could be about anything or anybody. But you had to be the stodgiest of puritans not to laugh.'

'And we've got more than enough of those, haven't we? Except not all reveal themselves in black and white, do they? You find some in velvet gowns. Or ermine even. So, Thomas, while you'd say your friend wasn't really an unbeliever, you'd agree he wasn't averse to a spot of blasphemous speculation presented as a joke?'

Was this a sudden trap? It certainly felt like one. I said, 'Perhaps.'

'Of course, jokes frequently depend on the tone of voice in which they're said, don't they?'

'Oh, yes,' I agreed.

'But once put down on paper they may not seem quite so amusing? Merely offensive or worse?'

'That can happen, yes.'

'You knew him intimately, I believe?'

'You change tack like a lawyer,' I said, half-laughing.

'I *was* a lawyer, Tom. And change tack is right. I used to have a high old time with maritime law.' He made it sound like seducing sailor boys. His wink supported this assumption.

I was disarmed. I said, 'Christofer and I lived together, worked together.'

'Tom taught his famous friend to write,' Pandora added.

This embarrassed me. 'No, not really,' I said. Because nobody could've taught Christofer. Not in any real sense. He knew everything just by being born. But we did collaborate. And to start with I did help him in the world of London's theatres. 'We often talked over plots together,' I said. 'And, yes, I was able to introduce him to Lord Strange who recognised his abilities at once. His lordship loved whatever was truly new, never heard before, and genuinely surprising. He used to say: 'All I ask is for a poet to astonish me.'

'Ferdy has a way with words himself,' Dick said. 'But I don't think I ever met your friend at Whitefriars?' He'd made this sound broadly speculative. As if to imply he could well have met Christofer somewhere else. But before I could query this Pandora interrupted.

'If you wish to question Tom further, you must do it another time, Dick. I came out to ride. Come along.'

At once he helped her remount and then got himself back into the saddle. His spring up from the mounting block was even more surprisingly light and quick than his jump down to greet me. Some big men seem to float despite their weight. Dick Baines did. His horse, however, grunted as he settled in the saddle. I allowed myself to wonder satirically if Pandora did that, too, when enjoying him. And for the first time in three months felt my prick tingle then twitch. The surprise of it and the sudden, living feeling made me smile. Quite unthinkingly for once.

'What's the matter, Tom?' Pandora asked. 'I've never seen you look like that before?' Her eyes were amused. Had she guessed the cause?

'How did I look, my lady?' I felt like a guilty schoolboy.

'Alive,' she said. 'You must smile like that more often. It improves you. Makes you look years younger.' She smiled too, and I felt warmed right through, as if the sun had at last pierced the dull August clouds. As she and Dick rode away I wondered if in a day or two I might ask her to lend me a horse. Perhaps I could ride again, after all? Certainly it would be easier than walking. She had offered only the week before but I'd refused. Out of self-defeating shame. Christofer and I had often gone riding. I'd had no desire to be reminded of that. I'd thought such memories would be too painful. But now I found they weren't. Had something changed within me? I doubted it and yet inside the doubt I sensed a budding hope.

We would hire horses at Paris Gardens and ride out into the fields of Battersea. Oh, the scent of lavender on Lavender Hill and of new mown hay on St John's Hill (the kindest air in Surrey blows there, they say). Sometimes we'd strike south from the Wandle's water meadows, loved for their kingcups and cowslips, as far as Mitcham or the heights of Norbury where we'd gaze out upon the pretty city of Croydon. And as our horses ambled through the lanes we'd invent the arguments of a dozen grandilo-quent plays. Each one more grotesque than the last.

Our shared ideal was to write the cruellest comedy ever heard. We weren't interested in tragedy alone. Tragedy was too pure, too remote, too rigid. Nor in comedy as such. To have people merely laugh was not enough for us. Just as to have them simply cry was not enough. No. Our aim was to make them do both at once and then howl like wolves at the beastly mystery of life. Ridiculous, you say? Perhaps. But we were young. We'd say, 'Who cares about applause or execration? When, if we're clever, we can induce our audience to lift their heads, stretch up their throats and bay the rising moon?' You must understand that we meant it, meant it with deadly seriousness while choking with laughter. Oh, yes, that was our aim, our fondest hope. And to that end we would consider any story, any legend, any fable however absurd, however repellent, however old, probing it, dissecting it, to discover if it possessed those hidden triggers, lurking paradoxes that promise savage truth, dramatic ecstasy. We told each other a play must first shock, then seduce, then attack. And at the end become so repulsively, so intricately beautiful that our animal natures are as exulted as our judgments. Oh, we aimed so high and yet so low. We called our work – it was our secret title for everything we did – *The Bestiary of Intellect*. And as we rode we'd bake babies in pies, rape nuns on altars, drag kings through dirt while plucking honeysuckle from the hedges and laugh and groan and kiss and feel like gods. Oh, those rides.

The sun came out on the Downs. The air was full of tiny blue butterflies, as blue as the harebells they fed on, floating above the springy sheep-cropped turf. As I reached Chancton Ring I counted seven magpies among the trees. My mother used to say if you saw seven at a time they stood for a secret never told before but soon to be revealed. My mother, mark you, comes from the Welsh Marches where the folk are superstitious beyond belief while professing to be sober Christians. My father maintains she's solid pagan from the neck down. I wish they'd come to see me in prison.

I stretched myself out in the freckled shade. The unexpected sun had warmed me and for the first time since May the ache had lessened in my knee. On my way up I'd purposefully made myself not think of Dick Baines in the hope that a blank mind might produce what it was about him that eluded me. As I lay back, cushioning my head on a tussock I'd swept clear of tawny rabbit droppings, I was rewarded. What it was came back to me. Baines had known Christofer in France. Several years ago. That was it. Well, when I say known I mean I'd understood they'd met briefly at Rheims. And spent the odd evening together drinking the sharp fizzy wine they make in that rolling region. Had Christofer told me anything more than that? I didn't think so. As a student Christofer had spent a term at Rheims. The English College of Douai had moved there. But he'd discovered he hated France and learned to despise the French. I used to tease him about it. Tell him he was too English. Indeed it would be true to say that if you mentioned France he became as English as a rabid dog. I thought it a curious quirk. But I forgave it because I loved him.

But now I wondered about this insular aversion. Was it based on something hidden from me? A never-told secret? And could this secret be joined with Baines? At this point the magpies set up a great racket, mobbing a carrion crow which had dared enter the ring. The crow was joined by its mate and together, cawing like cross-cut saws, they defied the magpies. Eventually the magpies swooped away leaving the trees to the hunchbacked crows. I returned to my reverie. What *had* Baines been doing at Rheims? He would've been far older than Christofer. Hardly a student. Christofer had been twenty-one at the time. Baines would have been at least thirty-five. Back when? '86? Yes, seven years ago. Had Dick been there as a divine? No, surely not? No more secular man existed than Richard Baines. And then the thought struck me.

It struck me so hard I found myself rising to my feet on the strength of it. Without bidding from my brain. Baines a government spy? An agent of the Queen? He'd denied any knowledge of Robert Poley as an intelligencer but of course he would, wouldn't he? If he too worked for Heneage and the Crown? Yes, it was plain as a pikestaff. Rheims was and is notorious as a training school for popish missionaries destined for England where, for eight years now, it's been a felony to entertain a seminarist let alone a Jesuit. And actually to be one of these within the Queen's dominion is high treason. But still they come, so dedicated are they to their cause. Once here they go about as laymen, never admitting to be priests at all, until they feel secure among their own in a private place. Then they'll celebrate mass, hear confessions, inspire martydoms. Had Dick Baines been sent out to France to observe them at their studies? To pose as a priest? While marking them down for their future execution?

Christofer had pretended to the old faith. He'd told me many times, seemed almost to boast of it. A curious, all-knowing look would suffuse him – it seemed to make him older, fatter, heavier – and he'd say, 'As a student I was Eliza's eyes and ears, you know? Yes, her devoted secret agent.' If you pricked his portentousness he'd shrug, laugh and become himself again and admit, his face flushing, that while at Cambridge he'd been invited to attend an interview with the Queen's intelligencers. As a scholarship boy from Canterbury he'd been offered certain increments to his pension in return for keeping an eye upon his fellow students – those especially who seemed rather too enamoured of the Jezebel at Rome. Later he'd been granted monies to spend a term at Rheims. My heart's ease had become a stipendary hypocrite, a scholar spy. When I said as much (self-righteously) he answered he would do anything to acquire knowledge. He needed to know more than other men. And what he'd learned from this was that the Privy Council could lie as well as any fishwife selling yesterday's haddock. Why, when the university questioned his fitness to proceed to Master of Arts (had he not been absent from his alma mater rather too often? even at Rheims of all abominable places?) the Council had stated – contrary to all truth – that Christofer had merely 'determined' to go there, not actually gone. At this blatant falsehood the Senate succombed, he got his MA and had never believed in officialdom since.

So was Baines the answer to the next question: *quis custodie ipsos custodies*? Had he in his turn been put in place to observe Christofer? Among others? Eliza's a stickler for detail and Secretary Walsingham was, in his time, said to be the most assiduous civil servant in England.

With such suppositions coursing through me I found I couldn't keep still. I had to move. I walked round the ring, even broke into a hobbling run. Then I stopped, partly from pain, partly because another recollection had occurred to me. Hadn't I once copied out a scene Christofer had written, intended for another of the dozen or so plays he'd never finished? In this scene a student of Christchurch, Oxford (for which read Corpus Christi, Cambridge – the author's college) had been given audience by a great lord known as Basildon (for whom read Walsingham). The student's name had been, yes – Leander. Of course! Who else? Christofer's favourite pseudonym. His other self. I walked round the ring again, snatches of dialogue half-heard in my head. It was as if the breeze was bringing them to me only to whisk them mischievously away. This way, that way. But eventually I seemed to have collected a passable dialogue.

> *'For what end would you go to France, my boy?'*
> *'To study, sir.'*
> *'To study treason?'*
> *'Not so, my lord. Divinity.'*
> *'And for this you would have money?'*
> *'If it please you.'*
> *'Come close, Leander. Close, boy. No, closer. Closer.'*

And hugging him Basildon whispered something in the student's ear, at which Leander drew back as if stung by a hornet and promptly denounced his potential benefactor in towering terms. Quite a theatrical surprise. Christofer was very proud of it. The essence of this outburst was that Leander would not agree to Basildon's whispered condition that he keep a watch on his fellows. How – he asked – could he barter his good conscience and still be a student of the divine? We'd both thought the last phrase of his tirade quite a meteor. Nor was I surprised by its return to me now. Who else had Christoferus filched it from?

> *'Am I to creep abroad a lawful spy? Never, my lord!'*

After this there was to be a long pause. Then Basildon would speak. Something about rewarding Leander richly.

> *'I spurn your money, sir.* Radix malorum est cupiditas.'

We were still at the stage of spattering our scenes with Latin tags to show how well-educated we were. It was, as I say, an unfinished script. A botch rightly neglected. The runt of his imagination's litter born out of exhaustion following the supreme success of his second play of *Tamburlaine the Great*. Its only value now was as a fiction obversely mirroring a possible truth.

I walked on but had hardly gone ten yards when again I stopped. If anyone had seen me he'd have taken me for a mad vagabond, a real Poor Tom just dismounted from his horse of air. I stopped because I'd suddenly sensed – was this remembering or seeing? – there'd been a note, a scribbled something, left in the margin of that scene I'd copied. Could it have said, 'Think of R. Let him stay silent so he may play his part later.'? I knew I'd questioned it and Christofer had said something about perhaps adding a bystander to the scene. Someone who wouldn't speak but who, by his watchful presence, would nevertheless be noticed as an important attendant on Basildon. A character to be used later. Suddenly I wanted to ride back to London and go through my papers – my raped and rifled papers. Wanted urgently to find this note and make certain I'd remembered it correctly. Because if I had – then 'R' could stand for Richard. Dick Baines? Or was this too tenuous? Yes. Surely. And yet he could have been Walsingham's trusted factotum. He could even had been present when Christofer was first recruited to Eliza's cause.

And what if there'd been another scene? The later one the margin's note suggested? It could have been drafted. Christofer and I didn't share everything. Even at our closest we kept something of ourselves for our own use. So there might be such a scene, lurking amidst the jumble of our dismembered past.

These urging speculations made me want to laugh and shout. I know I yelled something incoherent at the sky. Several sheep grazing nearby skittered away, baaing plaintively. As they departed their complainings became part of the air I breathed. Their cowardice reminded me of me and brought me back to my more prosaic senses. What was there to exult about? Very little. What was this vital truth I'd dug out of myself? At best a byway. At worst a nullity. It explained nothing. Allow that Dick Baines had kept watch on Christofer. What then? Assume that he'd continued as a spy, transferring his allegiance from Secretary Walsingham to Heneage? Again – what? Simply that Baines had remained in the Queen's service while Christofer hadn't. And of that I was certain anyway. He'd been too clever, too impatient, too much a genius to remain in thrall to anyone but himself. Christofer was loyal to no one else. His universe was he. And to be a spy is to be one of many cyphers who reflect power yet cannot create it; moons to suns. He'd never have put up with that for long. As a student at twenty-one perhaps but no longer. Christofer couldn't make a career out of being invisible. He needed to be known, he wanted his name on everybody's lips. He had to have applause or die. So avid was he for constant recognition he'd even tried to act. He was hopeless. Quite the most embarrassing actor who's ever appeared at the Rose Theatre. He forgot his moves, he fidgeted while others spoke, refused to study his lines (his own or other people's) and when called upon to speak would make up new ones. Often magnificent but usually irrelevant to the scene or the part he was playing. Who needs a 4th Citizen to bawl out for no reason: 'Villain, I say, should I but touch the rusty gates of hell the triple-headed Cerberus would howl and wake black Jove to crouch and kneel to me?' No, crave approval as he might, Christofer never received it as an actor. But as a playwright theatres shook for him. I've seen the galleries quiver as the audience stamped its applause.

He revelled in his fame. It changed him from a pasty-faced dwarf into a dainty giant. He ordered two-inch heels to his shoes and found creams for his skin that made him glow like Adonis. Do I exaggerate? A little. But not much. With success Christofer became beautiful. So I can't believe he stayed a spy.

But even so I decided I would ask Dick Baines what he could remember of Christofer in France. I had no doubt he would cheerfully divulge another's lifelong secret if it suited him. Or lie like Lucifer if it didn't. But whatever the outcome I decided to ask him when next we met.

As I made my way back the sun disappeared behind bellying cloud and ill-tempered bursts of rain whisked already brittle leaves out of the coppices flanking the Downs. I was glad to get home and shut the door upon this premature autumn. Once inside I was even more pleased to find that Pandora's servants had left a dinner of soup and lean beef to keep warm by the fire and also a bundle of broadsheets and pamphlets sent from London. I had an appetite for both. From the broadsheets I learned that the theatres were still closed. As well they might be: deaths from the plague had risen to over a thousand a week. May the Lord yet have mercy on us. A woman of Greenwich had given birth to a mermaid – well, a girl-child with her legs joined together – and both had been thrown into the Thames for their pains. The price of bread was to rise. It was only then that I found a note tucked in at the back of the bundle. I did not recognise the hand. It had a professional look to it. I read the following: 'A word to the wise. Take care. You have more enemies than you know. Keep your own counsel. *Ave atque vale.*' No signature. No seal.

My mind raced like a mouse in a toy treadmill. Who could've sent this? Baines? Pandora herself? Someone from my former life?

Only with the dawn did I find sleep. Just as the unknown author of this note intended, I am certain.

For the rest of that week I saw no one except in uneasy dreams. Dick Baines never returned and Pandora did not call. The only living creature I encountered was the girl who brings my milk each morning. By rights I should call her a milkmaid but that might conjure up a picture of cream and strawberry prettiness when here's a country Jane who can barely bring herself to mumble a good morning. I think she's put me down as a beggarly dependant of her ladyship and a townsman to boot. Though I may be her superior in degree, my impoverished state places me, in her peasant opinion, beneath her. Or so I imagine. It could be she has no brain at all and thinks nothing.

Our conversations are invariably one-sided. I greet her. She nods. I remark upon the weather. She pretends not to hear as she measures milk from her pail into a jug. I say truthfully her milk is quite the creamiest I've ever tasted. But compliments seem to mean nothing to her. I daresay she's been taught to see the devil in them. Exasperated with her I wish her a heartfelt good day. At this she nods quite vigorously, glad to be dismissed. I escort her to the door and watch her go without pleasure. But then suddenly – well, suddenly this morning – I realise she walks far better than she talks. Because as she goes out through the garden gate, she lets her hips swing, deliberately, saucily, as if to signal that within herself and among her own kind she enjoys great satisfactions. At this I wonder if she's willed her sullenness upon herself? Has her wooden comportment made her the plain Jane she's wanted me to see? But now does not? Or could this sudden flaunting change be a final demonstration of her contempt for me? Not just as a penniless townsman either, but as a man? Perversely, this thought of myself considered as a lover (however derisively) quite outweighs any other. If she meant that then that's a challenge!

By mid-afternoon my mind's made up. I've decided that the minute the opportunity is offered, tomorrow or the next day, I'll provoke her, force her to smile, make her eye understand mine. No more placatory platitudes, vapid compliments. No. I'll flirt unashamedly with her and melt her rustic hardness. By suppertime I see myself as a second Pygmalion and wonder if I shall fall in love with this new creation of mine. Already I've invoked Aphrodite twice to help me turn this rustic block into a soft and pretty mistress! These fantasies hearten me. I welcome them as harbingers of hope especially as last night I dreamt of nymphs, sleek as eels, bathing by moonlight.

The next day I tried out my resolve. And got an even stonier reception.

'It's time you told me your name, my dear,' I began. No reply. 'Surely there's no harm in divulging it? I think of you as Jane but I suspect that's too severe a nomination for one such as you?' Why was I talking like a drunken schoolmaster? No wonder she was silent. I tried again. 'You walk well,' I said. This sounded worse. What had come over me? Had I lost my powers of natural speech? 'I mean you walk very gracefully. I noticed only yesterday.' That was better. 'I'm sure you can't be as stony-hearted as you pretend? Especially now I look at you again. Your hair is softer, finer spun, than I thought. Your eyes more mysterious. Do I detect the light of pity in them?'

And then, convinced I'd redeemed myself in her eyes, I allowed mine to slide from hers by way of her cheek and neck to her breasts, her belly and back again. An all-seeing caress to which I added an eyebrow raised in what I hoped was admiring speculation reinforced by a winning smile. But then, so out of practice was I with the world that I – oh, I hate to tell it – I let my tongue lick my upper lip. Quick lizard lascivity. I agree I've never aspired to be a gentleman but to behave so coarsely! I confess I surprised myself. And felt myself offended by myself.

At this miscalculated moment her right hand swept up to sketch out a gesture which, had it been completed, might have carried a blow. Or was she perhaps preparing to ward me off? Human motion can be as ambiguous as human speech. But whatever her intentions I can hardly blame her. I must've seemed a danger. A hideous hunched-up cripple talking like a pisspot pedagogue while licking his lips at her? What would this slobbering gargoyle from London do next? But before she or I could declare our intentions further the door swung open to reveal Pandora poised on the threshold. To my amazement my stone milkmaid reddened and almost forgot to curtsy. For the first time in my presence her composure wobbled.

'What are you doing here, Mary?'

So common or garden Mary was her name. I might've guessed.

'Seeing to the gentleman, your worship.'

'You're blushing, girl. Why? Thomas, what have you been saying to her? You've made her blush.'

'No, madam, you've done that.'

'Me? How?'

'By your sudden arrival.'

'Mary – you can go.'

Mary-cum-Jane recovered her wits, curtsied again for good measure and sidled from the room, squeezing past my lady who shone like a dark star.

Pandora smiled. 'Poor Mary. Between us we've confused her completely.'

Once again I was obliged to disagree. 'No, as I said, madam, you did that. I came nowhere near to confusing her. I admit I tried to. Ergo it was your arrival caused her blushes.'

'Really?'

'I wish I had been able to make her blush. But no, I failed. In fact I think she was about to hit me.'

This produced the effect I'd hoped for. Pandora, for once, stood astonished. 'Hit you? What had you done, Thomas? What?'

I laughed, and prevaricated. 'Won't you please be seated, my lady?'

As Pandora sat at my table I thought I sensed something different about her. To say there was a new determination in her would be to disallow her very character. Nevertheless, she seemed more imperious than ever. I also sensed sadness in her and something locked away. As if doors in her mind had closed. She saw my look, smiled with some warmth and then scanned my papers. Rough drafts of my Garnier translation lay in neglected confusion before her.

Pandora said, 'Your translation bores you?'

'Yes. But it's I who am at fault. I distract myself constantly. Sparrows only have to squabble outside my window for me to break off.'

'Perhaps Garnier's play is bad? I enjoyed it but I'm no real judge. Unlike you.'

'It's good enough in its solemn way.' I fell silent. So did she. But not coldly. No, there was warmth in her silence.

Finally she said, 'Now, Thomas, tell me truly, what was happening between you and Mary?'

Now it was my turn to blush. I said, 'Well, I tried to – you won't laugh, will you?'

'I might. I can't say yet, can I? Not till you tell me?' Already her eyes shone in hope of laughter.

'Well, I tried to flirt with her.'

Pandora's hope was realised. She laughed and laughed. 'Oh, Thomas, how sweet. My crooked shepherd. What did you say? What terms did you use to address her? Honeyed phrases, I've no doubt?'

'Not really. I just told her she was – well, graceful. And that I was sure she wasn't as adamantine as she looked.'

'Adamantine? That's poetic, Thomas.'

'Well, I didn't actually use the word. She wouldn't have understood it, would she?'

'No, I'm sure not.'

'But I spoke to that effect.'

'Whereupon she was tempted to strike you?'

'No, not then. Well, not quite then.'

'Oh? There's more to tell? What?'

'I do wish you wouldn't laugh, madam.'

'I'm trying not to, Thomas.'

'But failing.'

She looked so unconvincingly contrite I was forced to wonder: did she know things I didn't? She said, 'Come along, man. What else did you say to the girl?'

'Oh, it wasn't my words that provoked her.'

'Deeds? Action? You proceeded to *do* something? But this is wonderful. What, Thomas, what?'

I hesitated to answer. I'm no puritan, Lord knows. Nor is Pandora. But to explain how I'd looked Mary so lubriciously up and down required a bravado I lacked. 'I'd prefer not to describe it, madam.'

'Oh, come along, Thomas. You can't start a story like this then stop. What did you *do*? As your hostess with a care for all her household I demand to know.' Pandora was brisk but mock-minatory. 'Did you seize her hand? Press it to your heart? Steal a kiss? Try to hurl her to the ground? Offer to rape her like Tarquin did Lucrece? What?'

'None of those things. Not even the first and least.'

'Probably as well. I'd say the girl's at least as strong as you. She might have given you best unless – '

Here she stopped. And eyed me almost as frankly as I had Mary. 'Unless,' she said, 'she suddenly discerned in you – as I do sometimes, as I do now – something of your former self, Tom.' I was Tom again, not faintly absurd Thomas. 'Perhaps that was it? Perhaps that stayed her hand?' Her voice was soft now, the register of it low. Her eyes no longer mocked me. 'Tell me.' When Pandora chooses to speak like this her voice becomes a precious liquid that seems to fall from heaven – as if the evening star was dispensing the milk of paradise.

I said, no longer afraid of her laughter, 'My eye flattered first Mary's cheek, then caressed her neck, lingered about her breasts

·39·

and then travelled to her centre. Fixed there I foolishly allowed my tongue to escape my mouth and then with my eyes returned to hers I traced the underside of my upper lip with the tip of it.'

Pandora frowned. 'A whore's trick, Tom,' she said.

'Yes, madam. Or else a would-be lover's?'

'You wanted her?'

'It was a passing fancy. Or so I'd have said of it before last Spring.'

'You should pursue your fancy, Tom.'

I laughed. 'You didn't see Mary's response. She was virtue outraged, madam.'

'Impossible. She has none. Ask my brother. He swears by Mary. His downland doxy he calls her.'

I gritted my teeth. What a fool I'd been. Now I knew why Pandora had been so eager to hear my story. She *had* known more than me. 'So that's why you were laughing,' I said, feeling something more than irritation. 'You knew all along.'

'No, that wasn't it. Well, not the whole of it. Mary's easy honesty was just a part. The other, far more important, was my own pleasure in seeing you, Tom, so revived. I liked the way you looked at her.'

What could she mean? She hadn't been present. I said, 'You saw? You can't have. Or did you see us through the window?'

'No, of course not. I've never snooped in my life. I came straight in.'

'Then how can you say you liked the way I looked at Mary?'

Pandora answered as to a child. 'Because, Thomas, in describing it you did the same to me. You looked *me* up and down.'

Had I? If this were true I was mortified. 'Surely I didn't, madam?'

'Oh, yes, you did.'

'Oh, no! Forgive me, please.'

'Why?'

'I wasn't aware I'd presumed to far.'

'Really? I supposed you were using one thought to promote another?'

'No, I swear it, madam.'

'Oh? Then I was mistaken.'

Her voice had cooled. Was she disappointed? Had I really failed to please her? Pandora is dangerous to anatomise; her quicksilver moods are contained in cut-glass. I apologised again.

She accepted my excuses. 'Very well, Thomas. But one day you'll need to dare far more than this. And I don't mean with women.' Her words chilled me as I'm sure she intended they should. And then – Pandora's delight in surprise is boundless – she said, 'Shall we ride?' And I heard grooms bringing horses to the door.

I had to be lifted bodily onto the horse. I did try to spring up unaided on my one good leg but there was less strength in it than I'd imagined so I fell back, knocking the breath out of myself among marigolds and feverfew.

Once I was pushed up into the saddle and settled there with my right foot in the stirrup and the left stretched stiffly down, I said, 'How did you know I wanted to ride?'

'I didn't.'

'You guessed?' She nodded. 'I think you can read my thoughts,' I said.

'No, Tom. I'm no wise-woman.'

'I beg to doubt that, my lady.'

'You shouldn't. Shall we go?'

And without regard for any reply she kicked her grey gelding into a trot. I followed carefully, praying the mare I'd been allotted was as mild in temper as Pandora's grooms had alleged. I didn't entirely trust them. If I was to stay in the saddle it had to be by courtesy of this unknown animal. My legs were almost powerless. I had no grip in my knees and my hands were mere cups to hold the reins. No proper grasp in them at all. But after only a few paces I'd got accustomed to my mount and my balance improved. I found I could trust her rhythm and soon that happy accord I've always had with horses returned. I felt myself begin to smile. My body seemed happier, more at home with itself than it had for months. The grooms hadn't lied. This mare was an amiable creature. I caught up with Pandora.

'I want to see the sea,' I said. She shook her head.

Instead she showed me the maze she'd had planted the week before. It was laid out beyond the knot garden at the back of the great house.

We came at it by way of the woods. And surveyed it from horseback. It looked raw. The turf had been lifted in a pattern akin to but far more complex than a walnut cracked in half. Within these precisely planned spiral beds, cuttings of box had been planted and secured to split chestnut stakes. The area was extensive, circular, a good hundred yards in diameter.

'Imagine, Tom. In twenty years time children will be hidden by these sun-scented hedges. Think themselves lost. In thirty years, us too, who knows?'

I didn't say, if we live that long. I said, 'I'm surprised, madam. I shouldn't have thought such a thing would interest you.'

'Then you don't know me, Thomas.'

'I think that's true, madam.'

'I adore puzzles. But that isn't all. A maze isn't just a puzzle, is it?'

'Not always, no.'

'What else would you, a poet, say it was?'

She seemed to want to play the pedant. I was surprised. This Pandora was new to me. Could she be ill at ease? She didn't look it. But if it was pedantry she required then I would supply it. I said, 'A maze might well be thought of as a garden parable, madam, preaching the journey of life as a green mystery.'

She smiled, approving the simile. 'Shall we walk it?' she said.

I shook my head. 'If I dismount I'll never get up again.'

'Of course you will. We'll call for help.' She waved towards the house. At once it seemed to contain a thousand servants impatient to please her. Perhaps it did? My benefactress is rich in her own recognisance beyond the dreams of Croesus.

I swung down from the saddle and landed without stumbling. I limped to Pandora's side and offered her my hand as she dismounted. She accepted it graciously, or rather, she gently rested hers upon mine without any hint of revulsion. At her cool touch my flesh felt hotly dry. As she slid to the ground her petticoats rustled against the silk of her skirt. She thanked me for my assistance.

At the start of the maze Pandora stopped to kick off her shoes and remove her stockings. 'You ought to walk a maze barefoot, Tom.' I pointed out that to pull off my boots was an occupation for an entire morning and to my surprise she accepted this truthful if exaggerated excuse.

Pandora took the walking of the maze with absolute serious-ness. She was completely absorbed, walking with her head bowed. But I found the walking this way then that tedious and after a while stepped straight across the planted spirals to reach the stone bench at the centre. Eleven hopping strides got me there. And left me free to sit and watch Pandora. She wove first one way then another, each curving path seeming to turn her back the way she'd come and yet always she was drawn inexorably towards the centre. Her progress, so wayward, so purposeful, made for a strange tension. Was it in me or in the air? I couldn't tell. But when she reached me where I sat in the middle it was gone and I felt glad. She looked at me, considering me, studying me more as an object than a person. 'You really should have walked it, Tom. It would've done you good.'

'Has it you, my lady?'

'Yes. I feel refreshed.'

She sat companionably down beside me and stuck out her feet. They were very elegant. Narrow, with perfect toes, smooth as ivory. I admired them. Pandora glanced at me and smiled. I kept silent, wanting her to speak. Barely begun this maze might be but I was convinced Pandora hadn't brought me here for nothing. It was clear that for her it was already a significant place with significance at its centre. But what she said was banal. She said, 'Dick's gone back to London.'

I couldn't tell from her tone if she'd told me this as a fact or as a criticism of him. I said, 'I supposed he had since he didn't come to see me again.'

'No. I told him not to.'

'Why?'

'I considered you'd been questioned enough. And not just by him.' I agreed. But was I grateful? I had promised myself another word with Baines. About Christofer at Rheims. 'But before he left – ' She paused as though to consider the accuracy of this statement before she continued. 'He said he could put in a word for you with Lord Strange. Restore you in his eyes. Since thanks to that busybody confessor, Father who was it?'

'Father Ignatius.'

'Fancy my forgetting. Yes, because, thanks to him your letters from prison never reached Strange. Would you like such a word to be said?'

'I don't know,' I answered. 'Those letters were written out of an abyss. I was desperate. But now? Well, thanks to you I'm no longer so desperate but – no – I'm not strong enough. I doubt I could look his lordship in the eye. Not yet anyway.'

Pandora said, 'That's what I told Dick. It was too soon. You must gather your strength here. Then we shall see what to do with you, Tom, won't we?'

'Even so I'm very grateful to Dick – '

'Don't be,' she interrupted. 'There's no need for gratitude with Dick. Dick never does anything unless it's to his advantage.'

I laughed. 'But how could I of all people ever hope to help Dick Baines?'

'Oh, he'd find a way eventually, believe me.'

Was there an undertone of contempt, disgust even, in her voice? When I'd last seen her with Dick she'd seemed fulfilled and cheerfully satirical – of him, of me. But now I divined a knife-edge of resentment in her. Had they quarrelled? I was tempted to ask. Did I dare? No, I told myself, don't presume. But then, being the paradox I am, I did. I said, 'Has Dick Baines offended you, my lady?'

Sharp glance. 'Oh, dear, I see I must be more careful. You're too observant, Tom. Or was it intuition?' This tacked-on question appeared to interest her more than her initial comment. Her eyes pierced mine.

'They're often the same thing,' I answered. 'Or so Christofer used to say.'

'You poets talk too much.'

'Our trade, madam. What else can we do?'

This made her smile. She said, 'Let's say I shan't ever invite him here again.' I'd been right. Doors in her mind had shut. Then she added. 'I expect an absolute loyalty, Tom, from those I chose to care for.'

Was this a warning addressed to me or a retrospective observation concerning her discarded lover? I couldn't tell so I guarded my reply. I said, 'I used to treasure loyalty to friends above all else.' But even in saying this so carefully I found I'd undermined myself. I felt barriers collapse inside me. I was short of breath, my eyeballs were stinging and I was back at Chelsea again with the clock striking five and the gulls screaming. I'd misjudged myself. Philosophy was still beyond me. And all this while my observant protectress pretended not to notice.

'Of course you did,' she said sympathetically. 'But your case isn't to be compared with Dick's.' So she *had* meant him? So he must have betrayed her in some way. Perhaps the usual way? With another woman? Was that the common truth of it? I didn't suppose Pandora would tolerate a real rival. Whores, yes. High-road rabbits and town minxes, too, I daresay. But never a coequal. She sighed, stretched out her bare feet again and in this innocently luxurious action I suddenly saw her younger self. She was a girl again. She caught my eye and wriggled her toes. 'I'm glad you admire my feet,' she said. 'Many have.'

In my former life I'd have been quick to say something suitable, charming, flattering. But I was tongue-tied. And in response Pandora got up abruptly, almost angrily, then stretched, arching herself backwards, her hands on her hips. 'Oh, Tom,' she exclaimed. 'I do so wish I'd known you before.' And with a sigh she walked away from me, tracing the maze this way, that way, back to her shoes and stockings. And all the while I kept my head bowed, wishing my teeming thoughts elsewhere, wishing I couldn't see her, wishing I wasn't who and what I was. Then she called me. 'Let me show you the house,' she said.

In the great hall Pandora became the complete hostess: gracious, charmingly remote, exquisitely bored yet warm. We nibbled tiny almond cakes and sipped lemon-water from Venetian glasses. I had fallen silent again after offering first an exhaustive admiration of the chequered marble floor (servants dressed as chessmen were a winter game), then several extempore flourishes upon the flowers and fruit with birds carved out of limewood, followed by a dissertation on the tapestries (I knew something of the techniques favoured in Brussels) together with a comparison of the ceiling's hammer beams with those of Scadbury in Kent. I hadn't meant to mention this particular place. I named it without thinking and the saying of it was more than enough to silence me. Scadbury! The seat of my undoing. Pandora made no attempt to prompt me or to question me about my sudden stop. Instead she studied me until I could no longer avoid her eye.

Oppressed by her gaze I said, 'I think I ought to go, madam.'

'I'll ride with you.'

'No, I can walk.'

'Of course you can't. It's far too far. And it will overtire your knee. I want you well, Thomas, well. You must ride.'

'Well if I must, my lady, then a groom can accompany me to bring the mare back.'

'No. I shall come with you.'

And she strode imperiously to the door calling for our horses. I followed, not relishing the prospect of her continued company. Something about her had become oppressive. It smelt of the hothouse. It breathed intemperance. I would have much preferred to go on foot, alone. It wasn't far – less than a mile. The walk to Chancton Ring was more than twice that, and uphill and downhill too, and I'd already done it several times. But great women like great men order the world to suit themselves. There was no gainsaying Pandora. I was her property, her guest, her prisoner.

We had ridden most of the way back when she said, 'There's something you should know, Tom. Something about your friend.' What had she heard? Had whispers reached her from London? From the Court at Greenwich? And if so what? What more was there to say about Christofer? He was dead. 'He's been seen in Paris,' she added. And smiled. A dance of triumph glittering behind her eyes.

I was struck dumb. A kind of poisonous panic choked me. It seemed to scorch my brain. I shook my head. I said, 'No, no! He can't have been. He's dead. Dead. Dead and buried.'

'You contradict me?'

'Yes, yes I do! I'm sorry, madam, but I must! I can't believe it!'

'Well, you should. He's lodged with the Jesuits of Clermont.'

'The Jesuits? Who's told you this?'

'The name would mean nothing to you.'

For once I was sharp with her. 'Oh?' I said. 'You employ spies, do you?'

She didn't bridle, rather she nodded amiably. 'A gossipy god-daughter. She's written to me from our embassy at Paris where her father serves the minister plenipotentiary. Her letter came yesterday. Had you not been in such a hurry to escape my hospitality just now I'd have shown it to you. She says your friend Christofer is known to everyone in the city as the English poet. Apparently he's about to receive a pension from the King – a signal honour for a foreigner.'

Still I couldn't believe. 'Does he use his own name?'

Pandora laughed indulgently. 'No, of course not, well, not quite. He's adopted a French name of sorts. One which smacks more of Brittany than of Britain but even so preserves something of his former identity. He's now known as Monsieur Saint-Malo. But this deceives nobody, my god-daughter says.'

My brain spun like a whipped top. Could this be? I had to admit the fake name sounded very like him. A typical Christofer joke. He loved puns – the more excruciating the better; a pun ought to really punish you, he used to say, spluttering with laughter. Saint-Malo? Yes, I could easily imagine him inventing such a name, the assonance would've delighted him. But no, it still had to be a mistake. He couldn't be alive. No. He was dead. Dead, my Christofer, my dear. I loved him so he had to be dead. And buried at Deptford Strand.

I said, fighting for breath (my thoughts had quite winded me), 'I want to believe you, madam, but I can't. No. Eliza's agents killed him. And arranged the evidence in such a way that the inquest was obliged to find his death an accident.'

'Unless the official account was intended to – '

But I couldn't listen to her. 'That *is* the official account, madam!'

'I know, Tom, I know.'

'It was approved by the Privy Council. To conceal murder!'

I was so angry I didn't care if she saw it. How could she be so obtuse, so wrong-headed? Everyone knows such official 'accidents' happen every day. They're common knowledge to the common people. Even if those above them choose to pretend otherwise.

'You misunderstand me, Tom. I don't doubt the evidence was so partial it was false. Of course it was. What I'm saying is it may have been a cloak for some other stratagem.'

'What?'

'Take breath and think. Think for yourself.'

I sighed, and did as I was told. She was right. Like a child I'd allowed my pent-up feelings to run away with me. I said, 'You suppose Christofer was smuggled abroad?'

She nodded. 'And a coffin full of stones or a pauper's corpse buried in his name.'

I said, 'No, no. I'm certain the people Christofer met at Deptford were determined to kill him, not remove him to France. And they did it for Eliza, for England.' My voice was rising. 'I know they did! Who better?' I was shouting, shaking. 'Who better than me to know? His friend, his betrayer?'

'Are you jealous?'

What could she mean? Again she'd outpaced me. Jealous? Jealous of what? I said, 'I don't understand you?'

'Of your own misfortune. You seem to me too anxious to give credence to your oppressors, Tom. Perhaps you imagine what they've done to you has made you their property? Or of their fraternity at least? However much you may complain of it? And of them?'

She was so right I sulked. 'Christofer can't be in Paris,' I said to divert her from this cruel perception of me. 'I only wish he were. But no, he's dead. Dead thanks to me. Me, me, me!'

'Yes, jealous,' she said. 'Jealous of your own defeat.' And before I could protest added, 'Would you recognise his handwriting?'

I was thunderstruck. Had she plotted this? How *could* she ask such a question of me? It had to be deliberate. Spoken to hurt, to wound, to cut me to the quick. Oh, yes, she knew what she was doing, of course she did. She'd seen how close I was to collapse. She knew I was heartsick with shame, consumed by guilt. And all because of Christofer's handwriting. There, that, was the prime cause of my condition. I half-yelled, half-sobbed at her, thick gobbets of words glistening with spittle, 'Why ask that? Why? Why that?'

Pandora remained as patient as a perfect mother with an imperfect child. 'So we can have proof,' she said. 'I'll write back to my god-daughter and ask her to procure a note from this Monsieur Saint-Malo. If you can then confirm or deny the hand we shall know for certain, shan't we?'

I nodded dumbly and then shook my head not in denial but out of anger at myself. After that I nodded again. Next I said shakily, 'Forgive me. I used to transcribe his work. He had a terrible hand. No one could read it except me. I knew every darting dash of it. He was so impatient, you see. His thoughts ran so quickly his hand couldn't keep up.'

'If this Saint-Malo is who he's said to be you could cross over to France and meet him again. I'd pay for you to go, Tom. From what you've told me I'm sure he would forgive you. You would be reconciled.'

Here was the coup de grâce! I stared at her. Me – meet Christofer again? Did she know what she was proposing? Had she any idea? Of course she hadn't. She hadn't been at our last meeting. I bowed my head and let sorrow drown me. I sat slumped on that sweet-tempered mare and made no attempt whatever to control my horror at myself. No, to say that is to flatter me. No, it's more honest to say I couldn't have controlled myself even if I'd wanted to. The truth is I was cankered with self-pity, rotted by self-regarding grief.

So locked inside my precious misery was I – Pandora was right, I hoarded it, guarded it like a dragon – that I scarcely heard her say, 'You disappoint me, Tom. I'd had higher hopes of you than this. Goodbye.'

When I looked up she was almost gone from sight – galloping furiously away.

No sooner had I returned to my cottage prison than I regretted the exhibition I'd made of myself. Though that hadn't been my first impulse. No, my first was to curse Pandora for not under-standing me. Later, however, I remembered I had never fully explained to her the twin circumstances that had brought me to my refuge here at her expense.

Perhaps now, as I sit at this ink-stained table, watching the day's light fade on the Downs so they lose all substance and become mere shadows floating on the vaporous dews rising from the valley below, perhaps I can describe both instances? The second is less painful to relate than the first so I shall let it be the first. I got here, to this solitary luxury, because I wrote a cringing, crawling letter to Sir John Puckering, Lord Keeper of the Royal Seal no less. In it I compounded the terrible slanders I'd already wished upon Christofer at Chelsea. I wrote this letter from the Clink in the same week I appealed without success to Lord Strange. When I say 'wrote' I mean I dictated my letters to the prison scribe – my hands were not yet healed. These letters were more or less identical except that those to Ferdinando attempted to play upon his past affection for me. Fond hope. But he was still – in name at least – my protector (or so I'd insisted to the governor of the prison to ensure the least worst treatment). I'd worn his livery – well, the embroidered badge establishing me as his obedient servant and bona fide member of his theatre com-pany. We all wore his emblem in case of difficulty with the authorities. I write ironically, of course; the protection of the great does not extend to investigation by Eliza's agents at midnight.

Sir John, aware of Pandora's enthusiasm for the theatre, showed her my letter. He hadn't heard of me, he told her. This frankly I doubt. But Pandora most certainly had. And of Christofer too, naturally. In fact she's since told me she met us both at the Cross Keys about four years ago, she thinks. I'm ashamed to say I've no recollection of this meeting. How I failed to notice her I can't say but it seems I did. Apparently it was after a performance of an old play neither Christofer nor I had worked on: *The Eunuch of Lisbon*. I remember it only too well (it was a feeble thing, or if you prefer, a neutered one) because by presenting it in Grasschurch Street we were defying a mayoral edict not to perform inside the city's limits. But so successful was our company at that time we decided to risk a performance of *The Eunuch*, telling ourselves so harmless a piece was incapable *sui generis* of offending anybody. How wrong we were. The Lord Mayor came down on us like a ton of bricks – an apt simile in the circumstances since he was a liveryman of the Right Worshipful Company of Master Masons – and we were required by statute to surrender our entire stock of playscripts for reappraisal by Archbishop Whitgift at Lambeth Palace. As a result many of our plays which up to then had been performed entire were now emasculated in earnest by those who prize power above knowledge, piety before truth and themselves as judges of everyone else. Of the manifold scenes and lines excised I remember one especially. It was by Christofer and can stand for all: *I count religion but a childish toy and hold there is no sin but ignorance.* The force of this had always impressed our audiences (you should've heard their in-drawn breaths) but now thanks to our bravado it was officially repressed. Our own fault perhaps but even so, if we might have shown more sense, surely the state could have shown more tolerance? But of Pandora's visit I recall nothing while she insists I was introduced to her after the play. She remembers me as tall with a bold stare and says I turned to nudge Christofer – who was talking to someone else – to pay attention to this distinguished lady, the sister of Lord Fitzwalter. It would appear

I minded my manners that afternoon which was a rare thing in those days when I was so full of myself I always felt about to burst – physically, intellectually, spiritually. Pride oozed out of me. I lusted after everything and everyone while aware of nothing, no one. So perhaps it was no wonder I didn't notice Pandora? Although I'm sure she must have been dressed to kill with looks, perfumed to disarm the sternest sense and when she spoke, if she spoke that day as she can now, then her voice would've pleased the tenderest ear.

It was this meeting that saved my life. But for Pandora's remembrance of me I'm sure I would've died in the Clink. Pandora told Sir John he need do nothing which, I suspect, was exactly what he'd hoped she'd say. I'm certain he wanted rid of me. She sent the chamberlain of her household in the Strand to the prison. And on her security I was released. I still couldn't walk. I had to be carried out on a stretcher. Anyone who saw me would've supposed I was dead of the plague and on my way to Houndsditch. But instead, I was conveyed by boat to the Strand where I was nursed until thought well enough to survive the journey down here. It was still a week-long daymare, nightmare; a jolting horror in a cart stuffed with cushions and me, moaning, yelping at every bump. Finally I was brought at night to this cottage which lies, as I say, at a safe distance from the main house. My benefactress may be kind but she's also circumspect. And for that I don't blame her. Pandora often appears as a law unto herself but I'm sure she knows she cannot be. Who can nowadays?

At the time of my arrival I had no proper idea of her. She was still only a resonant name in others' mouths, spoken with respect and not a little fear. Her servants were in constant awe of her. And when I met her so was I. Who wouldn't be impressed? She came to see me here the very next day and her first words have stuck in my mind since, not because they were in themselves particularly memorable but because I had grown used to thinking their opposite. They were: 'Welcome, Mr Kyd. It seems you're lucky to be alive.'

I said, 'Do you think so, madam? I don't.'

She pooh-poohed this, telling me for the first time what she has since frequenlty repeated, that I must teach myself to forgive myself and to begin my life again. It's excellent advice. I don't quarrel with it. My only problem is in following it.

After my arrival her doctor visited me every day for a fortnight and I must admit he's worked miracles when you consider that at the beginning of August I could neither walk nor write. That I can now do both, albeit imperfectly, is entirely thanks to him. Dr Thwaite is a pleasantly serious man from the north who's practised much of his medicine with the Huguenots at Rochester. He also knows surgery and speaks warmly of the schools of Paracelsus he attended in Switzerland as a young man. His visits alone have done me quite as much good as his cures; I dare to believe his presence is medicine in itself.

During this time I've also discovered that my hostess is not only better read than I am but also more widely travelled (as a girl she lived in Venice where her father was ambassador). Furthermore she's shrewder than any man I've ever met. Her knowledge of the Court is comprehensive, her grasp of politics formidable, her contempt for politicians heartening, her distrust of the Queen bottomless. She says Eliza has become a perfect tyrant. Her Majesty's vaunted impartiality being nothing of the kind; she's as intolerant as she is insensible; a whited, bewigged, bejewelled sepulchre. Pandora's even hinted that the Queen herself could have ordered my arrest last May. When I gawped open-mouthed she laughed but continued to insist she was sure I was the victim of someone's hidden purpose. And that I should allow my speculation concerning that person's identity to rise above the level of Heneage and Poley. If not as high as the Queen then at least up to the Lord Treasurer – since Burghley is the royal right hand and the left, too. When she said this I suddenly saw myself as I had been when I appeared before the Privy Council: a shambling wreck neatly dressed. And once again I heard Burghley's dry pumice voice congratulate me upon the loyal service I had rendered the state. 'England may not know it, Mr Kyd, but England has cause to thank you,' he said. Could this great one have engineered my downfall for reasons that still elude me? Pandora believes in conspiracies both by the state and against it whereas, up till now, I've always thought that humankind is invariably too fallible to conspire with absolute success.

When I repeated this to Pandora she smiled indulgently and said that minor intrigues might answer my description but major ones did not, since powerful men can overcome this world's vicissitudes more frequently than is popularly supposed. She said my theory was the false comfort of the weak.

Was this the moment when I first realised how unusually, strangely beautiful she was? I think so. If her words are often sibylline so are her looks. She seems to have stepped freshly out of antiquity to shame these present, ugly times.

In proof of her contention Pandora confirmed what I'd heard whispered before but doubted: that the followers of Sir William Babington had been tricked into plotting against the Queen's life by Secretary Walsingham himself. His intention was to create history. To present the brutal interrogation, measured trial and memorable execution of those deluded young men as a public example of Eliza's unsleeping resolve to root out papistry from the land. If Walsingham (and Burghley too) could arrange *that* for Eliza then neither I nor Christofer need necessarily have suffered at lesser hands, she said.

Pandora's brutal anecdote wasn't easy to dismiss and, what was worse, it carried a corollary I didn't dare to contemplate: that eventually, if I'm ever to make peace with myself, I need to enquire after those who've conspired against me. And then, and then – 'Am I to revenge myself upon the Lord Treasurer?' I said, trying to laugh. 'Or is it the Queen herself I am to aim at?' Pandora smiled but didn't deny my outlandish suggestions. Instead she said I should consider every possibility for redress. She believes I can only truly recover what I've lost by discovering who wronged me and why. In this she is as implacable as a pagan goddess.

My supper's arrived, brought by two dour footmen with instructions to remove the mare. They rode off on her together;

the patient, lightly boned creature visibly sweating under their combined weight.

I see now I've used these recent memories as a shield against the realities I face. Or rather which face me as a consequence of my outburst this afternoon. My anger and despair have utterly offended Pandora – of that I'm sure. Her revulsion was undisguised. Will she turn me out? She could. Without her I'm nothing. I'd be a bleating beggar, a naked moonman wandering the roads and whipped or stoned at every turn for a vagabond. A poor Tom indeed – barking at the dog-star.

Can I take reassurance from this supper that's been sent? That I've got no appetite for? Yes and no. Yes, in that my lady's solicitude continues without countermand for today; but no, in that tomorrow she can quite as easily order my departure. Those two servants who came would just as gladly throw me out as supply my food.

Should I write to her? Explain? Say I realise now she could've had no idea of the effect her words were bound to have on me? Those terrible words: 'Would I recognise Christofer's handwriting?' A sensible question, a proper question, a reasonable question – for anyone but me. Even to repeat it brings back the heart-thudding panic I felt that night when they banged on my door. Three deadly, deliberate knocks as at the beginning of a play performed in the French style. How could Pandora have known of this?

I called out, 'Who's there?' And for answer the door burst open with the two large bolts I'd placed my trust in splintering out of their housings with so sharp a noise that in my half-sleep, half-wake I mistook them for pistol shots. Lantern light danced in my face. I sat up to see three men. The one in the middle I soon discovered to be Robert Poley. I've never found out the names of the other two but the man on the left was the first to speak, announcing himself simply as an officer of the Lord Mayor while requiring from me my full identity.

He said, 'Is your name Kyd? Thomas Kyd, son of Francis?'

I said, 'Who are you?'

For reply he pointed again to his badge of office – his faith in brass and enamel was obviously absolute – and then introduced Poley by name and the other man as Poley's subordinate, both of the Queen's service.

'She has thousands of such servants,' I said. 'Not all their duties extend to – to interruptions such as this – at such times as this.' My words were bolder than their delivery. They stumbled into each other like a crowd panicked from behind.

Poley said, 'We have a warrant to search these premises.' And for a brief moment, a few seconds no more, he waved a piece of paper in my face that might or might not have been a warrant. After that it was gone as quickly as it had appeared, deftly pocketed. A true conjuror of authority is Bob Poley.

'On what grounds?' I managed to ask.

'Security. The security of the realm.'

'What – what address have you been given?' I don't know why I imagined I ought to verify their mission. I suppose I had some quaint notion of judicial propriety in need of observance. Perhaps this shows how startled I was? After all, as subjects of the Queen we're all only too constantly aware she may investigate where, when and whom she chooses.

But despite this Poley answered my question. 'Above the sign of the Green Man at Bucklersbury in the ward of St Stephen Walbrook. Would you accept this as correct?' I nodded. Poley's tone now changed from polite irony to direct command. 'Good. That's a start. Stand over there.' He pointed to a corner of the room.

I was yet to learn that Poley can reduce anyone to a shamefaced dunce if he chooses. I said, 'Why?'

'Stand over there.'

'May I dress?'

'No.'

'Come along, Mr Kyd,' said the third man, gripping my arm

in an attempt to pull me out of bed. I flung him off. In those days it should be remembered I was not the lame dog I am now. I was well-knit and rudely even crudely healthy. I gave ground to no one save pretty girls. And sometimes not even to them, especially the puritans among them. I'd dodge this way that way – not letting them pass until they'd blushed scarlet at the very least. So no court-spy was going to pull me from my bed. He came at me again. I sprang up, mother-naked as I was, and kicked out at him, a heel-kick to his jaw. He fell back. Poley stepped aside as the other man, the Lord Mayor's officer, struck at me with his stick. I seized it from him and slashed him with it across the nose. I heard gristle squeak around cracking bone. His hands covered his face as he yelped at the pain and I was just turning to deliver a similar blow at my first assailant when Poley levelled a pistol at a point between my navel and my prick.

'Please, Mr Kyd, that's enough. Or shall I empty this into your stomach? I'm not here to take part in a beerhouse brawl. Please stand over there.'

I decided discretion was the better part of valour, snatched up my breeches from the chair and pulled them on, glad to be covered again. 'I'm not standing here or anywhere else bollock-naked for you or the Queen,' I said. Poley grinned and shrugged. And ordered the other two men to start the search.

First they ripped my bed apart. Did they think I kept gold among the goosefeathers of my mattress? Then they ransacked the cupboards, piling all my papers onto the table and the denuded bedstead. Next they levered up the floorboards to peer between the joists. After that they returned to the papers which Poley was already picking over with cursory distaste. As an author I hardly blame him. There's nothing more depressing than to view the stacks of paper you've defaced in the writing of a play. Two hours to hear a play, two score quires of paper to make one, we used to say.

Poley looked at me then back at the dismal disorder his subordinates had produced so efficiently. He said, 'Is this all your work, Mr Kyd?'

I wondered what I should reply since so much of it wasn't. I decided to return his question to him. 'Why do you ask?' I said.

'Just answer, please.'

I hesitated again. Then said, 'Most of these manuscripts are mine.'

'And those that aren't?'

'A friend's.'

'Who?'

'I can't quite see why that should really concern you, Mr Poley?' Now that violence had been offered and as quickly quelled we were all determined to be jaw-crackingly polite, it seemed. I certainly was. A pistol pointed at your naked stomach is a potent inducement to politeness. 'With respect, I supposed your interest was in me?'

'Not necessarily.' If only I had known then how truthfully he spoke. 'Whose are these other papers? And please reply as quickly as you can. It'll save all of us so much trouble.'

I decided there was nothing to be gained from withholding what was common knowledge – at least in my playhouse world. A gossipy world as full of chatter as a communal washhouse. Which was that the other scripts were by Christofer. And that they'd been left here when he'd moved out the year before. After we'd lived and worked together for almost three years. Oh, the fun we'd had. I plotted his *Edward II* for him, he rewrote some of my *Spanish Tragedy*, especially the play within the play, and I suggested the Jew's catastrophe at the end of his *Maltese Comedy*. We were perfect collaborators. Oh, and let it be stated now, our separation was amicable. These lodgings had simply grown too small for us both but I didn't want to move, being sentimentally attached to the place – not to mention the beer in the Green Man below, the best double ale in London. So Christofer found accommodation more in keeping with his success near Ludgate while I stayed put in Bucklersbury. If Poley didn't know all this already he could easily find it out so I said, 'Some of these papers belong to this country's leading playwright – Christofer Marlowe. We often worked together and I often transcribed his work. I used to be a professional scribe. Before joining Lord Strange's Company.'

Poley laughed and I wasn't sure why. I couldn't see that anything I'd just said was particularly amusing – a little tight-lipped perhaps but not funny. I know why now. Poley's laugh was not at me but with himself. In his pleasure at what he was about to do.

He pulled some papers at random from one of the insecure, teetering piles – a draft of *Faustus Act III* fanned to the floor – and held up his apparent discovery. If before I'd thought him a conjuror with the warrant for my arrest he'd since been even more dextrous. First to place, then to produce in ill-curbed triumph this fistful of foul papers. His hand had deceived my eye utterly.

He pretended to scan the first page of his find. '*A lecture offering New Thoughts upon the New Testament. As given at the behest of W. R.,*' he read aloud.

He looked up at me. 'What's this, Mr Kyd? Is this by your friend?' Well might he ask. By which I mean I knew only too well that it was. But not, since it was surely an impossibility, how it had come to be there. 'Do you recognise the handwriting?' he added for good measure.

There. Pandora's question had been Poley's. And that's why I'd crumpled so ignobly in the wood. That same question! At once I'd seen myself as I was that night, half-naked in the corner of my room, being obliged to submit myself to Robert Poley of all people. A soft-voiced interpreter of other men's minds. Gentle-eyed but with the crab of ambition griping his stomach. Too like me for comfort or for safety. The danger for me in such eternal subordinates is that I find I rather like them. Or dare I say I did? But no longer? That I'm wiser now? I hope so. Otherwise I'm a fool twice over.

In reply to his question I said, 'Show it to me.' As I looked at the manuscript I ordered myself to display convincing mystifica-tion. My face, I hoped, was blank while my mind raced against itself. Could I really maintain that I didn't know who wrote this? Why, the room was full of other scripts exactly like it. And besides I'd already said I'd often transcribed Christofer's work. No, to deny it was impossible; I couldn't plead ignorance however much I wanted to. It was too late. 'Yes, I said. 'This hand is very much like Christofer's.' A feeble semi-evasion, I agree. But what else could I say?

'This lecture appears heretical. Who's W. R.?'

'I don't know.'

'Well, never mind. I expect you'll remember when you need to.' He rolled the pages into a neat scroll. 'Now you'd best come with us.'

I protested. 'Why? I've done nothing? And those papers you say you've just found – they weren't here – you must've brought them. Placed them here yourself. You did, didn't you? Didn't you? Why? What's your reason? Why?'

'I believe we're more experienced at asking questions than you, Mr Kyd. I suggest you stick to answers. Good answers will serve you better than poor questions. Come along.' And his two accomplices (oh, yes, that's the word to describe them when the state itself's a criminal) seized me, twisting my arms behind my back and securing my wrists with a leather loop. I've learnt since that for this purpose the Queen's agents favour strips cut from the thickest part of a pig's bladder – there's just enough give in it to allow its quick imposition on an unsuspecting person. Again I protested but now a hood went over my head to be laced tautly round my neck. Half thus garrotted, choking in thick woollen darkness, I was hurried from my lodgings. They led me, barefoot, half-naked, to Downgate, to a wharf where I was pushed into a boat and taken up river. My inglorious progress was accomplished in silence except for the slapping of the oars. The waters that windless night stank more than usual as the nightsoil carts laboured at every pier and road end . . .

At this moment I broke off, got up from my table and went outside to piss. A simple call of nature coincidental with this narrative. The air from the Downs was as welcome as my memories were vile but as I emptied my bladder they faded. And

I felt suddenly and strangely blessed. I remember looking up as the moon rose over Chancton Ring. It was almost full, rather lopsided. And I laughed. Such was my unlooked-for change of mood that I found this moon amusing, absurd – like a fat lady at a fair. I wanted her to break into a comic song. I began to hum, to invent nonsense words for her. My singing moon-lady! 'Call me Lady Cynthia, I come from far-off India.'

I must have stopped outside in the garden a good quarter of an hour enjoying the night as my funny fat moon flooded the slopes of the Downs with light. Sharp shadows lengthened across warm silver spaces. Grateful for the peace that had descended so unexpectedly upon me I turned to go inside.

At once I knew something was wrong. Something had happened behind my back. As I approached the door I became convinced it was not quite so ajar as I had left it. This could've been a trick of the breeze but instinct said otherwise. Someone or something had entered the house behind my back. An animal perhaps? A cat tame or wild? A stray dog? As I stepped inside I called out cautiously: a questioning hallo. No answer. I looked round. My room seemed as it was. I'd been mistaken. Nothing had happened. Then I realised one of the candles was missing from my table. So I was wrong again. Here was no animal, or any ghost. A thief? I reached for my stick by the door. Having got what grip on it I could I called again. Still no answer. Except the inner door to my left creaked. Whoever was here was there. I hobbled across. I said with what pugnaciousness I could muster (not much), 'I know you're here. Show yourself.' No reply. 'I warn you I'm armed,' I added as I took breath on the threshold before pushing hard at the door. It swung back. No one. I stepped into the moonlit room. No one. But the missing candle burned on the mantelpiece and the bedclothes were pulled back so the linen sheets gleamed like snow.

Someone giggled. What a fool I'd been not to look behind me! I turned as sharply as I could and – and there was Jane – I mean Mary. I stared at her. She smiled and reaching forward gently removed my stick from my awkward grasp. She set the brutal thing aside. Then she took the hand that had held it and kissed the palm so that her face was cupped within its curled-up crippledness. I can't remember when a gesture touched me more.

I said, 'Who sent you?'

For reply Mary pulled a letter from a pocket in her skirt. I took it to the candle and read: 'I send Mary with this. I was in a mind to turn you out but the girl has spoken for you. You have quite misunderstood her. The contempt you thought she showed you was pity. Pity that has since increased as I've now told her something of how you came by your injuries. Her motive in visiting you tonight is as mixed as most motives usually are. She comes to you out of her own simplicity of heart and natural need of men but also for gain since I have promised her rich rewards for comforting you. Enjoy your milkmaid. Goodbye. Postscriptum: Mary knows the contents of this letter, I've read it to her.'

I looked at Mary. 'You pity me?' She nodded. I put the letter down. 'You spoke up for me?' Again she nodded. 'Tell me,' I said. She looked from me to the opened bed. 'You'll tell me there?'

'Aye,' she said in no more than a whisper.

'No. Tell me now. What did you say to my lady?'

'You won't be angry, sir.'

'I don't know till you say it, do I?'

She surveyed her shoes then looked up at me and said. 'I told her I reckoned you must've been a proper young man once, sir. But now you looked aged. Aged beyond your years. It wasn't only in your body, I said, but in your eyes. And that I found a shame, sir.'

'And what did her ladyship say?'

'She said I spoke true, sir. And asked me what could be done.'

'What did you answer?'

'Well, I said I thought you needed loving, sir. Most men do I find.'

'And you, Mary? What do you want?'

'The same, sir. All of us are the same, sir. Men and women. Rich and poor. Great and small. We all need love's goodness, don't we?'

'I've met some who didn't, Mary. Who've grown fat on other pleasures.'

'Wicked creatures, I daresay.'

'Perhaps. But suppose I tell you that since my ill-treatment in prison I fear I'm no man at all?'

'I shan't believe it, sir. Not until we've made trial of it.' And she stepped out of the door into the other room. She took a pan of simmering water from the fire and poured it into the bowl I used for washing. Then she took up my sponge and brought both back into the bedroom. 'Shall we wash, sir? The both of us?'

'You do surprise me, Mary. You sound so gentle. And look it too. When I first saw you I thought you hard, unfeeling.'

'Well, I'm not, sir. Not once I know a person.'

'Do you think you know me?'

'No, I don't, sir, no. But her worship tells me I can be myself with you. So I shall be if it pleases you.'

I believe she meant this even if she did relish the prospect of reward from Pandora. And now the thought of my lady's managing spirit amused me. I should have expected to resent it. Perhaps in my former age I would've done but now I didn't. Was this the influence of the moon staring through the lattice at us? I don't know. But as I looked at Mary it seemed to me that both these women might mean well towards me, after all.

'Why did her ladyship say goodbye at the end of the letter? Is she leaving here?'

'I don't know, sir. Her worship does as she pleases.'

'Yes.' I laughed at the plain truth of this. 'Yes, she does indeed,' I said.

'Will you undress, sir?'

For reply I held out my hand. She took it gently and allowed me to draw her close. As our lips almost touched I said, 'A kiss first.' My motive, I'm afraid, was of the worst. I wanted to discover if her breath smelt or her spittle was tainted by onion or garlic. I can't bear either manifestation – any hint of such and all desire is gone.

Our lips touched, pressed closer, her mouth opened and her tongue flicked out at mine. Her breath was sweet. She tasted of milk and honey. I drew back, smiling. Her hand unbuttoned my shirt, then unbuckled my belt. I wanted to do likewise with her but I knew my hands would be too clumsy. Besides being ugly and too slow.

'I want to undress you, Mary. But I can't. My hands won't do it.'

'Then you mustn't.'

And straightaway, without artifice or coquetry, she pulled her bodice over her head, placed it aside, untied the drawstring at her waist and kicking off her shoes stepped out of her skirt. And at that she was naked. Before I could exclaim at her handsomeness so matter-of-factly revealed she had pulled my breeches to the floor and was nudging me to step from them. I did as I was bidden. Like a child. Now she took the sponge, dipped it in the water and wrung it out. She turned to face me. She regarded me and I regarded her. Her skin was without blemish unlike my freckled shoulders. Her breasts were a little imperfect with the left larger than the right – an endearing difference this. But who was I to find the slightest fault when my chest curved inwards below my rounded shoulders? Her nipples were dark rose-madder and already alert to caresses from the night air. Mine were sad ha'pennies. Her belly was flat. Mine, I realised was slack. Not fat especially but flabby and defeated. Her cunt was lost to view below a bush of bright gold. Far brighter than the hair of her head. My prick, I knew, was shrivelled to a timid dormouse peeping out at a world of promise spiked with terror.

'You put me to shame, Mary,' I said, my eyes still fixed on the burnished gold at her crotch.

She laughed. 'My mother taught me how to do that, sir. She mixes the dye for it. I paint it on. She says a girl's head hair may be the colour of last year's hay but below the waist let her hoard secret gold. But you must carry yourself better, sir. Your flesh looks afraid of itself.'

'It is,' I answered. 'And so is my mind, Mary. I'm full of fear. Night and day.'

'We must find what cures for that we can, sir.'

And she rinsed the sponge again in the water and then washed my chest, making me lift my arms up like a child. Then she dried me before washing my stomach, my prick – using the sponge to push back the foreskin so she could wash all round the tender crest of it. At this I felt a stir of desire. And then again as she turned me round and squeezed the sponge between my buttocks. Taking the towel she dried me briskly back and front. The sensation was almost painful and I reached down quickly to pull my foreskin forward. Suddenly it was as if I was dressed again. Mary laughed, kissed me on the breastbone and handed me the sponge.

I washed her neck, her shoulders, her breasts, her back. As I used the sponge to tickle her navel she giggled and suddenly her hips swayed as they had when going through the garden gate and she was standing with her legs apart inviting me to sponge her spun-gold crotch. I rinsed the sponge again and drew it slowly up her leg. When at last it reached its goal, hers, mine, her breath caught and she bore down on it. Quickly, to make her want more, I pulled the sponge away and reaching for the towel, dried the place. Whereat she crooned yearningly, pleasurably.

She whispered (how her breath tickled my ear), 'You may towel me, Master Tom, but you'll never dry me now, not there, not now.' And her teeth took my ear lobe and nipped it playfully.

At this – her action and her words – I found my prick filling. For the first time in months it became heavy inside itself, of itself. I felt newborn. I laughed. My Methuselah years dropped away.

Mary laughed too and without another word she took my crippled hands in hers and led me to the bed.

·I·I·

And so began my life in proper time again. At each sundown Mary would arrive, appearing out of the shadows like a healthy ghost, and by each dew-drenched dawn be gone. But only to return at seven with the milk for my breakfast whereat I would at once waylay her. She would protest that she had work to do – a whole morning churning butter – but I'd insist *I* was her work. Remind her she'd been expressly commanded by her absent ladyship to restore me to health. Oh, yes, Pandora's farewell had been real enough – she had gone and was said now to be at Greenwich. It was Mary's job to create rude health in me, I said. Of body, of soul, of mind. I must have no more frenzies or sick fancies. And here my tongue would lick my lips lasciviously – then hers until they opened to admit me. This breach achieved I'd draw back and argue like a lustful Jesuit that my restoration was far from complete, she still had lots to do and so did I, much of which we hadn't even imagined or invented yet. And then she'd laugh, then interrogate me with dancing eyes, then melt. Words, provided they were swift and sweet, captivated Mary. A sonnet breathed in her ear or upon her breast could bring her to ecstasy. With her a poet had hardly need of touch at all.

One remedy she employed upon me, after we had rioted together, died upon each other and I was yet to rise again, was to stroke my hands. Or rather to press and gently pummel them so that the taut tissues around the ill-set bones loosened and grew suppler. My left hand improved more than the right. Soon the first three fingers and thumb were almost like any other man's.

Now I thanked God for being born ambidextrous. I trained the left to do more and more: to grip a pen or a knife or tweak Mary's ear. My right remained stiff – an awkward signpost, a half-broken butter paddle. It could steer things to me or push them away but the fingers couldn't move let alone dance as my left hand's could: doing little jigs down Mary's back and across her buttocks, quick voltas upon her breasts, veritable sword dances around her navel. How we laughed as her cunning ways released me from care. I was becoming my old self, I told her. And it was all her doing. She had transformed me from a cringing beggar to a benevolent despot and I would tell her ladyship so when she returned. For reply she ran the edge of her fingernail down my back from the base of my skull to the tip of my spine. My answer was in kind. We spoke no further.

As the days and nights passed, my mind, in imitation of my body, seemed also to win itself new liberties. Where before I had brooded sulphurously upon my sufferings now I found I could dwell upon them to some purpose. Because, having hung upon Top's pillar and after had my knee and hands broken for my pains, it followed, as the night the day, and as Pandora had insisted, that someone had betrayed me long before I was forced to betray Christofer. That agent, that creature must have stolen the blasphemous document which Poley had placed between my papers. And that same cabinet thief must have purloined it to please another. Who? And passed it into the hands of God knows how many others before it reached Poley? Therefore who were they? I could think of one or two who might have done it. But not, I guessed, enough. Power commands so many eager disciples.

To discover who had first engineered my downfall I decided I must dissect my past life like a surgeon demonstrating anatomy to a class of students. Especially those inward parts of my history which had linked themselves with Christofer. Yes, I would cut, I would flay, never minding what repulsive mysteries I might lay bare.

But to do this I found at once that I needed to grant this unknown agent of my misfortunes a provisional identity. A name that would fix him in my mind, make him a target I could shoot at. I couldn't search for a nameless nobody, a cypher. And the instant I told myself this I found I'd already called him Ishmael. The name leapt like a fox into my head scattering the thoughts which had propagated it like so many farmyard fowls. Snap! Just like that! In the twinkling of an eye. Or rather two eyes. Mine first, then Mary's. I saw she'd caught this sudden flicker of invention.

'What is it?' she said as we lay side by side; Venus and Vulcan burnished by candlelight.

'I've thought of a name,' I answered. 'Or, to tell true, it seems to have found me out.'

'What name?'

'Ishmael.'

'And that makes you happy?'

'Yes.'

'I thought it did. I could tell from the look of you.'

'It's perfect,' I said, my hands in her hair, my lips brushing hers.

'Who for?'

'My enemy. My secret enemy.'

'Ishmael?'

'The wild man in the book of Genesis.'

'I know *that*.' She was offended. And to prove herself she chanted the verse at me. '"And he will be a wild man. His hand will be against every man – "'

I clapped my hand over her mouth and continued the chant for her. '"And every man's hand against him. And he shall dwell in the presence of his brethren." And he does, Mary, he does.' I took my hand from her mouth and kissed her. 'I forgot you were a scholar, my dear.'

'Now don't you tease me, Tom, or I'll not come to your bed tomorrow.' But her threat was as empty as her spun-gold quim was soon full of me again.

The next morning I found this determination to search out Ishmael had taken firm root in me. It had been no night thought. I would hunt him down methodically. Smoke him out from his hiding place inside my head. Somewhere I must have seen him, perhaps even met him without knowing what he was. To discover him I would need to order my memory most punctiliously; scrutinise every recollection, resurrect every encounter. I vowed I would shake my life through a sieve until I shook out Ishmael. From that moment I, Tom Kyd, would be a spy inside myself.

I decided to begin my new, model enquiry among my more recent memories of what had seemed my usual life. I mean those weeks in April before my arrest. I'd spent them in Kent. And it was there that Christofer's foul papers had last been seen (by me at least) before Robert Poley pretended to find them among mine in Bucklersbury. Yes, I would begin there, among Thomas Walsingham's many guests at Scadbury. It wouldn't be easy. He had filled his house to bursting with what seemed like all the youth of England. And that's not to mention his myriad servants and frequent day visitors some of whom, I now recall, were among the highest in the land.

But here comes Mary with the milk.

·I·I·I·

Scadbury is heaven on earth, a morning's ride from Deptford. The house is embraced by a moat which is joined to a lake shaped like a sheep's kidney set in a wooded park Herne the Hunter would be pleased to haunt. Fallow deer bring dappled sunlight to the oak trees' shade even when the day star is hidden; some are so tame they'll eat quartered apples from your hand. The air is sweet. Stinking London seems a world away.

I didn't want to go there. But Christofer petitioned me so urgently I gave in. He'd risked the plague to come to my lodgings from Ludgate. His only protection a linen bandage soaked in oil of rosemary and Dutch gin wound three times round his mouth and nose. He sounded like a drunk speaking inside a laundry bag. Outside a funeral bell tolled steadily while across the street two muslin-shrouded corpse collectors were loading their cart with the ragged bodies of three small children and their mother. The man of the house stood watching, stiller than his own doorpost.

'Please, Tom, please, my darling. You must come with me. You must!'

'But what would I do in Kent?'

'Escape the pestilence, man! Live and laugh. Walsingham's invited all his friends. We'll play at shepherds. Enact a pastoral. There'll be masques and balls and banquets. Sport of every kind. We'll eat and drink ourselves supine. And you can have your pick of the girls – you will anyway, won't you? And me too, I promise. I'll be your Ganymede whenever you're tired of Venus.

Oh, my dear, do say you'll come. You can't stay here. You'll die.'

'But I've promised to join the company at Epping.' The theatre had been closed since February; Lord Strange's Men, for fear of the plague's virulence increasing as the year advanced, were embarked upon a major tour.

'The company can manage without you, Tom. Beside it's time you wrote another play.'

'You too.'

'We'll work on one together.'

'Oh no! I'm not collaborating with you again. Look at the last time.' But I was smiling inside, outside, remembering the towering quarrels, the fabulous reconciliations we'd created between us as we worked on *The Damnable Life of Doctor John Faustus*.

Seeing I was tempted he said, 'Yes! But a comedy this time, Tom. A wicked comedy. A comedy with a heart of stone. *The Heretic's Comedy*! There – we've got our title already. That's an omen. An augury of vast success. We can start with the crucifixion. Yes! On comes the mob with three crosses. They nail Christ and the two thieves to them. Effigies of wax that look so real they seem to breathe. Guy ropes haul them upright to the beating of drums, the snarl of trumpets, all the Jews screaming like screech owls, together with great rolls of thunder – stabs of lightning.'

'Lightning? How shall we have lightning?'

'Fire crackers of course! Thrown from the heavens by the property boys. Oh, Tom, I can see it, can't you?' Christofer's eyes shone. I longed to agree. Yearned to recapture those heartwarm days when we had worked or consulted together on almost everything; read scenes one to the other, or both together, teased out arguments between us, roughed out speeches for each other. But I knew such lovely times were gone, and so I think did he even if he couldn't admit it. His next work, whatever it was, would be, had to be his alone. He'd outgrown me. But none of these sentimental considerations prevented him from continuing to entice me with false fire. His imagination was at full tilt – a galloping, snorting warhorse bearing down on me pell-mell. 'And meanwhile, my dear, our chorus enters! Two stupendous whores on six-inch buskins and ablaze with jewels. One male, stage right, tricked out as an oiled and perfumed nuncio – the other, female, stage left, dolled up as a certain majestical virgin, shrivelled, powdered, bald!'

I groaned pointedly. 'And these two familiar monsters will announce the argument of the play?'

'Of course! Turn by turn. Verse for verse.'

'And what will the argument be?'

'Why – whatever we hit on together so long as it paints religion as the sword of the State, the law the overseer's whip, the Church the chains that bind us all. Do come, my dear. Escape the sickness. Forsake the city. Come to Scadbury.'

'Well, perhaps I will!' I said. 'But I refuse to write a play with you.' The bandage across his mouth vibrated as he lip-farted at me. I ignored this urchin interruption saying, 'And I don't like Walsingham.' This was mildly said. The truth was I was close to detesting him. Master Thomas, cousin of the late Sir Francis, was Christofer's latest conquest and would-be patron. Tall, rich, bat-eared, unchinned, Walsingham wor-shipped my Christofer while neglecting his mistress, Lady Audrey Shelton.

'You've no cause to be jealous of Corin, my dear.'

'Corin! Is that what you call him?'

'It pleases him. He sees himself as a passionate shepherd.'

'Corin! How coy. How winsome.' It was my turn to express myself coarsely but not through my lips, rather I exercised the back of my throat as if eructing phelgm. 'And I *do* have reason to be jealous. He's in love with you.'

'No, he just thinks he is. It's calf-love, puppy-love, silly sonnet-love. Besides – ' But here he deliberately cut himself short, inviting me to ask him why he'd stopped.

This was an old trick and I was inclined to disregard it. Then I didn't. I shrugged just to let him know I'd noticed but didn't care and said, 'Why? What else is there *besides?*'

Christofer grinned. Well, his eyes glinted and the bandage puckered. 'I was thinking, my dearest Tom, thinking he'll have Lady Audrey with him in Kent. If he doesn't behave himself –

and I promise you I can make quite sure he doesn't – ' he laughed loudly and lewdly ' – then she'll be in need of consolation, won't she?' He eyed me like a whorehouse huckster knowing perfectly well that my jealousy of Walsingham was double-edged. On the one hand I was still possessive of Christofer, on the other I was violently drawn to Lady Audrey. Rarely had I had so many dreams and fancies about a woman and like a fool I'd confided some of them to him.

I said, 'You're certain Lady Audrey will be there?'

'Of course! With all her equally nubile waiting ladies. I tell you, Tom we shall have a tumultuous time! We'll re-invent the Golden Age. And while I have my Corin you can enjoy his Corinna, can't you? Why not? Is it a bargain? Tell me it is.' Still I pretended to hesitate. Knowing he had won me over he fell to his knees, became a grotesque mock supplicant, exclaiming untruthfully that I was his muse, his mentor, his talisman, what would he do without me? I laughed and agreed to go with him. He leapt to his feet and kissed me heartily through his plague-defying bandage.

The next morning we set off, taking a boat from Queen Hithe down river to Deptford where we hired horses and so came to Scadbury.

Christofer's promise of Arcady was fulfilled. Even as we entered the home park we could hear well-matched voices singing. At that distance the words held no meaning; they were simply notes afloat on the air but as we rode closer they spoke of love and loss most tunefully. Soon we saw our host and some twenty of his guests seated beneath an ancient, stag-headed oak which must have been a sturdy tree when King Stephen was knee high to a grasshopper, as Mary would say. Walsingham was living up to his shepherd's name of Corin. He was dressed in homespun breeches and rough linen shirt. He had a crook across his knees and a frayed straw hat lay on the ground beside him. And yet despite this rustic simplicity he retained an air of consummate if careless authority. The girls appeared not so much as shepherdesses as nymphs. While a few wore honest jersey most sported dresses of silk so gossamer fine you would have thought them more suited to be petticoats or nightshifts. Their hair was equally undressed. The ground about them was strewn with flowers: hyacinths, jonquils and lenten lilies had been cut for use as rushes on the parkland floor. A tethered nanny goat was munching them methodically while two tiny kids tugged greedily at her udder.

For their part the men conformed exactly with their host – only the softness of their hands, their unblemished cheeks and the downiness of their chins proclaimed them other than shepherds or goatherds. Except for one who stood apart. This was a big, muscular fellow with tightly curled, goose-greased hair. His beard was thick, cropped close. His teeth white as whalebone. His chest was uncovered, ornamented only by a gold medallion on a chain. He wore heavily belted breeches cut from some shaggy animal skin – wolf or bear perhaps. Evidently he saw himself as a forest faun of some substance. His insolent grin and continual flexing of every supple joint and swelling muscle proclaimed as much. Even as we rode up this self-made satyr turned three dashing cartwheels an Italian tumbler would have been proud to perform. But it struck me that this display was not in honour of our arrival. Oh no, there was nothing of welcome in it. Rather these antics seemed to be a warning – though of what I couldn't say. His name, I was soon informed, was Francis. But as secretary and chamberman to Walsingham he was known to all at Scadbury as Master Francis. These offices were precisely those I had enjoyed with Lord Strange when he first plucked me from Gray's Inn to serve in his household. But this Francis (was it Christian name or surname?) appeared much older than is usual with such protégés. I had been scarcely twenty-three when first I served in such a fashion whereas this preening creature must have been almost forty. Also it soon became apparent that he was excessively even uxoriously protective of his employer.

The moment Walsingham recognised Christofer he jumped up with a shout of joy and ran to him, almost pulling him down from his horse to embrace him.

'Christofer, my dear! Welcome, welcome. I'd begun to think you'd spurned me in favour of some grander host! Oh, you must stay for ever. And you've brought Tom, too. That's wonderful.

My house is complete. We're now a true fount of the muses! Welcome, Tom, welcome.'

His greetings were genuine but still I couldn't warm to the man. There was something too sugared in his manners.

He hugged us both and then with his arms about our shoulders he turned to the assembled company. 'Dear shepherds, sweet nymphs,' he proclaimed. 'Allow me to present the two finest poets of our age – Christofer and Tom. You've all seen their plays now you may admire their persons.'

Everyone laughed and to our pleasure Walsingham's beautiful guests applauded us. We clapped back as if we'd come from farthest Bohemia not London. Francis (I cannot bring myself to call him *Master*) did not applaud. He merely smacked one palm against the other. Just the once. It sounded like a pistol shot. Oh, he grinned freely enough with his mouth but his eyes were flintstones.

As Walsingham conducted us to sit on either side of him a caravan of servants arrived with covered baskets and creaking hampers full of an outdoors banquet. A picnic, Lady Audrey called it, pronouncing it in the French fashion. She pressed my hand as I sat beside her, I was laughing, so was she. And for one tingling instant we admired each other in each other's eyes. Then both of us looked away, taking breath, and bread, and wine.

To find yourself mirrored in Audrey's regard was to dream you'd become a favourite of the Queen of Love. Her gold-flecked eyes, freckle-dusted cheeks and burnished hair gave weight to such hyperbole. Or so it seemed that day. As I've said I had dreamed of her many times – often with explosive results. But never once in any of our actual encounters had I given her the slightest indication of my inmost urgings; I had, I was sure, behaved with a remarkable propriety. But now as I was seated next to her and observing that her nymph's apparel was both the richest and the finest of all those ladies present, I decided (was this silk across her breasts woven from spiders' webs?) I decided (I wrenched my eye back to hers only to find I dared not dwell within them!) I decided that this April must allow for more than dreaming, that I would keep Christofer to his pander's promise.

'Tom,' she said, taking my hand again. 'I told myself not to hope you'd come. I knew Christofer would but I wasn't sure of you. But despite my resolution I kept silently praying you would come and now you have and all my prayers are answered. Oh, I feel so glad.' She blushed and glanced across at Walsingham who was sharing a silver kissing cup the size of a chamber pot with Christofer. I laughed, her blush turned to a sudden frown at what she'd seen and my spirits soared like a lark even as cocky *Sweet William* ever alive in my breeches did likewise. A shameful admission I daresay, but most truths are, I've found.

I said, 'You supposed Christofer and I were no longer inseparable?'

'I'd heard you lived apart. That Christofer now entertained his friends at Ludgate.' Another glance at Walsingham who this time was offering Christofer pepper to season a quail's egg.

'That's true,' I said. 'But we haven't quarrelled.' Was she disappointed? This time I felt equal to her gaze but relinquished my grip on her hand (how soft it seemed) inviting her to withdraw it if she wished. She did, but not I noted immediately. I thought I detected a shadow of regret in her which while it flattered me also made me quick to reassure her. 'But,' I added, 'we have agreed we may follow whatever fancies we choose. We love each other still, of course. And yet we're free.'

She drew breath almost audibly. 'I'm sure that's only right,' she said. 'People should be free. How lucky you poets are. Your lives are so simple compared with ordinary mortals.'

'If only that were true.'

'It is, Tom, it is,' she sighed deeply. And was there a welling moistness in her eyes?

I said (wanting only to kiss them shut), 'There was another reason for our parting. A very ordinary one. My lodgings had become too small for two. We used to work in the same room together – the only room fit for the purpose – sitting opposite each other at my old table. But nowadays we find we write better alone. Unless we're deliberately collaborating, of course. Christofer wants us to work together while we are here but I'm not sure. I don't know if I want to. And besides I think we may both be far too busy – each in his own way, don't you?'

She smiled and said, 'Couldn't you afford somewhere larger to live? A successful playwright like you?'

'I don't know. Perhaps I could. But I have no share in the company and my Lord Strange has got himself another favourite. Besides I could never leave Bucklersbury. It's the hub of my world.'

Audrey shuddered. 'But what of the noise? Doesn't the constant traffic disturb you? I once had the misfortune to walk through from Walbrook to Cheapside – oh, the din! The carts! The people! It was beastly. And the smells! I don't think my nose has ever encountered so many different stenches in so confined a place.'

'I put a clothes' peg on my nose,' I said. 'And I can shut my ears like a toad.' We laughed. 'But I don't need peace and quiet. I love to hear the world outside my window.'

'Oh, dear. Then you're bound to hate it here. It's more than quiet here. The most you'll find to disturb you here are turtle doves.'

'No cuckoos yet?'

'I heard one only yesterday.'

'Well, that's a happy coincidence.'

'For whom?'

'For me, I hope.' I squeezed her hand but this time she removed it at once. I had spoken and acted too soon. Lady Audrey despite her dress, despite her warm regard, required subtler persuasion than this. To repair the damage I said, 'It won't be quiet here now. Not any longer. Not now Christofer's arrived. I promise you, it will soon be chaos. You've invited a natural lord of misrule. You'll have a riot of laughter, tears and tantrums.'

'Oh, I do hope not. I can't bear – '

But before Lady Audrey could explain herself further – I discovered later, that unusually for a gentlewoman, she abhorred public displays of private feelings – a huge guffaw larded with violent protests exploded all about us. Christofer had proved me right. Whatever he'd just said had obviously been outrageous. Walsingham was remonstrating with him even as he slurped more wine into his guests' proffered glasses. 'You can't *say* that, Christofer,' he yelled, red-faced, thrilled to the marrow by the enormity of whatever it was. 'You can't. You mustn't. It's monstrous! My God, man, suppose someone overheard?'

'What did he say?' asked Audrey.

'I can't repeat it, madam,' Walsingham answered. 'Nor must he.'

'I only said – '

'No, Christofer! Not again. I forbid you to speak. You'll have my head on the block for asking you here.'

But no one yet had ever prevented the Christofer I knew from expressing an opinion, however extreme. Uptil last Spring – may God help me – the sheer exuberance of his pronouncements on people, politics and religion had protected him: his hearers took them as the inordinate jokes of a genius – a poet's privileged excess. They assumed Christofer couldn't really mean what he said which was some distance from the truth. Or else they thought he must be drunk which wasn't necessarily true either though I confess he often was and me with him. No, the rooted reason for Christofer's outrageousness was far simpler: it was just that he was as easily intoxicated by words as wine. Words heated his brain quite as well as liquor. Better. They led him by the nose, snorting and curvetting, braying and neighing into an enchanted wilderness of savage thoughts, ferocious doubts, brutal laughter and wild Apollonian harmonies.

'I only said – '

'No! I'll stop your mouth!'

And Walsingham did. With a kiss. A demanding, thrustful kiss. Everyone laughed except Lady Audrey. I found her hand on my arm, her nails digging hard into my sleeve. When they broke apart her hand returned to her lap. The velvet's nap now showed four tiny crescent moons.

She said to those of us close by, 'It seems we may not know what Christofer said.' Her voice was a bright knife.

Nor did we. Each time Christofer threatened to speak

Walsingham would stop him with hand or mouth, once with a handkerchief as a makeshift gag. This teasing game continued until Christofer bit his patron's finger. Walsingham cried out, swore he'd drawn blood, then sulked for a while only to recover his usual cheerful spirits as four of his guests (those same matched voices we had heard from afar) honoured him with a graceful, pre-prandial madrigal. It was that old song *In Youth is Pleasure*. Here, I thought was Christofer's chance? While they sang he could declare himself at last. Surely?

But he didn't. Looking across at him I said, 'Quickly! Now! Say it, Christofer. Come on, man! Astonish us.' I was quoting Ferdinando at him.

He did – but not in the way I'd expected. He surprised me by denying me. By shaking his head. 'The moment's gone,' he said.

I couldn't believe my ears. I berated him, called him a coward put down by wealth, ordered him to say what it was or lose my respect for ever – I too can overstate – but still he refused to speak. Except that this last time he glanced dartingly at one of the shepherds perched on a knuckle of the oak tree's spreading roots. I didn't know the man. He had a round seemingly foolish face and a belly threatening to match it. His eyes were the palest I've ever seen; a wintry blue possessed them. I persisted at Christofer no further. Instead I asked Lady Audrey who this shepherd was. She said he was one of Walsingham's oldest friends and a great gambler. His name was Nicholas but he was known to all as Nick. Or Old Nick. His surname was Skeres. She quite liked him. This left me not much the wiser. I advised myself to question Christofer once we were alone.

We feasted the rest of the afternoon away, lining our stomachs with miniature sea crabs spiced with chillies, Kentish ducks baked among candied peaches from Portugal, sweet herb salads, pippin tarts and more junkets and custards than I have names for – except for one called snow cheese. Oh, how I gorged myself upon that! Lady Audrey said it was made out of whipped eggs and the zest of lemons but to succeed it needed the finest, purest sugar in the world which came from turnips grown in Picardy. As for the delicate wines, well, some were icy cold, others warm as blood. Together with the food they first provoked fierce philosophy, then gossip accompanied by waves of knowing laughter and much unbuttoned singing, both musically and lyrically. We ended at last in languor, lust or sleep. Several of our grosser swains merely lolled and snored where they were – their heads in their ladies' laps. Others more expeditious, took their nymphs by the hand and led them away – the girls objecting with a notable lack of conviction – towards the house or deeper into the park. As they departed their giggling protests seemed to float behind them like soap bubbles left hanging in the air. Unseen above us doves cooed insistently, crooningly, just as Lady Audrey had said they would. It seemed as if each and every trembling leaf and bursting bud were catching their breaths for love. How I longed to reach out and take Lady Audrey's hand and, as the others had done, draw her apart to some damask-curtained bed or brackened bower. But such a thing was quite impossible while my host remained among us – even if he lay, as he did now, with his head cushioned upon Christofer's shoulder.

After a while Lady Audrey rose to her feet with ill-concealed impatience. At once those of her closest female companions got up to join her. I too began to scramble upright but she – too peremptorily I thought – told me to stay where I was. I felt aggrieved; my fancies concerning her had not prepared me for such brusqueness. Something in my look must have conveyed my pique to her for suddenly she smiled – a quick, tight smile pleading forgiveness. Then she and her girls drifted away like silent shades. Once they were gone I resisted sleep no longer.

The next thing I knew someone was shouting he needed exercise and, opening my eyes, I saw Christofer hauling Walsingham to his feet. Beyond them Francis hung from a low bough performing chest-heaves with ape-like ease. Another shepherd was running on the spot, trying to hit his buttocks with his heels. Others simply stretched modestly or groaned eloquently.

'Come on, Corin!' Christofer was yelling. 'Let's race. I bet I'll beat you! Come on.'

'How much?'

'A hundred crowns of yours to a poem of mine.'

'How many stanzas?'

'What are you? Some backstreet moneychanger?'

'How many?' Walsingham insisted, outfacing Chrisofer's bawling derision. 'I know you poets. Market men the lot of you – for all your airs and graces.'

'No stanzas. Couplets. Fifteen couplets in pentameters.'

'Fifteen is that all?'

'Twenty? How's that? That's forty lines, for God's sake!'

'Still so few?'

'Still so honeyed, sweet shepherd, so scented, so bee-sucked I promise you'll die of pleasure at them. Agreed?'

'Agreed. But only because you're you, my dear. Here's my hand.'

And they shook hands heartily, hugging and patting each other the while. Then Walsingham asked which way the course should lie, suggesting the western gatehouse as the finishing post.

'No,' said Christofer, ever contrary. 'To the lake. We may need to cool ourselves.'

But Walsingham protested that this was not far enough for a true test unless they were to go by way of the orchards and the home wood. This in its turn proved too far for Christofer who objected that he and I – 'You'll race too, won't you, Tom?' – we had only that minute arrived whereas Corin and his fellow swains had been living off the fat of Arcadia for weeks on end and enjoying all kinds of exercise unknown to us. I intervened with a diplomatic compromise. 'Couldn't we run to the lake by way of the west gate? That'll be a matter of two miles not four?'

Our host accepted this and calling us all together we lined up in a row like schoolboys. Francis took it upon himself to give us our starting orders. Nine gentle shepherds and two underbred poets were suddenly at the command of a swaggering satyr who with military precision made sure we all stood level with each other before screaming in a falsetto more coercive than any baser note: 'On your marks, gentlemen! Get set. Set, set, set! Back Master Thomas! Back, back, back! Are we in line? Yes, we are in line, gentlemen! Yes, yes! Get set!' Final eldritch squeal. 'Go!'

As we sprang forward he did too. It seemed he intended to

supervise us as we ran. Furthermore it soon became plain this self-appointed umpire could if he chose – and he did – run the lot of us into the ground. From the start he sprinted ahead, running as if this were a course of two hundred yards not two miles. Very soon he was lost to view but some minutes later as we laboured after him he reappeared, full of prance and puff, to urge us on, jeering at us, running backwards beside us or else scissoring sideways alongside. Having proved his Olympian superiority he waved us forward to the gatehouse which now stood only a furlong ahead. When we returned we found him waiting where we'd left him, only now he was entertaining himself by walking on his hands. From this topsy-turvy point of vantage he observed us pass before flipping neatly to his feet and coming after us. In less than fifty yards he'd outstripped us and was gone again. I think we were all glad to see the back of him. I certainly was.

The rest of us, until now evenly matched, began to separate – teased apart by effort. At the next bend in the path Christofer and I saw our chance and we spurted ahead of Walsingham and the rest, grinning exultantly to each other. But our advantage was short-lived. I tripped on a tussock, Christofer turned his head to see what had happened and in that instant Walsingham and five other of his lordly bumpkins had galloped past us. I regained my balance almost at once but our lead was lost. We never recovered it. Corin and his cronies had found their second wind. Their heels were winged and we were left far behind, mere clods whose every breath was now a knife. We prayed – well, I did – for that blessed moment when the pain in your lungs evaporates and the air becomes your friend again, your legs lengthen of their own accord and the ground no longer clings to your feet. But we were too city-bound, too clogged by food and wine to cross that threshold whereby you pass from earthbound agony to heavenly lightness. We were two suet puddings sweating in their juices. Finally Christofer stopped, bent double, eyes popping, clutching his chest. I halted too, glad to give up.

'A stitch,' he gasped. 'Oh, my dear, why do I do these things?' He fell silent, his face screwed up against the invisible bodkin piercing him from belly to breast.

'You wish you hadn't challenged Walsingham?'

He nodded. 'I knew he was bound to beat me. Why? Why did I do it, Tom?'

'I expect you were bored.'

This minor perception got me a weasel grin. 'Trust you to notice. But then you notice everything about me. And know everything too, don't you?'

'No,' I said with truth but I needn't have spoken, he wasn't listening.

'I was bored with his maunderings, his dull conceits, his leaden comparisons. My lovesick shepherd has a brain like a bifurcated sponge.'

'And a bum to match?'

Christofer roared with delight. 'Oh, Tom, no wonder I love you!' And he would have folded me in his arms there and then had not another stabbing stitch transfixed him. Perhaps this was just as well because at that moment Walsingham appeared, naked, shining with water drops, a towel draped over one shoulder.

'There you are,' he said.

'Yes. Here we are,' answered Christofer. And from the evenness of his tone it was impossible to divine his meaning. Who exactly was or were *we*? Christofer was – I knew – perfectly capable of referring to himself in the royal plural. On the other hand had he meant him and me? Or else all three of us? Or again himself and Walsingham? I couldn't tell. My prince of outrage was also a prince of ambiguity.

Such subtleties were lost on Walsingham however. 'We've been swimming,' he announced superfluously.

'We had to stop. I got a stitch.'

'So I've won?'

'Yes, Corin. I owe you twenty couplets.'

'Oh, no. I forgive you the wager. You needn't write a single word.'

'Oh, yes, I shall! You'll get them!' Christofer had bristled. 'I shall honour my word if nothing else!'

'As you wish.' Walsingham shrugged with that smiling condescension the truly rich employ quite unawares. And he took Christofer by the arm. 'But now, my dearest, you must swim with me.'

Approaching the lake we heard shouts, laughter, great splashings and soon saw several shepherds frolicking in the water observed by Francis who stood, ever watchful on the bank. He had the expert air of one who expected any moment to leap in and rescue another swimmer less accomplished than himself.

Christofer and I needed no encouragement to swim. We stripped at once and ran into the water. It was shockingly cold but we struck out boldly, determined to prove that if we hadn't been as swift as hares we were at least as buoyant as ducks. Once we reached the middle of the lake we paused to tread water and look about us. And there was Walsingham swimming strongly to us with the dark, curled head of the ubiquitous Francis beside him.

Once joined with us Walsingham said, 'There! You can't escape me, Christofer, can you? Let's swim to the island.'

As far as I could see there was no island but the wave of his arm indicated a timber construction like a landing stage built upon piles away to our left. It looked raw and uninviting. But we all obeyed our host's suggestion. As we swam together Francis (who was, as I'd suspected, a most accomplished waterman) kept striking out to one side of us only to swim back underwater and surface on the other, grinning. Or else he'd suddenly appear breaking out and up from the water, turning and laughing, between Christofer and Walsingham. Then he'd submerge again. Twice I felt his hand slide across my shoulder and my hips. Once his fingers brushed my belly. I think the others received similar attentions but I couldn't be sure. I wasn't especially offended (in the theatre such familiarities are common currency) but I was irritated. Had the man not noticed my instant distaste for him? I determined to make it clearer. But then, to my surprise, I heard Walsingham shout something sharp and Francis swam meekly away.

Having gained the so-called island we climbed out to bask in the gentle sun. After the chill water the raw-sawn planks felt warm. Walsingham, whom I was pleased to note was less well *tooled* (as we cockneys say) than me or Christofer, explained that this island-in-the-making was to play a vital part in the May masque he was devising.

Walsingham told us the climax of his show was to be a sea battle between a galleon full of knights and several canoes bristling with cannibals. The battle was for possession of this island and its inhabitants who would be a dozen or so virgins, figuratively speaking that is, who had been marooned there. Presumably by the villain of the piece, I said. Once a plot man always a plot man. Walsingham replied that there would be a prologue to explain the argument to the audience who would then be invited to accompany the knights seated upon rafts decorated with trellis and hung about with flowers and ribbons. Amidst horrid clamour the knights would fight, win and rescue the virgins (he hadn't yet decided whether they were really hamadryads, water sprites or high-born ladies but whichever they were they would wear beautiful costumes appropriate to his decision) from the cannibals who had been planning to rape and then devour them, naturally enough. Christofer approved heartily of this invention. And hoped some of them would. In full view. Walsingham also had plans to dye the water blood red during the course of the battle and he was hoping to persuade some of his guests to float about as dreadfully gashed corpses. Neither Christofer nor I volunteered for these particular parts.

Once the knights had won each would choose a virgin for himself. I suggested there should first be a grand chase of these wonderful girls all over the island in which they would pretend to be as fearful of the knights as they'd been of the cannibals. He agreed this was an excellent idea and I felt obliged to confess it wasn't my own but one taken from a Portuguese poet whose name I couldn't pronounce but which sounded like a sunlit sea breaking upon a rocky shore. Christofer said all the best authors stole ideas while mediocre ones merely borrowed them. This made Walsingham laugh but I don't think he understood what Christofer meant. In fact I know he didn't. And his masque when it was finally performed proved that beyond a doubt.

Finally when the cannibals and the virgins were all subdued Lady Audrey would appear as Queen of the May and bless the happy outcome of the expedition and then, since by that time it would be growing dusk, there would be fantastic fireworks organised by an *artificier* from Cracow, it being well known that the Poles were the finest pyropractioners in the world.

The island was to be dressed with turf and planted with hothouse trees and shrubs: everything from nodding palms to bamboo groves with parakeets in cages (else they'd fly away) hung upon every convenient branch. Christofer pointed out that neither palms nor bamboos provided branches but was told not to be a bore whereupon he demanded that he be allowed to play the Chief of the Cannibals and to qualify for the part he promised to practise wearing his head between his shoulders as thus: his wild contortions made Corin not only laugh uproariously but roll towards him to embrace him overpoweringly.

Since it was soon apparent that no further discussion of the masque would take place while Christofer lay locked in our host's arms I slid back into the water – it seemed colder than before – and swam ashore.

Degree at Scadbury was depicted in stone, wood and plaster. Our rooms were on the sinister side of the house where all our neighbours had artistic pretensions similar to ours; waiting women and a few senior serving men were billeted on the dexter side while guests of gentle birth were housed centrally, lodged beside Walsingham's magnificent apartment which gazed out across the courtyard to the main gate.

My room adjoined Christofer's, in fact there was no way to it except through his. But he had the convenience of two doors, one from a corridor and one which gave egress to a small dressing room which in its turn led to another bedroom at that moment unoccupied.

The beds were large and soft, the linen got changed every day and the chamber pots were washed in lavender water. Never had I known such comfort. I felt like a pet spaniel. I think our fellow

guests in the *Muses' Bower* as this side was immediately nicknamed felt the same. Among them were two painter brothers
whom Walsingham had hired to depict his entire party in
miniature – John and Jeremy Willoughby. They seemed almost
twins, although John was the elder by a year. Both were timid
souls except when at work: then these sparrows became eagles.
The likeness Jeremy made of Christofer was a miracle but I was
less satisfied with John's portrait of me although Lady Audrey
said she'd often seen me look like that. But when I asked when
that was she couldn't answer. Instead she laughed and pinched
my cheek.

Next came Amos Bullivant. Amos was a composer; a bearded
giant with two voices: a normal bass and a skin-crawling counter-
tenor which he guarded like gold. But that was the limit of his
mystery. The rest of him was an open-hearted, uncomplicated
soul with a bittern boom of a laugh who took a boy's delight in
practical jokes (hedgehogs found their way into the bed of any
maiden who rebuffed him) and beer. In other words he was a
typical music man. When we arrived he was already at work
composing the songs for Walsingham's masque.

I can't believe any of these three to have been my Ishmael.
This may be naive of me but they seemed too childishly absorbed
in the practice of their arts to have room for evil-doing. By no
stretch of my imagination could they be hole and corner men.

Of our other neighbour I'm less certain. His name was Chapman. George Chapman, a solemn, pedantic fellow, said to be a
poet and at that time translating Ovid and Homer. He certainly
had too much Latin and even more Greek. He had a habit of
stuffing out his sentences with far too many versions of the same
word. For example, should he happen to mention earth he would
also dub it land, soil and sod. Meanwhile his adjectives came in
cow-like droves mooing at the subject noun. I once heard him
describe an innocent villager as not only unlettered but also
unpolished, untrained, unwashed and, to cap it all, unpruned –
all in the same breath. Perhaps it was the translator in him which
made him offer so many equivalences of meaning? Despite this
foible he had impressed Walsingham with his verses. And when

Christofer was given some to read he said they showed great learning and a sinewed strength.

Later in our stay George gave us to understand he was a frequent visitor at Cerne Abbas where Sir Walter Raleigh (still out of favour with our vixen Queen) had his seat. There in Dorset – and now George lowered his voice conspiratorially – sweet Sir Walter held a secret court. Not a state beehive such as buzzed at Greenwich but a court of the head, the mind, the intellect; an informal academy for enquiring spirits, mathematical speculators, rebellious sceptics, ingenious philosophers, new astronomers – in fact innovators of every kind. All such were welcome. At Cerne Abbas thought was free, speech was free, free as the air on Black Down.

It was only then I learned that Christofer already knew George, who had aspirations to be a playwright (may God have mercy upon us all!), and that George had introduced him to Raleigh. What was more, and to my envious mind worse, Christofer had read a private paper to this college of freethinkers which the entire company had praised without stint! Especially Henry Percy, the Wizard Earl and disciple of Hermes Trismegistus, and Thomas Harriot, the mathematical magus. When I asked what had been the subject of it, George said with a patronising smile that it was probably best for the likes of me not to ask.

To say I was annoyed is not enough. I boiled like an outraged lobster in a saucepan. 'Speech being free in Dorset but not in Kent?' I said.

But this man was impervious to irony. 'I doubt this house is as safe as Sir Walter's,' he said. 'After all Walsingham's guests have been less carefully selected.' Was he sneering at me? 'Or perhaps I should say they've been chosen for reasons other than their intellect?' Yes, he *was* sneering at me! 'Therefore most of the guests here will be loyal to themselves, to their own advancement in their host's esteem rather than to the pursuit of unadulterated, unallayed, untarnished, undiluted, nay pure *ab origine* knowledge.'

Phew! Once again George had made stale most of the vocabulary appropriate to the subject supposedly under mutual discussion, leaving his hearers with no room to speak and almost nothing to add.

Christofer had read the anger in me. He said, 'You wouldn't have enjoyed it, Tom. Far too esoteric a place for you. And so solemn. No one laughs much at Cerne Abbas.'

Despite this I remained resentful at my exclusion. And I told him so. I really should've liked to have been invited. Nor had I needed George's stage whisperings to inform me of the school's existence. Raleigh's arcane academy was virtually common knowledge. Gossip accounted it either a nest of atheists or else a military college for Rome's assassins or even a witches' coven which regularly offered child sacrifices to Moloch, god of Hell, whose giant effigy was carved deep into the chalk of the hill close by. But as always the truth was more interesting than any of these predictable inventions. That's why I wished I'd been invited.

Christofer sought to placate me. 'Very well, Tom,' he said. 'If I'm asked again I shall insist you must come too.' I noticed he didn't ask George if I would be welcome. Presumably having secured his entry into Raleigh's favour Christofer had no further need of so saturnine an intercessor? George however at once took pains to point out that – should I go – I would be expected to present a treatise entirely of my own making. A paper upon an abstruse theological crux perhaps or an astronomical observation never before advanced. His tone made it obvious he considered these requirements quite beyond me.

'Are you a student of the heavens?' he enquired, knowing full well I wasn't.

'No,' I said. 'I can hardly tell one of God's candles from another. I leave that to my mistresses. They are my best astronomers.'

'Your mistresses your astronomers? How?'

'Why, when I pleasure them on their backs under the stars. I remember one who in her transports named a whole constellation after me.' I smiled, inviting him to run into my snare.

He did. 'Which constellation was that?' he asked.

The waxed thread of my noose tightened and I'd caught my fat rabbit. 'Oh, the Plough, of course, George. What else?'

Christofer laughed but George viewed me with reinforced contempt, marking me down as a male flibbertigibbet, a weight-less man of feathers if not a man of straw, whatever my success with women.

Today, I suppose, all his assumptions about me must seem proven to him. I'm sure he now reviles me voluminously when-ever the awkward subject of Christofer's sudden death is dis-cussed. I can picture him, I can give him voice, hear him pontificate at the assembled company: 'Oh, I could tell at the time, last April, when I first met Tom Kyd at Scadbury that here was a nullity, a nobody, a non-entity, a vacuity not to be trusted. I put no faith in him then and how wise I was, how very wise I was, gentlemen, not to say sagacious.'

But while it's easy to imitate George it's less easy to dismiss him as a possible Ishmael. His dislike of me was visceral. So he could have been the instrument of my betrayal.

But against this I must admit I can see no reason why he should bring down Christofer. Me, possibly. But not Christofer. He could have done – like almost everyone else at Scadbury he had the chance to spy, to inform. But would he? At this distance it is difficult to say. I remember he sang Christofer's praises above all other poets, even himself. Did he protest too much, I wonder? Was he jealous of Christofer's genius while concealing it beneath a cloak of adulation? Perhaps. Or had he, by aiming at me brought down the two of us? Me, intentionally, Christofer not? If so then George must be mourning him as bitterly as I. Again I can't say. So I won't. I shall allow him for the time being to be a paradoxical suspect: a possibly improbable, probably impossible Ishmael.

After that I heard nothing about Cerne Abbas for several days. Or was it weeks? Time vanished at Scadbury. Christofer didn't refer to the matter again and since I for my part avoided George's company whenever I possibly could I heard nothing from him either. I don't doubt given the opportunity however he would have cheerfully reiterated my intellectual unsuitedness to Sir Walter's notorious night school – as some have termed it.

Of the other guests on our side of the castle I remember only one: a skeletal man aged fifty or so who never spoke to any of us. He was once a soldier and explorer, Walsingham said. But had become a timid recluse whom our host had rescued from poverty. Apparently the man had visited many barbarous places in his prime. He had sat upon the roof of the world which is, I was informed, covered in perpetual snow and situated just south of Coromandel. I have since discovered that Walsingham's geography was as arsy-varsy as Christofer's who always insisted Ireland lay to the east of Scotland. Walsingham hoped this silent cadaver would one day write an account of his marvellous travels. I have forgotten his name. But if he's my Ishmael I'll eat my hat, feather and all.

·I·V·

At this moment as I was sifting Walsingham's guests through the sieve of my memory I was interrupted by Dr Thwaite, Pandora's Yorkshire physician, who has been the initiator of my recovery here in Sussex before Mary took a hand to even greater effect.

I welcomed him warmly, glad of his unexpected company. His visit, he announced, was at Pandora's request. At once I wondered if she had returned from wherever she was? But no. She was still away but that morning he'd been given a letter from her written at Greenwich where she was in attendance upon Eliza.

'No letter for me?' I said. And I was surprised by the sharpness of my chagrin.

'Nay, I fear not, Mr Kyd. But she's asked me to cast an eye upon you.' And he looked at me across the froth on the beer I'd poured for him.

'Oh? Recruited you as a spy, has she?' He laughed. So did I. Then I wondered if I really should be laughing. Perhaps I'd spoken more truth than I knew? I like Dr Thwaite and I respect his skills but hadn't I sworn to myself only yesterday that in future I must trust no one, simply no one? 'Well, what do you see, doctor?' I said, returning his gaze with an equal inspection of him as he sipped his beer. He looked so honest it hurt me.

'I see a changed man, Mr Kyd. I do, I do. You're standing straighter. Your eye is clear, the blood in your cheeks restored. May I see your hands?'

I held them out like a child whose nails must be inspected for cleanliness. Dr Thwaite felt the joints with careful, considerate pressure, testing and admiring their renewed suppleness.

I said, 'My mistress, Mary, kneads them most tenderly. Thanks to her I can write without pain – at least of the fleshly sort!'

He nodded his approval. 'The lass has worked wonders. I shall tell her ladyship so. She'll be well pleased. She wrote in her letter I was to report how you did in every particular.'

'In *every* particular?'

'Aye. In body, in mind, in soul.'

'But surely each is monitor of the other, doctor? You cannot separate them?'

'They are, lad. Oh, forgive me. Mr Kyd I should say.'

'No you needn't. I like "lad". Coming from you it sounds right,' I answered imitating his northern brogue with gross exaggeration.

He laughed. 'And I can tell you – these three estates of your being are in better health and accord today than I've yet seen them. Do you feel the same yourself?'

I nodded. 'Yes, doctor, I do. But I'm yet to be tried and tested I think.'

'How? How tried? What must you do?' He looked puzzled as well he might.

'I don't know,' I answered quickly. But I did. I had spoken more than I meant. I could hardly tell this decent man I was at present examining my life in search of someone who had sent Eliza's secret agents to me in the middle of the night. Let alone that when I had identified the author of my ruin I would be obliged to discover and confront him. And then? But I put that thought aside. Meanwhile I had no means of knowing how much Dr Thwaite knew. I had told him I was an actor and a playwright but what had Pandora said? After all, my torture and Christofer's death might be the talk of town and court but that didn't mean a country doctor knew of them. Pandora could have told him anything; she had the power to impose her reading of events upon us all. For aught I knew she could've informed Dr Thwaite

I'd been run over by a fish wagon or trampled by bullocks stampeding across London Bridge.

My good doctor, seeing I was not going to elaborate upon my unwelcome future, decided this was the moment to spring his surprise. He took out from his creased leather satchel a small silver casket embossed with the figures of the zodiac. It measured not more than five inches long by three wide by two deep but its effect upon me was immeasurable. To say I recognised it at once is to state the fact too slowly.

'Where did you get that?' I said, breathless with remembrance.

'Her ladyship sent it to me with her letter.'

'From Greenwich?'

'Aye, from Court. She said I must give it you at once. Here's the key to it.'

And he produced a tiny brass key which I also recognised. He placed it on the table while I turned the box over in my hands. Something shifted inside it. Suddenly I couldn't wait for him to go so I could inspect the contents of this only too familiar casket alone. Equally I found my hands trembling with the effort not to seize the key and open it there and then.

But Dr Thwaite was a man of good understanding. He required no urging to leave. He said, 'Well, that's about the sum of my errand, lad. So I'll be on my way. I'm glad your health's mending. Good day to you.'

I regret I only stammered my farewells to him so intent was I upon the box. This box lined with ivory which I'd been obliged to give to Lady Audrey last Spring. But what was now inside it? Would it still contain what she had placed there?

I took up the key. It seemed no longer to fit. Then I got the trick of it again, the lock turned sweetly, the box opened. First there was a note addressed to me, to my initials *T.K.* that is, in what I took to be Lady Audrey's hand and beneath it a soft leather pouch such as pearls are kept in. But here were no pearls. Here was a miniature. The likeness John Willoughby had made of me. Painted on a playing card cut into a roundel not two inches in diameter. I remember him considering me when I first sat for him, then taking his rule and muttering somewhat to me but mostly to himself, 'Yes, a round of one inch and seven eighths will do for you, yes.'

This was the portrait Audrey had paid him sixty shillings for. A sum only a little less than what I'd received on delivery of my play *Hieronymo*. How overpaid these courtly painters are. A bricklayer could hardly earn as much in a year!

The shock of seeing myself as I was barely four months before sent me for my looking glass. And despite what Dr Thwaite had said I immediately noticed dreadful differences between my two selves. Of course he hadn't known me in my heyday. Before I was plump of cheek, bold of eye, with my hair dressed to one side in a buccaneer's swathe falling to my shoulder. Now I'm lean-faced and although my eyes are bright enough they're also quick like a fox, alert as a hunted thing. My hair's cut short and dulled by grey – what's called a salt and pepper mixture. Compared with this portrait I'm now a ghost.

I set glossy miniature and truthful glass aside remembering how Audrey, having bought my picture, at once complained she'd got nothing to keep it in. This was quite untrue. She had dozens of caskets, boxes, jewel cases. But this did not prevent her insisting she couldn't keep my precious likeness openly beside her bed. What would Walsingham say? It was then her eye fell upon this silver box in which I treasured my buttons, earrings, buckles. Oh, I was a fashionable poet, believe me. I glittered modestly by day and night.

The box was on my table at Scadbury. She picked it up most acquisitively, exclaiming at its beauty as if she hadn't seen it many times before. Nor had she any objection to the inscription engraved inside the lid which read: 'From F.S. in whose regard T.K. shall ever dwell upon the occasion of his *Amleth* first crying: Revenge.'

Ferdinando had given it to me to mark my first success with my play of *Amleth* – as the Prince of Denmark was at first known to us. I had worked it up at his request from a Frenchman's account of this famous history by one Saxo called Grammaticus. It was in rehearsal that we changed the prince's name. Hamlet had a crisper note to it – the final T making the name easier to speak and hear. The effect of the ghost on his first entrance was tremendous and his final cry of 'Hamlet, revenge' became the talk of London. People cried out 'Hamlet, revenge' to each other in the street or sang it out as a drunken catch. I didn't mind the raucous comedy they made out of my tragedy. I took it as a compliment which proved I'd reworked that rough history to some real purpose. Sadly the play has fallen out of fashion; it now seems wooden and contrived; it needs revising. If Christofer was alive, the plague abated and I restored to Ferdinando's favour I'd be tempted to propose we revise the play together. There's a fierce life in its story and a powerful mystery in its prince of folly. But what am I dreaming of? It's too late. Some other hand must do it.

I opened the note I had thought must come from Audrey. It wasn't. It came from Pandora. I would quote it verbatim if she had not instructed me to burn it the moment I had read it. The gist, however, still flames in my memory. Pandora wished me well conventionally enough and then informed me she had received the box at Court from Lady Audrey who upon hearing regretfully of my continued existence had asked her to return this unwelcome memento of me. Pandora said that upon inspection of the box and its contents (she too has no shame) she had been inclined to keep both for herself since she did not, as I must know, entertain quite so poor an opinion of me as Lady Audrey did. What *had* I done to make the woman dislike me so?

Her note continued with the news that she had written to her god-daughter in Paris asking her to secure an example of the mysterious Monsieur Saint-Malo's handwriting. She hoped for a reply soon. Again I flinched but at least this time I didn't break into tears. Finally she trusted I had quite outgrown that petulance which was now my only enemy. P.S. Wasn't I beautiful last Spring?

At this I raised my hand in fury. I needed no further urging to burn her missive. But even as I did so I recognised she'd written this on purpose. I was fulfilling her command. This thought arrested me. But then I laughed, saluting her. Now, instead of hurling it onto the logs, I laid her note most soberly – quite unpetulantly – upon the fire. It flamed at once. Then the draught caught it and in another moment it flew away up the chimney as if it were the phoenix.

Assuaged I looked again upon my portrait but this time I did not compare my superseded self with the one I had become. Rather I remembered the sittings I had had with John Willoughby. How flattering it is to have someone other than a lover peer at you so closely. And then make you new. This bright miniature seemed to me yet to contain something of that glow of shared esteem John and I enjoyed while he painted my likeness. Lost in these self-pleasing thoughts I didn't hear Mary enter with my supper.

But here she is and I am glad of her. 'Mary,' I say, 'you're as welcome to me as water in the desert or the fruit of the vine.'

'And tonight I shall comfort you with apples, Tom,' she answers. She loves to quote the bible at me so I encourage her with Hebrew rhythms and similes of Judah. She lifts the lid from the pot to show me two pink pork chops (each with its moist kidney) half-hidden in a bed of blond apple slices dotted with butter.

'The earliest apples of the season,' she says. 'Sent up to the house from the west country.'

And with that she places the supper to bake upon the fire and lights the candles. But for some reason, I'm not sure why, I do not show her my picture of me as I was.

·V·

In Kent Walsingham presided not just as host over all his guests – often forty or more – but equally as undisputed president of an inner group, a cabal which began with five of us but later increased to seven with the arrival of the Earl of Northumberland and his Italian mistress, a certain Marchesa di Torremaggiore. We five appeared to be his favourites and our order of precedence in his affections was as follows: Christofer tremendously first; Audrey first too but in a civil sense and unequally; next Nick Skeres, the gambler, of whom Christofer had since said – after his warning glance to me at that first picnic under the great oak – that he was a man to beware of; then George Chapman (but I've already described him more than he deserves) and finally coming a long, long way behind: me. I'm certain now that only at Christofer's continual insistence was I of that inmost five. Perhaps Lady Audrey put in word for me as well? If she did her word would have been most carefully chosen. Walsingham might be bewitched by Christofer but he was also a rich and jealous man.

I made shameless use of Christofer's hold upon our host. He had kept his promise to me most bountifully. Having sworn I should have Lady Audrey he had so engrossed Walsingham that our host hardly acknowledged his mistress's presence except in the most formal ways – at supper, at dancing in the great hall, at chapel. Otherwise, thanks to Christofer, Audrey was studiedly neglected. I was free to pursue her as I chose.

And I did. I was constantly beside her in public, at our cabal's private suppers or at Walsingham's morning receptions when we sipped lime-flower infusions or sweet muscat wines from the Rousillion to the accompaniment of a consort playing Amos Bullivant's latest composition. While Walsingham rose and dressed household bills, begging letters and villagers' petitions were presented to him. What a lordling our Corin became dispensing judgment upon his estate.

With equal ease Audrey and I could ride together ahead of everyone else, even of the cabal itself. She was a good rider but putting her Arab at a fence one afternoon she fell and I had to run to her assistance. She was unhurt and rose almost at once to her feet, smiling foolishly. I couldn't resist that unguarded smile. I kissed her for the first time and she seemed to melt, opening her lips. But then her eyes widened and she drew back shaking her head. But whether in denial of me or against a dizziness she felt I couldn't say.

Until she spoke, 'Never do that again, Tom,' she said. 'Unless *I* command it.'

This infuriated me. I wanted to reply, 'And suppose I then refuse you?' But I didn't. I acquiesced to the power she had over me both in love and rank. Thus she became my tyrant. What fools we are to let our lives be ruled by great ones; to accept degree; to be the lowest stones bearing all the weight of the stately pyramid.

She saw my angry look and took my arm and squeezed it hard. 'Don't frown. I didn't mean it. You know you're my favourite. If Walsingham must have a poet, so must I.' And with that she laughed. So that was how she rated me, as a mere tit-for-tat companion? A waiting man? I laughed with her but without pleasure. And that night dreamt of violation at a volcano's edge.

But the next day I was besottedly at her side once more aboard Walsingham's barge off Greenhithe, fishing. After an hour in which our lines twitched not at all, not even with a mackerel, and Audrey spoke relentlessly of Christofer's genius as a poet as if to ameliorate her jealousy of him, her rod suddenly bent double. In a great arc. She exclaimed, almost screamed. I leapt to her assistance and at once our hands were joined together on the rod, our bodies close, then closer, as we struggled in convulsive union to land her unknown prey.

For ten or fifteen minutes we fought, seeing nothing, only feeling the weight of the thing first one way then that. But then I sensed a slackening of pull and we glimpsed a dark shape a foot below the surface of the water. It looked like a huge subaqueous kite, black, menacing. We pulled harder, locked together, laughing harshly. We were become complicit hunters. The water boiled beneath us and the creature exploded into the air, flapping deleriously but however much we heaved, conjoined, conjointly, we could not raise our monster to the deck. We let it sink back into the sea and for an instant I thought we'd lost it but then the line tightened again and I knew this time we'd won. We let the fish (it seemed a normal creature now) run this way and that, playing with its life while we exchanged looks of savage satisfaction. I thought I detected a reddening in Audrey's eyes as if the fight had brought blood to them and I wondered if mine were the same? Eventually – we sensed it together – we hauled again and this time, so co-ordinate were we, our wearied catch sailed out of the water in a burst of froth and like a great submarine harpy came flying over the rail onto the deck. The thud it made was heart-stopping. It lay stunned. We howled in triumph, laughing and hugging each other united by success. The monster revived. Began to heave, to wriggle, to slither forward, but Francis, abandoning the helm, ran forward with a knife and stabbed it in the head. Straight through the eye. Blood drenched his hand, splattered his face. Lady Audrey screamed and it was as if she were no longer the hunter but was voicing her victim's ecstasy at its violent end. I shivered as death rippled through the fish from head to tail.

Francis grinned. He told us such a death was merciful really. The eye was the quickest way to the brain. Christofer and Walsingham came up from below asking what was to do? We all gazed at the fish together. Audrey and I still had our arms about each other. Christofer noticed first and winked dirtily at me. Walsingham appeared less pleased while pretending not to care.

'Tom and I caught it together, my dear,' Audrey told him unnecessarily.

'I can believe it. It would take more than one to catch such a beastly thing. Look at it. It's disgusting.'

I had to agree with Walsingham. It looked dreadful. But George who at once professed to know more than most about piscation as he called honest fishing, pronounced it to be a monk-fish. A true monster of the deep but highly edible, he opined. The carbuncular head was as deformed as any lobbish child's; the gaping mouth an expandable horror tricked out with spines and antennae. And the whole of it was black as new-spilt ink. But once relieved of its evil head, winglike fins and elastic skin the slippery meat was white and translucent as alabaster.

Coming ashore at Sheppey Island we roasted the flesh of it stuck upon sticks over a driftwood fire. Seasoned with salt and accompanied by crunching mouthfuls of freshly gathered samphire we feasted like pirates. Audrey and I were toasted for our success and she smiled upon me as if she was to be mine at last. I told myself she would be. She would come to my room that very night, or I would go to hers at some further signal I was bound to receive shortly, and at last my lusts for her would be assuaged. But when we returned from that excursion she resumed her teasing ways again. As we danced that evening in fancy dress – she as Minerva, me as Neptune – she was as sharply coy as ever. Audrey, like the Queen, wore her virginity like an invisible, impenetrable caul. That she was no more a virgin than the mother who bore her was known to everyone – but our great ladies must never be seen as such while still unmarried. It is an obligatory fiction maintained to the point of politic disappearance abroad should they, by natural mischance, conceive.

That night Audrey even kissed me briefly as Christofer and Walsingham left the great hall hand in hand. But the way she brushed my lips made it plain I was to proceed no further. Her kiss was planted upon me to show the other dancers she cared nothing for Walsingham's infidelities. Once again I was the instrument of her *amour propre*. My blood boiled. I took my leave of her.

Coming towards my room I realised my way to it was barred. Not physically. The door through which I must pass to reach it was ajar. Candles glowed within. Voices whispered, murmured, sighed. Christofer was entertaining Walsingham in his bed. How could I go through there to reach my own? It was impossible. But still I could not resist taking a peek at them. At once I regretted it. They lay side by side in the open bed. Illuminated by candles all about them their nakedness appeared golden. Walsingham was dipping a finger into a glass of equally golden wine and anointing Christofer's lips with it. I drew back as if bitten by a viper. The action seemed so curiously intimate, so delicately lascivious that it was worse to me than if I had seen one mounted on the other. I retreated into the adjoining dressing room, realised that I might be discovered there when Walsingham finally withdrew to his own apartment, and not wishing to encounter him that night or indeed ever again, I ran out through the corridor and down to the courtyard.

I persuaded the gatekeeper to let me out through the postern door, crossed the bridge over the moat (it could still be raised at times of trouble) and came into the moonlit park. As I walked the length and breadth of it I determined first to leave Scadbury and return to London, next to remain but make myself indifferent to my teasing goddess who forever promised what she would not give. Had I not grievously deceived myself with Audrey, assuming from her melting looks an equal spirit? I must escape such tyranny; she was too far above me ever to fall below me. Or was my anger really jealousy of Christofer? Was I here, pacing these shadowed paths beneath these oaks, not because of Lady Audrey's abuse of me as a compliant lover (or should I say a mooncalf?) but because of what I'd witnessed only an hour ago? Perhaps I hated Walsingham more than I longed for his mistress? If that were so then my best revenge would be to remain and lay such cold-blooded siege to Audrey that despite herself she would surrender to me.

Driven by these serpentine thoughts I remained in the park until the first birds began to call to one another heralding the dawn. But now I heard horses behind me. And the sound of little bells, tinkling, clacking, ringing. Were these sheep or what? I turned and towards me came two armed outriders in black and silver livery ahead of a coach, also black but dressed all about with the bells I had heard. They hung everywhere. Upon hooks, upon cords or from looped chains. Their tintabulation was both soothing and curiously painful. You could not see inside the coach since every black velvet curtain was close shut. If I'd had a hat I would have removed it so like some funeral cortège did this procession seem. Behind the coach came a file of packhorses and more black liveried outriders. At the rear was a cart (also decked with bells) upon which a wooden crate longer than a coffin lay amongst other boxes and bales. Two final guards kept guard. Never had I seen anything so sinister yet so frivolous.

I let the strange procession pass but stepped out from where I stood to accost the last two riders. I asked them who they served. They seemed unwilling to reply and when at my second enquiry one of them did he spoke with an accent of the north so extreme he was incomprehensible to me. Was this Scots or an even more foreign tongue? Norwegian or Danish? I tried again. Again I didn't understand. At that I waved him on. Not that he needed any dismissal, he was already on his way.

When I returned to the house every window of the courtyard was full of sleep-bleared faces staring down in wonder at the scene below. Walsingham dishevelled, undressed, with Lady Audrey beside him also in deshabille, was greeting the new arrivals. Servants were already unloading the great coffin from the cart and, at Walsingham's direction, carried it straight into the house by way of the main door. Avoiding the increasing hubbub I went up to my room. Christofer was standing at the window.

'The Wizard Earl has arrived,' he said.

'Is that who it is?'

'Together with his consort – the Marchesa di Torremaggiore – just look at her, Tom. Look! What a tun of blubber!'

I looked. The Italian marchioness was as barrel-ish as Christofer had said. She seemed to have no form but roundness. The earl, Henry Percy of Northumberland to give him his proper name, looked like a bodkin's shadow beside her. She was dressed entirely in cloth of silver, he entirely in black but negligently: his shirt was unbuttoned at the neck, his jerkin too, his breeches unpadded. His feet were covered in soft slippers. He wore no gloves nor any ornament of any kind.

'I met them at Cerne Abbas,' Christofer said. 'She's the cannonball to his feather. To imagine them in congress is to giggle. And yet by some hidden art they seem to weigh evenly with each other.'

'Rumour has it Percy's a follower of Pythagoras?'

'Rumour's right. And of Hermes Trismegistus.'

'Is he wise or foolish?'

Christofer laughed. 'Both, Tom. Like me, like you, like most of us.' He put his arm around my waist. Despite myself I wanted to throw him off. 'What?' he said. 'Have I offended you?'

Without thinking I lied. 'No,' I said. 'No. You can't. We can't offend each other, can we?'

'I hope not. But I think I have – even so.'

I sighed and reflected. Why try to keep anything from Christofer? He would guess come what might. And almost without exception his guesses hit the mark. What had I just done but spend the best part of the night resenting him, Walsingham, Audrey and myself? And all because he had his lover while I still burned for mine. 'Forgive me,' I said. 'I'm full of envy.'

'Of course you are, my dear. Lady Audrey loves to tease. And I say that with authority, Tom. Not just upon the witness of my own eyes but on Walsingham's word, too.'

'Oh? You laugh at me together, do you?'

'Thomas, Thomas – shush. And listen, sweetheart, listen.'

What he told me concerning Lady Audrey I could not believe. Well, not at once. But later I decided he had to be right. If there was anyone who understood humankind's inhuman secrets it was Christofer.

But now the breakfast bell was sounding.

I yawned and said, 'I must go to bed, I haven't slept all night.'

'Sleep well, my dear. And then disdain her, hurt her and

dream of beastly victory.' He kissed my cheek and this time I
didn't flinch.

Walsingham's cabal is now complete. We're seated at his private
hearth two days later. The fire flickers. Lady Audrey has seated
herself close to me (Christofer's latest advice is working admirably) while Henry Percy and Lucrezia di Torremaggiore are close
to Walsingham. We're waiting for the moon to rise. In the
meantime Christofer is honouring the bet he had with our host
upon arrival. He's paying for his lack of prowess as a runner with
twenty couplets from his latest poem. We laugh with delight at
them. They are full of savour. But Percy and his Italian concubine
do not. They think us less than high-minded. We are.

   The subject of Christofer's amorous poem is Leander's love for
Hero. To set the scene he gives us a taste of five couplets which
are not part of the promised payment. These are his thoughts, he
says, upon Leander when he sees Hero, votary of Venus, for the
first time. He reads, rather well for him.

   Christofer:

> *It lies not in our power to love or hate,*
> *For will in us is overruled by fate . . .*

Walsingham nods profoundly.

> *When two are stripped, long ere the course begin*
> *We wish that one should lose, the other win.*
> *And one especially do we effect . . .*

Audrey grips my hand, and to endorse this sentiment, her nails
bite into my palm. How right Christofer's been. My nails bite her
palm back. Her breath catches. She smiles as Christofer
continues.

> *Of two golden ingots like in each respect.*
> *The reason no man knows: let it suffice*

What we behold is censured by our eyes.
Where both deliberate the love is slight . . .

Is this true? I wonder.

Whoever loved that loved not at first sight?

A concerted sign of agreement, approval. Once again Christofer wins a doubtful argument with a feline rhythm and the pounce of rhyme. He looks up from his papers. Walsingham asks him how he can possibly decipher his own writing? Christofer laughs and so do I, not reckoning the future because I do not know it. A log collapses in flames. Christofer speaks again, but as himself in prose. 'I pass now to the scene in which Leander swims the Hellespont to enjoy his Hero in her lonely tower. He strips and dives in. But Neptune mistakes him for Ganymede and in his lust pulls the boy down into the depths. Being only human Leander nearly drowns so Neptune lets him go but – well, you'll hear the rest in verse.'

'Must we?' murmurs Percy. Walsingham explains yet again that the occasion is the fulfilment of a wager. His noble guest shrugs nobly and lies languidly back, his head almost disappearing from sight among the billows of Lucrezia's lap. It seems she never wears anything but silver satins and taffetas. She's a shining sea; a swelling ocean in herself; vast and I suspect unfathomable.

She murmurs something fond in Italian and strokes Percy's thinning hair. Every one of her fingers bears a ring, some of which carry cabalistic signs especially those for Mercury, Mars and Venus. Christofer reads again.

Leander being up began to swim
And looking back saw Neptune follow him . . .

I groan at this rhyme. Christofer grins, unabashed.

Whereat aghast, the boy began to cry,
'Oh, let me visit Hero ere I die.'
The god put Helle's bracelet on his arm . . .

Trust Christofer to mention Helle, the most loose-living god-dess of them all. She who laid the world egg and, in the guise of a dove, hatched it upon the waters.

And swore the sea would never do him harm.
He clapped his plump cheeks, with his tresses played
And smiling wantonly his love betrayed.

Christofer suits action to words by smirking horribly. We all smile too. Beaming beams in firelight. Christofer continues, his eyes aglint, looking from me to Walsingham, inviting us to recognise the source of his inspiration.

He watched his arms and as they opened wide
At every stroke betwixt them he would slide
And steal a kiss and then run out and dance,
And as he turned cast many a lustful glance
And throw him gaudy toys to please his eye
And dive into the water and there pry . . .

I begin not just to smile but to laugh. Walsingham's seen the point, too. He's laughing and for once the two of us see eye to eye. We've got something in common: the remembrance of Francis, Scadbury's pet satyr, disporting himself between the three of us as we swam out to Walsingham's half-built island. Audrey's puzzled. 'What, what?' she hisses. But I withhold any explanation. 'No,' I whisper. 'You must stew in the mystery, madam.' 'Damn you,' she whispers back and bites my ear. I almost cry out. Christofer's advice is good but double-edged. Christofer, noting this diversion, suggests he should repeat his last line. We all agree, except Percy.

> *And dive into the water and there pry*
> *Upon his breast, his thighs, and every limb*
> *And up again and close behind him swim*
> *And talk of love. Leander made reply,*
> *'You are deceived – I am no woman, I.'*

Christofer stops. Everyone claps, even Lucrezia, but not Percy. And Walsingham protests he's not heard enough. The wager was for twenty couplets. Christofer has offered only nine. He's kept count. Christofer is furious. On his feet. Bull-necked with rage. His face bright as the fire. He shouts, 'You horseleech! You demand blood do you? Very well! Here's blood for you! Virgin bloody blood!'

In his raging Christofer rifles through his papers, scattering them everywhere. But out of this spewing chaos he seizes what he wants and standing bolt upright reads out the following as if it were a grocery list.

> *Love is not full of pity (as men say)*
> *But deaf and cruel where he means to prey.*

I feel Lady Audrey shiver deliciously beside me.

> *Even as a bird, which in our hands we wring*
> *Forth plunges and oft flutters with her wing*
> *She trembling strove . . .*

Walsingham, I realise, is quite unaffected by Christofer's outburst. He's taken no offence at all. Indeed he's smiling. Can it be that he shares with his betrothed a deep desire to be abused? Can Christofer's understanding of Audrey be applied to him? Again Audrey's nails impale my palm. This time I do not return the compliment. She digs deeper. I shake my hand free. She grins with happy dissatisfaction. I begin to fear I've stirred a wasps' nest.

Christofer continues.

> *. . . this strife of hers, like that*
> *Which made the world, another world begat*
> *Of unknown joy. Treason was in her thought*
> *And cunningly to yield herself she sought,*
> *Seeming not won, yet won she was at length . . .*

Nicholas Skeres laughs suddenly, coarsely. Christofer glares at him. Quickly he drinks to cover his faux pas.

> *In such wars women use but half their strength.*

Despite himself his voice is softening. Christofer's anger is being soothed by his own music. How many times have I seen it happen so? Hundreds. I'm glad. Extempore savageness doesn't suit him. He's best on paper. There he can howl and curse with anyone. Better than anyone.

> *Leander now, like Theban Hercules*
> *Entered the orchard of the Hesperides*
> *Whose fruit none rightly can describe but he*
> *That pulls or shakes it from the golden tree.*

Christofer stops. Silence. Now George begins to clap in measured approval. We all join in, even the Wizard Earl. But Walsingham has not applauded. He says 'But that's only six couplets. You still owe me five.'

Christofer says, 'God damn you, Walsingham!'

'Pay the wager!'

'There! Take them all! All my verses! You can count them at your leisure!'

Christofer, pale, trembling, breathless, hurls his papers at Walsingham and himself from the room. I'm inclined to go after him. If Audrey tries to prevent me I shall. But she doesn't. I hesitate, remain.

George says, shaking his head, 'You don't understand us poets, Thomas.'

Walsingham answers, 'I understand *you*, George.'

We laugh. Our host has put down our resident pedant neatly enough. But I suspect Walsingham really wants to follow Christofer, have a terrific spat and fall into bed with him. He gathers up the scattered papers, glancing towards the door. Percy stalks over to the window, unlatches the shutters. He turns and speaks with sacerdotal solemnity: 'Her Serene Highness Luna has risen.'

Out we go.

Up on the roof the contents of the Wizard Earl's prodigious crate had been assembled. And become a wood and canvas cannon, or so it appeared. The barrel was some five feet in length and slung in a leather harness between two timber uprights upon a turntable. The wider end of it pointed at the heavens while the smaller was in reach of a standing man's hand. This device amazed us all.

Percy spoke of it in Italian, calling it his *telescopio*. He had invented it on paper, he said, but had had to travel to Amsterdam to get it built by a Dutchman he termed an optic genius. Within the wood and canvas barrel (tarred to keep the light out) were two glasses such as are used in spectacles; although, of course, they were much larger and their manufacture in Köln had cost him dearly. They were placed one at each end of this barrel. These two glasses – he called them *lentes* – magnified anything at which the telescopio was pointed by virtue of the light rays from that thing penetrating these glasses. Whatever they revealed could be seen by way of the eyepiece. Here he demonstrated to us a leather cup with a hole in it set against the nearer glass at the end of the barrel. This perspective trunk, he said, brought the heavens closer.

He swore us all to an absolute silence, assuring us that if news of his machine were to escape from Scadbury it would be held to be the work of Satan. And he had little doubt that the Privy

Council would call for an investigation of him as an atheist. While laughing heartily at the stupidity of authority we all agreed it was more than likely. For his part the Wizard Earl was convinced he could lose his head if word of this mathematical invention got out.

Walsingham had a bible brought up from the library and we all swore silence very earnestly upon it. Fittingly it was a breeches bible from Geneva. One that is, in which our original parents in their shame at having eaten of the tree of knowledge cover their nakedness not with aprons made of fig leaves but with breeches of the same. This translation has always struck me as apt enough, and unworthy of a smile. Fig leaves are frequently as tough as leather and more extensive than any moleskin. Surely our first mother could have fashioned breeches for Adam and herself? It wouldn't have been beyond her wit surely? Had she not just eaten of the apple of all invention?

Thinking of our hands placed in turn upon that book I see first my own, then Audrey's, Walsingham's, Chapman's and finally Nicholas Skeres'. Should I reflect further upon Skeres? Can he qualify as my betrayer? Despite Christofer's warning against him I'd found him harmless. Inclined to drink too much – that night on the roof he was as thick-voiced and slow to speak as usual; several of us had joked that we must keep Old Nick – as I too by then had learned to call him – away from the parapet lest he imitate his namesake's headlong fall from grace. With the moat doing service as the lake of fire. I'd put him down for a genial ninny and only wondered why Walsingham admitted him to the cabal. Apart from wine and cards and dice he seemed to have few other interests except hunting. But that season was now gone. He detested books, was deaf to music, preferred cock-fighting to play-acting. He was a close companion of Francis although he averred he hated exercise, declaring he never exerted himself except at stool. His jokes rarely rose above the shit-house kind – his jakes-jokes he called them. However, just once, he did boast of an escapade which made me wonder if he was all he seemed. In it he and Francis, together with Walsingham, had for a wager disguised themselves as cut-throat beggars and set upon a packhorse train making its way to Rochester by night. They had come away with considerable booty which Walsingham had graciously returned to its outraged owners the next morning thus proving them ridiculous and himself a gentleman. They had humbly thanked Walsingham for their humiliation and gone on their journey praising God for His hand in the ordering of things. But if this loutish incident makes me doubt Skeres then in logic I must also doubt Walsingham and Francis. Any of these three could be my Ishmael. Especially Walsingham who very soon had cause to truly hate me.

But that night our only interest was the moon. She was at full. Percy trained his device upon her and exclaimed in wonder at what he saw. He then allowed Lucrezia to look and she too expostulated upon the vision the telescopio had granted her. After her came Walsingham, and the rest of us. I was to be last. All were bedazzled. They babbled. Said they would never have believed it. Their voices rose, pitched close to alarm, even fear. Audrey said, who would have thought Her Majesty the Moon to look like that? Now my turn came.

At first I could see nothing, then Percy touched a lever in the body of the barrel and Luna swam into my sight. I was struck with horror. Dumbfounded. Can you imagine a goddess of flawless crystal revealed as raddled chalk? A queen stripped of her state and seen to be decayed? Here was Diana (or Belphoebe or Cynthia – call her what you will) shown at last for what she really was. Percy's invention had pierced her every veil. This was she for ever now – a whore dead of the pox, her beauty cratered by past eruptions, a heavenly corpse luminous with its own corruption. I fell back. I felt sick. I felt angry. How dare this telescopio do this to me? The Wizard Earl had destroyed the moon.

I looked up at her with my naked eye and she seemed herself again except I no longer believed my eye. It knew better. I knew better. Here was a machine which could make me see things as they really were.

Like a child I said, 'I wish I hadn't looked.'

'Why?' said Audrey, knowing perfectly well. Hadn't she cried out in equal astonishment?

'What shall we do without the moon?'

'Without her? We can see her more clearly than ever before.'

'Yes! But now she's ruined! Ravished by Percy's one-eyed cock! This standing glass! This optical erection!'

Audrey laughed at my wild comparisons. 'No, she's still the same, Tom. Look with your own eyes.'

'I have! Her virtue's lost and so are we. We'll all go mad. But not from her. She's dead and gone. No, we'll all go mad from mathematics.'

Was I already so? I was well-filled with canary wine, I admit. My brain was on fire with it but that wasn't all, no. I was truly overcome by what I'd seen. And I cursed this new knowledge. How could my chaste moon ever be restored? Impossible. Wax and wane as she might she would never hunt through my dreams or inspire my verse again. Her rottenness was mine. Her corruption my corruption.

Percy proceeded to lecture us most learnedly upon the wandering courses of the moon and her six celestial companions. But I couldn't listen. I wanted no more instruction. I was deaf to information. I had to guard my ignorance. I left the roof taking a flask of canary with me and went in search of Christofer. I found him fast asleep. How could he sleep? Here were the heavens destroyed yet he was snoring like a bull-mastiff. I nearly shook him awake but then I didn't. I went on into my room where I wrote a rambling letter to Lady Audrey in which I tried to describe the sensations Percy's enlarged vision of the moon had excited in me. But as I sipped more wine the letter turned away from philosophy to become an inflamed harangue against Audrey herself. I abused her most feelingly, I called her cruel, deceitful, and I drew a besotted parallel between her apparent flawless beauty and the moon's diseased condition. I suppose by then I was drunk. I remember I signed the thing: 'Your pet poet, T.K.'

Having sealed this bibulous missive I decided I would deliver it to her rooms while she was still on the roof. I crept out past Christofer who now bellowed and snorted as if he were become the bull itself with the mastiff fastened upon his nose and made my blundering way along corridors, down stairs and up again until with one last ricochet off the panelling I reached Audrey's apartment. I took breath, knocked more steadily and in a while her outer door was opened by Agnes, her ladyship's maid. She apologised profusely for her delay in answering my knock. She had fallen asleep, she said, waiting for Lady Audrey's return. Would I forgive her? She had little or no chin and looked most fishlike as she swallowed her yawns. Poor Agnes. Like most servants she was obliged to be ashamed of her own humanity.

I was about to hand her my letter when I heard the recipient's voice. I turned quickly. I didn't want to meet Audrey. My letter was intended to say everything I meant without my being there. But there she was, bearing down upon me. No way of escape – my exit was her entrance.

She arrived, accompanied by Nick Skeres who was lighting her to bed. 'So this is where you are, Tom?' she said in something like triumph.

'Why? Have you been looking for me?'

'No. But we all wondered at your deserting us. Especially Corin. He became quite concerned – even jealous I think. I expect he thought you must be enjoying his dearest friend. Were you?'

'No,' I said, suddenly detesting her enamelled assurance.

'Well, whatever you've been doing I've been forced to ask dear old Nick to light my way here.'

'A pleasure, madam,' said Nick, smiling foolishly but swaying dangerously. Suddenly, compared with Skeres, I realised I was sober as a mill-stone.

'But now you may leave us, Nick my sweet. Before you set my favourite tapestry on fire.' Audrey pointed at a gruesome cloth depicting the flaying of Marsyas which I had scarcely noticed before. Had it been painted rather than woven the scene would have been unsupportable.

Old Nick announced he would he happy to take his leave, adding, 'I'm sure Tom can be of infinitely more service to you than me, madam.' He leered at her, winked at me and clicked his tongue like a costermonger. 'Good night, my lady.' He backed away unsteadily; the candelabra bobbing, splattering wax everywhere. Audrey ordered Agnes to accompany him lest he set the house on fire. Agnes hurried after him only to find herself encompassed by his flailing left arm. Thus supported he disappeared among his own dancing shadows.

'Now you may come in and explain yourself, Tom. And that letter in your hand.'

She swept into her room but held the door wide – was she mocking me? – so I might enter. But then, as she shut it she shot the bolt across. And laughed. And to me it seemed suddenly that her lips rode up too far above her teeth revealing too much gum. I was reminded of a Barbary ape we'd once employed as a pet for Abigail, daughter of Barabas, in our *Jew of Malta*. The creature pissed everywhere which pleased the audience excessively but us not at all. The boards of the Rose stank for days after.

'Now you're my prisoner,' she said. 'Give me the letter.'

'No,' I said, not wishing to be present at her reading of it.

'But it's for me, isn't it?'

'It was, madam, yes.'

'But now you don't want me to read it after all?'

'Yes. I do. Once I've gone.'

'Why? Are you ashamed of it?'

'No. But a letter loses its chief purpose if the writer is present when the reader reads it.'

'Does it? I think I must be the judge of that.' And she reached forward to snatch the letter from me. But I held on and we struggled for possession of it. Our closeness heated both of us. Perhaps as she intended? Audrey made to bite my hand but I slapped her head away harder than I meant. She fell sideways into the heavy curtains of the bed, pulling them apart. There she half-lay, half-sat, looking at me, her hair loosened, her painted mouth smudged. I stood back and surveyed her as if her room had become a common brothel. Her disarray should have moved me to desire but I felt nothing. I dropped the letter beside her.

'Good night, madam,' I said.

'No, wait. Wait, Tom. Please. I won't read it now. I promise.'

And she smiled, stretching out to feel for something concealed beneath the pillows. And brought out a key. She pointed with it at an iron-bound travelling coffer which stood at the foot of the bed. 'Open it,' she said, handing me the key.

A knock came at the door and Agnes's voice announced her return but Audrey told her she could go to bed; she had everything she needed. Agnes murmured good night and there was silence.

'Open the box, Tom.'

I did as I was commanded. Within it lay such instruments as may be used by some of a phlegmatic humour for spiritual advancement: chains, a leather whip, several knuckled canes of malacca, even a pair of iron manacles. Revulsed by this store of implements I turned to question Audrey. She was nowhere to be seen. The bed's curtain had been drawn across. What new game was this?

Audrey called from within the damasked bed. 'Bring a cane and the whip, Tom.'

Here was plain proof of what Christofer had meant about my Lady Audrey. She could only be heated by hurt. Either felt by herself or by another. Was she of that numerous sort who cry out in ecstasy at a public execution? Or could she only admit a man after due correction? Or was the pain itself her satisfaction?

'Quickly, Tom, I'm waiting.'

Sick with dismay I scooped out all her chosen instruments and I strode to the bed, feeling ridiculous. Somehow I elbowed the curtains apart. And there she was, crouched with her skirts pulled over her back, her bum openly displayed, her head twisted round and peering upwards at me out of a pillow.

'Use the cane first, my dearest,' she said.

The sight of her filled my eyes, my throat, my heart, my stomach with horror. Her buttocks were already a tapestry of weals and bruises (from whose hand?); her vulva already split with ripeness; her topsy-turvy smile already a Maenad's leer. So this was my pure Audrey? My nymph of Arcady within whose eyes I'd hoped to drown in perfect innocence? Very well. So be it. I'd surfaced into truth. And truth now told me how to punish her truly.

I flung all her evil instruments at her, shouting. 'You witch, you hell-hag, you worse than both! You strike yourself! You work your own damnation!'

And I ran to the door, pulled back the bolt and fled the room, choking back my bile.

·V·I·

Someone's just tried to kill me. Yes. Here in Sussex. In the full light of day. I'm still not sure how my assailant failed in his task. Let alone who assigned him to it. Or if he was his own commander. How can I say? But it would seem the author of that anonymous note knew of what he wrote. I have got more enemies than I supposed.

Sickened by my recollection of Lady Audrey (my whited sepulchre) I had taken myself for a walk upon the Downs. For once the sky was clear although the clouds in the west were already rubbing shoulders and threatening to obscure the sun at sunset. But as I walked the air was warm and the heat in it seemed to ease my knee yet more. I felt a newfound spring in my step. Or perhaps I should say a newborn bounce in my hobble?

I got to the crest of the Downs where the sight of the docile sea glinting in the unusual sun refreshed my soul. But as I approached Chancton Ring my ear filled with the cries of lapwings and my eye was caught by a great wheeling flock of them suddenly risen up beyond the trees. They streamed towards me, tumbling and calling. Then at the sight of me (did they presume I was a scarecrow?) they turned again and fled away northwards, passing over Pandora's great house to become mere specks blinking white and black against the standing murk of the charcoal works and smelting foundries of the Weald. So taken by the lapwings' plaintive beauty was I that I quite forgot to ask myself the obvious question: what had disturbed them?

I reached the ring and finding my favourite spot settled myself down with my back against an oak tree whose trunk's contours were now familiar. Once sat there I instructed myself to dismiss Lady Audrey from my mind for a moment. I needed to separate myself from the dross she embodied in order to see the events at Scadbury more clearly. Otherwise to continue to sift my memory so hectically might mean I'd miss what really mattered. In future, I instructed myself, I must see everything as if it had happened to another, to a someone else, a stranger who by chance was also called Tom Kyd. Yes, I must henceforth be my own creation; a character in a play of mine: a kind of Hieronymo or Hamlet. My recent past must no longer be coloured by anger or resentment or I would never shake out my Ishmael. Or if I did I'd be too perturbed to recognise him.

Having made these resolutions I allowed myself to think once more of Audrey. Had my rejection of her that night turned her mind against me? Even though the next day she'd begged we might continue as before – as platonic lovers? Could she herself be in some sense an Ishmael? Could she have incited others against me? It was then, as I examined these suppositions, that my unknown assailant struck.

How to describe the event? Well, to begin with what must be most apparent: I survived it unscathed – in body at least. Next, that a teasing fly saved my life. Then that the phrase 'a bolt from the blue' might serve here except the description would be inaccurate twice over. One, because the bolt came not from the blue but out of green shade; two, that the fly's assault upon me anticipated this other attack. The insect flew straight at my nose with a furious, insistent buzz which made me duck violently forward to avoid it. At that very instant the crossbow's bolt struck the trunk above my head. The brutal thwack of it was eloquent of death. Without thinking I sprang to my feet looking everywhere but the way from which it had come. And then, like a blind fool, I shouted. 'What? Who's that?' Stupid questions deserving only another bolt for answer. It came. I heard the stiff quills of it shriek past my ear. I fell flat, knowing now – too late – that I must make myself invisible. I lay rigid as a hunted rabbit, sniffing the air, every sense alert, trying to peer between the trees. Was that a shadow beyond that thorn? Did someone move behind that oak? Were those leaves rustling with the breeze alone? Was that creak the bow rewound or one bough rubbing against another? What was that thudding? Booted footfalls? No. My heart. My own heart. I drew breath and pushed myself up a little on my elbows. What could I see? What hear? Nothing. Nothing except the wind among oak, ash and thorn: all held to be the most beneficent of England's trees or so the country folk say. I'd heard Mary say it only the day before. But beneficent to whom? Me or my assailant?

I must have lain there for twenty minutes or more. Certainly till every part of me ached with cramps. Finally I could endure my immobility no longer. If death came from this impatience then so be it. I rose up with the thought. And found my foolhardiness rewarded. Nothing happened.

Standing, stretching, groaning as I eased my limbs I was an easy mark for anyone to shoot at. As big and bold as a Finsbury butt. But no one did. Next, as if I hadn't challenged providence enough, I walked forward. Still no one shot at me. My calmness interested me. Where had it come from? I cannot call it courage – I'm a notorious coward even to myself – because it wasn't. No, it flowed from an inner certitude, a quite unreasonable conviction, an animal knowledge, that all immediate danger was removed.

Soon I found the place where the bowman had taken aim. Grass and earth were pressed and scuffed by his knee and boots beside an ancient thorn. From here he'd had a perfect sight of me not thirty yards away. He must have thought me already dead even as he loosed his bolt. So why hadn't he pushed his advantage home? There being no immediate answer to this I walked forward again, out from the trees, to survey the Downs beyond. The sun still shone. Harebells still danced above the sheep-cropped turf. And a mob of seagulls screeched and squabbled around something which lay just below the curve of the hill. A dead sheep, perhaps? But several crows and jackdaws joined them and then, high above them all, I saw four buzzards circling. At the sight of these great carrion birds I decided to enquire further.

I hadn't gone a hundred yards when I saw my attacker with

one of the crows already standing majestically upon his back. He lay face downwards, the crossbow abandoned beside him. I ran forward as best I could waving my arms at the rout of birds. They merely circled higher and called the more urgently. The man was of medium stature with a dark leather jerkin, thick breeches and well-made boots. He looked a ruffian for all seasons.

At first sight there seemed no mark upon him but then I noticed blood under his collar and more, much more, soaking into the wiry grass about his head. Swallowing my repugnance I pulled at his right shoulder to turn him over. The body behaved naturally enough but his head slewed horribly forward and then fell away to one side. The birds above me screamed and swooped as blood spewed everywhere. But I'd got him on his back. I wished I hadn't. His throat was cut, his face and chest curtained by blood, his eyes wide as a hooked fish's. Those eyes! I recognised them at once. That palest of blues, that washed-out indigo. Those once seen not easily forgotten eyes. Eyes such as belonged to Old Nick – to Nicholas Skeres who only last April had lived for the hunting season to return. Now it had. And here he was. And I had been his quarry.

This thought was bad enough but the next was worse. Knowing Nick I couldn't believe he'd hunted me at his own behest. No, the man relied for his very existence upon Walsingham. However much he pretended he lived for pleasure Old Nick paid for the privilege in services to his friend and patron. So his attempt upon my life must have been at Walsingham's direction? This corpse therefore was Walsingham's and rightly should be laid at his door.

But who had cut his throat? Who had caught him from behind, stretched the neck back, hand over mouth, and butchered him with such swift dexterity? No wonder I'd heard nothing. Old Nick's murderer was surely to be feared far more than he, eager hunter though he was?

I looked around me, suddenly afraid. Was I observed? No. I was viewed only by my carrion companions whose feast I was preventing. The flank of the hill concealed no one. Even so I remained watchful. My inner certainty had fled as quickly as it had advanced. I was apprehension's apprentice once again. I had heard – who has not? – of practised assassins who lie in wait for those who enquire after a corpse or seek to succour such a one. These demons employ their victims as baits to catch another.

I wondered what I should do. Should I tell of this body? Tell whom? Or should I leave Old Nick (perversely I felt almost fond of him) for others to find? Yes, that I decided would be for the best. Let a passing shepherd discover him – not me. Besides, Pandora, I suspected, would not thank me for announcing my presence on her estate to the county magistrates. Albeit I was known of locally – to Mary, to Dr Thwaite, to the servants of the great house – nevertheless I felt sure it would be better to remain no further known. Few at present knew who I was and if they did I doubted they were much the wiser. But the law was different. The law's a creature with many tentacles. At their furthest ends they may be no more than ignorant orifices but what they digest nourishes the centre where intelligence has its seat. After all, I had brought disgrace and death upon Christofer, my dearest friend. That was enough evil for one lifetime. It would ill-become me to bring my benefactress into danger too. For danger was here, I knew. And not for me alone. It was present in equal measure for those who tried to help me.

I left Old Nick to his hungry confederates and hurried down-hill. I looked back once. And saw the buzzards descending, their huge wings outspread, to scatter the gulls and crows like sparrows. As I half-hopped, half-ran, my fears increased. By the time I reached the cottage I was sweating like a galley slave. So was my mind. My brain pulsed and dripped with trepidation. I drank a gallon of water from the bucket and dunked my head in the butt beside the door but still I sweated. I sat on the bench that has its back to the cottage wall and commands a view of the garden and the track beyond.

Seated there I felt a little better. No one, I felt sure, could creep up on me without my observing his approach. Now I could call my thoughts to order. Two crossbow bolts had been fired at me. The first by Old Nick surely? But was the second? Hadn't I thought, even as it happened, that he'd had no time to rewind his bow? So could the second bolt have been fired by his murderer? If so, were they accomplices who'd quarrelled? Or was Skeres himself the other's chosen prey? Had this second shot been aimed not at me at all but at him? And missing its mark come on at me? If that was the truth of it then Skeres could have run down the hill to confront his enemy. But only to die in the ensuing struggle. Instinct told me this was so. And reason added that this explanation accorded well with what had happened since. Or rather what had *not* happened. Because Nick's assassin had let me be.

Could Pandora have appointed someone to be my protector? Had I indeed been saved by this shadowy warden? It was a comforting fancy in which I could not quite believe and yet Pandora had cared enough for my welfare to provide Mary. It wouldn't be beyond her powers to instruct a bodyguard to keep an eye upon me. Had she heard something at Court and sent out instructions to this end at the same time as restoring my miniature to me? Had Lady Audrey given her cause for alarm? Perhaps. But would such a bodyguard resort to murder on my behalf? And then disappear? This thought gave me pause. The manner of Skeres' dispatch seemed too butcherly for this imagined guardian. Or was that sentimental? A countryman could cut a throat just as well – if not better – than any city ruffian.

Dissatisfied with these unravelments I wove myself another web of ugly likelihoods. Suppose Pandora had taken no steps at all to shield me? If that were so then Skeres had either been killed by his own enemy or by an enemy of Walsingham who had struck at the master by way of the man. And this other, whoever he was, might wish me to remain alive for reasons yet to be revealed. At this conclusion I shivered and not because a sharp breeze had suddenly sprung up as the clouds in the west smothered the declining sun. Was I being allowed to enjoy a doubtful liberty while two superior forces, Walsingham's and this other's, strove for mastery? Mastery not of me – I was only a toy, a puppet, to live or die within the suburbs of their purposes – but of each other? Was Walsingham's rival my true Ishmael? If so, who could he be? How hidden was he? The mystery deepened with the dark. I went inside and barred the door.

Driven by these misgivings I made up the fire, lit every candle I could find and shuttered all the windows. Even so I still didn't feel secure, although I told myself again and again all immediate danger must have passed. Whatever else might be one thing was sure: Skeres had failed to kill me. At the worst Walsingham would have to appoint another agent for my destruction and that event could not, of necessity, be now. Even so I took a kitchen knife and honed it to a stiletto's keenness.

That evening Mary was late – for the first time since she had come to me. And when she did arrive it was already fully dark outside. She had run all the way, was out of breath, and overflowing with news of the dead stranger. Hearing it I could only express a false surprise. It wrenched my heart to deceive Mary but I knew I must.

'Oh, Tom, I'd have been here long before but there's been such a turmoil! I had to look after young Martin – my sister's son. He found the body.'

'The body? What body?'

'A man's body. Up on the Downs just below Chancton Ring. His throat was cut from one ear to the other. Little Martin kept shivering and crying, crying and shivering. The boy's beside himself with what he saw. He's only six year's old. He came running back to tell my sister. She was in the cowshed milking. It's a wonder his tale didn't turn the milk, she says. And Martin says he saw someone close by the body. A man with a hobble, he says. Was that you, Tom?'

'Me?'

'I thought you might have gone for a walk up there? Like you do sometimes.'

'Oh, yes. Yes. I did go that way. But I saw no body. Whose was it?'

'No one knows. A stranger's they say. But he weren't a beggar. There was money in his breeches.'

I was tempted to suggest they put Old Nick on a carrier's cart and have him sent to Scadbury, back whence he came, with the carrier to be paid upon delivery. But I didn't say it. My situation's too precarious for irony. Irony's for those secure inside their own complacencies; for well-armed hunters not for the hunted.

'They've told the beadle and he's to have a proclamation cried. For murder. They say it's murder but no robbery.'

'I daresay there'll be a reward offered for information.'

'What good'll that do? Folks about here won't know anything. All they know is themselves. He was a stranger, wasn't he?'

Her simplicity touched me. I took her in my arms and kissed her. I said, 'Hope of reward can often make people see things they thought they hadn't noticed.'

'It leads them into falsehood?'

'Or to unregarded truths.'

'Are you sure you didn't see the body, Tom?'

'No!' I hoped my denial hadn't sounded too vehement.

'Martin said the man hopped just like you. He showed me. I thought it was you I was seeing. He's a clever young monkey.'

'Oh, I don't doubt your nephew saw me. But I didn't see him, Mary. Nor the body.' There! I'd lied three times over. All that was needed now was for Chanticleer to crow. But it was the wrong end of the day and I'm no St Peter, not even in potentia.

Mary continued to speak of the mystery throughout supper and upon our going to bed. And the more she chattered the more I longed to tell her what I knew. But I didn't. I couldn't speak. Instead I told myself I must not compromise her ignorance: she would be safer if she knew nothing. This argument had not an iota of logic in it. Not in this iron age. Lack of knowledge is no protection nowadays. Under duress we can all remember anything. Am I not a living proof of it? No, the reason I held my tongue had little or nothing to do with Mary's safety but much, indeed everything, with my own. For the time being I'd been saved from death; though whether by chance or design I couldn't say. But however it had come about I had been given some further time to discover the true nature of my predicament. But this meant I must first disown my unlucky murderer. I knew that for my very life's sake Old Nick must remain the stranger he was to those hereabouts in Sussex. I needed him buried six feet down in a nameless grave. Meantime I only hoped young Martin's witness concerning me would be forgotten or else discounted as boyish babble. I had no wish to repeat my shameful history to a rustic magistrate.

These unquiet thoughts drove both desire and sleep from me. Only with the dawn did my eyes close. When I awoke Mary was long since gone and I had no one in whom to confide my reviving hopes let alone my newly resurgent desires.

·V·I·I·

Was there ever a more deceitful Spring than this year's? Having enticed us into an Arcadian dream it next engendered in us the dangerous idea that we might become more serious. The Wizard Earl, supported by Lucrezia – 'there are seasons for the head as well as for the flesh, *amici miei*' – proposed one soft afternoon as we of the cabal sat beside the lake that we should establish an academy at Scadbury in imitation of that at Cerne Abbas. At once George Chapman objected, huff-puff, protesting that the company here was too numerous, multifarious, polyglot, not to say lightweight (with this his eye dwelt heavily upon me). But Walsingham, flattered to think himself a Raleigh, overrode George and agreed at once to appoint himself President of this new School of Light, as our folly was quickly dubbed. Admittance to so rarified an academy, we decided, would have to be by private invitation only. Thus those excluded – so we argued – would not feel slighted even though they were. This in itself gives some measure of the school's intellectual rigour. And looking back it was a pity no one had the gumption to question it then and there. But no one did simply because we founder members never doubted our election nor our right to choose from among the rest of Walsingham's guests.

Each member, as in Dorset, would be expected to deliver a paper upon some matter of substance. No subject would be barred, all thought would be free, any censoring must be begot out of logic never upon prejudice or superstition. We were to be shining apostles of pure knowledge. The first convention, Percy pronounced, could take place that very evening if our host and president agreed. He did. And that night Percy delivered a stupefying discourse upon a new science called 'economical projection' or 'paper commonwealths' as practised by his friend Thomas Harriot while attending the ill-fated foundation of the new-world state known as Virginia. Harriot had invented a method, Percy said, by which we may deduce the wealth of a newfound country long before the natives of it have been subdued and put to useful work or its natural goods harnessed or extracted. Thus you may look at a flat meadow and say in Harriot's terms: there, unseen, lies a treasury of invisible gold we can now pretend to measure so let us weigh it in our heads and, like projectionists, call ourselves already rich.

It was after this opening lecture that Percy begged Christofer to repeat the dissertation George and he had heard him read at Cerne Abbas in which the sacred nature of the Gospels was dissected and their historical veracity examined. Christofer agreed to search out the paper. He knew he'd brought it with him. It wasn't, he said, the kind of manuscript he particularly cared to leave unattended. We all smiled wisely like the fools we were and repeated yet again our vows of secrecy.

In vain! Within two days our academy was known to all. And all had clamoured to enroll in it. So vociferously that we of the cabal were forced to accede to the appeals of our fellow guests. By the end of the week each and every former nymph and shepherd had become a scholar!

Walsingham's library was ransacked. Whole yards of shelves stood empty. No one walked without a book in hand. No one talked now of anything save what was serious. And behold, Aristotle was found inadequate, Plato platitudinous, Lucretius specious. The park filled with dour discussion groups. The house fell into a bookish silence where no reader dared disturb another except in the most charnelhouse whisper. Even more mysteriously people's manner of dressing changed. Where before they'd clothed themselves either with a flowery simplicity which promised and provided all kinds of country pleasures or else with a bold desire for peacock excess, now everyone affected black.

Black, black, black. We were become a university of crows. Each and everyone of us a cawing malcontent. Never have I seen sadder faces or heard more saturnine laughter than at Scadbury in those latter days. How we weighed the world. And existence. And found both wanting.

If anything the girls showed themselves more assiduous in their studies than us men. What was worse they now reserved their favours to themselves insisting we should flatter their minds rather than their bodies. And – imagine it – we wretched males agreed! As one man we all acquiesced with this nunnish edict, compounding the girls' new-fangled hypocrisy by strenuously proclaiming the virtues that enforced chastity bestowed upon the masculine intellect. I was especially glad of this turnabout of events. So puritan a rule enabled me to hide my aversion to Lady Audrey's lacerated bottom under the fashionable guise of pure principle.

When Christofer, after much nagging, pulled his Cerne Abbas lecture out of the quagmire of foul papers at the bottom of his trunk it was pronounced illegible. Not by him nor by me but by Walsingham who suddenly insisted he must know the matter of the discourse before he could consent to Christofer's delivering it to our enlarged academy. At this Christofer sulked. I intervened. And like a fool I took Walsingham's part, arguing with him that since our cabinet academy had been translated willy-nilly into a common university then as the founders of it we should take some care. Free thought among private friends was one thing – among a multitude another. This craven argument led to my undoing. Especially when I said I would gladly make a fair copy of the lecture.

Christofer glowered and cursed me under his breath but agreed. Walsingham thanked me profusely, dismissed Francis upon estate business, tousled Chrisofer's hair and walked him away to view the planting of palm trees upon his May masque island. I took the lecture to the library but the place was crowded with a gaggle of our nymphs-turned-nuns furiously discussing female education. I listened for a while and even attempted to say that my old headmaster at Merchant Taylors' had advocated as much if not more than they were proposing. They turned on me like snakes. I left hurriedly to the sound of their hissing. And took refuge in my room.

Having prepared pens, ink and paper I settled down to copy out Christofer's lecture. At that time I still had three scripts to choose from: Italian Chancery, Financial and Running Secretary. Now I have none save Hangman's Scribble. For Christofer's *New thoughts upon the New Testament* I chose plain Running Secretary.

Was I shocked by what I copied? Hardly – for two reasons. One, I'd heard most of it before. Christofer had often maintained the Gospels were poor poetry and worse history. Two, as a copyist you scarcely read what you transcribe. Your mind is a waterfly moving across the surface of the subject under your hand. You make tiny dents in the fluid skin of it but considered comprehension eludes you. All I really remember is that I sat up most of the night to do it. I was out of practice and Christofer's lecture was longer than it looked – his scrawl got smaller and smaller as his argument progressed.

When blear-eyed the next morning I presented my fair copy to Walsingham he exploded like a tun of saltpetre. I swear my eyebrows caught fire. He declared Christofer's opinions abominable. The lecture was an enormity. It could not be delivered in public. Not in his house. No. Never.

Henry Percy disagreed. He told Walsingham it was neither blasphemous nor atheistical, merely modern: a well-argued *critique* of conventional pieties and received ideas which had been much admired at Cerne Abbas otherwise he would never have suggested its repetition at Scadbury. Walsingham ought to be proud to count himself alongside such as Raleigh. Christofer weighed in too, doing his cause no good at all by denouncing Corin as a hypocrite who having pronounced himself a libertarian now sought to strangle free thought at birth. The argument raged all day, drawing in Lucrezia (for), Nick Skeres (against – why did I not note that at the time?), George Chapman (for), Lady Audrey (didn't know) and me (for-ish). Yes, as ever I compromised suggesting that if our host really thought the lecture too inflammatory to be given to all, then why should it not be given to some? In other words, by invitation only? This daft proposal was seized upon as if it were a consummate solution of diplomatic genius instead of the social wedge it proved to be. We lost half our academy at a stroke as those not invited packed their bags and left in a huff, taking out into the world dangerous talk of Scadbury as a nest of unbelievers preaching doubt of God and Eliza. Once again, as in volunteering to copy out Christofer's manuscript, I had woven my own destiny.

The lecture itself, addressed to some thirty of us squashed into the library, proved far more acceptable than Walsingham had feared. Several auditors even declared themselves disappointed. After the fuss of who was and who wasn't invited, and why and why not, they'd expected an evening of spectacular intellectual fire and brimstone from the wildest poet in Christendom. Instead they got a sober discourse which set out to discover the historical accuracy of the Gospels by a painstaking comparison of one text with another. Here were no rhetorical flourishes, treasonable analogies, or poetic hyperboles teetering on the brink of blasphemy. No, this was Christofer the divinity student of Cambridge. An earlier, studious Christofer I had never known but sometimes heard about. A subfusc fellow quite unlike his later self. Only once did I hear his audience draw breath in concerted surprise. At a moment when he remarked in passing that he presumed Jesus had died quite as much a sodomist as his bedfellow John the Evangelist. Apart from that small frolic even our Archbishop Whitgift could have listened to Christofer without overmuch fear of hellfire. At least for himself.

But if the lecture itself proved harmless the aftermath wasn't. On returning to my room I found Christofer's foul papers missing. I'd left them on my table held down by a dog-eared copy of Holinshed. It had gone too. To begin with I exclaimed more at the loss of Holinshed's *Chronicles* (every playwright's bible) but common sense soon informed me that this book was replaceable whereas the papers weren't. Had Christofer taken them? No one else would want them surely? Yes, Christofer, of course. And while he was about it he'd borrowed my Holinshed. That was obvious and typical. I looked in his room just to be sure. Neither my book nor his foul papers were there.

Very well. Someone else had wanted them. Someone else had taken them. But who? Well, any of the servants – even if Walsingham did boast of their trustworthiness. But what would be the value of such a theft to them? Since most if not all were illiterate? The value of a bribe perhaps? Yes. Money. Naturally. Then who would've paid a servant to do this? The answer was as plain as it was disquieting: almost any guest or even Walsingham himself could have ordered the manuscript's removal. (By this time I had discounted the theft of my Holinshed as a superfluity intended to confuse the true issue.)

The more I thought the more I convinced myself it had to be Walsingham's doing. And although I hadn't a shred of evidence for it I kept seeing Francis as its perpetrator. Walsingham's preening secretary seemed to me the perfect instrument. He was his master's confidant – hence his insolence. And furthermore he'd been present when I offered to make the fair copy. Could he even have advised his master to safeguard himself in this way? After all, while the lecture had proved less inflammatory than Walsingham had feared it might yet be construed as heretical by zealous guardians of the State. A damp squib at Scadbury could be a fire-bomb at Whitehall. Yes, Walsingham persuaded by Francis had ordered this confiscation to protect himself from the law. So in my innocence did I reason. And I determined to have the matter out with Walsingham the next day.

But in the morning neither he nor Christofer nor Francis were to be found. They had gone to Deptford where an important shipment from France had arrived bringing effects and properties essential for the May masque. Consequently I was obliged to relate my loss to Lady Audrey whom I found sitting demurely in an arbour on the south side of the knot garden. At my approach she smiled guardedly. There was an open book on her lap. It was my copy of Holinshed.

'You took it?' I said not hiding my surprise.

'Yes. I found it in your room. I've always meant to read it.' No shame. No apology.

'Did you take the manuscript, too?'

'What manuscript?'

Was she lying? 'Christofer's lecture. The papers I made a fair copy from? They were on the table, under that book.'

'I didn't see them. And what would I want with them anyway? I'd heard the lecture. It was rather dull, I thought. So predictable. I thought we were all meant to be brilliant and original?'

I regarded her, doubting every word she'd uttered. She smiled more freely at me – there was even warmth in her eyes. 'Oh, Tom,' she said, 'you can look such a little boy lost sometimes.'

Was this reproof? Was I to grow up? Was that her meaning? Or did she consider it an endearment? I couldn't tell. Ever since the night of the telescopio we'd conducted ourselves like politic strangers. I had been quite unable to respond to her repeated pleas for us to continue as platonic lovers sharing everything except our bodies. In fact as far as I could I'd avoided her, finding other places at table, at chapel, in our *conversazioni* as Lucrezia called our academy's self-conscious seminars. My difficulty was that to see Audrey was to desire her still. But not in the vile fashion she desired me. I could not use her, abuse her as she wanted. I would not be her whipster. Foolishly I wanted her as I had first imagined her: as the embodiment of the Age of Gold, as my May queen, as Primavera herself. She could look the part why wouldn't she play it?

Or was she deceiving me? Calling me childish so as to hide the truth: that she had taken the papers at her betrothed's behest? As an intimate thief her presence in my room would be more plausible than Walsingham's or Francis's.

'Are you quite sure you didn't see them?'

'Why do you ask?'

'Because it's important. In the wrong hands those papers could be dangerous to Christofer. Surely you can see that? We may find his ideas unexceptional but others wouldn't. Corin realised that at once, didn't he?'

'Walsingham panics about almost anything these days. He's always in a lather. If he knew what knowledge you now have of

me, oh, I tell you, my sweet silly Tom, he'd dissolve with fear.'
She laughed.

I didn't. I said, as severely as any Holy Brother of Amsterdam,
'Well, you may keep him for that service, madam, if that's your
pleasure. It isn't mine.'

'I know. I've learned that lesson, Tom.' She looked contrite.
'And so I wonder – would it please you to hear I'm allowing my
body to heal? Already my mirror tells me the marks are disappearing. Soon I'll be unmarked again. Can I then call you to
account? I want to. I want you as you wish I were. Please.' Her
voice was low, her eyes held mine. Was this mockery or subter-
fuge or both? Was she perhaps more than a little crazy? I couldn't
decide. But whatever it was she'd come close to disarming me. I
sat beside her. She took my hand. 'Do forgive me, Tom. Until
now I thought it pleased men to be cruel. I judged you by the
others I've known and by myself, too. I'm sorry. I was wrong.
Who knows, perhaps you can teach me purer pleasures, higher
delights? Will you?'

Flattered thus, I was, as you may imagine, tempted to say yes
of course I can and I will. Yes. But still doubt held me captive.
This mixture of the profane and the political was too pat. Put
crudely her sweet talk, sweet reformation, sweet cajoling of my
carnal preferences could only – in my reckoning – be aimed at
one end: to distract me from my enquiry into the disappearance
of Christofer's papers. After all I only had her word she hadn't
seen them. I couldn't bring myself to trust it.

I got up. 'I can't think who would've taken them, can you?' I
said, keeping my eye upon her.

'No.' Her candour seemed impregnable. 'Do stay, Tom.'

'No, madam, I mustn't.'

'But you'll remember what I've said?'

'Most certainly. I want to believe you.'

'You can, you can. It's the truth, I swear. But upon this other
matter I'll ask Walsingham if you wish. Would you like me to?'

'No need. I shall. As soon as he returns from Deptford.'

'How stern you sound. Can't you smile anymore?'

'Good day, madam.'

As I walked away I think she wanted to make one last appeal to me but one of her ladies appeared to call her to the tennis court so I was spared further temptation. Which was perhaps as well since, as I say, she'd come near to redeeming herself in my eyes – rather as Aphrodite could always restore her virginity by the magical expediency of going for a bathe in the sea. Or so the ancients liked to believe.

When Walsingham and Christofer got back that evening they rode at the head of a cavalcade of packhorses and groaning waggons. They looked like triumphant brigands. Both were well-wined. They had dined magnificently, they said, at an excellent hotel (hic) belonging to a formidable widow (sic) by the name of Bull. Eleanor Bull. Her house was to be recommended (whoops). Quite the best in Deptford. Most exclusive. Renowned for its table, cellar, comfort and (sway) seclusion standing as it did beside the Strand yet within ample (stumble) gardens enclosed by high walls (better sit down).

At this initial encounter they received my news with convivial equanimity. But an hour or so later Walsingham sent for me to attend him in his apartment. He was damply pale, very sober. He'd taken an emetic, he said. He demanded full details of the missing manuscript. As I explained Christofer came in. He too was sober. He caught Walsingham's concern and agreed a search should be made. Walsingham called in Francis and Old Nick to organise it. The whole house was ransacked from top to bottom. No guest's coffer or cupboard was sacred. Some took offence. The atmosphere soured. The manuscript wasn't found. All that remained of Christofer's lecture was my fair copy. Walsingham burned it himself page by page. Christofer did not protest. Nor did I. To be honest I was glad to see it burn. I had no wish to be mistaken for its author. As I watched the flames consume it I felt safer. What a ninny I was four months ago.

A general convocation was called for the next day. At noon the academy would be addressed by its president. We all gathered under the great oak where Christofer and I had first encountered

Walsingham, Lady Audrey and their company of carefree arcadians at the beginning of April. On All Fools' Day itself I suddenly remembered.

Walsingham voiced his present concerns to us saying that while he had absolute confidence in our discretion nevertheless he would be much reassured if as bold freethinkers and new philosophers we took a collective oath never to breathe a word outside Scadbury about Christofer's lecture. This, he said, was for Christofer's sake. Of course nothing could be done about the missing autograph papers but the least we could do would be to deny the lecture. It hadn't in fact been given. In this way, Walsingham argued, Christofer could never be held to ransom by the unknown thief. Private papers were after all private. What a man wrote for his own consideration was a different thing from what he preached abroad. Even the Privy Council would agree with that. We all accepted our host's less than convincing argument and filed up one by one to swear to it upon that same Geneva bible which had provided surety for Henry Percy and his telescopio. Looking back it seems strange to me now that we proud humanists placed faith in a vow made on the very book we'd all joined Christofer in doubting. And also that we were quite so ready to revise the truth even if our intentions were of the best. But we did. Walsingham was visibly relieved. He congratulated us.

And with that the damage was done. From that instant our academy decayed. It cankered from within. Killed by partisan loyalty to itself and to its own. The effect was soon apparent. Books were cast aside. People reverted to prettier clothes, brighter colours. They began to laugh and sing again. They started to flirt, suggest games to be played. Impromptu parties blossomed. Where before we had resolved to eat modestly and drink nothing but herbal infusions and spring water we now demanded exotic dishes and spiced wines. Gossip became the only conversation (any mention of moral matters was howled down or yawned away). Jokes verbal and practical became de rigeur and as the days passed they grew perceptibly coarser, openly crueller. Soon we would laugh at nothing unless it had a razor's edge of viciousness and a heart of stone. George Chapman warned us against this ruthless frivolity and for once I thought him right. But Amos Bullivant composed ruder songs and even found a viper to place under one unfortunate chambermaid's pillow. The girl was bitten and nearly died. Even the Willoughby brothers chose darker backgrounds for their portraits. The Wizard Earl, ever circumspect, took his leave transporting Lucrezia and his equally massive telescopio with him. Meanwhile Christofer insisted he welcomed the change that had come over us. We had encompassed the history of the world in the blink of an eye, he said. Passing from the age of Apollo to that of Mercury and now to Saturn in thirty days instead of sixteen thousand years. Christofer had no patience with present dogma that's fixed the world's beginning at a mere six thousand years ago; his argument being it was clear from their works that many heathen authors wrote long, long before Adam was moulded out of dust. After the school at Scadbury he declared, there could be nothing but chaos come again and an eternal dark. We laughed and danced and romanced the more frenziedly.

But however hectically we guests comported ourselves Walsingham's army of servants continued to wait decorously upon us while yet more prepared for the May masque. How they laboured. A kind of clapboard Dover was built on the bank of the lake with two curving jetties to form a harbour large enough to contain the various craft needed for the entertainment. There was a miniature galleon, a Portuguese caravel and cannibal canoes for the performers, together with various punts and rafts for the audience who would follow the knightly expedition out to battle. We were determined to out-panto Lepanto. The island was now not only planted with palms but with bamboos and roses. It was also turfed except at the water's edge where pink sand imported from Britanny had been carefully spread and raked into a tiny similitude of a sea shore.

And while Walsingham supervised his toy world outside, Lady Audrey inside (with the help of the brothers Willoughby) designed the costumes and had them made up by a flock of patient seamstresses who ruined their eyes round the clock; the poor creatures looked like peahens making peacocks.

Next, almost as an afterthought, rehearsals were called. I was asked to copy out the parts but I declined. I'd had enough of scrivening. And besides, Walsingham's work was scarcely worth the copying, unlike Christofer's. I insisted another penman be found. Francis got the job.

Christofer was granted his wish and cast as chief of the cannibals. I became his comic henchman. Our cannibal costumes were mostly garish bodypaint, pheasant feathers in our hair, chicken bones stuck on either side of our noses to make them look hideously pierced and leather harnesses round our loins from which dangled papier mâché dildoes which erected cheerfully at the pull of a string. Walsingham seriously insisted he had classical authority for these horselike appendages but he convinced none of us. He knew and we knew they were there for the dirty laugh. They got it. And after the show became treasured souvenirs. As cannibals Christofer and I had to learn a song to sing. It went: 'We like Christians spread on toast or else long-pig for feast-day roast.' Oh, dear. Courtly masques have a way of degenerating into doggerel . . .

·V·I·I·I·

A letter's come. Dated three days ago. Delivered by a groom from the great house. I think it best to record it verbatim.

My dear Kyd

I write to you from Whitefriars where I am lodged in the house of our mutual patron, young Ferdinando. I have returned here from visiting his lordship at Knowsley. Alas, poor Ferdy remains in miserable health but yours I hear improves daily if not hourly. But to our muttons, dear heart and fellow favourite of our good Lord Strange. For so you are, Thomas! You are returned to your lord's favour. If you recall I swore I would speak for you. I did. At first he pouted and looked at me as if I'd let flee a fart as our excellent poet Chaucer puts it. But upon persuasion, and I dare tell you, sweet boy, I am an adept at this necessary art, yes, upon persuasion his love for you has revived. Your name may once again be spoken in his presence. He is delighted to hear of your recovery from the detestable attentions of Poley and Topcliffe to name but two of Eliza's ever watchful myrmidons and further he is on tenterhooks to see you. Hence this letter, dear boy. He has charged me to command you to come with what speed you can to London but by any event not later than the end of this month of September. From Whitefriars you will be conducted to Lancashire to be reconciled with his lordship and placed again in honour as his personal secretary, household bard and private friend. What else can I say? Your fortune is restored, your disgrace annulled, your ills redressed and ready to be yet further recompensed. Reply immediately and a munificent purse shall wing its way to Sussex to ease your return into the arms of your bountiful lord and merciful patron. Not to mention those of your eternal friend and ever-loving servant,

Richard Baines

Post-Scriptum. If you will accept my advice do not stay for the return of your present benefactress. I shall make good your excuses with her at our next encounter at Court. I journey to Greenwich tomorrow. Therefore have no fear. Your future is assured.   R.B.

As I finished reading I jumped for joy. And promptly cracked my head on the ceiling's centre beam. The pain made me curse and think. I read the letter again. And thought again. Of my leaving Mary (how much did she mean to me?), of venturing back to London (how far was the plague abated and why had Baines made no mention of it?), of Lord Strange and finally of Pandora. Of ingratitude to the one person, that singular woman, who'd rescued me, befriended me when all the world – Baines and Strange included – had deserted me. How could I leave Sussex before her return? Baines might urge all speed but I knew in my bones I couldn't go until I'd seen Pandora again. Nor was this simply a sense of obligation. I *wanted* to see her again. And I wanted her to see me. Me as I am today. Not as I was when she left for Greenwich. How long ago? Almost a month. No, a month yesterday. Yes. Suddenly I longed to speak to her. To question her again about the author of this letter, this erstwhile lover, this Dick Baines. What did *she* know of his past? Had he ever spoken of attending the English College at Rheims? Had he talked of Christofer to her? Was he really a government agent? Was his letter to be trusted? I liked him but how far could I believe him?

Instinct, cold as bad luck, told me his news was too good to be true. Yes, too good for poor Tom. And Pandora was the one person who would know. Who would answer truthfully. But how long might I have to wait for her return?

I tried to write her a letter but gave it up to the fire's embers. The half-started thing didn't even burn – just smouldered into blackness. I told myself to examine my dilemma the next day; to put it to one side and return to my quest for Ishmael. But neither of these resolves could still my mind. The fact was I had to talk to someone other than myself, someone other than Mary. Who could that be if not Pandora? The only other person was Dr Thwaite. At this thought my spirits revived. Of course! Yes. I would consult Dr Thwaite. Not as a physician but as a man of rooted sense and pleasing humour. His house was no more than a mile away. I set off at once, taking my blackthorn shillelagh to help me along.

I was directed at once to the second-best house in the village. Decent brick, good timber. Dr Thwaite was not yet home from visiting a patient at Steyning but his wife was there, surrounded by eight children who, upon my arrival, arranged themselves about her, sitting or standing, like a choir of well-scrubbed angels. Rarely have I seen a family so well ordered. The three eldest seemed to have a special care for all except the youngest who sat boisterously upon his mother's lap. My heart seemed to leave my body at the sight of such contentment. Here was a happiness quite prohibited me. Here was a shining emblem of Dr Thwaite's worth, his goodness. Why, oh why, I thought, why had I forsaken this world for the world of the theatre? This real world, bonny world, which defines itself by honest dealing, thrift and care. Which exists below and yet above any gloss put upon it by a poet. For however much we poets may proclaim the world's a stage, our life a play of passion, at heart we know our vainglorious pleading's false – a convenient conceit. For all our bragging we whistle in the dark, cringe before our patrons and are prey to every fashion of thought or dress. Suddenly, in my mind's eye, I saw my parents' home in Fen Church Street. As solid as this, as worthy as this. How I had despised it before I left it.

These reflections were deflected by one of the children coming to take my hand. The youngest but two, a little petticoated boy called Adam, who wished to show me his pet rabbit. We went out to look. He pulled it smartly from the hutch by its ears. A small black and white morsel of life. I asked its name. Adam answered Goliath. I said he didn't look big enough to be called Goliath whereat Adam gave me Goliath to hold while he took a white mouse from his pocket and announced its name as David. I laughed. The boy's logic was faultless. We set Goliath-rabbit and David-mouse together in the hutch and they played together most prettily. I congratulated Adam upon the naming of his creatures and his grasp of the relative nature of existence. I told him I was sure he would be a poet when he grew up.

'I hope not,' said a voice behind us. Dr Thwaite had come upon us unawares. 'Good day to you, Mr Kyd. I meant no disrespect to your calling, sir, but I have Adam pricked down for a doctor.' And he lifted the boy high in the air and then kissed him. Adam wriggled and nuzzled against his father's neck.

I said, 'You echoed my thoughts, Dr Thwaite. Seeing your house and family calls my poor vocation into question.'

'Nay, your verses will outlive us humdrum folk, lad.'

'You'd best leave such hollow boasting to us, Dr Thwaite.'

He laughed and led me through to his study, telling Adam to run along to the kitchen where he was sure he'd seen gingerbread men taken just then from the oven. Adam was gone in the instant.

The study was a scholar's room. Books, pharmacy jars upon shelves, a work table and a work bench with several pestles and mortars. Two good windows flooded the place with light.

Dr Thwaite invited me to be seated while again declaring himself professionally satisfied with the look of me and pleased my walk there had neither tired my knee nor, as he put it, brought upon me any unlooked-for mishap. This last comment puzzled me, even rather unnerved me, but before I could question him further his wife appeared with a tray bearing Kent cider in a jug and hot chicken pasties. I told her I considered myself fortunate to have arrived on baking day. I was. The pasties were delicious. As she closed the door behind her I opened my mouth to ask Dr Thwaite what he'd meant by his last remark but once again he forestalled me.

He said, 'Your visit surprises me, Mr Kyd. I thought you liked to keep yourself to yourself? Your health, sir.' We supped our cider. 'Has this visit owt to do with that body on the Downs I examined last week?'

At once I wondered guiltily (though what had I to be guilty of?) if Mary had gossiped? For while I had denied seeing the body I had allowed her young nephew might have seen me close by. But then I realised that others quite apart from Mary could have talked. The boy's parents, for instance. What would be more natural than for them to repeat what their Martin had said? Perhaps the only oddness here was that no constable or county justice had come to question me.

'I hope it hasn't,' I said. And meant it. Could there be a connection between Skeres' death and Baines' letter? Had Skeres been known to Baines? Had Baines heard of the murder? Could Skeres have died at Baines' behest? Was Baines my unseen protector? Or my Ishmael?

My head buzzed with these questions while to Dr Thwaite I hoped I looked as dull and blank as a winter beehive.

He said, 'I was asked by our coroner to determine the cause of death.'

'What did you say?'

'It was so sadly obvious I put it in Latin to make it sound better. I ask you, Mr Kyd, would you write *stuck like pig* on a death certificate? The poor fellow was deserving of more dignity than that whoever he was.' Despite myself I smiled. So did he. 'Of course by the time I saw him I couldn't say if he'd cut his own windpipe or had it done for him. You didn't see the body by any chance, did you, lad?'

'No,' I said, unashamedly compounding my lie to Mary.

'Oh, a pity. It crossed my mind you might have known the man?'

I sat very still. I said, 'No. I've only heard of the matter by report. But why should you suppose I might have known him?' I hoped my voice didn't sound as spittle-dry as it was.

'Well, I reasoned one stranger among us might bring another after him. Some unfinished business maybe – from a life elsewhere?'

Thwaite was too shrewd for comfort. Playing for time, seeking sea-room like a ship blown too near a rocky shore, I said, 'No. No, I wish I *had* seen the body. My Mary's nephew – young Martin – discovered it, you know?'

'Aye. So I heard.'

'Apparently I passed close by without seeing it. I'd gone up to Chancton Ring that very afternoon.'

Suddenly I was tempted to confide in Dr Thwaite. To tell him what had really happened. But something, as with Mary, held me back. Yes, it was the same thing. Here was too good a person to be involved with this side of my predicament. I could not, would not wish it on him. Let him remain as ignorant as her.

'Happen it was as well you missed seeing him, lad. He was a sorry sight. Another pasty?'

'No, thank you.' My appetite was gone but I was glad of more cider. My dry mouth moistened, I said, 'Was there really no way of your telling if it was suicide or murder?'

'Nay. Not once they'd brought the body down here. Maybe if I'd seen him where he lay. But since they never found the knife I'd guess it was murder. I don't suppose we'll ever know for sure. But to return to you, Mr Kyd, and the reason for your visit?'

I was glad he'd changed the subject. I said, 'I need your advice, Dr Thwaite. I've just received a letter. I'd like to show it to you. Do you know Mr Baines? He's a friend – a close friend – of her ladyship.'

'Dick Baines?'

'You *do* know him?'

'Aye. I attended him for the colic last winter. A pint of warm sherry as an enema. Works wonders for the wind. He was most promptly relieved – upwards and downwards. Is it he who's sent you this letter?'

'Yes. But is that all you know about him?'

'Nay. But before I go further let me ask you a question, Mr Kyd. What do you know about her ladyship?'

Yet again Dr Thwaite had outflanked me. 'Why do you ask?'

'Because I believe it matters, lad.'

'Oh. Yes. Of cours⌐ Well, I know very little really. Except she's rich and saved me from certain death in prison. I've heard from Mary she would be a widow had she married the man to whom she was betrothed. But he died in the Low Countries, I believe?'

'Aye. In '86. At Zutphen. Killed alongside Sir Philip Sidney, they say.'

'Mary also thinks her ladyship would make a better inheritor of the title than her brother.'

'If she were a man she would.'

'I once met Lord Fitzwalter. He came to see a play of mine. I took him for a fool.'

'Most do, and they're not wrong but don't say I said so. Is that the limit of your knowledge?'

'More or less except – ' Dared I say it? Yes, I would. I said, 'Except I find her strangely beautiful. I say strangely because each time I see her she appears to have gained in beauty. And yet her features aren't regular, there's something too aquiline about her nose – ' I stopped, feeling too embarrassed to continue. 'I'm sorry,' I said. 'That's hardly an answer is it?'

Thwaite laughed. I blushed like a boy. He said, 'Her ladyship inspires great affections.'

'She can count on mine. And that's why I've come to see you, doctor. This letter – ' I took it from my pocket and proffered it to him. He took it but then placed it to one side.

'In a moment, Mr Kyd. Has she ever told you why she plucked you out of prison?'

'No. All she's said is she heard of my plight from the Lord Privy Seal. I've always assumed it was pure benevolence: a noble damsel come to rescue an ignoble poet in distress?'

He smiled at my small joke. 'She's told *me*, Mr Kyd. She sees you as a challenge. To her you're a possible Lazarus who may perhaps be raised from the dead.'

'To what end?'

'I've no idea.'

'You're sure of this?'

'Aye. She aims to make you new.'

'Then she's got her work cut out, doctor. A silk purse out of a sow's ear.'

We both laughed. He said, 'Her worship makes of people what she pleases. She wanted children, never mind wedlock, but she's never conceived. Nor never will. She's barren. The remedies I've mixed her. All to no avail.' He sighed, then reached for the letter. 'But now to this letter of yours, lad.'

He read it twice. When he'd finished he looked at me for a good minute without speaking. So finally I said, 'I can't leave before her ladyship returns, can I?'

'I daresay you could. But would you?' His eyes weighed me.

'No.'

'I'm glad to hear it.'

'You said you know more of Dick Baines?'

'Aye, I do. And you've done well to come to me to ask. He's dismissed.'

'Dismissed?'

'From her ladyship's service.'

'Why?'

'For disloyalty.'

'How? In what way?'

'He took her ladyship's name in vain. Pledged it as security for a loan.'

'Without asking her permission?'

'Aye. And what was worse he used the money thus got to purchase jewels for his latest paramour. A negro hermaphrodite who's just run off with a Lombardy banker.'

I couldn't help laughing. It was so louche somehow. Exactly the kind of escapade Christofer and I had loved to put into a play. I said, 'Was it for a great deal of money?'

'It was, aye. A sizeable sum. Five hundred pounds.'

'Sizeable? That's a fortune!'

'But the money's beside the point with her ladyship. With her it's the trust that matters. Dick Baines had that trust but abused it. Do you see? So he's gone. Fallen like Lucifer. And if you want any more advice from me you'll show her ladyship this letter the moment she gets back.'

'She's returning?'

'She sent word this morning. She'll arrive on Saturday.'

I tried to conceal my delight and failed. I said, 'Why didn't you say before?'

'She asked me not to tell you.'

'Oh? Why?'

'I don't know. She gave no reason.'

'But you've just broken, well, ignored her request?'

He grinned. 'Have I, Mr Kyd? That depends on you, I reckon. You needn't give me away, need you?'

'No. And I won't, I promise.' But why had he told me? I asked him and he said in order to make sure I confided in her ladyship before answering Dick's letter.

'Her goodwill is more germane to you than that of Dick Baines or your former employer, Mr Kyd. Not that I know the noble lord, of course. But that's how I see your position. And that's my advice.'

He rose to his feet and I got up, too, thanking him for his hospitality and wisdom. It had been good to talk to him – even if some of his questions had cut closer to the bone than I might have wished. He patted me on the shoulder and called a man-servant to accompany me home.

I said, 'I can go alone.'

'Nay, lad. It's getting dark. I'll be happier to know you've got company. John here's a reliable man. Wrestles for his village.' I could believe it. John was as heavy shouldered as Old Bruin the blind bear in Paris Garden. I thanked Dr Thwaite again, shook his hand and took my leave, content to follow his advice in everything.

·I·X·

In one of the many stoppages during the second dress rehearsal of Walsingham's masque (the caravel had sprung a leak, several Knights of Primavera had tried to swim for safety in their armour and half-drowned) Christofer let me into a secret. We were, he said, to have a real play performed at Scadbury. He had written to our company at Hornchurch where they were now playing before going on to Chelmsford. They would cross the river to come and play *Faustus* in the great hall the day after the masque.

'Walsingham must have offered them a pretty penny,' I said. 'To break their journey.'

Christofer said, 'He has. A very pretty penny. I told him that anything less than a hundred marks would be seen as an insult.'

'And he paid up? That much?'

'Like a lamb.' He squeezed my arm, tweaked my ear and looked triumphant. 'I told him it was time some real verse was heard spoken here.' We laughed, two poet-cannibals together.

Christofer was right. Walsingham's verses were mostly sing-song rhymings of the 'Hail, jocund May' variety. But the costumes were astonishing. And despite the many hold-ups and hitches in the extensive dress rehearsals the actual performance proved smoothly enjoyable and genuinely spectacular.

Since almost every guest was to take part in the masque Walsingham invited more to watch it. They came from nearby and beyond. Some appeared from as far afield as Devon. And the majority of them were older than us – forty, fifty, sixty. I realised then that for the last few weeks I'd lived in a society which was artificially youthful. Apart from the servants we had not had amongst us any wiser heads or more experienced voices. Now there were and it was a shock. Here were men and women who might not be so easily amused as we, who might find our wit-laden cavortings puzzling. We had grown used to thinking we knew everything. We had forgotten we might need indulgence. Some of the new guests' grave faces made me shiver. Here was frost in May indeed. Could we ever hope to entertain them?

In the event I believe we did. Walsingham, a resourceful host, feasted the audience at length in the great hall while we masquers prepared for our performance. We certainly needed plenty of time. It took over an hour for Christofer, me and the other eighteen cannibals to paint ourselves all over. Inevitably ours was the most ribald dressing room. Or should I say undressing room? A score of naked men all slapping each others backs and buttocks with handfuls of black dye out of buckets. Not to mention sticking feathers in our hair and strapping on hand-modelled genitalia which worked at the pull of a string. Christofer said our room was the best boys' bordello outside Southwark. But if we cannibals took a long, bawling time to get ready, the girls took even longer. As for the company of knights they were soonest ready because their costumes were only richer, bejewelled ver-sions of what they always wore except for the addition of various chivalric devices: helmets, shields, the occasional breastplate, the obligatory sword, odd greave, optional spear and spare mailed fist.

Having diplomatically wined and dined our captive audience Walsingham led them out to their seats on the bank of the lake overlooking the harbour with the island in view beyond.

Amos Bullivant, dressed as a pirate, conducted a mixed band which included not only the usual strings and woodwind but also an entire military section of drums and brass together with two massive serpents. These bellowing instruments were needed for the battle scenes.

Once the audience was seated, Walsingham retired to change while Mercury appeared to announce the argument of the masque. Mercury was Jeremy Willoughby. He had wings in his hair and on his sandals. In between was a tubby silver tunic. And of course he carried the caduceus: a most inventive property this because the twin snakes curled around the rod appeared to be alive. They were made of meticulously concertina-ed paper and nodded their flat, evil-looking heads most realistically. Several of our audience thought they were real.

Jeremy, accompanied by a gently twangling continuo from Bullivant's band, told the audience what to expect. His message as herald of the gods was that Lady May and her ladies had been most unfortunately delayed by a violent storm which had ship-wrecked them on an equatorial island. This meant they couldn't hope to celebrate the Spring with their May Lord and his fellow knights. Indeed it was incumbent these gentlemen set sail at once to rescue the ladies. As you can imagine the brave knights needed no further encouragement even though they hadn't actually been present to hear this prologue. But now, on cue, they appeared, a magnificent mounted procession headed by Walsingham and flanked on all sides by the girls dressed as Votaries of Primavera all waving branches of may blossom. The rich smell was over-powering; its curious odour suggestive of rumpled sheets and love-dampened limbs. I noted several elderly matrons sniffing the sweet air reminiscently. The Votaries sang a hymn to Spring which did in fact begin as I have quoted: 'Hail jocund May.' It continued in the same vein ending with the predictable resolution of: 'Fairest month of all the year.' But the tune was good, the voices too – especially when the men's tenors and basses joined in at the end.

During this choral offering gangplanks were placed ready for the company of knights to enter the galleon and the caravel (now re-caulked and waterproof) and set sail for the tropics. But before this Walsingham had a speech in which he dedicated himself and his colleagues to the goddess Primavera whose help he craved during the perilous voyage to fetch Lady May home to her proper place in a proper climate.

Once the Knights of Primavera were embarked the audience was invited to follow suit and take their seats upon the rafts moored to one side of the harbour. Most took up the offer although some of the staider kind preferred to remain on the bank and watch the knight's voyage to the island from terra firma. At a great fanfare the galleon and the caravel set sail or rather were poled out by servants dressed as sailors. An early attempt to employ sail had been abandoned at the second dress rehearsal. The wind had been in the wrong direction and since no one, not even Walsingham, could predict its behaviour this more reliable if less poetic means of propulsion had been devised. Which was as well since in the event there was no wind at all except that of Bullivant's blowing.

No sooner had the two warships with their glittering cargo of household chivalry left the harbour to be joined by the audience ensconced sedately on their rafts than Walsingham made another speech to the effect that they were now traversing a particularly dangerous spread of ocean close to what his verses termed 'the dread Africk shore'. A watery waste notorious for man-eating sharks and Turkish pirates.

Cue for both. Oh, yes, this was the masque's first moment of drama. The pirates suddenly appeared in a longboat rowed furiously by four Kentish Christians recruited from the village. The infidel pirates commanding them were for the most part as noble as they were insolent: two viscounts, three baronets and Nick Skeres Esquire. Meanwhile our heroic knights clashed swords on shields and shouted suitable battlecries, mostly 'Cry God for Walsingham' or 'To Hell with the Ottoman'.

But now as the opposing ships threatened each other with these warlike exclamations six fabulous sharks appeared, scenting blood. Powerful swimmers led by Francis. Naked save for silver breeches and most ingenious masks which they wore upon their heads. These were conical cages constructed out of whalebone but boasting glaring eyes and gaping jaws full of fearsome teeth. The sight of these sea monsters slicing through the water, the swimmers propelling themselves only with their feet, provoked the first spontaneous applause of the performance.

The grinning sharks circled the combatants as two toy cannon appeared on the poop of the galleon. They took aim at the pirates and fired. Two impressive pops. Quite a lot of smoke. The pirates pretended to be rocked from stem to stern and keel to gunwale and the longboat began to sink as two of the Christian galley slaves wrenched open hatches made ready for the purpose beneath their feet. Thus the Turks were sunk and at the mercy of the sharks who in a dazzling aquatic display dived and surfaced and snapped at their floundering prey. Eventually the sharks escorted their victims ashore and our gallant knights sailed on singing a hearty hymn of victory.

At this point the masque changed tack. By which I mean that the auditors on their rafts found themselves anchored in front of the island which, now they were drawn near to it, provoked exclamations of admiration and delight. It looked a paradise especially as grouped daintily about on the lawn between the palm trees lay any number of pretty young women apparently asleep. These were none other than the shipwrecked ladies of Lady May (lately Votaries of Primavera but now sporting different costumes) who had been surreptitiously brought to the island by a different route while the audience was entertained by the sharks feasting upon the pirates. Meanwhile as the ladies began to bestir themselves the Knights of Primavera disappeared from view so as to be ready for their next triumphal entrance.

The ladies' awakening developed from a mime to a dance and thence into a song which painted an entirely false picture of the trials and tribulations they had suffered during the shipwreck. The more they sang about death, terror, wind and rain, the prettier they looked in their loose, flower-silk dresses which floated about them as loosely as their hair. Rarely has such fashionable undress been so cleverly contrived. As they moved you glimpsed here a narrow foot, there a fleeting arm, then perhaps a peeping breast followed swiftly by a swelling thigh. It was enough to bestir the sternest puritan either to righteous indignation or else to a declaration of profoundest boredom even as his eyes popped out of his head. I noted that several of the older men in the audience leaned forward sharply. Those younger simply beamed.

At the end of this fetching song and dance Lady May herself appeared. She was played by Lady Audrey and her costume was a more sumptuous version of those worn by her ladies in waiting. She looked wonderful. Like a young Cleopatra. And she too sang. I wasn't surprised. I had heard her take part in many madrigals. She had a bright soprano which that day sounded softer, more tempered than I had yet heard it. Her song was the simplest and most affecting of the masque. It was a lyric of a maiden longing to be one no longer. Could this be the same Lady Audrey, tawdry Audrey, who'd wanted me to whip her into pleasure? Perhaps not. Perhaps this was the new Audrey she'd promised me she was when I found her reading my Holinshed? As I listened my heart melted. I forgave her everything and longed for her again as I had when Christofer and I had first arrived at Scadbury.

When Audrey's song ended there was a palpable silence and then concerted applause – that unmistakable approbation actors, playwrights long for, when clapping hands become extensions of the heart, that single heart all audiences have in common if only the poet and his performers can find it, touch it. Lady Audrey's song was the masque's true triumph. All honour to Walsingham's suddenly true lyric and to Amos Bullivant for writing a melody which gathered its hearers together into one commonwealth of feeling. But most praise of all to Audrey whose singing had, for a brief while, restored her to that innocent age, that golden world I thought I had entered a month before.

Two shipwrecked mariners now appeared bringing with them a huge lobster pot. Ten tick-tock pentameters between Lady May and the First Mariner informed us that the pot contained a portent rather than a lobster so once this point had been established the pot was opened. And a tiny, wide-eyed negro boy aged two was pulled out. This caused the matrons in our audience to coo with conjoint sentimentality. Understandably enough – the baby was charmingly plump and wore not a stitch except for a gold anklet. Lady Audrey took him in her arms whereupon he made a pretty play to find her breast but when she held him from it he promptly bit her ear. This action was vital to the plot since it impelled the First Mariner to reveal that this bold child of nature was really a cannibal and so not quite as endearing as he had first appeared. What was worse he'd been discovered playing with seashells on the shore not far away which meant that other, more mature cannibals must be close by. At this a delicious shudder rippled through both cast and audience and sure enough baleful drumming was at once heard warning Lady May and her ladies to withdraw and leave the island free for its original inhabitants to bustle in. Us.

On we cannibals pranced accompanied by more Bullivant drumming – Amos surpassed himself that day – plus eldritch squeals from fifes and whistles. The audience roared with laughter. We snarled back. They laughed again. We stopped prancing and stood stock still with our primitive knees apart. Still they laughed. So we barked out a single savage 'Ha!' That silenced them. Ha! Now Christofer strode forward. You could tell he was our chief because the feathers in his hair were longer and brighter than ours as was his papier-mâché cockalorum not to mention his ridiculous shield and spear.

He made a heart-rending speech concerning the loss of his cannibal son ('proud Nature's princeling' as Walsingham put it) but the audience was too busy commenting among themselves upon the base essentials of our cannibal physique to pay overmuch attention to it. My suspicion, which was confirmed afterwards, was that they were universally wondering if our generative equipment worked. Not that their inattention to Chrisofer really mattered because now it was our turn to exit and leave room for the girls again.

Our exit however was more false than real. In other words we lurked menacingly among the palms while Lady May's ladies wondered in rondo form about the whereabouts of the Knights of Primavera who were supposed to be rescuing them from this ordeal. There was a lot of unconvincing looking out to sea in mime but not a sail was to be discerned. The girls became visibly more and more disheartened but just before the audience joined them in the dumps we cannibals were cued to attack! With a savage burst of drums and yells we stood forth from behind our palm trees. And when I say stood forth I mean it because we not only brandished our spears in a most barbarous manner but we also, simultaneously pulled our prick-strings. And at once our papier-mâché erections laid the audience's speculations to rest while alarming Lady May and her maidens most stupendously. Horror, squeals. Then began what we had termed in rehearsal 'the rout'. A semi-formal gallop of a dance in which we cannibals stamped and grabbed and growled while the girls fainted, screamed and allowed their loose gowns to get even looser. Just as it seemed we were each about to have our primitive pleasure with our respective ladies Nemesis – ever a spoilsport – struck.

Walsingham and his company of knights arrived. How did you guess? And at once we cannibals were involved in a different form of hand to hand combat, and needless to say those of us who didn't die choreographically at the end of a sword ended up kneeling abjectly before the victorious May Lord and his gorgeous Lady May. Since it was only a masque our lives were spared on condition that in future we seriously refrained from (a) despoiling Christian virgins and (b) eating them afterwards. Reluctantly we agreed (Christofer waxing elegiac at foregoing stuffed breast of spring maiden with roast parsnips) but were finally reconciled to the ways of civilisation – most unconvincingly and sentimentally – by Lady Audrey announcing as Lady May that she would adopt the little cannibal lad caught in the lobster pot. At once he was dubbed Prince of the May and we savages became his slaves. More speeches, dances and at the very last great fountains of fireworks washed the dusklight with glory. Now we could all sail home. And we did – cast and audience side by side – lantern-lit. And there on the bank to greet us and to receive yet more applause were the drowned Turkish pirates (dry now) and the sharks (dressed now) still wearing their wicked whalebone heads.

Is it a trick of memory or was this the second time I thought of Francis as something more than Walsingham's arrogant secretary? And if so was this because of his proximity to Nick Skeres? And the remembrance of their escapade of the baggage train on its way to Rochester? Pirate and shark stood side by side to take their bows. Or was the thought induced by the way Francis grinned twice over? There before me was an ambitious chamberman openly rejoicing in the possession of two sets of teeth. His own, perfectly neat and unusually white, and these others, this vicious fish's maw which, thrust forward as he bowed, became alarmingly sharkish. Or have I inferred this from another incident that evening?

This other event was equally negligible – in itself. Coming out of the great hall for a breath of air after a particularly strenuous volta I came upon Francis and Old Nick conferring together in a window corner. At my approach they abruptly changed the subject of their discourse but not before I heard Francis pronounce the words: ' – expect him tomorrow afternoon or evening.' Innocent enough perhaps except for the sudden manner of his breaking off. And their consequent over-jocular enquiries as to my enjoyment of our Maytime festivities.

Looking back I think they may have been referring to another guest who arrived the next day. An important guest who took Walsingham by surprise. But at the time I dismissed it from my mind.

We danced until four in the morning. By then Christofer was misquoting interminable chunks of *Tamburlaine* to anyone who would listen. Finally we all became so exasperated by his drunken mangling of his own magnificences that we hauled him bodily out of the house and threw him – one, two, three – into the moat. He made a huge splash and as he surfaced he protested bitterly that the water stank. He was right. It did. Of every kind of stale. Especially now he'd broken its mantle of green weed. Cursing us all he clambered out and ran, tearing off his clothes, to the clearer waters of the lake. We raced after him. And by the time rosy-fingered Aurora had touched our tender cheeks (as Walsingham inevitably put it) we'd all joined a cleaner Christofer in the lake – every stark Jack and uncovered Jill of us. And so it was that I discovered my Audrey was indeed new-made. Her scars had healed. She was no longer a lacerated maenad but a wholesome mistress who led me away – the pair of us toga-ed in towels like Romans – to a summer house I'd often glimpsed but never entered on the eastern side of the park. There beneath dried bunches of last year's flowers and among sweet-smelling baskets of tumbled rose petals we fed upon each other's eyes and lips until we thought we'd die unless we opened further to each other. And thereupon we did. And whereupon – at last – Audrey was mine. And afterwards she too professed herself satisfied and I believe she meant it whatever may have happened since.

On making our way back to the house I found our company had arrived. Here was their property cart in the court with Lord Strange's badge upon the canopy. And all of them grouped about it. How glad I was to see them! And how much, as we embraced, did I discover I had missed them. We all hugged each other tumultuously. Here were Bill and Ned and Tom and John and George and, delaying his entrance as always, dimpling, ever-angelic Augustine whose voice will never break, whose cheek will never fade, whose gilded hair will always curl. How we joked and teased. They called me traitor for deserting them and swore they would re-enlist me in their company. I protested I was at work on a new play. They mocked me, saying where was it, might they read it? I lied further saying, soon, soon. None of us believed the other most professionally.

Then – before I could prevent her – Audrey requested a speech from the players. Just as my Hamlet had. How brazenly life imitates art! Has it nothing of its own to invent? Ned at once refused with unctuous charm. To my mind correctly. Already I was an actor again. How could Audrey patronise our leading actor, our pole star, Ned Alleyn thus? To perform extempore as at a fair?

Ned having denied Lady Audrey the pleasure of a speech, Bill Kempe came – roly-poly – to the rescue. With a quick wink at me (and a knowing eye rolled all over Audrey) Bill offered a jig instead. And, even in his proffering was already doing it: dancing then singing with new words to the old, old tune of the wind and the rain, hey-ho. Your every jig-maker's standby.

When later that day the company rehearsed I couldn't keep away. I was hungry for their fellowship. So was Christofer but he was hampered by Walsingham's presence. He was obliged to explain everything while I was free to joke and clown with my peers. I was also beguiled into playing several roles since this touring version of *The Horrible Life and Damnable Death of Doctor Faustus* required much doubling, trebling even quadrupling of parts. As a result that evening I found myself playing a vintner, a female devil, the deadly sin of Sloth and the Archbishop of Rheims. Since the vintner appears immediately after the Archbishop has dined with the Pope I had to underdress. Off with the magnificent cope to reveal the wine-stained apron and grubby shirt and onto the stage again.

The dinner with the Pope, as with that half-remembered scene with Lord Basildon, now gives me cause for reflection. In it the Archbishop compares Faustus to a troublesome ghost who's crept out of Purgatory. During the action, Faustus, made conveniently invisible by Mephostophilis, boxes the Pope's ears and then throws fireworks at his priests and friars. This knockabout scene is invariably a success since it pillories the Pope. But today, I wonder if that is all it does? Especially when I think of Dick Baines at Rheims with Christofer. How does this particular buffoonery now translate? Well, first we have Faustus as an unseen presence in the Vatican, a spy in other words. Next comes Mephostophilis, a fellow agent from Hell, who can grant Faustus anything – at a price. Call Faustus Christofer and Mephostophilis Baines, who then serves whom and who, come to that, if the Archbishop? Answer: an important papal authority from the very seminary Christofer attended. The Archbishop refers to a ghost – the Cockney name for a spy or informer is *ghost* – and says Christofer comes from Purgatory. On the face of it an unexceptionable provenance entirely suited to such a restless spirit except Christofer once told me there were three courtyards at the seminary of Rheims which were commonly known as Heaven, Purgatory and Hell. And the English students always took the air and exercised themselves at football in Purgatory. Did Baines find Christofer there? And become his Mephostophilis? In which case for which side?

If only Christofer were here to ask. Or Baines for that matter. I could consult him soon enough if I were to obey his letter – but I've sworn I won't. Perhaps Pandora can illuminate me once she arrives? Who knows what Baines may have confided to her before they quarrelled?

To relate what happened next I must resort to hearsay. I was too engaged in the performance of *Faustus* to witness the matter fully for myself. All I can say of it is that the play began promptly at six o'clock in the great hall and was proceeding smartly (what a joy it was to experience once again a brisk, workaday tempo, to find every cue snapped up, to hear Alleyn's sinuous voice and observe his presence – the man can sound and look like an angel) when Francis strode in. Just as Faustus was writing his soul away. Handing a deed of gift written in his own blood to the first agent of Hell. Francis came to Walsingham and whispered something in his ear. At once he rose and left the hall at a great pace. From where I stood backstage I saw heads turn at his flurried departure and heard a rustle of whisperings. Shortly afterwards Christofer got up, his face chalk-white, blasted by fury. He too left the hall. We proceeded with the doctor's damnation.

The cause of these upheavals was the arrival of Walsingham's unexpected guest. At least by him if not by Francis and Skeres. A personage far too important to be kept waiting by a play. This was none other than Sir Thomas Heneage himself, except of course he has no self, by which I mean parts of him do not exist – officially that is. Here was the Heneage of whom Dick Baines had spoken so cheerfully, perhaps even served cheerfully, the master intelligencer I had encouraged not so cheerfully, at Chelsea. Oh, if only I'd known then what I know now.

But this is where Christofer must take up the story and I must try to impersonate him as he spoke reluctantly of Mr Vice's visit that same night in my moon-shadowed room.

He said, 'Oh, Tom, I regret it now.'

'So you say. But what? What do you regret?'

He sighed. He seemed lost for words. Could he be? My Christofer? He said, 'I thought, well, I assumed, when Corin was called out from the play that he'd only be gone a minute. But when that minute stretched to five I went after him.'

'I saw you leave.'

'I was so angry! I can't tell you how angry. How dared he walk out of my play? I know now he'd got good reason but I didn't then. I was stupid with anger, Tom.' He fell silent, hunched upon himself.

To prompt him I said, 'Lady Audrey tells me Heneage is an old friend of the Walsinghams?' He sighed but still didn't reply. 'Oh, do come along, Christofer. Say it whatever it is. You can trust me.'

Oh God, to think I said that and what's worse to think he believed me.

He said, 'I rushed out to the courtyard but Corin wasn't there. Just a pair of Heneage's bodyguards supping beer with Master Francis. Who said they'd gone inside and his lordship had left strict word they were not to be disturbed.'

'So you immediately burst in upon them?'

He almost laughed, said, 'You know me too well, Tom. Yes, I did.'

'Where were they?'

'In that cubby hole Corin calls his cabinet – it's at the back of his dressing room.'

'I don't know it.'

'No, you wouldn't. It's his private closet. Where he writes his lousy verses. Even I was told I was privileged to be shown it. Oh, Tom, how our petty gentlemen have to prove themselves at every turn, day and night.'

'You'd just entered,' I said, prodding him back onto the high road of his story.

'Oh, yes, so I had. Yes. Well – ' More hesitation.

More prod. 'Yes?' I said firmly, as at a wayward bullock.

'I went straight for Corin. Told him either to come back to the play that instant or forfeit my love forever.'

'You ignored Heneage?'

'Completely.'

'Couldn't you have suggested they both hear your play?'

'Why?'

'Why? As a matter of politeness, of course.'

Christofer looked blank. His incomprehension was so deep I decided it wasn't worth plumbing. Instead I said, 'What was Walsingham's answer – to your ultimatum?'

'Nothing! He just sat there white as a lily and as open-mouthed. But Heneage spoke. Oh, yes. Or rather he barked, emitting gob-flecked noises. The man's a lurcher, Tom. A gipsy's lurcher. All skin, bone and snap.'

I sighed. 'Rhetoric apart, Christofer, what did he say?'

'He asked me who I was. No, he didn't. He said who did I think I was? So I told him. I said, I'm a poet. A poet insulted by his lover. Him! And I pointed at Corin.' He started to laugh. 'And Corin went cross-eyed at my finger! I jabbed it right up against his nose end!'

His laughter continued but I couldn't share it. Some weevil of doubt, some intimation of danger was already at work inside me.

I said, 'And this forced Walsingham to speak up?'

'No. Just made him look pleadingly at me.'

'Provoking you yet again?'

'Of course! Except Heneage forestalled me by demanding through a fountain of saliva if I knew to whom I spoke? To which I said I didn't give a damn who he was or what he was. And rather ostentatiously I pretended to brush spittle off my shirt.'

'Oh, no.'

'Oh, yes! But don't worry, my dear, it gets worse.' He laughed again but less heartily. Had he sensed my unease? 'I told Heneage no one but no one, not even our Blessed Belphoebe Herself interrupted a play of mine. He didn't reply. Just stared at me as if I was a hare to be coursed and eaten alive. But now Corin found his voice. Well, a kind of rusty axle of a voice which squeaked as he tried to introduce us. And, so it was, Tom, I understood that there before me stood none other, God help us, than the Vice-Chamberlain of Eliza's household and a Privy Councillor to boot. A courtier to reckon with! Subordinate power parading as a mongrel bred out of a greyhound, a sheepdog and God knows what.'

If only that had been all that Heneage was. If only Christofer had known, or perhaps even more importantly, *I* had known, whom exactly he'd offended that evening. I might have escaped Top's pillar and he would not have died at Deptford. These considerations do not however make Heneage my Ishmael. Rather they make him Ishmael's most likely master. If not his dupe? What dreadful thought is this? Another circle of Hell? Chelsea has been likened not only to Hell but also to the tree of knowledge but shrouded in spiders' webs. Such trees are to be found, if traveller's tales can be believed, in Africa where the natives declare they are the seat of many malignant spirits.

I said, 'And upon this introduction you shook hands with Heneage?' No reply. 'You didn't shake hands with Heneage?'

'No.'

'Was that wise?'

'Wise? What's wise? Whenever were we wise, Tom? But yes, yes, I did offer my hand, yes! When Corin begged me to, yes. I did. But he refused it.'

'Oh? It was too late by then, was it?'

He half-laughed, said, 'Let's say the moment had passed. Passed over us like a lost cherub.'

'I see.'

And that was that. I could picture Christofer only too well: first outfacing the man then flicking out his hand to shake as if it were a knife. No wonder Heneage hadn't taken it.

'What happened next?'

'More spit and snap to herald his departure. He tells Corin to be sure to remember what he's said and off he goes, slinking away down the corridor. I'd half-expected him to cock his leg against a doorpost to mark the place as his, but he didn't.'

'So you were left with Walsingham?'

'Not quite. Corin wanted to run after Heneage!'

Another silence for me to break.

'Yes?' I said, breaking it.

'I stopped him.'

'You did? Why?'

'I told him he wasn't to see Heneage out. The man was so vile.'

'And he accepted that?'

'Oh, yes. Once I'd cracked his head against the wainscot, that is.'

'You fought?'

He grinned. 'We had quite a tussle. I won. My headbutt to his armlock.'

'So that's why you haven't seen him tonight?'

'He'll come round. He always does.'

But what had Heneage said to Walsingham that Walsingham had to be sure to remember? I asked Christofer. He hesitated but this time there was no need to prompt him. He spoke soon enough.

'He'd heard rumours at Court apparently. About our academy. Of atheism being preached here.'

'He'd had news of your lecture?'

'I don't know. But gossip had got to Greenwich – that's for sure.'

'What did Walsingham say to that?'

'Oh, to be fair, he kept his word. Stuck to our oath of silence.'

'Denied you'd ever given the lecture?'

'Oh, yes.'

I didn't think he sounded certain enough of Walsingham. I said, 'You don't seem convinced?'

'I am! I trust him, Tom.'

'I wish I did.'

He was onto this like a trout at a mayfly. 'You liar! You don't wish anything of the kind! You distrust Corin utterly because you're jealous of him.'

'I'm not!'

But however hotly I denied it there was a residue of truth here. Part of me was jealous, part wasn't. And thus divided I was prey to further doubt. Had Heneage really come only as an influential friend who'd heard dangerous talk in the corridors at Court? Was he simply warning Walsingham to take care what company he kept, what ideas he entertained? Or was there something more to his visit? I think now there was. But now I enjoy the luxury of hindsight. At the time I simply wondered if Walsingham had told Christofer the entire truth.

I said, 'Suppose he hasn't kept his sworn word? What then?'

'He has, Tom! He has! I know Corin!'

'Let's hope so. This man Heneage could do you dreadful harm if he chooses.' Silence. 'You've made a real enemy of him from the sound of it.'

'Don't, Tom, please. I told you I'd been a fool.'

I nodded. And poured salt into the wound. 'Perhaps Heneage has seen your manuscript? After all, it must've disappeared from here for a reason, mustn't it? And Heneage must employ informers. All great men do. What could be simpler than to place someone here at Scadbury? To eavesdrop on us?'

Christofer shook his head, not in denial, but in acceptance of these all too plausible probabilities.

'Such evidence,' I concluded, 'could be used to – well, I needn't say, need I?'

'For God's sake, Tom! My lecture was mild enough.'

'Not to a determined enemy at Court. These days they can make a heresy out of a child's hornbook. I think you should ask your Corin again. Make doubly sure of what he said.'

He sighed. But promised he would. It had grown late or rather it was become early. The first birds were calling. Christofer took my hand, asked me to come into his bed but I said I had no wish to usurp his lover's place. Besides he might return with the dawn. He did. I heard him. First I heard his whisper then Christofer's, next angry words (I stuffed my head under the pillow) and finally their gathering reconciliation.

It was left to me and Lady Audrey to say farewell to our company. We rode part of the way to Deptford with them. I congratulated Ned Alleyn once again upon his Faustus. Never had I seen him better than he was that night at Scadbury. But he was as proud as Christofer (or should I say Lucifer?) and try as I might to explain that Christofer had been as angry with our host as he was with Christofer for neglecting the performance, I could not mollify him. And indeed it was a shame that Heneage's coming and its aftermath had prevented Christofer from witnessing the play –

especially at the end. Alleyn's counting of the clock up to the stroke of midnight was almost impossible to watch for terror. Christofer's words and Alleyn's voice froze your blood. And the closing of the mouth of Hell as it finally swallowed him up was no old mystery. Here was God's modern man-trap at work like a sausage machine. As for the spectacle of Faustus's torn off head, truncated torso and chopped up limbs hurled piecemeal onto the stage at the very end – well, the audience literally shook, moaned, shuddered. Just as we had always hoped they would. Waxen simulations those gobbets might be but they seemed real beyond belief. Our property master knows his business.

When we took our leave of each other upon Black Heath I found myself, almost without thinking, promising to rejoin the company after their tour of Anglia – from Chelmsford they were to travel to Colchester and Cambridge. Having embraced them all heartily (it's the way of our fraternity to profess undying loyalty to each other and not all of it is false) Lady Audrey and I returned to Scadbury where, later that day, Christofer categorically assured me Walsingham *had* told him the complete truth. I wanted to believe him but couldn't because as we made our way back through the park Audrey had inveigled me to stop at the summer house. To be fair to her I needed little or no persuasion. There, post-coitum, in a sweet melancholy, while her hand idly sifted the dried petals so the ghosts of last year's roses filled the room, I questioned her and she said something quite other than Christofer. She said Heneage had most certainly spoken of a manuscript of an essay or lecture doubting the Gospels as the Word of God. And forced Walsingham to admit it had been given. He'd also mentioned – as if in passing – a poor ploughman, a Matthew someone (the name escaped her) who, a couple of years before, had arrived at the same conclusion and been executed for a heretic. And his friends who'd harboured him had been publically flogged.

Naturally I was biased in favour of my informant while Christofer was inclined to his. For a moment it seemed we might quarrel about who was right: Corin or Audrey? But somehow we didn't. Something had grown tired between us. We'd exhausted our caring for each other – unless the caring was of the most undemanding kind.

I said, 'I think it's time for me to leave Scadbury.'

'You do? Why?' I didn't answer. 'Where would you go? You can't go back to London. Far too dangerous. The plague's got worse. Ned Alleyn's worried sick for his wife.'

'Ned always exaggerates. The fact is, the plague's abated.'

'Wishful thinking, Tom.'

'It's true.'

'It'll be back.'

'Perhaps. But meanwhile there's work to be done. A play to revise. Bill Kempe's already put me in the way of it.'

'But you can work here with me. We'll start tomorrow. Yes! That comedy we talked of – our *Heretic's Comedy*.'

'You've still got an appetite for that? After Heneage's coming here?'

'Yes! Why not?'

'Well, I haven't.'

'Coward!'

'No. I'd do it if you meant it. But you don't, do you? Not really.'

Silence. Then Christofer nodded, admitting I was right. Oh, Christofer! Here was his saving grace. He could be as meek as he was arrogant. How many times have I seen him brimming over with contempt for everything and everyone, and then, as suddenly, become humble in the face of a plain truth or a true person. The child was strong in him.

We wrangled a little longer for old love's sake but as I say our hearts weren't in it. He knew I would go and so did I. His argument that the plague's retreat was surely transient had some strength (and by God it has returned with a vengeance since) but I was determined to risk it. I had to break free from Walsingham's precious world for my soul's sake, if not my health's.

'I shall leave tomorrow,' I said.

Scadbury, despite Lady Audrey's submission, had become a prison to me. Her body might now pleasure mine but her spirit aggravated me. Within her remained an essential dross, a sort of mendacious sediment that was demonstrated yet again that evening when I told her I was leaving the next day and she claimed as a memento my silver casket to contain John Willoughby's likeness of me. When in fury I'd dubbed her 'tawdry Audrey' I'd been right. My anger had spoken truly. The cheap rhyme expressed her accurately. She valued her possessions quite as much as her lovers. I realised she'd bought my miniature from Willoughby not out of any feeling for me but so she might have it as a trophy. And my silver casket was required to give a further veracity to the conquest she would claim she'd made of me.

As I made my round of the house to say goodbye (Amos Bullivant guffawing hugely, declared himself 'undone' at my departure, George Chapman pretended to regret it and Walsingham wished me well with eyes of steel) certain thoughts still nagged at me. Had Christofer deliberately withheld from me what I'd heard from Audrey? Had his loyalty to Walsingham outweighed his outworn love for me? Had he lied by omission? Perhaps. But what of it? He was the one in danger, not me. What had Heneage to do with me? He didn't know me from Adam and my fair copy was safely burned.

Upon that surge of ignoble renunciation I left, kissing Christofer farewell at the park gates. He stood there waving as I rode away on a borrowed cob I was to leave at Deptford at the house of the widow Bull. It was the fifth day of May. I mark it thus because one week later my measuring of time became a different thing from that of other men.

·X·

Pandora has returned. I was sent for on Sunday. I was led by her steward to her presence in a gallery overlooking the gardens and the maze. The moment I arrived she dismissed the two waiting women who were in attendance. The steward withdrew too.

Instead of speaking she held out her hand. I took it, kissed it as if she were an empress. I was puzzled by her appearance. She seemed changed. A foreign being. But could she be? She'd only been away a month. Was this change due to her dress? Possibly. Her stay at Court had provided several expensive embellishments – her ruff, for example was a miracle of scrolled gossamer sparkling with seed pearls, her wrists were braceleted with skeins of jet and she carried a purple feathered fan.

It wasn't just her clothes. The difference went deeper. It was in her eyes, and along the line of her mouth which did not smile. She looked older certainly, but that wasn't all, no, she was younger somehow, too. Older in mind, younger in spirit. And so to me more of a living mystery than ever.

Her first words to me were a command.

She said, 'Stand still, Tom.' And took several steps back to survey me as if I were a piece of statuary presented for her appraisal. This impression was reinforced when she walked right round me.

Without turning I said, 'Am I to be set up to ornament your outer court, madam? Or your inner garden?'

She laughed. 'I think you might do well in both, Tom. Yes, I do. And on your plinth I shall have carved "Here stands a true poet".'

She was in front of me again, smiling.

I said, 'You flatter me, my lady.'

'Oh, my dear man, how well you do look. You're quite another one from the cripple I left behind.'

I'm sure I blinked at her words. Never before had she addressed me as her dear man. What was this? Condescension or affection?

I said, 'You too, madam. You've changed too, I think.'

'No, I'm much the same. What's new in me is superficial. The effect of fashion.'

'I disagree, my lady. That was my first thought but on looking more closely as I do now – ' And I did, I held her eye quite boldly while saying, 'I find you older yet younger.'

'Not better?'

'That I can't honestly tell, madam.'

'Well, I can – with you. You've definitely changed for the better. Mary's worked the transformation I looked for. What a clever girl. Now all you need is more exercise, fresh experiences and a good tailor. I shall arrange for all of these.'

'Have you spoken to Mary?'

'The instant I returned. Her report delighted me. All I needed after that was the proof of my own eyes. Shall we walk?'

And she offered me her arm to conduct her the length of the gallery. And back again. It seemed I had become a gentleman in her eyes as well as a poet. The two are said to be synonymous – by gentlemen, that is. As we trod the polished boards I praised Mary, extolled her loving ways, her simple heart, her goodness. Told how she'd given me new hope, new determination to discover who had wronged me. And I thanked Pandora for her part in my redemption.

Throughout my account she smiled, shrugged, seemed slightly bored.

'I'm glad,' she said. 'You deserved such pleasure after so much pain.' She stopped, stemming a yawn, and looked about her.

'There are several other matters we must speak of, Tom. But not here I think.'

I followed her look along the tapestried walls and across to the deepset windows illuminating them.

'You suppose we might be overheard? A spy perhaps behind these cloths? A listening dwarf in that coffer or beneath the lid of that window seat?'

'Not really. Such things are too subtle for Sussex. Though I daresay my stay at Greenwich has made me aware again of such malpractices. Anyway – I love the open air too, Tom. So why don't we satisfy ourselves on both counts? Pleasure and safety?'

With this we went downstairs and out into the walk of pleached limes which led down to the physic garden. There we sat on a bench set against an old wall of flint and brick. Our feet rested upon a patch of camomile which beguiled our noses even as rosemary, golden thyme, hyssop, sweet savoury, marigolds and marjoram delighted our eyes. The air was alive with bees, especially all about the blue-flowered borage that some call bees' bread, gathering nectar for Pandora's hives that stood in a neat row at the other end of the garden.

The sun shone.

I accord this fact a line to itself because such shining was still unlooked for. After all, great Phœbus, King Sol Himself had hardly deigned to appear for months on end. He'd sulked like Achilles in his tent all through July, August, September but now just as October was arriving his heavenly majesty was in progress once again. As we sat he emblazoned us with his glory. I could scarcely believe it.

'I feel warm again,' I said, my whole body smiling.

'You like the sun?'

'Don't you?'

'No, you must answer first, Tom. You're the one under examination.'

Not once, so far, I realised, had she called me 'Thomas' – her former way of mocking me, goading me, or bringing me to heel.

I said, 'I'd worship Phoebus if it weren't a sin.'

'As a poet or as a pagan?'

'As both, madam.'

'How predictable you are, Thomas.'

There! Just as I thought she was yet to put me down she did! But at least she was laughing. And perhaps my mind, my being *is* a commonplace? I've often feared it was. If so, Pandora would've been the first to observe it. Even more than Lord Strange she loved the new, things original. On the other hand her proven concern for my well-being surely suggested she did not find me quite so dull as I did?

'But now you must answer,' I said. 'Do you pay homage to King Phoebus?'

'Of course,' she said. 'His Majesty shall have tribute of me.'

'You're quoting my play?'

'I'm glad you noticed.'

'I'm flattered.'

'I intended you to be. But now to the world as it is – not as we wish it were. I've heard from my god-daughter in Paris.' My heart stood still. 'Monsieur Saint-Malo isn't your friend Christofer.'

I found a sort of voice which said, 'How does she know?'

'Very simply. She enquired of the Jesuits at Clermont.'

'She hasn't sent an example of this man's writing?'

'Oh, yes, of course. She's an obedient child. There – you can judge for yourself.'

She drew out a note from her cuff. As I unfolded it I tried to keep my hands steady but still the scrap of paper shook as I examined it. It wasn't Christofer's script. This was a controlled cursive hand such as he could never have encompassed, close in style to what we scriveners call *lettres financières*.

Pandora said, looking at it with me, 'What do you say, Tom?'

I said, 'Christofer could never have written like this.'

'So we have proof?'

'Yes.'

'Good.'

But I didn't know what to feel. I was sad, I was intricately angry and even crudely relieved. Christofer alive, harboured in exile by Jesuits, would've quite unravelled my new-knit resolve to search out my betrayer. I'd have been distracted from my self-appointed purpose. I'd have needed to go to France straightaway. I'd have had to make good our love.

Hadn't Pandora offered to pay for just such a journey? Where before I'd recoiled from the thought of travelling to meet a living Christofer at her expense now I knew I'd have had no such compunction. I'd have flown there like Mercury, winged with her money. Now it was proved impossible I was frantic for my Christofer. Desperate for him. No! For *Christoferus*! There I've said it! *Christoferus*. That silly, secret version of his name which meant so much to me. My lover's name for him. It began, as such things so often do, as a joke. We were inventing mock epitaphs for each other. In Latin naturally. Well, in dog Latin or, if you prefer, in Latin doggerel. *In obitum honoratissimi viri Thomassi Kyddus* – that kind of stuff. Such as you see carved in plaster beneath any pudding-faced bust of any worthy in any church. But out of our foolery *Christoferus* stuck. It became a private emblem of our friendship. A code name, if you like, signifying everything I've since betrayed: love, genius, truth, the muse herself. All these found their seat for me in Christofer whose cypher was *Christoferus*.

Pandora said, 'No one at Clermont knows anything about your friend. The Monsieur Saint-Malo who resides there is an elderly clerk from the Breton town of that name. He speaks good English apparently and has even written some verses in our language.'

'So the rumours were wrong?'

'Rumours often are.'

'Not always.'

'In Paris invariably, my god-daughter tells me. Apparently they consider anyone from Brittany a foreigner. And so by the natural progression of a happy falsehood this versifying Saint-Malo became Marlowe, the English poet.' I still couldn't express what I felt because I couldn't define what I was feeling so instead I nodded. 'I wish I could have brought you better news, Tom.'

'Well, yes, but – oh, I don't know.'

'Of course, this doesn't mean your friend couldn't have been smuggled abroad, does it?'

'Please,' I said. 'I prefer to think he's dead!' And my voice sounded angrier than I'd meant.

To my surprise Pandora gently inclined her head in acceptance of this unreasoned reason.

'I agree it makes the affair clearer,' she said. 'And at least this time you haven't burst into tears, thank God.'

'No. I'm much more sanguine than I was.'

'You no longer blame yourself alone?'

'No. Like you I think others must share my shame with me.'

'Good. Who?'

I grinned. 'If I knew that, madam, I shouldn't be sitting here beside you. I'd be demanding money from you – to hunt him down.'

This reply pleased her. she smiled, she laughed, she shone with delight. Words tumbled out of her.

'But this is wonderful, Tom! You're truly reformed. More than I dared hope. And you're right. Others must take the blame. And its consequences. What do you know of a man called Nicholas Skeres?'

Again I was shocked into silence. But this time I was able to breach it with a question of my own.

'Before I answer,' I said. 'May I ask – did you appoint anyone to act as an unseen warden or bodyguard of me while you were away?'

She shook her head. 'No, I didn't.' Smile. 'As a procuress I'm afraid I only found you Mary.' No smile. 'Why? Should I have? Do you wish I had?'

'Yes, I do, madam. Most definitely. Especially now. Now you ask about Nicholas Skeres.'

'Why?'

'Because – well, I'm sure you will have heard of the body discovered on the Downs?'

'Oh, yes. Dr Thwaite sent word to me at Greenwich and Mary says her young nephew saw you close by it?'

'He did. But even so I lied to Mary. Told her I hadn't seen the corpse when I had.'

'Why was that? What was your reason for lying?'

'Because, madam, the man had just tried to kill me.'

'Oh, no! Oh, Tom!'

'And when Dr Thwaite asked me about it I told him precisely the same as I'd told Mary.'

'You lied to him too?'

'I was as consistent with the truth as I was sparing of it, my lady.'

'Why?'

'I told myself the less they knew the better. Hardly a reliable argument nowadays, I know, but the best I could do to keep those two good people safe.'

'I see. But you won't be so – so careful of me?'

'You're a great lady, madam. You can protect yourself in ways they can't.'

'Perhaps. Very well. Now's your chance to be more bountiful with the truth. Speak.'

Our eyes met. Hers danced. Amity seemed confirmed between us.

'Yes,' I said. 'I shall speak.' But I didn't. I drew breath instead.

'Well, what, Tom? What?'

Having created the pause I wanted I said, 'The dead man on the Downs was Nicholas Skeres.'

Her exhaled receipt of this information was like a sigh of sensual satisfaction.

She said, 'So you do know him? Or rather you did?'

'I met him at Scadbury. He was a follower, a friend, a dependant of Walsingham. To me he seemed dull and feckless but Christofer told me he wasn't to be trusted and – yes – it was Skeres together with Master Francis, Walsingham's secretary, who organised the search for Christofer's manuscript.'

'What are you talking about, Tom?'

I apologised for running ahead of her and explained. I spoke of the disappearance of those very pages which later appeared with Robert Poley in my lodgings. Now the link was clear. Skeres must have taken them and delivered them to his superiors at Chelsea.

But as I spoke I seemed to hear a scuffle behind me. I looked round.

'What, Tom?'

'I thought I heard something.'

'Where? Behind here?'

I'd risen to my feet and was attempting, clumsily to mount the bench to look over the wall. Pandora, with two good legs, was quicker than I. She was up on the bench in a swirl of silk and peering over.

'You!' she shouted. 'You!'

And she was down again and running towards a little gate in the wall. I followed as she disappeared from sight. Next I heard a sharp cry and an outburst of tears. I hurried to the gateway.

Pandora was returning with a small boy held firmly by the ear. He yowled relentlessly. There was a raw pink graze on each of his knees.

'If he hadn't tripped I'd never have caught him.'

'Who is he? Do you know him, madam?'

'Yes. This is Martin, Mary's nephew. Shush, boy.'

But her command had no effect. Pandora transferred her grasp from his ear to his hand and the sobbing ebbed.

'Now,' she said. 'What were you doing, Martin?'

But the boy was too overawed to answer her.

I said, 'Were you listening?'

Still there was no reply.

Pandora said, 'Did someone send you?' More wide-eyed silence, except for a lingering sob.

I said, 'I'll ask Mary about him.'

'Do you hear that, Martin? This gentleman's going to ask your aunt what you've been up to.'

But even this threat had no effect. The boy was made mute.

I said, 'I don't suppose there's any harm in him. What could he hope to understand of our conversation?'

But Pandora was less complacent. She said she too would make enquiries. She wasn't having the children among her household employed as spies. Martin was dismissed with a warning that she would speak to his parents that evening. The child left us still without having uttered a single word.

I said, 'Since neither your house nor garden seem proof against eavesdropping, madam, I suggest I show you the place where Nick Skeres tried to kill me.'

'Yes, Tom, do. And also where he died.'

'It's close by.'

We rode up to Chancton Ring. And on our way Pandora explained that her purpose in attending the Queen at Greenwich had been not only to remain within the royal favour (although that was as necessary as it was distasteful) but to learn what she could of the shadowy circumstances surrounding my arrest and torture.

Eliza, in her view, was worse than ever; she'd gone quite beyond any common perception of her; the public could not and did not know what she was really like.

'She panders to the people, Tom, while terrorising those who govern for her. As for her harrowing of our papists, why, she's a perfect hypocrite. Unlike her sister. At least Mary genuinely believed in burning protestants! To save their souls. Eliza believes in nothing! Nothing, Tom. Except the state. Her state. Her realm. Everyone and everything is subservient to that. To its security and her safety. And to this end she'll pervert justice, kill and torture. You. Your friend. Anybody. Without mercy, without compunction. What can be said of such a monarch? Who's become as insensible as she is intolerant.'

'Well, I can think of one thing, madam.'

'What?'

'That those who serve her too zealously are as bad as she.'

'Such as Nicholas Skeres? He was – I'm told – an agent of the Crown. Recommended to her by Essex, it's said.'

'I guessed as much, my lady.'

'Skeres worked for or with another in the service. I've not been able to discover their respective ranks. But this other's name is

Frizer. He in turn answers to Poley. That Robert Poley who interrogated you at Chelsea.'

I didn't say what I thought because I was reluctant to mention Baines or his letter just then. I considered it prudent to keep these matters separate. Yet Baines had expressed (or feigned) surprise when I'd told him of Poley's presence at Chelsea. He'd appeared unwilling even to believe Poley could be an agent. But here we were approaching the very spot where I had first remembered Baines' connection with Christofer. And first conceded to myself that Baines, too, might serve the Queen by the backstairs.

Pandora said as if she'd read my thoughts, 'Of course Dick knew Poley, didn't he? I remember you both talking about him that day I brought him to the cottage.'

'Yes, madam.' And since she'd mentioned Baines I felt obliged to forego the first part of my resolution not to mention him. I said, 'He had a poor opinion of Poley, I remember. He appeared to doubt he could be an intelligencer at all.'

Pandora laughed. 'Dick has a poor opinion of almost everyone.'

'Is Dick a spy, too, madam?'

Pandora checked her horse and looked across at me.

'What makes you say that, Tom?'

'An impression I got that day. Together with certain other things I've remembered since.'

'What other things?'

'No. I think you should answer first, my lady.'

'I don't know, Tom.'

I couldn't believe my ears. Pandora not know if her former lover was a hole and corner man? She saw my disbelief and laughed.

'You must believe me, Tom. It's true. I don't know. Oh, I agree he could be. I suspect he is. But I have no proof. Indeed I've enquired many times – of him, of others. But I've never heard a word or whisper yet to that effect.'

'Well, I have. I heard it long ago. From Christofer. He met Dick at Rheims in France. He was attending the seminary there as part – '

'Oh, *that*!' she interrupted. 'I know that. Dick told me. He happened to be at Rheims buying champagne for the Cecils. He bought the entire '86 vintage of the Abbaye Hautvillers. It cost a fortune but of course the Cecils can afford such things.'

'Could he have been a spy at the seminary as well?'

'I'm sure he could. I would say Dick was capable of anything. Shall we go on?'

And she spurred her gelding up the hill again. I followed. Soon we reached the ring. I dismounted and came to Pandora to offer her my hand. Speaking of Dick had seemed to chill the air between us. It was as if the sun had gone behind an all too familiar cloud. Not that it had. Sol was a little lower certainly – but he still shone warmly.

Pandora swung down from the saddle more easily than I had. As we stood face to face I asked another question.

'Did you gather anything more at Court about Nick Skeres?'

'Yes. And you may let go my hand, Tom.'

'I'm sorry,' I said, genuinely confused. 'I hadn't realised, madam.'

'You mean you hadn't noticed you were holding it?'

'Well, yes, of course but – ' I was blustering now. What could I say? 'Forgive me, my lady. But your hand in mine seemed the most natural thing in the world. So much so I hardly remarked on it.'

Would this semi-ironical impertinence earn me a rebuke? If it did I didn't care. And because I didn't care it didn't. Instead Pandora laughed a little to herself as if I wasn't there and hitched her gelding to a windbent thorn. I followed suit.

'To answer your question, Tom. Yes, I did discover more at Greenwich. Skeres was present when Christofer was killed. Or smuggled abroad.'

This was news indeed!

'You've seen the coroner's report?'

'Yes. I sent to Deptford for a copy of it.'

'Do you think it can be believed?'

'Yes and no.'

'Why do you say that?'

'Because as I told you once before I don't doubt the coroner's findings were dictated to him. But that doesn't mean there's no truth at all in his report. The Privy Council is perfectly capable of ordering events to protect itself and others.'

I sighed. She was right, of course. I asked if she could remember the chief facts in the report and being Pandora she could. As we walked into the ring of trees she told me it said that Christofer had been killed on the thirtieth of May in self-defence by one Ingram Frizer in the company of Nicholas Skeres and Robert Poley at the house of Eleanor Bull, on Deptford Strand.

Here was confirmation, with date and names, of what I'd heard in the Clink. The official account agreed with prison rumour. There had been a dispute concerning payment of the bill for supper. And all three men involved were agents of the Crown, just as the world had said even if it had no names to give them. Now it had. And of the three, I knew two, but not the third. Ingram Frizer? The name meant nothing to me. As for his accomplices, well, Old Nick was dead and Poley had earned a death – preferably at my hands.

This thought pierced me even as we reached the tree where I had sat and but for a fly's buzzing would have died. I stopped. Pandora looked quizzically at me.

'I've never known anyone like you, Tom. In you thought is at once reflected in your body, your face, your eyes. But what's reflected is often unclear. What is it this time?'

'I've just realised what I must do, madam.'

'What?'

'Revenge myself. Kill Robert Poley.'

But Pandora laughed.

'Oh, I don't think you should bother yourself with him, Tom. He's only the tool of others.'

'At least I might reach him! At least I know who he is! At least I have true cause to hate him!'

But my words were hollow. And Pandora was right. Despite everything Poley had done to me, arresting me, taking me to Chelsea, questioning me, I could not hate him. I despised him, loathed him, feared him but such feelings do not add up to hate.

Hate is a purer passion. Only he – or she – who'd brought me into Poley's net was worthy of my hatred and its first-born – revenge.

Nevertheless in choosing the wrong target I had for the first time defined and voiced to myself the necessity of revenge. My hunt for Ishmael must lead inevitably to vengeance on that person: the bloody revenge of a cripple against someone doubtless stronger and more supple than I. But even so only his blood would do.

I said, 'You're right, madam. I must aim beyond Poley.'

'Of course you must. Is this where you nearly died?'

She pointed to the foot of the tree where I'd sat. I nodded and explained how it had happened, pointing to a splintered gash in the bark where the bolt had struck home. I even demonstrated in mime my ducking forward at the fly and how my head had been exactly in line with the gash the bolt had made. Pandora shivered at my re-enactment of the scene. Especially when I showed her where I'd crouched and how the second bolt had whistled past my ear.

Next I rose and led her to the spot where Nick had taken aim, then out of the trees and down the slope of the hill to where I had found his body. It proved a little difficult to locate precisely – wind and weather had erased all signs of murder. Rain or dews had washed his lifeblood into the earth. The grass looked as innocent as ever.

But by looking back to the ring, measuring the distance with my eye and remembering the busy wheeling and swooping of the gulls with the buzzards high above I managed to locate the spot.

As I described how Nick had lain face forward, his crossbow fallen to one side, I knelt on my one good knee the better to show Pandora the shock I'd felt on turning the body over. Why was I so at pains to relive these experiences? Was it only as I thought then (and I said as much to Pandora) that I wished to see if by these re-enactments things previously unapprehended might come into my ken? Yes, that was true but only partly so. I also wanted to involve Pandora in my narrow escape from death. Luckily she appeared eager to share in this experience and even more fortunately my kneeling there produced what I can only describe as a material token or proof of it.

As I straightened up Pandora pointed at my knee.

'What's that?'

I looked down and there caught in the nap of my velvet breeches was a plain gold ring. An earring. I picked it off my knee between finger and thumb. It was a little twisted but complete. I unscrewed the tiny barrel sleeve which opened it. Foolishly – I can't say why – I was tempted to insert it in my own ear. I used to have an earring. It was stolen from me in prison.

Pandora said, 'Did Skeres wear an earring?'

'No, madam.'

'Most men do.'

'That's why I remember Nick didn't.'

'Then this must belong to whoever killed him. Give it to me.'

I placed it in her palm. As she examined it I suggested it needn't have belonged to the murderer. It could have fallen there long ago. Dropped by human hand or beak of jackdaw.

Pandora said, 'There's something inscribed on the inner side. But I can't read it. Can you?'

I couldn't either however much I urged my squinting eyes to decipher it.

I said, 'We need a jeweller's glass.'

She said, 'We shall have one. But now I've seen enough.'

We returned to our horses. Riding down to the cottage we discussed every possibility imaginable concerning Nick's death. That he had been murdered by another who had aimed at him as he had aimed at me we had no doubt. But the only new question was had Nick in his death struggle torn the earring from his assailant's ear? If so then in my pocket was something close to certain proof – if what Pandora had seen scratched within the ring could be read and reconciled with someone able to be found. The thought that such a man would be dangerous to accost occurred to us both. In a strange way it made us laugh.

The head groom was waiting at the cottage to take my mare and escort my lady home. But she sent him back for a magnifying glass that was kept in the library. And she ordered supper to be brought to us there at the cottage.

While she gave these orders I hurriedly cleared my table of these pages and reinstated my neglected Garnier translation in false pride of place. I feared Pandora might construe my composition of these confessions adversely. See them as a breach of trust, even an abuse of her hospitality. I needn't have bothered. She already knew of their existence.

'You may leave your writings where they are, Tom,' she said as she entered.

'You've heard about them?' I answered guiltily.

'Of course. Didn't I tell you? I questioned Mary very closely. I know all about you, Tom. Your doings, your thoughts, your private papers. Mr Tom's secret book, she calls it. Is it?'

'I should like it to be, my lady.'

'Between us? Or between you and your maker?'

'I don't know. When I began, it seemed to be for no one. Not even me. But now perhaps I think I could share it – when it's finished – with you. But I warn you – you'll need plenty of patience. My hand is as disgraceful as the events I describe.'

'I love solving puzzles.'

And I remembered her looking at me before she walked her newly planted maze. And I saw her bare feet – as narrowly beautiful as Persephone's.

She said, 'Tom, I think it's time you addressed me less formally. At least when we're alone. At times like this for instance. Yes, you must use my Christian name.'

'Is that a request or an order, madam?'

'Both. You do know it, I suppose?'

'How could I not? Living as I do at your pleasure on your estate?'

'Well, say it, then. I want to hear it from your lips.'

'But I've already got a name for you, madam. Of my own. I thought it advisable not to refer to you directly in these pages so I invented another for you.'

'You seem to have the instincts of a natural spy, Tom?'

'Never, madam. Or if I have they've been forcibly impressed upon me.'

'Well? What name have you given me?'

I hesitated. How would she take it, I wondered? After all I'd named her before I knew even the little I had come to know about her.

I said, 'I call you – forgive my presumption – but I call you Pandora.'

'Pandora? Oh, no.'

And she burst into disgusted laughter, repeating the name with ever-increased contempt, eruptive indignation.

'Pandora! Oh, Tom, how could you?'

'I thought it a beautiful name, madam.'

'But I'm not beautiful, am I?'

Dared I say what I thought, what I wanted to say? I did. I said, 'Yes, madam, you are. Your beauty increases each time I see you.' She almost smiled. Had she accepted the compliment? I couldn't tell. I continued, 'But since you command it I shall from now on name you as you really are.'

'Good. Say it.'

'Lycia.'

'Thank you.' And now she did smile and her voice was soft as swan's down.

But if by this interlude she had intended to breed equality, perhaps even intimacy, between us then for me it had quite the opposite effect. I felt I was more her property than ever. And in using her real name I felt more a sense of affectation than affection – if that was what she wanted. As a result I soon found I was addressing her as nothing. Neither as Lycia, let alone Pandora, nor as *my lady* nor as *madam*. And this omitting of any name or title created a kind of tension in me, not of desire though God knows she was desirable, but of expectation. An expectation of revelation. And a growing conviction that here was a person beyond anyone, even Christofer, I had ever known before. No wonder she despised the Queen. She was a very queen herself. And I felt sure she could teach me mysteries if she chose.

Now I thanked Heaven I'd consulted Dr Thwaite and not answered Dick Baines' letter. I took it from the table and handed it to her. She sat in my chair to read it.

I said, 'I showed that letter to Dr Thwaite. The same day I received it.'

She looked up. 'What did he say?'

'He advised me to do nothing about it until your return.'

'And was that all he said?'

'No. He told me you'd rid yourself of Dick Baines.'

'Quite right, I have.'

And she continued to read the letter. I fell silent. When she'd finished it she said, 'Dick abused my trust.'

'So I believe.'

'Do you wish to return to Lord Strange? As he suggests?'

'No.'

'Why not?'

'He's a sick man, with a sick man's fancies, I don't trust him.'

'Whatever Dick might say?'

'I no longer trust Dick either.'

'Very wise of you.'

'Nor Father Ignatius, come to that.'

'You prefer to stay here?'

'Or return to Bucklersbury. To my own lodgings.'

'Would you be safe there?'

'I don't know.'

'I'm sure you wouldn't be, Tom. If you aren't safe here you'll certainly be in deadly peril in London. Thank you for showing me this letter.' And she returned it to me.

'What's your advice?' I said, taking it.

'To tell *me* everything, Tom.'

'Everything?'

'Everything you've been writing and everything you're yet to write.'

'I meant about Dick's letter.'

'Oh that? Ignore it utterly. Do precisely nothing. Be full of an absolute negligence in your own interest.'

'And stay here?'

She smiled.

'I wish you would, Tom. I'm beginning to enjoy your company.'

Before I could acknowledge the qualified graciousness of this extension of her hospitality a pair of footmen arrived with our supper and the magnifying glass from the library. Lycia seized it at once and demanded the earring. Taking both to the door to find the best of the light (the day was gently dying) she squinted fiercely at it, tilting ring and glass first one way then that.

'I think it may read: *sapere aude*,' she said.

'Dare to be wise?'

'Mm. Horace, isn't it? And then come what look like initials: *F.T.W.*'

'May I see?'

'Do.'

I looked through the glass. What I saw agreed with what she'd seen except there appeared to be another scratch rather like an *I* in front of the *F*.

I said, 'There could be four letters: *I.F.T.W.*' Lycia looked again and nodded.

'It would seem this earring belonged to someone of gentle birth.'

'The rich being rich with names as well as riches?'

'Exactly.'

'Then *sapere aude* could be a family motto?'

'Yes, perhaps.'

'Do you know a family with such a motto?'

'No.'

'Then your glass has told us everything except what we need to know.'

'Food may help us think, Tom.'

And even as she spoke (such was the ordering of her world) the servants called us to the supper table and then withdrew outside whilst we ate. I was hungry. And so was my lady whose appetite surprised me. I had never eaten with her before, save for the nibbling of an almond biscuit or two on my first visit to the great house. I'd assumed she would pick at her food like a bird but she ate her spiced beef as heartily as I did.

There was red wine from Bordeaux too, and as I swallowed it with relish, having drank little but water or beer for a month, the taste reminded me of our feastings at Scadbury where Walsingham had particularly prided himself on his cellars full of clarets from that region of France. And with that unique taste came two possible names to fit two of those four initials: *I.F.T.W.*

I said, 'I wonder if – '

But Lycia interrupted me with exactly the same words. We laughed and I invited her to speak first. She insisted I should.

So I said, 'I was wondering if these initials really belong to two people not one. If so *T.W.* might be Thomas Walsingham.'

Lycia said, 'I was thinking the same and had just remembered the name Ingram Frizer. The man said to have killed your friend in self-defence. And who has since been pardoned for his crime.'

I was cannon-struck. Bowled over. I hadn't known this.

'Pardoned? Christofer's killer pardoned?'

'Oh, yes. The Queen's pardon. His case was heard in Chancery and he received his pardon on the twenty eighth of June.'

'The day you got me out of prison.'

'Was it? I forget.'

'I don't. So this Ingram Frizer went free the day I did?'

'So I was told at Greenwich.'

'Well, that proves it, doesn't it? He must have acted under orders of the Crown. Poley must've ordered him to kill Christofer.'

'Perhaps.'

I shook my head trying to separate my teeming thoughts from one another. Suppose we were right about those initials? Then the earring must have been torn from Frizer's ear by Nick Skeres who'd been sent to kill me. By whom? By *T.W.*? Possibly. Except – if Frizer was also known to Walsingham (and well enough to have his earring inscribed with both their initials) then Walsingham could either have sent both men to carry out murder or else sent Frizer in pursuit of Skeres to prevent it. Had he had second thoughts, perhaps? Knowing Walsingham it was possible. On the other hand if my first thought was the right one Frizer and Skeres could've been accomplices who had fallen out. And furthermore they need not have been sent by Walsingham at all. Others could have commanded them. Poley again?

But why suppose any of this? We could just as easily be wrong as right. This earring need not have belonged to Ingram Frizer at all. The initials need not stand for him or Walsingham; a myriad other names would fit just as well.

I said all this to Lycia concluding it might well be a castle of conjecture built upon a bog of coincidence.

'But I believe in coincidence, Tom,' she said.

I protested, telling her that as a candidate for assassination, I was trying to be as level-headed as possible.

'Do you feel afraid here, Tom?'

'Occasionally. But I comfort myself with the thought that whoever sent Nick Skeres may need some time to hire another killer.'

'I'm glad to hear you sound so sanguine.'

Next I told Lycia of Heneage's visit to Scadbury and she agreed that Heneage might not have called merely as a friend of the family. Walsingham, she informed me, was well thought of by Eliza which meant that very soon, if not already, he would be required to demonstrate his loyalty to the Crown. He would need to do the state, she said, some service. That might be either to beggar himself entertaining Her Glorious Majesty, or more cheaply but more dangerously, by providing her intelligencers with information Heneage could present as potent evidence of Walsingham's love for her and hatred of Rome.

I said, choosing my words, 'I expect you met Walsingham at Court?'

'Several times.'

A stillness grew between us. 'And Lady Audrey, too, of course. Since she returned my likeness to you?'

'Yes. And Dr Thwaite tells me he delivered it safely?'

'Oh, yes. I have it here.'

'May I look? I only viewed it briefly at Greenwich.'

I got up to fetch Willoughby's miniature. Lycia admired the casket, calling it a pretty thing for what it was, and raising an ironic eyebrow at Lord Strange's dedication inside the lid. She said something to the effect that the notion of revenge appeared to permeate my life. For here was Ferdinando Stragne commemorating my *Amleth* with the word.

I agreed. 'I begin to believe my work hasn't just forecast my future but forged my destiny, madam.'

'Madam? I thought – ?'

'I'm sorry. Lycia, I should say.'

'Yes, you should.'

She took the miniature from its pouch. She gazed at it closely, then across at me. I said nothing.

'You pose as a constant lover againt black?'

'That was at Lady Audrey's insistence.'

'Ah. Yes, she described you as quite the most passionate of those shepherds who attended her at Scadbury. Is that true? Were you?'

'Yes and no. Or rather, at the start yes, but later no and then at the last we reached a kind of accord it was as easy to relinquish as to enjoy.'

'For you perhaps. But not for her.'

'Is that what she says?'

'Most furiously. It struck me she nurses great hate for you, Tom. She gave me to understand she had changed her ways to please you but despite this you left Scadbury soon after?'

'Yes, and a week later I was hanging from Top's pillar.'

'Her doing, do you think?'

'I hope not.'

'Or Walsingham's? She could have turned him against you.'

'He'd come to dislike me.'

'Well, there you are.'

'Did he say as much to you?'

'No. Rather the reverse. He spoke warmly of you. But that's the way at Court. We all smile all the time. But he did say – and I believed him – he missed your friend Christofer most dreadfully.'

'He loved Christofer. Out of reason.'

'So Lady Audrey told me. And I can see why she was so taken with you.'

She slid my picture back into the pouch, placed it in the box and closed the lid. Then she leant forward her hands grasping the box as if to help her crystallise her thoughts.

'Tom, attend to me. I believe the Walsinghams have a great deal to do with your fate and your friend's. I think you made two powerful enemies at Scadbury. And for the most banal of reasons. Love. Audrey may or may not have known that Skeres was a spy but could she not have confided in him?'

'Oh, easily. Skeres was something of an intimate. He would light her to bed.'

'Well, there you are. And doubtless she expressed her feelings to him – after you'd gone.'

'Whereupon Skeres informed Poley I was a sitting duck once I'd returned to London from Scadbury?'

'It seems likely. But you cheated death at Chelsea. And then four months later, Lady Audrey hears that I'm harbouring you. So Skeres is sent here.'

'But only to be killed by another.'

'Well, as you say, Walsingham may have had second thoughts.'

I allowed her theory had some likelihoods within it but said it still didn't explain Christofer's death. She smiled and reiterated her conviction that Christofer hadn't died at Deptford. That his death had been a charade to hide his removal abroad. Not to Paris, she agreed, but to somewhere across the water. And who had arranged it? Why, Walsingham, of course. To save his friend, my friend, from certain execution.

Perhaps my behaviour was proof of my recovery? Because on this occasion as Pandora – Lycia again advanced this supposition I found I could consider it quite coolly. And to admit it could be so even if every instinct told me it wasn't.

I said as much and added that I could give many reasons for my doubts but not then, not there.

'You're tired?'

'Yes, forgive me, I am. I've grown unused to company. Well, to such exacting company as your ladyship provides.'

'Exacting?'

'Yes, very. Who else have I seen save Mary and Dr Thwaite?'

'For the last time, Tom, please, please use my name.' I grinned. 'There. Now you may see what I mean when I say you are exacting?' She smiled. And I added her name. This time as I pronounced it, it felt easier on the tongue. Her smile widened and she held out her hand. I took it.

'Goodnight, Tom.'

'Goodnight, Lycia.'

And this second time it was easier still. Lycia withdrew her hand and went. I heard her speak to the grooms and then ride away with them.

·X·I·

I've got up early to resume my search for Ishmael among the residue of my former life. And to do it the more punctiliously I've decided to furnish myself with a calendar of those latter days, those few remaining days, in which he may have appeared, before I was thrown as little more than a bag of offal into prison.

My bare-bones horary goes like this: on the fifth of May I leave Scadbury to return to London. On the twelfth Poley arrests me. On the fifteenth I say anything. On the seventeenth I'm warmly congratulated by the Privy Council for betraying my dearest friend. On the eighteenth, thanks to me, Christofer's arrested at Scadbury, brought to Chelsea too, but allowed bail provided he reports daily to the authorities. On the nineteenth of May – no, I cannot write it, no! Not even in brief – no! No, no, no! I can more happily recall the twenty third, yes, because that was merely the day Topcliffe crippled me for life and is thus the more tolerable in the tablets of my memory. By the thirtieth I'm in the Clink and close to death but unknown to me Christofer is even closer. In fact he's killed that very night at Deptford.

But where is Ishmael in this? Let me retrace my steps. Back to the day I left Scadbury . . .

·X·I·I·

Had I known what was to come I would've looked more closely at that house on Deptford Strand where Christofer and his Corin had dined and drank so well the day they took delivery of the properties for Walsingham's masque. Because this was the very same house in which Christofer supped once again some six weeks later, less felicitously.

But the afternoon I got there it was just a discreet hotel where I was to leave my borrowed cob with the head ostler: a weighty man of few words who received Walsingham's regards without expression and only smiled when I pressed a penny into his instantly accommodating palm.

After a stroll along the quays to note the bondhouses (all of stone or brick and gravid with merchandise) and the scores of vessels unloading there (here were wherries from Holland and Hamburg, coalers from Newcastle – their dust hung in the air – and several three-masters of the Turkey Company as fat as fishwives' cats, not to mention Drake's *Golden Hind* at Mast Wharf now retired from service round the globe and serving shilling suppers for discerning businessmen and their Deptford dolls), after all this I took to the water myself and was rowed upriver by a garrulous waterman who swore he'd sailed as a boy with Hawkins running slaves out of Africa. And you may believe me that by the time he'd brought me to below London Bridge he had fought and killed six Spaniards, got two Indian princesses with child, been given up for dead of the yellow fever as well as the black, married his childhood sweetheart at Plymouth and leaving her to bear him triplets, returned to sea.

Before stepping ashore at Billing's Gate I congratulated him on his adventurous life, assuring him that never had so short a river-trip encompassed so much worldly experience. Especially when – interrupting his flood of salty reminiscences – he'd shipped oars to point out two weatherworn barges whose tawny sails bore crude red crosses and whose open holds emitted a thin white vapour. These decrepit vessels had been lately put back into service, he said, as pest-boats. Twice a week they took those dead of the plague out to sea, covered in quicklime, there to be shovelled overboard. Many feared they would infect the fish. But despite this melancholy sight he assured me the sickness had lately diminished and people were returning daily to the town – just as I was.

And certainly as I walked along to Downgate Hill and up its familiar incline to Walbrook it appeared he'd spoken with some truth – not a virtue I ordinarily associate with watermen. The streets were almost as busy as I'd known them before the disease had crept silently into the bosom of the city. But now here was everyday traffic again and hurrying people determined to do business even if every fourth or fifth house was still shut up, the doors and windows boarded, and thereupon the telltale crosses warning that all inside had been forcibly sequestered and left to survive by God or rot by chance.

When I got to the open place that stands before my lodgings in Bucklersbury I was overjoyed to see it had returned to its former busy state. The grass that had grown up between the cobbles was worn away once more and the market stalls which had spilled down the lane from Cheapside were back where they'd always been. Their trade was as multifarious and raucous as ever; the market men grossly bawling their wares, the public daintily picking and sniffing at them. The baker's was under new management with a quick-moving queue at the door. The pie shop was busy, too, and the Green Man stood open. Three druggists and four sweet shops further up the lane were doing a brisk trade – if you've got a sweet tooth come to Bucklersbury where you may buy every marzipan and sugared delicacy you can dream of. Oh, and chocolate too, if your purse is deep enough. But beware, it breeds in the eater a ruinous madness for more and more. And toothache too – for which Bucklersbury can as readily supply an opiate.

The stairway to my lodgings stood to the left of the tavern and as always the door was ajar. I went in, eager to reach my rooms again. I ran up the stairs, two at a time.

A man stood knocking at my door. As I appeared he turned. I didn't know him but he knew me, he said, announcing himself as a messenger from across the river. And he handed me a letter. I thanked him and he clomped down the stairs.

I unlocked my door and entered into the shuttered dark of my lodgings. I couldn't wait to let the light in, to see my place again. I opened every shutter. All was as I'd left it. No sign of any break-in, pilfering or damage. Six weeks dust lay everywhere however and the very first thing I found myself doing was to seize a cloth to dust my table, chest and chairs. Only then did I open the windows to let the air in. And with it the lovely noise from the street below.

Although I had extolled the virtues of my lodgings to Lady Audrey I was still astonished by how much pleasure I felt at this return home. It's a dog's instinct, I know, this need for one's own place. But none the worse for that – if you like dogs as I do.

I kept moving about my room, regarding it from this position then that. I fussed at the placing of chairs and stools, pushing one a little to the right, another to the left. I made a soldier-like row of my twelve candlesticks on the chimney piece and then greedily contemplated my books. I have three long shelves full and I suppose if I have any wealth at all you could say it lies in my library.

Having performed these rituals I went into my bedchamber to open the shutters and windows. I stripped the bedclothes back to air them and contemplated my table where Christofer and I had so often sat, working opposite each other in those happy days before success embraced him and toyed with me.

Only then did I open the letter I'd been sent. It was from Ned

Alleyn's father in law, Philip Henslowe, owner and manager of the Rose Theatre where our company had performed before the plague struck. Henslowe hoped God continued to uphold my health as He did his even though almost all his neighbours were dead. He had heard, he wrote, from Alleyn by way of his step-daughter Joan who had received a letter from him written at Chelmsford, that had come to her that selfsame morning. (Never have I known anyone talk so fast as Henslowe and the writing of his letter seemed equal to this headlong verbosity). Never was a man so blessed in his son-in-law, he averred, as he was, even if he wrote oftener to Joan than to him but surely this proved it was a good marriage despite the wagging of certain malicious tongues – some now stilled for ever, perhaps visited by the pestilence for their wickedness. But to the purpose, he wrote, I heartily commend me to you, and I beg leave to state that since you are come out of Kent again and since, as my son writes to Joan, you might welcome some employment then should you be of a humour to call upon me at the theatre I would be happy to present you with a play in sore need of revisions of such a kind as only you, my good friend, can provide. This comedy of *God Speed the Plough* while requiring repair yet offers good opportunities for the players as you with your working knowledge of the theatre will immediately observe.

He went on to say Alleyn hoped to open next season with this particular piece since it told of the misadventures of several good city folk who had fled into the country to avoid the pestilence. What better topic could be found for a play once the law allowed the Rose to reopen? He was further instructed by Alleyn to pay me six marks in advance for this work. Meanwhile I was to accept his friendship till death and the fervent hopes of his son-in-law that I would keep my word and join the company at Bristol at the end of July or sooner if I wished.

This letter pleased me. It seemed an augury of more purposeful times to come. Others, apart from me, were already looking to the future when the plague would be past for good. I determined to go over to the theatre the next morning but in the interim I would reward my return to London with a skinful of beer, supper and gossip in the Green Man below.

I learned a lot that evening. And much of it was as disquieting as it was to be expected. Now the sickness seemed retreated a little, people had, I was told, the energy to search for scapegoats for it. Who could they find to blame other than themselves? My fellow drinkers at the Green Man (their number depleted by the fall of three bright spirits) spoke first of the Pope's responsibility for the visitation, then of bad air with no wind from the west to clear it, next of stray dogs being thought the source of the infection and finally, their voices somewhat lowered but not much, of hardworking and prosperous foreigners who had brought it with them from the continent. These last were the present favourites for the guilty prize and already pamphlets signed by such valiants as 'Jack England' or 'Albion's Son' were being passed from hand to hand denouncing these 'scrofulous strangers whose breath reeks poisonous garlic, whose oily ordures render the natural composture of an honest English cesspit impossible thus breeding those foreign flies and alien vapours which convey the barbarous disease – ' Etcetera. I don't suppose I need elaborate further. The language of intolerance never varies. Posters saying much the same had been printed and were now stuck up round Paul's – some in the church itself whereat the Dean had laughed – or so rumour had it – and let them be. I doubted this and most agreed it was probably false but I was yet, they said, to see the graffiti painted nightly upon walls. Every morning more were to be seen: 'Huguenots go Home', 'Fuck off Flemings' or 'Dirty Dutch Depart'. We agreed these daubs together with the pamphlets and posters must be the work either of rabid young gentlemen of the Inns of Court or hired trouble-makers. Clearly they hoped to provoke ordinary people into protest and riot. Already a Flemish weaver's house had caught fire for no reason save arson while others complained of filth thrown in at doors and windows.

So far the authorities had done nothing. But surely they would? Indeed they were bound to or else the city would boil over. At least that was the general view in the Green Man on that evening of the fifth of May. One important aspect of the business was however neglected. Had it been voiced I might well have quit London at once. But then our lives consist, do they not, as much or more of what we might have done as what we do? This omission may have been a mistaken kindness to me or, rather more likely, may not have yet been known to those present. What wasn't said that night was that official wisdom had concluded these incitements to civil unrest were *not* just the work of unruly youth at the Inns of Court. No, they were also, and much more dangerously for me, thought to be the inventions of discontented poets and trouble-making playwrights. Since the latest bills carried such pseudonyms as Friar Bacon, Tamburlaine and Old Hieronymo. Naturally it never crossed authority's mind that poets were far more likely to champion a minority than persecute one. More sinisterly it's possible officialdom did realise this only too well but dismissed the notion as unhelpful, even obstructive to the greater good of putting the fear of God and Eliza into each and every author they could lay their hands on? And issued warrants of search and arrest accordingly.

Before crossing over to the theatre next morning I walked through St Paul's and saw for myself the posters and graffiti. My informants hadn't exaggerated. These exhortations were cruel.

When I reached the Rose later that morning Henslowe had gone out. Either to his new tanning business or the dyer's yard or else to collect his rents – the theatre doorman knew no more than that. But he didn't suppose he would be long. Things were very quiet roundabout.

While I waited I went into the theatre itself and stood upon the stage. Oh, how can I convey the feelings I felt as I stood there once again? To say I shivered is to understate. My blood thrilled. I was covered with goosepimples. How fierce, how demanding a vacancy a theatre encompasses! My eyes made their way around the silent galleries from top to bottom until they reached the empty pit. I tried to imagine the place packed again with eager auditors. But I couldn't. My fancy failed me. But this mattered not a whit such was my certainty that one day we would all –

players and playgoers together – return to reconvene the world –
our world, I mean, of our choosing, our making.

Meanwhile the vibrant quiet of that wooden vessel, that giant
tub, that expectant omega, was tempting me to speak. Cajoling
me like a lover. And I felt bound to respond. To offer it a speech
to savour. The Rose demanded a keepsake of me.

The words of my Horatio to his mistress came back into my
mind. Out of context they meant little but I told myself the dear
place had heard them often enough before and so might warm to
a reminder of them. I began to speak very softly, with the word
expelled on the breath, off the tongue, upwards and out (an old
actor's trick) while making each syllable as clear and every
consonant as crisp as I possibly could.

> *Now that night begins with sable wings*
> *To overcloud the brightness of the sun,*
> *And that in darkness pleasure may be done,*
> *Come, Bel-imperia, let us to the bower*
> *And there in safety pass a pleasant hour.*

To be plain my words speak better than they read. As is often
the case with a play. Certainly when I spoke them that morning
it seemed to me the Rose grew kind at the hearing of them. The
building smiled again. Became a fraction smaller as if it were
leaning forward, inward, downward to catch the purport of my
speech.

Having pronounced my offering I bowed to the empty space.
My homage was, I believe, accepted. I made a clean, swift exit.

A quarter of an hour later Henslowe returned. And out of the
welter of his garrulous welcome I gradually discovered that he
did not share his son-in-law's optimism concerning the plague's
eventual departure. It had come sooner than expected, he said,
and would leave later. The present lull would prove a short-lived
blessing, an exceedingly small mercy. But nevertheless he was
happy to be the instrument by which I might turn an honest
penny over in my pocket though he doubted the play would see
the stage (at least in London) for many a month. If at all. Here

was the script and here Ned Alleyn's money, not his, he was at pains to point out, patting my back, as if his parsimony was somehow proof of his professional regard for me. Yes, he said, he'd heard tell of the libels stuck up in St Paul's, jumping clean over my question concerning them, but no, he hadn't bothered to see them for himself. He was too busy trying to survive on this side of the river to risk the virulence of the other. Business was bad enough without unrest as well. Half his tenants couldn't pay their rents, his dyer's yard was failing for lack of orders – why dye a winding sheet? – he'd opened a pawn-shop as much for charity as gain and of course he was denied all profit from his whorehouse. It had paid better than the theatre but like the Rose had been shut by law since February. And would remain so, he reckoned, till he was a beggar at the road's end. His sincere advice to me was to take the script and Ned's money and depart as soon as I could to join the company on tour. Why wait? The town was dying on its feet whatever people might say to the contrary and I would do well to believe him and mark his words.

Why didn't I take his advice? It couldn't have been better. I wish I knew. Except I think I've already partly answered the question. I was – I accept it now – just so pleased to be home. And I told myself I could work on the play in Bucklersbury, enjoy this truce in the plague's war but still depart the instant it was broken. Henslowe had been too pessimistic; things weren't as bad as he said; theatre owners like farmers were veteran complainers; they made quite as much moan as money; never believe them. So I argued to myself.

I began work on the play that evening. And I did what I always used to do when asked to revise someone else's work. Or in this instance several others' work cobbled barbarously together. That is I read it through trying not to have an opinion, good or bad, about it. It wasn't easy. The play invited contempt.

That done I filled a tobacco pipe and sat at the open window with the street below me growing quieter and more sweetly dark by the minute. With the scented smoke soothing my heart and lungs while sharpening my mind (oh, the blessings of tobacco for a writer) I allowed my thoughts to order themselves to face the task I'd been set.

The play was a mongrel bitch of a piece. But the subject was good and several characters promised well even if they performed little because the machinery of the action was so ramshackle. The argument – essentially town mice versus country mice – attracted me. And how shrewd of Alleyn to invite me to rework the play – was not this theme my most recent experience? But here the plague was merely a pretext for selected Italian gentlefolk to flee the town of Mantua only to meet token resistance from the peasantry outside. After that the action collapsed into sentimental misunderstandings among the haystacks.

As I sat there in the darkling air I determined to reset the play in England and make the action serious, severe. I would have the plague stalk my protagonists as in a stately death hunt. With this solemnly procreant thought I tapped out my pipe and went to bed.

And thus it was I was seduced by the pleasure of my craft. For the next five days I thought of nothing but my work. I was back in my old routine and it was good. I rose early, worked all day, ate and drank all evening and went to bed alone.

By the eleventh of May I had replotted the action and promised myself I'd be up early the next morning to begin the writing proper. And it was that evening that I heard of the arrest of three poets I knew. The Green Man simmered with the news. Few doubted the three would be lucky to return alive from 'helping the Queen with her enquiries' as the sour joke had it. Some even asked me if I had any fears of arrest? I honestly answered I had none, pointing out that I'd only just returned to London and that whatever my faults inciting the stupid to harass the helpless was not one of them. What a fool I was.

That same night on the last stroke of midnight as the eleventh of May became the twelfth my door was broken down, the bolts were burst and I was standing up in bed without a stitch facing Robert Poley and his hired associates. What monsters dictate our lives. There I was shouting my defiance, standing on my already forfeit dignity, while Poley was planting Christofer's manuscript among my papers like a rare Dutch tulip. Only to unearth it with theatrical surprise saying 'What's this, may I ask?' How can you answer when the question itself is a lie?

But since I've told of this before let us hurry along a little further. As I was. Rowed by night in a double-oared skiff to Chelsea. My head hooded, wrists bound behind my back, half-naked and shivering in the fetid night air.

Not a word was said as we proceeded upriver. Well, not that I could hear. If they'd whispered I doubt the words would've been audible within the felted thickness of the hood. But I could hear the regular squeaks of the rowlocks and the steady grunts of the waterman nearest to me.

When we reached Poley's covert destination I was hauled out into the shallows and then along a stretch of greasy duckboarding up to what I took to be a substantial gatehouse at the river's edge. For now there were flagstones beneath my naked feet. And here we stopped for some time. I asked for the hood to be removed, my words muffled in sweaty darkness. But the more I begged to be heard the less I was. This was the first Chelsea lesson I was to learn, a lesson so simple it hurt. To wit: a person held for questioning is only heard when he says something Chelsea wishes to hear. Otherwise Heneage, Poley and the rest consider themselves deaf and you dumb even if you're screaming your head off.

A little later I could hear jocular voices, assentive laughter: the easy rejoinders of persons brought together by a common routine. Then I smelt bacon frying and beer. Poley, I concluded, must be refreshing himself with his subordinates in the suburbs after his labours in the city. I was offered nothing. Merely stood in a corner like a child who had neglected to learn the alphabet. After half an hour or so of genial supping I heard steels struck, lanterns lit and boots stamp purposefully upon the flagstones. Then I was hauled away along a corridor to what I supposed would be my prison cell. But no. Instead I heard a voice at my swaddled ear saying: 'Mind your step, Mr Kyd, as you go down.' And with that I was propelled abruptly into a void. Inevitably I missed my footing on the unseen stairs but the man who had me by the other arm kept me roughly on my feet with a grunt of 'steady now' as if I were an animal unloaded from a cart. We reached the bottom after some ten steps or so and I heard other boots descending after us and Poley saying: 'On we go, gentlemen.' Here was another trick of Chelsea. Everyone there is a gentleman even the prisoner. But if irony begot this joke its parentage has since been quite forgotten.

We trudged for a long time, my feet in a conduit of running water. I believed and hoped it was fresh water. There was no sewage stink in the air. Just the dankness of a tunnel. Its gentle incline bore away, I thought, to my left but I had no real means of judging where I was or where I was going. Once again, as on the river, no one said a word. There was only the sensation of water running over the silk-smooth stones, the splash and thud of boots and then, just once, an unusually resonant belch from one of my escorts followed by his cronies' echoing laughter.

Coming at last to what I supposed must be a wider area I smelt a different smell and heard another sound. The sound first. It was that of a drum. Intermittent, irregular, relentless. Next the smell. That of humanity: the combined stench of sweat, urine, ordure. As we drew nearer the sound and stink grew stronger. And then with only the squeal of hinges for a warning and without a word from Poley or his assistants I was shoved into a somewhere I had no immediate way of assessing at all. I felt my feet in water again and my forehead against brick. But little else. I think I heard the door slammed shut and locked behind me. But I can't be sure. I could be remembering that from later times at Chelsea when I counted myself fortunate to hear those selfsame sounds.

For the moment that seemed to be all. My midnight's journey was at a stop. And I was at leisure to explore my new accommodation. Not that I wished to discover it. Not to begin with. I was too numbed in body, too shaken in mind. Apart from still being hooded and bound. But I was aware that the water I now stood up to my calves in was no longer running and fresh but stagnant and stale; that the brick walls all about me sweated with a mildewed wetness.

I learned later that this underground cell was one in a double row of six. All identical. And that what I stood in was a common amenity. These vaulted cells were part of the basement of a great house. Each measured some six feet by four. A barred door gave what light there was. And that was all except that the cobbled floor of the cells was set a foot below the level of the central causeway outside them. In this way the cells were flooded with water and other matter with connecting pipes to ensure that all prisoners enjoyed each other's effluent. Inevitably once you became too tired or weak to stand you had no choice but to sit in this disgusting tub like a latter-day Diogenes and listen to the drummer. It must be said that a cynic's contempt for comfort is required of you at Chelsea. Especially in respect of the drumming. While I was there it never ceased. Or to describe it more precisely, it forever stopped and started. It would first find a rhythm only to discard it. Then bang monotonously for half an hour, pause, and on the off-beat resume in a different manner. Before any particular drummer's natural predilections and rhythms became familiar to us, another replaced him. Thus we, the tormented, could never be sure how the sounds would compose themselves. Soon – sitting sleepless, hunched in filth – any thought of accepting these irregular riffles, uneasy syncopations, and bonging thumps, became impossible. Even as your brain tried to make sense of them it was destroyed. Kneaded into a bloody lump at the back of sand-dry eyes. And that is to discount the other injuries your body ached with.

Like every newcomer there I didn't appreciate the full purport of this incarceration straightaway. I assumed someone would soon arrive to release me from my hood and unstrap my wrists from behind my back. And then supply me with food, however meagre, however unappetising. I told myself that since the state had taken me in for questioning then it was within the interests of its upholders to have me in a condition to answer their questions coherently. This was nothing more than a sharp reminder of their power. A shock from which I would shortly be released. How childish hope necessarily is! I remained there all night comforting myself with the thought that since I'd had nothing to eat or drink I wouldn't be obliged to foul myself. But of course I did eventually. I can't say when. But as I felt the trickle of piss down my leg I felt equally the trickle of a tear down my cheek. My subjection to Eliza was truly begun.

The next morning or rather the same morning – this was still the twelfth of May – I heard my door unlock, swing open and felt hands pull me up and out of the water. I can't remember at what moment I had capitulated to my need to sit down but sat I had and after that my existence see-sawed between sitting and standing with ever increasing shame. Voices said, 'So this is the new gentleman, is it?' and 'This way, Mr Kyd.' And I was dragged to a guardroom where they took off my hood at last, untied my hands and removed my breeches. A bucket of water was thrown over me and I was given a grubby towel to dry myself with. But my hands after being strapped together for so long could hardly hold it so one of the guards seized it and pummelled me more or less dry. After this a coarse linen smock was pushed over my head which when pulled down barely covered my privates. No other clothes were supplied. At Chelsea all male prisoners are unbreeched babies. I begged for water, for food. Superfluously as it happened. Both were brought even as I spoke. What's more I was invited to sit at table and enjoy them. Bread, a pickled herring, water. I was also offered beer. I accepted everything. My spirits revived. The guards smiled. And when I'd finished one allowed me a puff or two of his pipe and after that I found I could speak more steadily. I asked the obvious question: where was I? They laughed and said I was now a guest of Her Majesty, God bless her. Did this mean I was at Whitehall? Or had I been taken not upriver as I'd thought but down river to Greenwich? But to these further questions there was no reply. It wasn't for them to say, they said. Chelsea may be an open secret to some (as it is to me now) but that doesn't mean its officers are free to speak of it.

Robert Poley arrived, greeting me as if nothing had happened. As if I hadn't been dragged from my bed on the last stroke of midnight and brought by force to that filthy basement, there to spend the remains of the night in sleepless terror. I told him as much but he didn't bother to apologise.

Instead he said blandly, 'Everyone's treated alike here, Mr Kyd. You can rest assured you've fared no worse than anyone else. But now I should like you to come with me if you would, please.'

I said, 'What happens if I refuse to accompany you?'

He shrugged. 'No one ever has.'

'Well, I do!'

'Please, Mr Kyd. Your show of spirit is admirable, of course, but we usually find it best for us to remain as polite as we can to each other. The more we all cooperate, the sooner certain truths can be established and the matter satisfactorily concluded.'

I stared at him. Did he really believe this courteous rubbish? It seemed he did.

I said, 'You've got no grounds for arresting me! You didn't have any last night and you've got none now!'

'I'm bound to disagree, Mr Kyd. But as I say all these things are about to be discussed between us. So why not come along?' This time he glanced towards the guards on either side of me. Each now weighted a truncheon in his hands. Poley's point was made. Chelsea's niceties have nice limits.

I agreed to accompany him.

The two guards escorted me behind Poley to a flight of stairs that led us up to a disused dairy. The place still smelt of cheese and butter on the turn. The insidious rancid smell followed us for a while along a corridor which gradually became less workaday. Soon we were passing doors to better scented rooms with windows overlooking well-kept gardens. It was then that it was borne in upon me that I was being led through the ground floor of a noble house.

But even so I wasn't prepared for what followed. Now my feet were treading polished boards and my eyes feasted upon a great carved staircase as we crossed the reception lobby and two liveried footmen threw open double doors into one of the longest rooms I have ever seen. It was over a hundred feet in length with tall windows on either side. I'd seen greater, loftier halls at court when we played at Whitehall but they lacked this room's most striking feature: a marble pillar some twelve feet high. Topcliffe's pillar.

It served no structural purpose since it stopped short of the ceiling by at least six inches. Its fluted column rose from a round foot set on a square base and it was completed by a capital of the Corinthian order: a marble explosion of sinuously carved fernlike forms supporting nothing. Beyond it I glimpsed a semicircle of comfortable, leather-cushioned, leather-backed chairs such as might accommodate the well-padded backsides of several privy councillors. Each chairback was embellished with a pattern of golden roses. What I couldn't see was the small stool on the other side of the pillar, nor the iron manacles and gauntlets cemented into the marble some seven feet above it.

Like every other innocent brought here I remarked at once upon this object.

Poley said, 'Yes, you all ask about it. It's quite a conversation piece.'

'What's it for?'

'That depends.'

'It doesn't even support the ceiling, does it?'

'True.'

'Is it some sort of monument? Or a treasure shipped from abroad?'

'I think you would do better to compose your thoughts, Mr Kyd, rather than engage in idle speculation.'

We proceeded to the other side of the pillar where I was instructed to seat myself upon the stool. I glanced up at the instruments protruding from the column above my head.

I said, 'What are those things?'

Poley replied, 'Mr Topcliffe will explain their use to you.'

I was appalled to hear this name. I hadn't dreamt he would be here. 'The Queen's executioner?' I couldn't hide my alarm, try as I could.

'That isn't his only skill. We value him in many other ways. But have no fear, My Kyd. While he sits with us Topcliffe does not act alone. There'll be others superior to him during the preliminary hearing.'

I looked at the semicircle of chairs in front of me. There were ten of them. My guards withdrew. Poley remained beside me. Several minutes passed. Then I heard a clock outside strike the quarter.

'What time is it?'

'Quarter past eleven.'

'Thank you. I lost count.'

'It can happen here. People do. Forgive me.'

And Poley strode away to greet a knot of richly dressed persons who were now arriving. I peered round at them from my stool like a hopeful invalid or pop-eyed bedlam. There were five of them. The first man to whom all deferred, I knew at once to be Heneage. Although I hadn't seen him at Scadbury, being too busily engaged in the performance of *Faustus*, Christofer's description of him had been exact. The man was a common lurcher however lustrous his fur collar, however fine the expensive worsted of his gown. As for the face, it was as sharp, as alert, as mean as a usurer's Christmas.

The second man I recognised at once as Topcliffe. He was as short as he was wide but evidently muscular. He gleamed with health and an easy conscience. He had an eager, boyish air. Beside him his assistant Roger appeared almost clerical: prematurely balding, stoop-shouldered, disinclined to smile, full of dismay at the wickedness of the world. I was not, of course, given these names straightaway: they only emerged during the proceedings. We might all of us be gentlemen at Chelsea but that didn't mean we introduced ourselves to each other. So I nicknamed the last pair, both large men, Gog and Magog. Gog carried a writing box which he placed upon his knee. He took out paper and several expensive plumbago pencils and settled comfortably to record the proceedings in deft shorthand.

As they gathered about me Poley requested me to stand. They seated themselves. Heneage in the middle, with Gog and Magog on either side of him, then Poley to the right of Gog and Topcliffe to the left of Magog. Roger sat a little apart. He too had a receptacle of sorts. A leather case. I discovered later that it contained various volatile salts and reviving cordials. Heneage placed spectacles upon his nose to inspect me the better.

He said: 'Good morning, Mr Kyd. I've been looking forward to talking to you.'

I opened my mouth to answer in no uncertain terms but he held up his hand, forestalling me.

'Please speak only when invited to do so.'

'But – '

'That is the rule here, Mr Kyd. Now kindly allow me to explain these proceedings to you. This morning is in the nature of a preliminary hearing. Mr Poley with whom you are already acquainted will outline the charges against you and then you will be invited to comment upon them. If your comments prove positive that may well be the end of the matter. If not then further hearings may be required. We shall see. So without more ado I'll call on Mr Poley to speak.'

Poley smiled and snapped his fingers. At once a footman appeared from nowhere with a leatherbound folder. Having handed it to Poley he backed punctiliously away. The protocol at Chelsea seemed almost as strict as at Whitehall. Poley took a key and unlocked a brass clasp on the folder, took out the first of several documents contained therein and promptly proceeded to read from it in a swift monotone.

'Gentlemen – acting upon information received from a source whose anonymity I am, as you will be aware, bound by oath to protect, I called upon Mr Kyd at his place of residence in the early hours of this morning. Having established his identity I then, in accordance with the instructions of the Privy Council, together with my assistants made a thorough search of the accused's premises in quest of evidence pertaining to the recent libels illegally published in the city against citizens of foreign extraction. We found none and I suggest with respect, gentlemen, that Mr Kyd be – for the moment at least – exonerated upon that particular charge.'

Heneage said, 'On what grounds?'

'Insufficient evidence, sir.'

'Proceed.'

'However, during our investigation another matter has come to light. A matter, possibly, of greater import and wider implications. This, gentlemen.'

And he held up Christofer's manuscript.

I protested, 'You put it there. I know for a fact you did. And then made a great show of finding it.'

There followed what I took to be a shocked silence. Except it's perfectly impossible to shock anyone at Chelsea. But they can shock you. Well, they did me. A glance from Heneage brought one of my guards with a leather strap and a sponge. He thrust the sponge into my mouth and secured it there with the strap as a gag which he buckled behind my head. The leather bruised the corners of my mouth unmercifully while the swelling sponge prevented me from voicing both protest and complaint.

Heneage said, 'I did warn you, Mr Kyd. Our rules are clear. You speak only when invited to.' He returned to Poley. 'Kindly continue with your report, Robert.'

'As I was saying, gentlemen, this manuscript was discovered by me among the accused's many papers. As you will be aware, Mr Kyd is something of a poet who has achieved a moderate fame. The manuscript in question – which I invite you to inspect hereafter – is not however the work of Mr Kyd. No. This is not his hand. A point I shall return to. Furthermore he has already informed us that it has been written by a friend of his – a Mr Christofer Marlowe of whom I daresay we all have heard something? Indeed I'm given to understand that he's considered by those qualified to judge to be our finest poet and most successful playwright. That may well be so but of course it has no bearing upon this particular enquiry since the document under examination is neither a poem nor a play. It is in point of fact a dissertation or lecture.'

Heneage said, 'Oddly enough I met Mr Marlowe only the other day.' And the very evenness of his tone gave the observation great menace. Especially as I knew, having heard Christofer's account of his meeting with Heneage, that it was deliberately incomplete. Hadn't Heneage come to Scadbury precisely *because* he'd got wind of the lecture? Oddly enough indeed! He'd come on advice. To warn Walsingham against Christofer.

Poley continued, 'The manuscript consists of twenty-five closely written quarto sheets and is prefaced by the words *A lecture offering new thoughts upon the New Testament*. I believe I can safely say that this heading alone could well cause us some disquiet. I put it to you, gentlemen: should tuppenny poets rush in where our best theologians fear to tread?' Poley's safe little joke drew appreciative smiles from all and even a chuckle from Magog. 'We are also informed that this lecture was given to an assembly of some thirty impressionable young persons on the twenty-first of April at the house of Mr Thomas Walsingham at Scadbury in Kent. But here, perhaps, you might care to say a word, sir?'

And Poley turned to Heneage who nodded.

Heneage said, 'Thank you, Robert, I would, yes. I visited young Walsingham on the second of May. As an old friend of the family I felt obliged to warn him that a number of possibly damaging rumours were circulating concerning various occurrences at Scadbury. Among them that heresies were being promulgated and blasphemies spoken. Not to mention general riot and excess. Of course youth must have its fling but we were, I intimated to him, a trifle exercised on his behalf. Free thought is, after all, a close cousin of treason leading as it does to tolerance of our enemies, not least those in Rome.' Did a collective shiver run through my corpus of inquisitors? I certainly fancied it did. 'But imagine my surprise, gentlemen, when this Mr Marlowe thrust himself upon us. Apparently some play of his was in progress at the time and he was incensed that Thomas had had the good manners to leave his place to welcome me. Marlowe's intemperance knew no bounds. Frankly he struck me as far too excitable and I have since warned Thomas to be rid of him. But, alas, to no effect. Marlowe remains a favoured guest at Scadbury. Of course his behaviour towards me is irrelevant to the weightier question of this document before us. I only mention it to give you a notion of the kind of unsound person we're dealing with.' His gaze turned upon me. 'And I have little doubt Mr Kyd here can, if he chooses, confirm my less than fortunate impression of his friend. Or I should say his erstwhile friend?' I held Heneage's eye as defiantly as I could. He remained unmoved – the owner in title of his face. 'Well, I'm sure he will in due course,' he added and turned once more to Poley. 'Back to you, Robert.'

Poley said, 'I now wish to draw your attention to a matter I touched on a moment ago. This is that Mr Kyd made a fair copy of the original we have to hand. That copy has since been destroyed. Mr Kyd, you should understand, was employed as a scribe at Gray's Inn before turning to the more lucrative world of the theatre. Fortunately, however, Mr Kyd carefully preserved the original – you may discount any protests to the contrary – bringing it with him to London from Kent where, until a week ago, he too had been residing with his loving friend, Mr Marlowe.'

Being gagged has one advantage. It heightens your awareness of the liars and smearers gathered before you. Poley and Heneage were clearly as practised a double act as any clown and his feed. With Poley to falsify the facts and with Heneage to cast doubt on the character of their chosen victim – already it was apparent to me that I was nothing but the means to their end: the arraignment of Christofer. The Queen's passion for security would soon be satisfied, it seemed. With the public execution of a popular poet.

So I assumed at the time as I sat there deprived of speech and breeches. For what it was worth which was nothing I shook my head at every lie, at every smear. I burned to make them hear the truth but I knew that even if they were to grant me the opportunity to speak I'd still be wasting my breath.

From what Poley had reported it was obvious that someone at Scadbury had been his eyes and ears. But who, I wondered? I didn't know then, of course, what I know now. Now it's only too easy to say, as Lycia has, as I have, that this spy was Skeres. That Skeres stole Christofer's manuscript from my room, passed it to Poley, that Skeres's reports brought Heneage to Kent, that Skeres informed Poley of my departure for London on the fifth of May, that Skeres was the agent in place whose anonymity Poley was bound by oath of service to preserve. All that is plain as a pikestaff now. But it wasn't then – not when I was perched on my stool in front of Topcliffe's pillar.

But does this knowledge make Old Nick my Ishmael? To be honest I hope not. Frankly I'd find it an insult to have had him for my hidden enemy. My self-respect requires a more substantial foe! Yes, I refuse to be brought to crippledom and beggary by such a one. Besides he's dead. I need my enemy alive. How else am I to have revenge?

The man I'd nicknamed Gog held up a finger in delicate query. Poley at once deferred to him.

Gog said, 'Are we to understand that this manuscript is of an atheistical tendency?'

'Yes, sir,' said Poley.

'Ah. And consequently blasphemous as well?'

'Yes, sir.'

'Thank you. Do go on.'

'One further point, gentlemen, before I sum up. The manuscript bears a note after the title which reads – "as given at the earnest behest of W.R." I asked Mr Kyd about these initials but to date he has professed ignorance of them. I would suggest that here is an interesting subsidiary matter which Mr Kyd might profitably be encouraged to think about. In our work, as you know, the apparently extraneous can often become germane. That aside, I would say in conclusion that it's my sincere belief Mr Kyd is in a position to contribute greatly to our store of knowledge concerning Mr Marlowe, who, as we are agreed, has always been, and remains, our chief concern. I'm certain that with Mr Kyd's cooperation this particular case can be brought to a solution satisfactory to the Queen's Privy Council. Not before time, you may say, gentlemen, and I agree. After all it is now almost seven years since we first put Mr Marlowe under observation.'

On hearing this I don't suppose I would've spoken even if I'd been able to. I was too appalled. Dumbfounded. Christofer watched for? Ever since he'd come down from Cambridge? I shook my head not in negation anymore but in disgust. How could Eliza treat us so? Her whole state was a lie. And we, her subjects, connived at it. Gave her ever more sustenance and credence. We self-styled, hearty, freeborn Englishmen were anything but. We were slaves. And as such we crept, we sniffed, we snooped. We glorified a spinster despot whose violent and now unfounded fear of Rome was employed to subdue us all. No, worse. By it each and every one of us was to some degree subverted; this green island turned into a dunghill breeding maggot spies, swarming informers. All in the name of a freedom not our own but hers.

Heneage said, 'We now need Mr Kyd to speak.' At once I was dragged to my feet, my gag unbuckled and the sodden sponge removed. I swallowed, licked the rawness at the corners of my mouth, wondered if my jaw was still upon its hinges. 'Mr Kyd,' Heneage continued, 'I have one question only to ask you before we adjourn for dinner and digestion of the contents of Mr Marlowe's manuscript. It is this: Have you anything you would like to tell us? If so, do feel free to do so. I need hardly say that anything spoken here is confidential. Also, that we are great believers in the voluntary statement. It often goes a long way to mitigate the ultimate fate of the accused. And please make no mistake, Mr Kyd, that if it is established beyond such doubt as a reasonable man might hold that you assisted an atheist in his criminal proceedings against God and this His realm of Her Majesty Queen Elizabeth, then the law must and shall take its course. So please, do help us. Help us all you can.'

What could I say? Nothing. So I said it. The silence grew like a toadstool in the dark.

'Have you really nothing to say, Mr Kyd?'

'No. Except I'm innocent.'

'Who isn't – in his own estimation, Mr Kyd?'

He turned to his fellow inquisitors.

'Well, gentlemen, I think we may adjourn. I'd hoped for a more helpful contribution from the accused, as I'm sure you did, but there we are.'

He and they rose. As they went I heard Heneage continuing to expatiate upon me to the effect that in his experience it was always the more minor poets who tended towards intransigence.

Poley, meantime, spoke briefly to my guards who seized me and frogmarched me (my feet barely touching the ground as they say) back to my cell. And there I remained in sodden famishment for many hours. No dinner for the accused. In fact it wasn't until early evening that I was hauled out, slopped down again, and presented once more to my inquisitors who on this occasion were already waiting for me.

I was ordered to stand beside the stool. Heneage spoke first.

'We have now considered the document found in your rooms, Mr Kyd. It wasn't easy. Fortunately Mr Skeate here (so that was Magog's name) is something of an expert in decipherment and he has been quick to disentangle the slovenly hand of Mr Marlowe. No wonder you were called upon to make a fair copy and would that it too had been preserved. However the lecture's contents have now been viewed and digested by us all and I think I may pronounce them comparatively harmless.'

He paused for effect, as if expecting me to be surprised by this example of the hearing's fair-mindedness.

I said, 'That's what everyone said at Scadbury.'

'They'd hoped for something more controversial?'

I realised I had to be careful. I nodded briefly.

'May I sit down?'

'No. Kindly continue to stand.'

'I haven't eaten and the cell – '

'Please, Mr Kyd. Remember our rule. Are we to infer that Walsingham and his young friends found Marlowe's lecture disappointing given the author's reputation for excess?'

'That reputation has been grossly exaggerated.'

'Surely not? Mr Skeate has read all his plays on behalf of the Cantuar Commission – Archbishop Whitgift, as I'm sure you're aware, has become increasingly concerned at the licence the theatre's enjoyed recently. There can be no doubt that your friend has largely contributed to this licence.'

'To read a play is one thing – to see it performed is another.'

Skeate said, 'Your friend says, and I quote: *I count religion but a childish toy*. What do you say to that, Mr Kyd?'

'That Christofer doesn't say it. The character of Machiavelli whom everyone knows is the worst of men, says it.'

Skeate snorted. 'Chop logic!'

Heneage said to Skeate, 'With respect, Sir, as Mr Poley has said, we're here to pronounce upon this lecture and its author as a likely atheist and blasphemer rather than as a playwright. After all his plays have enjoyed the protection of Ferdinando Stanley with all that that implies. I think we may safely leave them aside and concentrate on what we have in hand: this manuscript and Mr Kyd, its copyist and friend nay intimate of the author. Especially as you yourself have pointed out there are within it two passages which really ought to give us cause for concern. Perhaps you would now be so good as to read them to us? I'm sure Mr Kyd would like his memory refreshed?'

Skeate read out the following.

'If you read the Gospels as I have without awe saying to yourself these stories are written by men not God you shall find them an almighty muddle. While preaching love they teach hate making of a rebel Jew a Gentile saviour. We cannot trust Matthew, Mark, Luke or John as historians since their purpose is not to record events as they were but to pervert them in support of an emergent cult of a new messiah.'

Heavy, frowning silence from all. Heneage looked at me.

'How did you feel when you copied *that*, Mr Kyd?'

'I can't remember. It's an odd fact but true for all that – that when you work as a scrivener you hardly ever take note of the substance of what you're transcribing.'

'Very well. But now you've had time to note it, what do you say?'

'That it is possible but perhaps imprudent to read the Gospels in that way. As suggested there.'

'How circumspect of you, Mr Kyd. You should be a politician.'

This raised a zephyr of amusement from my inquisitors. I wondered whether to explain about our school of light at Scadbury but decided any elaboration upon the notion of free thought or philosophical speculation might prove unwise. Chelsea did not appear to welcome original thought: was it not, after all, as Christofer had often said, the original sin?

My silence won approval from Poley.

He said to Heneage, 'I believe Mr Kyd now respects our first requirement, sir. That is, to speak advisedly. I wonder therefore if he might not be invited to sit down?'

Heneage considered, nodded. I sat, very gratefully. Just as Poley intended. For here was another demonstration of their practised double act: Heneage hard, Poley soft. But as my backside found the seat of that tripod stool the whole of me suddenly shivered, shuddered. With the shock of comfort, I suppose.

I think I must have looked as if I were about to faint because Topcliffe glanced at his assistant, boot-faced Roger, who opened his bag and took out a small glass and a phial containing brownish liquid. He measured a thimbleful into the glass and brought it across to me.

'What's that?'

'A restorative. Drink it.'

But before I could even say yea let alone nay a guard jerked my head back, forced my jaw ajar as if I were a dog to be cured of the worms and Roger tipped the concoction neatly down my gullet. I had the impression that this too was part of a routine; I was a performer in a private play of their making. And though I had an important role there was no need for me to learn my lines. I would be prompted with the correct speeches all the way through. The draught of whatever it was tasted of nothing but smelt of juniper. I daresay its basis was Dutch gin. Its other ingredients were a mystery but the effect of it was immediate. At once I felt warmed, then alert. My shivering ceased, the throb in my head diminished. I felt ready to answer my accusers with conviction. And to refute them where necessary.

Heneage spoke to Skeate.

'Why don't you come to the second passage that concerns us, Mr Skeate?'

Skeate cleared his throat portentously; he was perhaps our huggermugger drama's crudest performer.

'Mr Marlowe says the following on sheet four: "and I daresay Jesus died quite as much a sodomite as his bedfellow John the Evangelist." What do you say to that, Mr Kyd?'

'It was a joke.'

'A joke. You joke about our Saviour and St John?'

'Christofer's young. So were the others who heard his lecture.'

'Youth is no excuse for blasphemy.'

'But Christofer doesn't blaspheme. His words are – well – ambiguous. He doesn't actually say Jesus used John in the manner of Sodom, does he?'

'A quibble, sir. The implication of the statement is quite plain.'

'It was just a light remark. What we call in the theatre a throwaway. It wasn't intended seriously.'

'But we are serious, Mr Kyd. And of the firm opinion that the first passage is heretical to the point of atheism and the second blasphemous. Furthermore as the copyist you were party to these crimes.'

'But that's like blaming the messenger!'

Gog spoke.

'The law is clear, My Kyd. Anyone who aids or abets an atheist or assists in a blasphemy is as culpable as the aforesaid atheist or blasphemer.'

Heneage intervened. Addressing me directly.

'Surely you understand the danger you're in?'

'I have to insist upon my innocence, sir.'

'Even though it has been explained to you that you are not innocent?'

'But the lecture was harmless, sir. You said so yourself.'

'My words were: comparatively harmless, Mr Kyd. I chose them carefully and I would advise you to do the same with yours.'

'It was a private lecture in a private house.'

'I don't consider an audience of thirty easily influenced young people private, Mr Kyd. And what's privacy to do with the matter anyway? A privy function can break the law quite as irrevocably as a public one. No, I insist you're in great danger, sir. And that you should consider how you might avoid the perils which undoubtably surround you.'

And Heneage allowed his eyes to turn to Topcliffe who grinned and flexed his fists and then cracked his knuckles in the silence Heneage had created for him. Topcliffe's relish of me as a prospective victim was as cheerful as it was blatant: he looked like a happy potboy. Heneage spoke again.

'As Gentlemen and Yeomen of the Queen's Chamber – to give us our official title – we value voluntary evidence, Mr Kyd, far more than that extracted by other means. In plain English we can – as I intimated before – protect those who provide us with what we call Queen's evidence.'

'You're inviting me to turn informer?'

'Do reflect, Mr Kyd, before you answer.'

'No!'

'You refuse?'

'Yes!'

'Think again. All we're asking is that you call to mind what you know of Mr Marlowe. His way of thinking, his opinions on this and that, his preferences of the carnal kind, his particular friends – especially the one designated by the initials W.R. – and anything else you may think relevant to the author of this atheistical lecture.'

It had taken less than half an hour for Christofer's thoughts on the New Testament to be transmuted from 'comparatively harmless' to 'atheistical'. So much for Heneage's initial show of fair-mindedness. That had been comparative, too.

'One other thing we shall ask of you, Mr Kyd. And here again the more you can contribute of your own accord the better. In our experience many of those who exhibit doubt or scepticism are later uncovered as secret adherents of Rome, agents of the purple whore of Babylon herself. Would you say Mr Marlowe ever showed signs of favouring Rome, Mr Kyd? Or did he ever to your knowledge consort with seditious persons of that persuasion?'

I did not reply.

'Well, never mind. As I've said all these things are to be

discussed between us. But an indication from you now before we reconvene tomorrow could make a difference to the accommodation you will enjoy tonight. What do you say?'

Again I said nothing.

'Oh, dear. You refuse to offer evidence?'

I nodded.

'You reject the clemency of the Crown?'

'I cannot betray my friend.'

'Nonsense. You not only can but you will. That I can safely promise you.' He turned silkily to Poley. 'Robert, I believe we've seen enough for the moment of Mr Kyd, don't you?'

Poley rose and my guards appeared at once. And as before I was frogmarched away to my cell. I won't describe the sleepless horrors of that night except to say they paled beside the terrors of the morning.

·X·I·I·I·

Lycia said to me, 'Go on.'

'I can't. It was too terrible.'

She reached out and took my hand.

'You promised to tell me everything, Tom. Everything that happened at Chelsea. You must. Not just for your sake, for mine too. People must know what really happens there. They know of Bridewell's horrors but not of Chelsea's. Or else they pretend they know more than they actually do, hint and nudge. Believe me, Tom, no one until today has told me what's done there. Now you have. And, by the way, I know your Magog – the Mr Skeate you mention. His full name is Sebastian Skeate, a papist now reformed, once of Hart Hall, Oxford. I didn't know he smelt out heresies for Heneage. And Topcliffe's assistant, whom you knew only as Roger, is Roger Shoesmith – a doctor and bonesetter of some distinction. He once removed a tooth out of no less a mouth than that of Lord Burghley.'

'And Gog? Can you think who he might me?'

'Describe him again.'

'As big as Magog. Bearded but quite bald. Aged forty or thereabouts. Broken nose. Three gold teeth.'

'No, I've no idea, Tom.'

'You wouldn't forget him if you saw him.'

'From the sound of it, no. Go on.'

But before I relate what I next told Lycia I must speak of where we were. Of the strange place, where, sitting by her side I had just described my first day of interrogation at Chelsea. We sat at the edge of a dewpond on the crest of the Downs. Despite its name it was bone dry. Away to the left our horses cropped the grasses amid a haze of butterflies. I hadn't known what a dewpond was until Lycia told me. These shallow downland declivities conserve the dews and rain for the sheep. During the wet summer I'd taken this place for a permanent pond but now in this autumn's unlooked-for warmth – already we'd been blessed by five golden days in a row since Lycia's return – all the water had gone, drunk by the sheep or risen away in vapour.

This grassy saucer lay some way from Chancton Ring. From its rim you could see the sea while at your back the Weald unfolded. It had become our preferred place – partly, I'd told Lycia, because up there out in the open no one could come upon us unawares.

Lycia had used a certain cunning to have me join her there. She achieved it by the straightforward expediency of animal attraction. She'd sent me a new horse to ride. Her groom arrived with this bay three year old on the afternoon following our supper together. He informed me Goodfellow lived up to his name and her ladyship begged me to think of him as my own. Though a stallion I could trust him not to throw me. He was a real gentleman, he said.

I inspected Goodfellow (I know one shouldn't look a gift horse in the mouth but I did) and found no faults in him. He nuzzled his nose at me out of sheer good humour. I rewarded him with a quartered apple. He eyed me as he munched it and I swear there was a smile, a twinkle even, in those eloquent eyes. Then he nudged at me again and I realised he was trying to push me in the direction of his harness which the groom had set on the bench by the door. It was clear he wanted me to ride. I laughed. He whinnied. I picked up the saddle and heaved it up onto his back. He stood stock still. I buckled the girth. He breathed out approvingly. As I set the bit between his teeth I could tell his mouth would be of velvet.

Once bridled and saddled Goodfellow cavorted gently to demonstrate his satisfaction at having successfully conveyed his meaning to me. I led him to the mounting block and hauled myself up into the saddle. I swear he'd have knelt like a camel for me to mount if I'd asked it of him. Never had I known such an accommodating animal. Had he no fault, I wondered? Yes, he had one but I've come to count it a virtue.

Once I was safely in the saddle with my good leg in the stirrup Goodfellow shook his head and reached out his neck to nod us forward. We set off. He needed no spur (not that I wore any), not even a nudge of the heel. He was determined upon exercise, adventure and, I can say it now though I didn't know it then, sheer pleasure.

I had no plan of where to ride. Our errand was quite errant. I let Goodfellow choose the way. His gait was easy, smooth as silk. On his back I felt I was a real rider again. I laughed and patted his neck. His ears pricked as I told him he had a clever and generous mistress to grant me such a ride as this. For reply – I believe he understood every word I spoke – he broke into a trot and then a canter along the lane that led the way I'd hitherto hobbled towards the Downs. I felt as brave as Christofer's Tamburlaine. Sussex had become my Persepolis.

Goodfellow conducted me across the flank of the Down away to the west of the ring. And when I tried to turn him to it he refused. So you have a fault, I said? A will of your own when you choose? He snorted so emphatically I again let him have his head. The incline soon brought him back to a walk, his breathing was deeper, louder. But he was far from blown. Quite the contrary. As we neared the soft summit he increased his pace and as soon as we reached that rounded levelness which makes these hills such a joy to walk along he broke again into a happy canter – whinnying as he went.

And I saw why. For ahead of us was a rider: a woman who could only be Lycia. She rode the mare I had formerly ridden. Something glinted in the sun. It was a gold visor she wore with a black veil thrown over her head and shoulders. At our approach she pushed up the visor, shook her hair free of the veil and laughed. I found I was laughing, too. From the sheer transmitted joy of the animal beneath me. Such was Goodfellow's joy in finding not only his mistress but also her mare. Who appeared as pleased as he at his approach. As he pulled to a halt and stretched forward to nuzzle her neck she whinnied softly.

Lycia said, 'Well, here you are, Tom. I knew if I took the mare I could count on Goodfellow bringing you to me.'

'Why? Is she in season?'

'How cynical of you. No. She's the light of his heart. He cares for her most daintily. They share a stable and are as devoted to each other as a pair of blackbirds. But when she's next on heat I shall put him to her. A foal of theirs would be worth breeding if only for the gentle manners it would inherit.'

'He's a beautiful horse. To ride him is to feel like a king.'

'And indeed you looked like one as you came up.'

'I don't believe you.'

'Well, you needn't. But you did. Why don't you help me dismount.'

I swung off Goodfellow and came to Lycia. I held up my hands to her. She took them and slipped most gracefully down from the saddle. As she stood in front of me she looked into my eyes and I believe had Lycia been any other woman we should have embraced then and there. But Lycia isn't any other woman. Her ways are subtler, labyrinthine. As I held her gaze she blinked quite deliberately and at once the eyebeams spun between us were cut. Then she shook her head but more in considerate wonder than denial.

She said, 'My dear Tom, there are still several things I need to know about you.'

And still holding my left hand she led me to the edge of the dewpond and there releasing me promptly sat, hugging her knees to her chest like a girl. Still standing I proposed we should tether the horses. Lycia smiled and enquired to what did I hope to hitch them? I had to smile, too. There was nothing on that open hilltop save grasses and harebells. However Lycia assured me her mare never strayed and that where she was Goodfellow would be sure to remain, so faithful was he. Whereupon I also sat.

Thus I came to speak of what I feared the most. At Lycia's coaxing I told of the initial hearing at Chelsea before I was put to

Topcliffe's pillar. That preliminary interrogation seemed at the time of telling to be recollected at some cost. I remember my mind cringing, my pride rebelling, before I could admit the humiliations I'd endured. But once they were told and I came to speak of the next caravan of cruelties they seemed as nothing. No, not seemed. They *were* nothing – compared with the events of the three days which followed. Though these again, in their turn, paled beside the final horror.

The next day was the thirteenth of May. My guards let me in as before and I was allowed to sit as before. It was exactly noon. I had been without sleep for thirty-six hours. My well-slept, well-fed inquisitors trooped in five minutes later. To my exhausted eyes they looked even more grandly dressed than before. They greeted me good-humouredly, still called me Mr Kyd, still pretended we were equals despite the disparity of our conditions.

Heneage said, 'Mr Kyd, when we last spoke together I asked you, as a loyal subject of the Queen, to provide us, her officers, with information concerning a certain atheist and possible traitor. That is your friend, Mr Christofer Marlowe. You refused. I now ask you again, and for the very last time, to tell us voluntarily what you know of him. We're certain you know much. And, as I said yesterday, the Crown looks favourably upon those who give evidence willingly in the great cause of keeping England free. I beg you not to refuse again.'

As he finished he turned to glance at Topcliffe whose eyes were fixed upon the manacles set in the pillar above my head. I hadn't got much of a voice despite having been given hot toddy an hour before by my guards as they got me ready for this noonday appearance.

Nevertheless I said no, audibly enough. And I remember feeling absurdly proud of myself, as well as a little surprised by my own staunchness. I was convinced I would rather defy my country than betray my friend Christofer.

Heneage sighed and rose.

He said, 'Then we must leave you for the moment, Mr Kyd. Come along gentlemen. It's a pity. But there we are.'

And he left, together with Poley, Skeate, Gog and Magog. But Topcliffe and Roger remained.

Here in my relation I stopped and Lycia was obliged to prompt me. She did so first by taking my hand again, then by saying, 'Please, Tom, please, you must speak. You know it, I know it, please.'

Her voice was gentle, low, excellently persuasive. How could I refuse her?

Caressed by her voice, flattered by her touch, I broke all bounds, became a flood, a torrent of facts and fury.

'Topcliffe's got two steel bracelets set in that pillar I mentioned. You'd say it was quite out of place in that long room but it isn't. Oh, no! I had to stand on the stool I'd previously sat on, lift up my arms like a child and push my hands up into these two rings above my head. They were ratcheted round my wrists. Once Topcliffe was satisfied by their tightness – what a keen artisan the man is! – he kicked the stool away, saying as he did that this was ever the best moment for him. He said it not as an evil joke, though it was, but as a fact. I cried out as my wrists and hands took upon themselves the whole weight of me. Later, after repeated hangings and as many revivals – you're right, Roger Shoesmith's an expert physician, his cordials can bring you back from the grave which is the only place you want to be – later I found I'd scream even before Topcliffe kicked the stool away.

'For how long exactly did you refuse to speak, Tom?'

'Three days.'

'Then I'd say you're a brave and proper man.'

'I disagree.'

'You shouldn't. But go on. Say everything.'

'Easier said than done! Words can scarcely describe Topcliffe's torture. It's simpler and worse than the rack. Suffice it to say my fingers' ends spouted blood, my chest and belly felt shot full of fire while my heels, kicking against the pillar, only increased the bloody excoriation of my clamped wrists. The various pains you yourself produce send your bursting head off into delirium. You know you're screaming for release but to you, sealed up in agony, your voice is faraway. It might even be another person's. As for your inquisitors, well, they've left the room lest their eyes and ears be offended by the grotesqueness of the spectacle. They only return once Topcliffe has temporarily brought you down to sit upon the stool or more usually to lie shuddering upon the floor since you're quite unable to support yourself and besides the cool boards offer a sort of solace to your cheek. And after each suspension Heneage or Poley would ask me if I was now ready to speak for England? And invariably I shook my head or whispered no. And they would nod as if the entire proceeding and my answer were normal and to be expected. They'd say, politely, when you're ready, Mr Kyd, we shall be happy to hear you. And retire again. They comport themselves as if they were aldermen not spymasters. I suppose they are aldermen of a kind. After all, at Chelsea, they govern what we may call "the Ward of Eliza Within" – a hidden parish which underlies the whole realm.'

Lycia smiled, said she liked this comparison. And yes, she could all too easily imagine the business conducted with just such civic decorum. State roguery had never yet lacked ceremony, she said.

I came then to tell of the third day. The afternoon of that day. The fifteenth of May. When I'd already been hung up three times, when my arms were swollen like blood sausages, my wrists were raw to the bone, my sight was almost gone, my voice a croak, my mind a mess of porridge. It was nearly five o'clock.

They dragged me up from the floor to bring me to the pillar, to the manacles once again. But this time the mere sight of them sticking out from the blood-flecked marble was enough. My resolution died at last.

'Perhaps you can imagine that, too?' I said and Lycia nodded. 'That's when I said I'd speak. When I'd tell them everything, anything they wanted to know rather than be hung up there another time. Heneage congratulated me and said he was sure I would be word-perfect in my new role.'

'Poor Tom.'

'And I was.'

'What precisely did you tell them?'

'You want an inventory of the lies I told?'

'Yes! These things must be said, Tom. Or they'll fester for ever inside you.'

I drew breath at the thought of itemising my disgrace. How could I possibly do what Lycia commanded? I looked at her. This time she did not cut short our gaze and from her eyes I seemed to glean a promise of miraculous happiness to come if her demand was met.

For answer Lycia smiled and said, 'I always try to mean everything I do. And everything I say. So please go on.'

So I did. I said, 'I began at the beginning. Told them how Christofer had come to me with his play of *Tamburlaine* and asked me to read it. He was just down from Cambridge and knew no one in the theatre. I told how I'd read it where I stood – in absolute amazement and then passed it to Bill Kempe who'd recommended it to Alleyn. I said how we'd become fast friends. And that Christofer being at that time penniless I'd taken him in at Bucklersbury. Where we'd lived and worked together in great harmony and with increasing success. But then, then I'd noticed I was failing to hold my inquisitors' attention. My tale was of no interest to them. And I knew that if I was to preserve myself I must offer more than truthful anecdote. These intelligencers wanted lies. Meaty, juicy, blood-red falsehoods. As I faltered Heneage told me to come to the point: was Christofer an atheist or not? Had I heard him express such views? If so where and when? So I said, yes, yes, oh yes, he most certainly was an unbeliever, that I'd heard him deny the existence of God countless times. Their faces softened. Warming to my mendacity I said he despised all religions but had some regard for the papists upon the grounds that their ceremonies were statelier than ours. Poley smiled. What was more he considered Protestants obstinate donkeys. A sparkle entered Gog's eye. Next I swore blind I'd argued and quarrelled with Christofer as I became more and more offended by his monstrous opinions. That I'd been tempted to denounce him to the authorities but out of misguided reverence for his poetic talent had failed to do so. The which I now regretted. At this enormity Skeate nodded appreciatively. But I said, I had even so, and eventually I'd turned him out of my lodgings on account of his blasphemies. Here all smiled at once. What cared they that in fact Christofer and I had parted in perfect amity? Poley said he'd heard that Mr Marlowe was prone to sudden violence? Perhaps I could comment upon that? Not that he wanted to put words into my mouth, of course. And he laughed but his eyes warned me to corroborate his statement. Thus advised I made Christofer not only overweening but malicious too in the most underhand of ways. Why, I said, turning treachery into further fancy, he had actually contrived to brand the buttocks of his boy-lovers with the letter M to mark them for all time as his beastly catamites. He'd heat the iron secretly and then hold the poor children down by force until this vile deed was accomplished.

'All untrue?'

'Absolutely. Christofer was often angry and always outspoken but never vicious. He kept such brutal actions for his plays.'

'What more did you say?'

'Much too much. Why, I even said he'd told me he had as much right to coin money as the Queen, who had no more divine right to it than he. Since she was no more appointed by God than he was. She was just another jumped-up bandit like her ancestors. A despot put in high place by fortune.'

'And they liked your lies?'

'Lapped them up. Like cats at spilt milk. Gog's pencil flew as he noted every item.'

'They congratulated you?'

'Several times. And I was rewarded. I was brought breeches with a belt to hold them up. Offered food, beer. My lowly stool was exchanged for a chair like theirs. I can't pretend I wasn't grateful. I was. My body was only too glad of comfort. Every fibre in me told me my hell's bargain was well made. Such was my relief at my ebbing pains I failed to notice Topcliffe's demeanour.'

'Why? Was he displeased?'

'Deeply. He sat still as stone.'

'Deprived of his prey?'

'Yes. He said as much later. When I was returned to his custody to be conveyed, as I thought, unharmed to prison.'

'You've jumped ahead, my dear. What other information did you lay against your dearest friend?'

'Everything about the lecture at Scadbury. How Christofer had given it once before at Cerne Abbas and therefore the initials W. R. on the script must stand for Sir Walter Raleigh since he has his house there. The minute I said *that* they were on to it like kites and crows! Did I know who else had been there in Dorset? Had I been there? I said no – the truth for once but no less damnable for that. With more to come since I knew for certain Henry Percy had gone there together with George Chapman – not to mention the notorious mathematician Thomas Harriot. I put all four of them in mortal danger.'

'I doubt you need fear for Raleigh or for Percy. Not with their deep pockets. They can afford their freedoms. But for the other two perhaps.'

'Now you see what a common informer I am.'

'Under duress, Tom, under duress.'

'I still don't forgive myself.'

'Well, I think you should. In fact I say you must. Do you suppose any of us would not have done the same in your place? Imagine Percy on that pillar – would he have held out?'

'I don't know.'

'Or Christofer come to that?'

'Don't!'

'I dare swear none of us would've shown more courage than you. Three days you held out, Tom. Three dreadful days and three abominable nights. That's enough for any man or woman. It's certainly enough for me. What else did you tell them? Come on. I want all your bad blood let out. I want your mind clean again, scoured of guilt.'

I laughed from sudden well-being. Lycia was right. By telling her the truth I was stripping my former lies of their power over me: they could no longer crush me. If Lycia could forgive me why shouldn't I? Or if not forgive at least no longer pretend to myself I should've held out till death.

I said, 'I also told them Christofer was a necromancer. Quite false. We'd got drunk one night when he was working on *Faustus*. And played some silly games. I'd read the story in a translation from the German and given it to him thinking the subject might suit. It did! He went wild with enthusiasm. Talked about it day and night. He blessed me, kissed me, said here was the best, the only story in the world. Did I not see how much subtler it was than the old moralities? What a genius I was to discover it! Was not Faust's bargain the one we all make by being born? Anyway he drafted the opening scenes in a great rush and then came to the moment when Faustus experiments with magic and raises that arch-agent of hell, soft-tongued Mephostophilis.'

'You mean you and Christofer conducted such an experiment?'

'Oh yes. But as I say we were both drunk.'

'What did you do?'

'We pushed our work table aside and drew a wobbly pentagram in chalk on the floor. And every mystic symbol we could think of. Then Christofer stood in the middle and called up the devil in Latin.'

'Just as in the play?'

'*Exactly* as in the play. Christofer put it all in next morning.'

Lycia laughed. 'And did Mephostophilis appear?'

'Well, no. But one of the candles suddenly flared and then on the wall was a shadow in a hooded shape – like a Franciscan friar.'

'What had cast it?'

'We couldn't tell. The nearest candle guttered and went out. And the shadow was gone. But then – then all the others burned blue.'

Lycia shivered happily. 'No smell of sulphur?'

'No. So next we tried to recite the Lord's Prayer backwards. Only we kept getting lost. You try: "Evil from us deliver but temptation into not us lead" when you've got eight pints of the Green Man's best mild under your belt. Oh, the whole business was quite ridiculous. But at Chelsea I made it seem the gravest matter in the world.'

'They took it seriously?'

'Gog noted every detail.'

'And was that all – for that day?'

'More or less. They asked me further questions concerning the lecture. Not what it was about – after all, they had Christofer's own script – but now they wanted the names of all who'd heard it at Scadbury. I gave what names I could remember but told Heneage he would surely do better to ask Walsingham for a guest list? Heneage concurred most agreeably that he would and thanked me for my help. The Queen's Council would be grateful to me, he said.'

'So am I, Tom. Thank you.'

'Why do you say that?'

'For doing as I asked. For unburdening yourself. Already you look years younger.

And Lycia pushed out her legs and lay back beside me with her arms spread wide. I was reminded of the way she'd stretched that day she'd walked her newly-planted maze. I suddenly felt free to lie back, too. She lay gazing at the sky. She seemed to breathe satisfaction. After a while she turned on her side to me, as if we were children in a grassy bed. I turned to her. Then, before our eyes could meet, she did a most extraordinary thing. She rolled away from me, down the bank, laughing, turning over and over until she reached the bottom of that dry mystery we'd sat above: that dewpond full of sun and air.

'You try it, Tom,' she said. 'I was always rolling downhill as a child.'

I did as I was told. And arrived at the bottom where by some quick magic, smoother and better than anything Christofer and I had devised, I found myself in Lycia's arms. She held me close and kissed my lips.

She said, 'What's left to tell can be told elsewhere.'

And at once she was on her feet, brushing clean her skirts. Then she held out her hands. I took them, and like Lazarus rose from the grave. Now was my turn to draw her to me and kiss her for myself. She accepted my salute almost meditatively. As if savouring the future she had so surely created for herself and me.

'Now we may go home, Tom,' she said.

·X·I·V·

Thus was I made lord of my lady's house. I ruled by whimsical decree. I could do exactly what I wished. And whilst I did it my beard was scissored to a daily perfection, my hair curled, my bath perfumed and my jewel box heaped with glistening trifles of unimaginable cost. I was a kept Mycaenas. My wardrobe became as multivarious as any Spanish grandee's. Six tailors, three hatters and two shoemakers were at my constant command. My measurements were their bible; their handiwork their prayers; my glory their salvation.

I rode every day. Soon I could put Goodfellow at any fence however tall and thanks to his easy motion and balanced judgment never find myself unseated. I went hunting, hawking and relearned the art of defence with rapier and dagger. Then at Lycia's insistence, the tricks of cloak and dagger. When I asked her why she wished me to revise such a back-alley skill she kissed me in a blatant evasion of the question. The next day she presented me with a set of rapiers with matching daggers the hilts of which were so cleverly crafted my grip became the equal of any other man's.

As for my diet – it was so dainty I became as slender as I was well-nourished. I felt ten years younger. I glowed with power, with health, with sheer possession.

Lycia still commanded me. But as a mistress. Her bed was my bed. It became our world.

It was curtained about with two sets of draperies. The outer ones were of a green and red damask so heavy it shut out all light.

When the candles were snuffed and they were closed we were buried in darkness. We became whispers, touch and smell. Invisible animals. We burrowed and tumbled and fed upon each other in coiling, moiling blackness. But once the damask was drawn back and dawnlight admitted we were again ourselves: pale as maggots, naked, human.

Another night and, with candles lit and the fire aglow, Lycia would call for the inner set of curtains to be pulled about us – when she needed service Lycia knew no prudery, she simply called for it whatever her state of nature – and straightaway we were created gods newborn in glory. These other curtains were golden gauze – a cloth of gold so fine all light shone through it transmuted into sunshine. This way we were enclosed in a flickering, flame-fed artificial summer. Bathed in gold we were made yet more desirable to each other; more beautiful than we really were. Now our eyes could revel in every embellished particular of ourselves, anatomise every part, note each and every hair, count every freckle, kiss any mole or scar, please a pap with a finger, tease an ear lobe with a bite, trace every crease. We became eagle-eyed surgeons of each other. I couldn't see or know enough of Lycia's body, nor she mine. And then as desire mounted again, and yet again, it seemed to me we formed (in that translucent cloister) our own sweet-axled chariot of the sun. We were both Phaeton's carriage, Phaeton himself and all his flying horses tumbling through sheets of cloud, riding the heavens, shooting out sunbeams like burning swords.

A poet's fancy? A word picture? Yes! Yes! Yes! For who doesn't know that everything is made in the eye of the beholder? Certainly Lycia and I begot ourselves in each other's eyes and by reflection became each other. Or so I thought.

One morning returning from a gallop along the Downs we saw Mary carrying milk to the dairy. She curtsied to us and I felt a pang of remorse at my removal from her. I suddenly felt I'd flown too far above her and wished I could stoop down. But that seemed now impossible. Mary smiled dutifully first at Lycia then at me, muttered 'my lady, my lord' and went on her way, the yoke across her shoulders, the milk in the two pails spilling a little before she steadied them.

Apart from my own changed circumstances was it only in my imagination that Mary too had changed? There was an air about her that wasn't as before. There was a containedness in her.

'She's with child,' Lycia said. 'With your child, Tom.'

I cannot pretend I was surprised. What more natural consequence could there have been of Mary's loving restoration of me? But I wasn't prepared for Lycia's frown. How could she be jealous of a cowgirl? Then I remembered what Dr Thwaite had said. Lycia was barren.

She said, 'I shall adopt the baby, Tom. That way it may be ours. I've wanted a baby of each, of all my lovers but never more than from you.'

'Yes. Dr Thwaite told me.'

'Oh, you've gossiped with him, have you?'

'Only once. He said you'd tried every remedy.'

'I have. Truly.' she nodded. 'I shall adopt it at birth and appoint Mary as wetnurse. It shall want for nothing.'

'Have you told Mary of your intention, madam?'

'Madam?'

'I may call you that if I choose, surely?'

'Yes. But why should you choose?'

There was a spark of anger in her and a glow of resentment in me at her imperiousness.

'Because it seems I'm the last to be advised about my child's future.'

'*Our* child! And I've told you now! Besides who but I sent Mary to you with my blessing? And my money? The girl's already been handsomely rewarded, Tom, believe me.'

'That still doesn't give you any right in her baby!'

'It does! Every right! Why – oh!'

To my astonishment Lycia sobbed, swung herself down from her mare and ran into the house, crying like the rain.

Some moments after I thrust aside her second chamberwoman who tried to bar the door and found Lycia sprawled across the bed, her face buried in the bolster. I was struck with wonder. I could not credit this grief I'd discovered in my lady. How could such apparent poise have been built on these glistening quicksands? Her sobs racked my heart. I was overcome with pity. My empress should not, must not cry. I would stop her.

I flung myself down beside her and began to kiss her tears away. I sucked them up and wiped her cheeks with a corner of the sheet. I told her Mary's child was hers. Suddenly I was as despotic as she; I freely offered what wasn't mine; another being in another's belly. But out of my passionate hypocrisy our desires were rekindled and with her tears dried the tinder caught. From my commiseration lust was born. Soon Lycia was calling her women to undress her. Did I not say she was quite above propriety? How they giggled as they unlaced her, glancing lubriciously at me as I stood by. One girl even had the temerity to offer to undress me but Lycia, stepping like a dark Venus from the seafoam of her petticoats, dismissed her from the room.

Soon we were one animal again and if sheer force could've made my Lycia fecund I swear that morning we should've got a child between us. At the last she gave a great cry, arched back over the pillows, and lay still as if in our final spending she had died in truth.

Eventually she said, 'May I count that as the making of our child, Tom?'

I agreed she might. And cradled her in my arms. If I was made new then so it seemed was Lycia.

It was during those days that I completed my confession. At table, on horseback, beside the dewpond, in bed, walking the maze. Lycia persuaded me to walk it barefoot as she did. I told her she was as foolish a philospher as the Wizard Earl but nevertheless I did as I was told and found the winding of the pathway curiously pleasant, and even beneficent to my knee. Though this may have been coincidence – a further easiness that might have occurred whatever I had done. But Lycia swore it was the maze's doing.

I told how I'd signed the indictment of Christofer. How Gog had augmented my catalogue of lies with some of his own – particularly a flourish in praise of tobacco and boys together with mention of someone I'd never heard of, a man called Chomley who said he'd turned atheist thanks to Christofer's evil instruction. This seemed entirely unlikely but I let it pass and signed.

The next day I was presented to the Star Chamber where I was required to read this Judas list aloud to the assembled council. I spoke like a repentant ghost. I'd been ordered to read the document with a will or risk a return to the pillar but try as I might I couldn't give my voice any real voice. The more I tried the more I croaked. But somehow I got through it and when I'd finished Lord Burghley smiled in my direction. He said I was to be congratulated upon my service to the state despite my initial reluctance to speak out. As a consequence any other charges would be dropped and my life spared. It was always a pleasure to him when people realised where their true loyalities lay. And with that I was dismissed, though even as I left I heard him call for a warrant to be issued for Christofer's arrest.

Two days later, on the nineteenth of May, Poley brought Christofer to my privileged cell at Chelsea. As an official informer I commanded a dry floor, a straw mattress and a slop bucket with a lid. The place still stank however. Mostly of remorse. Christofer's hands were pinioned behind his back just as mine had been.

Poley said, 'Your friend asked to see you, Mr Kyd. You've got five minutes.' He then withdrew but kept watch through the grill of the door.

We stared at each other. Christofer still looked much himself. His clothes were still fresh, unstained; his eyes still clear; his chin more or less shaven as always. I could tell he was shocked by what his eyes showed him of me.

He said, 'I was going to curse you up hill, down dale.'

'Well, you can. You should.'

'Oh, my dear. What have they done to you?'

'Very little. '

And I explained Topcliffe's genius to him. How he did the least while you did the most and Eliza's state watched, waited, listened. When I'd finished he kissed me.

'I don't blame you, Tom. I thought I would but, of course, I don't. Oh, my God, how vile, how vicious, how dare they?'

'I've given up complaint. It's of no use here. Here everything's devised to outwit indignation. You'll find they'll let you say anything you like for as long as you like. Have you heard the drum?'

'No?'

'Then you haven't been shown the basement. Do you remember when you invented a drum to keep poor Edward awake in the depths of Killingworth Castle?'

'Yes.'

'Someone from here attended your play. He thought it a good idea. Now a drum beats continually down below. Oh, Christofer – I held out for as long as I could. But in the end – oh! I know I should've held out – '

'No, Tom, no! They'd only have tortured you to death. Then made up their own lies and put them into your mouth. Your dear, dead mouth. The dead can't contradict, can they? There's no more loyal a subject than a corpse, is there?'

'Have they questioned you?'

'Not yet. Look at me. I'm quite whole. They assure me I shall be held in decent comfort till the trial.'

'They're planning a trial?'

'A very grand one, apparently. Of the kind usually afforded only to our nobler traitors. As a piffling playwright I ought to be well flattered, they say.' Christofer laughed. I wished I could. 'So you see, Tom, for the moment I'm safe. Besides Corin's gone to Greenwich to plead for me.'

'Where are you held?'

'At home. At Ludgate. They call it house arrest. But I'm obliged to present myself either here or Whitehall every day. At my own expense. Oh, yes, I pay the waterman. Our Blessed Eliza's nothing if not thrifty.'

'I'm sorry. Forgive me.'

'No, Tom. I've said!' Suddenly Christofer was ablaze. 'I *do* forgive you. You *are* forgiven. So just accept that, will you?'

'I can't! And there's no need to be angry.'

'Oh, yes, there is. Look at you! Look what they've done to you. My God! You're a living corpse!'

Silence fell between us like a stone.

I said, 'You'd better go.'

'I forgive you, Tom. Please understand that. I forgive you!'

'Go.'

For reply he kissed my blood-sausage hands. I tried to push him from me. But still he refused to go, saying he would stay until I accepted his forgiveness.

I called for Poley. Told him to remove Christofer from my sight. In cold blood I asked the very man who'd brought me to this hell to take my dearest friend, my furious forgiving Christoferus, away from me! Oh, how could I have done such a thing? Here was my final treason. Everything else pales beside that request to Poley. Poley! Of all people! I still feel sick at it. To have parted like that. For ever. How could I? How could I?

But when I told Lycia of this last meeting between us, between two friends lost for words, out-flanked by policy, torn apart by guilt and pity, love and contempt, she put her finger to my lips to hush me.

And said, 'Don't say any more, Tom. Just listen. Please listen. You've managed to forgive yourself once, haven't you? Nod if you agree.' I nodded. 'Well, now you must forgive yourself again. You must. And you can. Hadn't you just been humiliated beyond all bounds? But now – listen! – now is the moment, the very instant, you must lay your Chelsea ghost to rest. That creature wasn't you! It was a ghastly parody of you. A thing created for another's purposes. That other you call Ishmael – your real enemy. And the way to give yourself the peace your spirit craves is to find out that bugbear and be quit of him.'

Never had I known Lycia more purposeful than at that moment. And to say that of my empress is to say much. Her whole being it seemed was recruited to reinforce mine.

I said, out of reason not prevarication, 'But how do I find him?

I've already scrutinised every memory, shaken my past through a sieve – all to no avail.'

'Perhaps you found him but didn't recognise him?'

'Perhaps. But where's the help in that?'

'Come, let's employ paper and ink.'

And she rose from the daybed where we'd been sitting and led me to her study. It was at the end of the long gallery where I had first been received on her return from court. To me it was a perfect room. Octagonal, book-lined, with a tiny gallery running round it to enable the conscientious student to reach the books above. A library in miniature with a single polished table at its centre, set out with fresh paper, ink, pens.

We sat side by side. Lycia took a quarto sheet, dipped a pen in ink and held it poised.

'Let's set down the names of all your likely and unlikely Ishmaels?'

'Very well. But where shall we begin?'

'With the highest in the land.'

I laughed. 'Eliza, then,' I said.

'And she could've spoken to Burghley, could she not?'

She wrote down both names. And added, 'He might have gone to his son Robert who would have gone to Heneage with the news that Her Majesty was rather concerned by the extreme opinions of a certain popular playwright.' She wrote down Robert Cecil and Heneage. 'Heneage in his turn would've come to his chief executant? Who is who? Skeate? Possibly.' She wrote down Skeate.

'And Skeate would've instructed Poley to arrest me?'

'Not at once. First someone had to pass Poley the manuscript he professed to discover at your lodgings.'

While she wrote down Poley's name I said, 'Well, we decided that had to be Nick Skeres?' She nodded and wrote down Skeres. 'But why note him? He's dead. And besides – '

'We must consider everybody, Tom.'

'But I thought we'd agreed – or rather you'd instructed me – to disregard such minions as Poley and Skeres?'

'I know. But I've revised my opinion. Today I believe we

should note down every single one of your persecutors. A false Ishmael may lead us to the real one.'

'In logic all those we've named so far are Eliza's instruments. Therefore she must be my Ishmael.'

'It's not impossible, Tom.'

'No. But I don't believe it. I doubt she even knows of my existence.'

'Oh, I'm sure not. But as I said she could've heard of Christofer. And disapproved. And besides, a prince may express a careless wish only to find an impetuous courtier has granted it. But since you appear to have been the means to an end your Ishmael may have had no opinion of you at all, Tom. To him, you were, perhaps, merely the sprat to catch his mackerel?'

I didn't care for this comparison and said so. She kissed my cheek. I turned to kiss her mouth. She shook her head.

'No, Tom, we must not stray from our chosen path.'

'We can always come back to it.'

'Don't you want to discover your Ishmael?'

'Of course but equally I want to cover you.'

'I'm not a brood mare!'

She was laughing. Another moment and she would've melted but there was a knock at the door and her steward appeared, breathless, anxious-eyed.

He stammered out his message: 'My lady, the cottage – it's been fired. Set on fire.'

When we got there the cottage where I had lived until my elevation to Lycia's bed was gone. It had become a smouldering, flame-flecked midden of ash and embers with one beam still standing, streaming flames in the wind like a defiant ensign on a field of rout. Two farmhands and a shepherd with his dog stood by with three buckets between them. They explained how ineffective they had been. Water bucketed from the well had been powerless to quench the flames, try as they had. Lycia nodded and dismissed them.

We gazed at the ruin as if our solemn contemplation was a

homage required by Prometheus – a silent acknowledgement of his fiery powers. I felt both sad and glad. The cottage had been a pleasant refuge, a cradle for my hurts – especially when Mary had come to me (or rather been sent to serve Lycia's future purpose) but against this had to be set the misery and remorse I'd suffered there. Not the place's fault I told myself but such logic can never wholly overcome inmost feeling; no more than three buckets against a blaze of thatch and timber.

But my gladness, I realised, had a further dimension: this burning had set me free: it was as if this fire had burned any last dross in me away. I felt like the phoenix. I must have smiled at the thought because Lycia queried me.

'What, Tom? You look pleased.'

'Well, I am. But I suppose I shouldn't be.'

'Why not?'

'Well, I expect you were fonder of the place than I.'

'Perhaps.'

'For me it was a pretty prison. A sweet place yet a sour one.'

'I used to play here as a child. And when I was no longer a child. Or rather it was here that I used to meet my betrothed.'

'Who died at Zutphen?'

'Did Dr Thwaite tell you that?'

'No. Mary did. But Dr Thwaite confirmed it.'

'Well, that's past. Nine years have gone since then.' She fell silent.

'You won't speak of it?'

'No.'

'You loved him?'

'I shall never love anyone as I loved Patrick. And don't say: not even me? Or I shall be obliged to say: no, not even you, my dear.'

'Well, you have said it anyway.'

'Yes.' she smiled in half-apology but there was an ancient sadness behind her eyes. As if to admonish herself she said briskly, 'Come along. There's nothing more we can do here.'

But there was, because as we turned to go the shepherd came back at a run. He was full of fear and trembling. 'Please, my lady, come quick – for Jesus's sake!' And he hurried us down to a hazel coppice beside the lane which lay below the cottage and led to the village where Dr Thwaite lived.

Is there any more grievous sight than a dead child? Young Martin, Mary's inquisitive nephew, lay as Nick Skeres had done, his throat cut. Beside him crouched the shepherd's dog, keening gently, eyes full of understanding.

I said, quite absurdly, 'Don't look, Lycia.'

The shepherd explained how his bitch Rosie, normally obedience herself, had run into the coppice and refused to return when whistled. He came through determined to teach her a lesson only to find her crouched by the boy. Nor would she leave him. He hadn't beaten her but come straight back to us. He knew little Martin well, so did Rosie. He'd heard how Martin had discovered the stranger's body on the Downs last month and he reckoned the lad must've seen too much for his own good.

Lycia said, 'Fetch Dr Thwaite. Run as fast as you can. We'll stay here.'

While he was gone we moved a little aside from the body, leaving the dog as guard and mourner.

I said. 'Surely this must be the same hand as killed Nick Skeres?'

Lycia agreed. Quickly we invented the events most likely to have led to Martin's death. The killer had come to kill me at the cottage. Finding I had gone he'd set the place on fire only to discover his act of arson had been observed by Martin. The boy had run away but had been overtaken by a superior runner, seized like a peddler's puppet and had the life sliced from him in an instant. We shuddered at our shared imagining of the scene.

'Who, Tom, who? Search your memory.'

Lycia's command released the only possible name: Francis, Master Francis. Everything in my recollection pointed to him: his strength, his speed, his alliance with Skeres.

I described Francis to Lycia, told her of his running prowess, his pride in his physique, his performance as a shark. She thought she might have seen him in the company of Walsingham at court.

She certainly remembered Walsingham calling for his secretary and had an impression of an insolent acolyte older than his master but then weren't all secretaries insolent? At least in her experience they were. But as for the man's name, well, she hadn't caught it, no.

'But I think you must consider him an Ishmael, Tom.'

'We'll include him in our catalogue.'

'Had he no other name than Francis.'

'No. He was known to all as Master Francis.'

'I shall make enquiries. Lady Audrey's mother is a cousin.'

'You're related to Lady Audrey?'

'Don't sound so displeased. Only distantly.'

She smiled and squeezed my arm.

It was dusk before Dr Thwaite arrived with the district beadle, two constables and a wheelbarrow for the body.

Dr Thwaite examined the small corpse and gave his opinion to Lycia and the beadle that it was more than likely the same hand had killed Martin as had slain the stranger on the Downs. As he said this he looked hard at me as if about to say more but Lycia intervened to invite him to eat with her that evening. But before we supped together she said she would go to break the dreadful news to Martin's parents while the constables brought the child's body along after her. I meanwhile should accompany Dr Thwaite.

As we rode back to the house he asked me again about Nick Skeres. He pronounced it a pity I had passed by the unknown body without seeing it. And then paused as if inviting me to correct this vagary, this curious inexactitude. As before at his house I was tempted to tell him the truth but resolved instead to wait till suppertime.

As we ate Lycia told the doctor how we had caught Martin eavesdropping but she now regretted she'd spoken so sternly to the boy and his parents. He'd been soundly beaten. But hardly cured of his inquisitiveness. If only he hadn't been seen by the arsonist.

Dr Thwaite took this as his cue to speak. He asked if we supposed that whoever had set the cottage ablaze had expected to find me at home there?

I said feelingly, 'No doubt of it, doctor. He did.'

Lycia said, 'We think he came to kill Tom. And Tom believes he knows who he might be. Why don't you explain, my dear?'

Here was my chance to apologise to Dr Thwaite for having been such a niggard with the truth. And to tell him why.

'My only excuse,' I said, having explained, 'was a good intent. I had no wish to involve you in my recent misfortunes.'

'I thank you, lad. But from what you say it looks like you're still in danger. With murderers coming for you twice.'

Lycia said, 'Well, at least he's secure here.'

I said, rather to my own surprise, 'But I can't stay here for ever, can I?' Lycia smiled, in sudden approval. 'Not that I want to go,' I added.

'I can understand that,' Thwaite said. 'But happen you'd feel easier with yourself once you'd faced up to your persecutor.'

I agreed but pointed out the difficulty of finding him. Told him how I'd invented the pseudonym Ishmael for this invisible arbiter of my destiny.

Dr Thwaite was nothing if not practical in his response. 'If that's the case I'd go for whoever's nearest and make sure he told me who he answered to. Then go for that bugger. And so on. Work your way up tree, lad, till you find the rotten fruit. And shake it down. Hard.'

Lycia laughed and applauded. 'There, Tom! What better advice can you hope for?'

I laughed too, warm with wine. But admonished Dr Thwaite even so. 'Fancy you, a physician, advocating such a course of violence.'

'I didn't say kill him, Tom. I said shake him to the ground.'

'It would amount to the same thing, I suspect.'

'That's for you to judge, lad. But I tell you, in my eyes, as a man, that if I'd suffered what you've suffered, I'd set my oath to one side just for a while and then do penance to Hippocrates after.'

We concluded that I would be justified in taking any revenge I chose and rose from the table to sit beside the fire where Lycia cracked green walnuts for us while asking Dr Thwaite a succession of questions concerning the health and welfare of her servants and estate workers. Mercifully only two had died of the plague (brought into Sussex by vagrants from Winchester – a city sorely visited) and by his insisting the afflicted families kept themselves in isolation this outbreak had been resisted. Dr Thwaite was of the opinion that cleanliness of house and person was invariably the best protection against the universal sickness.

This talk lay outside my cognisance, except for the names of those servants and gardeners closest to my lady and so, by my translation from humble guest to lordly lover, known to me too. Consequently I held my peace and stared at the burning logs. A fiery cave had grown amongst them. Add a fresh log and this blazing cavity would collapse. I didn't. Instead there was salt to hand for the walnuts. Idly I flung a good measure of it into the fire. The cave burned brilliant blue. Blue enough to change the light upon our burnished faces. Suddenly we were become shadows without eyes. I shivered, wishing I hadn't acted so childishly. Lycia's questioning glance at me seemed in this quick dullness to be almost malevolent. Then the flames turned gold again and so did we. And the brief evil I'd conjured was gone.

I got up and wished Dr Thwaite good night, thanking him for his advice. I would heed it, I said. He wished me well and rose to take his leave but Lycia begged him to stay a little longer. I kissed her hand and retired to my room.

But first I went to Lycia's study and collected the list we had been making when news came of the fire. I took it to my room to review it and complete it.

We had got as far as Nick Skeres. Who else followed? Well, first his murderer and Martin's. Who was either unknown to me or else was Master Francis or Frizer (if the earring were his), Nick's one-time friend and possible accomplice in the theft of Christofer's manuscript. I wrote down Francis-cum-Frizer with a question mark. After him I added Walsingham and Lady Audrey. Both nursed hatred of me. Either could have sent Skeres or

Francis. Either could have contradicted the other's command. If so – here was confusion – but the confusion of life, of human motives mixed beyond conspiracy into deadly mischief: a burnt-out cottage and murdered child.

Who next? George Chapman? I started to write the name only to cross it out. I still couldn't believe him to be the agent of anyone except himself. No, not George, he was too much a literary sobersides dreaming epic dreams of the day when he'd be crowned with laurel.

Having rejected George I came to Dick Baines. And on his heels, as night the day, Lord Strange and his confessor Father Ignatius who according to Dick had resented my appointment as Ferdinando's secretary. Was he the man?

As I brooded on this I realised that, without thinking, I had made two columns of my likely Ishmaels. One long, one short. The longer list descended from Eliza herself by way of Burghley, his son Robert Cecil, Heneage, Skeate and Poley down to Skeres, Francis-cum-Frizer, and Audrey Walsingham. The shorter column consisted of Dick, Strange and Father Ignatius. The last a steadfast papist. Could Dick also be of Rome? Hadn't that knockabout banquet in *Faustus* made me wonder upon that?

If this were so – and I told myself to dismiss no theory out of hand – then my two columns (formed so unwittingly) defined our age's argument. My Ishmaels made two opposing factions of an all too familiar kind. Here was the old war in little: a cohort of Eliza's loyalists on the one side and on the other a triumvirate of the Pope's adherents.

But what then? Suppose Christofer *had* changed allegiance? That surely exonerated Dick, Strange and Father Ignatius from plotting his downfall through me? I could discount them and concentrate upon the other side. Especially upon Heneage, Skeate and Poley. Since all three were dedicated executants of Eliza's policy. They most certainly would've brought a treacherous poet most cheerfully to justice and if that meant implicating and torturing his innocent friend so be it.

And yet a doubt still teased me. As with George so with the Christofer I knew. Put crudely poets have more important things to do than play at spies. Besides – Christofer's passionate doubt-ings were legion and infuriatingly even-handed. He always mocked both sides of every question. Say chalk he'd say cheese. Praise the good he'd extol the bad. Whatever was denied, he'd affirm. Bless Eliza, he'd curse her. Defy the Pope, he'd defend him. Such contradictory spirits do not make good functionaries of any cause. And therefore –

While I sat wrestling with these thoughts Lycia's maid appeared with a candle to say her ladyship awaited me in her chamber. She would light me there, she said dimpling prettily. I obeyed at once.

The next morning, as we lay in each other's arms, I told Lycia of my night thoughts. She said they supported Dr Thwaite's advice which was also hers: to root out the nearest villain and shake what truth I could out of him. And so go from him to the next until everything was known and quittance made. I agreed. Whereupon we lay in a long silence. And within it we both became aware that here was our farewell. Without another word we turned to each other and, swaddled thus in this quietus of our own creation, we slowly and stealthily caressed, cajoled, and tantalised ourselves into an ecstasy of love as frenzied as it was mute. Even at the zenith we still stifled our exclamations. Lycia's hand on my mouth, mine on hers. I kissed away her joyous tears as I slipped from her while she murmured in my ear a loving conspirator's goodbye.

·X·V·

I travelled back to London in charge of a packhorse train of thirty heavily laden mules and ponies, and six massive waggons. My duties were mostly nominal however. Lycia's London steward had come down to Sussex expressly to conduct the fruits of the harvest back to the family palace in the Strand. The huge responsibility of their safety was therefore not mine but his. Even so he deferred to me as if I were Bobby Spend-All himself not her ladyship's latest plaything. For that, I knew, was how I was regarded by her household whatever the depths of love we had sounded in ourselves.

As the miles between us increased the more I realised what Lycia had made of me. I was no longer a cripple, neither in mind nor spirit. As for my body, well, even here I felt I was pretty well myself again, albeit with one or two awkward provisos such as an uneven gait and a pair of hands like gargoyles. Even so these hands could now grasp a sword and dagger, provided the hilts were fashioned to assist their limited grip. Such weapons I possessed and expected to use: indeed I wanted to. My determination had become as fixed as the north star.

We passed the first night of our journey at Horsham, travelling on the next day by way of Redhill. Our intended halt that night was the Mitre at Coulsdon but several vexations prevented this. First one of the waggons broke an axle which to repair necessitated the unloading of its entire contents: eighteen sacks of flour, three dozen boxes of custard apples, quinces and white peaches from the glasshouses not to mention seven hogsheads of double ale. Second, no sooner was the axle made good again than the heavens opened and in less time that it takes to say the Lord's Prayer the road was turned to a bog. Nor was there enough brushwood handy to place under the waggon wheels. All six were stuck fast. There was nothing for it but to wait with patience. Mr Bunnage, the steward, politely suggested I might care to ride ahead and make myself comfortable at Coulsdon but I declared I was no fairweather friend and stayed with the column.

The rain lessened but persisted as a penetrating drizzle. Soon it became apparent that we were not going to go another yard that day. Not until the weather cleared, more brushwood was procured and the road dried out. We were bound to bivouac – as the Switzers say – where we were. This we did. Sheltering as best we could among the boxes and bales (at least we would not go short of food and drink) while a premature dusk shrouded us in drumming darkness. Bunnage ordered all the mules and pack-horses to be tethered in a ring close about us and appointed four successive pairs of servants to keep watch against marauders. A trial was made to make a fire but when the blaze was kindled we found we hadn't enough dry wood to keep it going. Jokes were made suggesting we take an axe to one of the waggons but Bunnage who could be of a jovial humour when he chose, did not smile.

The night passed in tortoise tedium but at about three in the morning a wind got up and the rain gusted before stopping entirely. Soon the pall of cloud was torn to shreds by the freshening wind and through the rents there gleamed occasional stars and a waxing moon. With this fitful lightness came shouts from our sentries. Bunnage and I jumped down from the waggon to answer their call. And came to see our two men surrounded by six others. Shouts and curses flew in the wind. Followed by an eldritch scream as one of our fellows dropped to the ground, clutching his stomach.

Without thinking I charged towards the fight, drawing my sword in anger for the first time in years. When had I last been in such a brawl? Five years before, I think, at Finsbury Butts where with Christofer I'd marked two jostling moonmen for life.

At sight of me the marauders fell back. But not far. We faced each other, eyes aglint. Bunnage joined me, sword in hand. The other sentry, too, with his cudgel. So there we stood: three against six. Except that the would-be robbers were a sad sight. But so was our companion. He lay huddled on the ground nursing the wound in his gut, crooning at himself as the blood spilled out between his fingers.

We advanced against our enemies: four wild men, two wilder women, all in rags you wouldn't dress a leper in. Their eyes flamed with penury, their meagre flesh (so pitiously taut about the bones) was blotched by sores and eye-despoiling ulcers. One half of me prayed they'd all turn tail; the other that the men at least would stand. They did. In fact all six stayed rooted to the spot, cemented together by adversity, their frail hands clutching knives, clubs, even a broken bottle. At this my better moiety wanted to cry out: 'Begone! I won't hurt you!' While my second half was eager to avenge our wounded sentry. Or so I say. But if the truth is ever to be true there was a worser thing within me: a grand desire to test my prowess with the rapier upon a weaker adversary than myself.

I chose for prey the tallest beggar with the longest knife and at once lunged forward. To my dismay, he parried neatly and came in fast, headbent, under my arm and sword. I stepped back and had just enough time (but only just) to draw my dagger and sweep his knife aside. But at least I now had two weapons to his one. I needed them. For he was far nimbler than I was. I soon discovered that my knee – Topcliffe's legacy – remained a handicap in a real fight. At practice in Sussex my fencing master had, I was rapidly realising to my cost, never put my footwork to the test, never pressed my legs beyond what hops and skips they could most easily execute. This vagabond was not so considerate. Sooner than I liked I had become first ashamed then frightened at my clumsiness. Here was I, equipped in every particular, warmly-dressed, firmly-booted, well-fed, doubly-armed, put to the extremest test by a barefoot bag of bones with only a kitchen knife between him and death. How did I suppose I might fare against a better enemy?

While I strove to defend myself Bunnage was putting two of our opponents to flight even as our other sentry belaboured the women with a brutal relish. Then, as Bunnage drew breath, the last man who'd held aloof from the affray came in at me – at my back. Now I was beset by two! I yelled forcibly for help. Bunnage, thank God, intervened at once otherwise I should've died quite ignominiously skewered from back to front and front to back. As it was he killed his man and I mine. In the nick of time. I shall not disguise the gratification I enjoyed as my rapier pierced my opponent's guts and my dagger his gullet. I felt the beggar's blood spurt upon my face. I let it dry there, telling myself I was a man again. The women fled.

We carried our stricken sentry back to the waggons and staunched his wound. Next we broached a pipkin of aqua vitae for him. And spent what remained of the night helping him to drink it. Our bravery burgeoned at every gulp. By dawn we were legends to each other.

As daylight spread I went to view the corpses. The two women had returned, and drenched in sorrow, were dragging the man I'd killed away. At my coming they stopped and stared at me. Before I could say a word, one of them began to curse me without pause: I must think myself a hero (she said) to have killed her husband and he a destitute farmer dispossessed of his tenancy a year since and sick of the smallpox too, as she was, God grant I also caught the disease in return for my cruelty to one whose only crime was hunger, was I come to claim their dead, was I covetous of a beggar's corpse, did I really think I owned what I had murdered?

Her unstopped eloquence pricked my heart. For answer since I had no words to equal hers I flung two pennies at her. She made no move to pick them up. Instead her companion darted forward. Whereat the widow set her corpse aside and fought for possession of them. In my fortified wisdom, the aqua vitae still warm in my head and blood, I was happy to watch them squabble. What revulsion I felt at their desperation. Fancy fighting over tuppence. The widow won the money for herself as I'd intended. But then she flung the coins back at me with the words: 'May my man's pox rot you, sir!' I turned away in fury – and in sudden apprehension for my health.

I was urgent to wash and change. To get away from that unhappy place. Exerting my dubious authority I announced I would, as Bunnage had originally suggested, ride ahead. Clearly he was competent to bring the caravan safely on once the road was dried out. And with that I took a satchel of fresh clothes and made off for Coulsdon. There at the Mitre I scrubbed myself fiercely, religiously, changed all my garments and breakfasted like Gargantua telling myself every devilled kidney and bacon rasher I consumed was a nostrum for my dead beggar's pox. But were they? Despite all, I was a sponge full of disquiet. Could the itch of smallpox enter through the pores of the skin? In my complacency I'd let the man's blood dry on my cheek. Had some entered at my mouth and been swallowed without my knowing it? What if to touch such a one were to contract the disease? I had put my hand to his chest when pulling my rapier free of him. I wished Dr Thwaite was there to consult. I didn't want to become like others we've all seen obliged to conceal their faces behind buckram lest we vomit at the sight of them. Nor could I paint an inch thick as Eliza does to hide her scars.

Behind these disquiets lay another: had I not killed a man no less unfortunate than I was only a few months back? Was not his misery brought about through no fault of his own? Heaped upon him first by the commonwealth (what a confounding of logic dwells in that word) and next by me – a poet of passage masquerading as a travelling gentleman?

Still disgusted with myself I decided to ride on to London. But before setting out I called for pen and paper and wrote to Lycia to assure her of my devotion and to advise her of my adventure. Once my thoughts were committed, signed and sealed, I felt better. I left the letter with the carrier, word for Bunnage with the landlord and departed.

Once past Croydon and ascending Whitehorse Lane to scale the leafy heights of Norwood I found I was again traversing those Surrey roads I'd ridden so often with Christofer in the days of our innocence when we had seen ourselves as lords of creation.

But where before these woods and pastures had been soft and green, now with the approach of winter they appeared stale and brown. Admittedly the day was overcast. Had there been a shaft of sunlight it might have brought a glow of gold and russet to the drifting leaves; a gleam of summer to the yellowed grass.

Travellers who passed said not a word in greeting. When I stopped to ask a ditcher for the right road to Herne Hill he turned away. When I got there the road was blocked. Here travellers coming out of London were required to halt to be examined for symptoms of the plague. Men, women and children stood, penned in by hurdles, waiting to be paraded before two hollow-eyed physicians. Once called for inspection they were ordered to remove their clothes lest beneath them swelled those purple blisters of the groin and armpit that herald death by pestilence. All this in public view. Those who passed the test were given a bill of health to show upon demand to any sheriff, innkeeper, constable or like person in authority throughout the county. All who failed the test were sent back the deadly way they'd come. This rule applied to whole families even if only one of their number had displayed the fatal signs. Some afflicted parents paid strangers to take their unmarked children as their own while others – it was rumoured – had bribed the overworked doctors to turn a blind eye to their condition. A shilling was quoted as the going rate. To be dropped into the money chest placed beside them – ostensibly to gather alms for the foundation of an hospital.

Meanwhile the wealthy leaving London were free to pass without examination no matter what lay hidden beneath their silks and furs. Closed coaches would pause so their embroidered occupants could peep out upon the poor coralled like cattle in furtherance of the nation's health. Judging from the tinkling laughter I heard behind brocaded curtains and velvet travelling masks many of the richer sort found the sight almost as amusing as a visit to the Bethlam Hospital.

Since I was a traveller coming to the city I was allowed through without question although I gathered from the looks exchanged by a brace of constables on duty beside the pens that I was more to be wondered at for foolhardiness than admired for courage.

One of them ventured to advise me at some length that the pest was once again worse than ever; that this week had seen a greater exodus than any yet; why, yesterday alone six hundred had died, it was said. I wouldn't recognise the place; the city was a graveyard with scarce a soul left strong enough to toll the bell. Folk no longer said 'God have mercy on us' but rather cursed Him for the ceaseless visitation and recked not the blasphemy neither. And whenever the sickness did seem to lessen, like it had last Spring if I recalled, it was only to gather more fury for yet another return like a storm going round and roundabout.

I thanked him for his warning but said I had urgent business in the city. He doubted I'd find anyone to transact it with. I replied I must discover that for myself whereupon he shook his head and wished me luck in tones which quite belied the word.

As I rode towards Southwark I encountered more and more people coming away. Whole bevies of them with all or more than they could carry upon their backs, on donkeys, ponies or in handcarts. Here was a flow of human misery such as I had never seen before. New burial pits had been dug at Newington Butts and here, holding my breath, I galloped past a line of plague carts waiting to discharge their cargoes into the trenches. The air swirled with clouds of quicklime and the sick stink of fleshly corruption. Breathe it once and you feel your lungs will never be clean again, your nose never free of that cloying smell.

I decided to change my route. I would not as I had originally intended cross over the river by the bridge. Rather I turned westward to avoid the city coming instead to the horseferry by Lambeth. At least that way I kept to windward of the city's vapours.

My welcome to Lycia's house in the Strand was warm. As warm as she had promised me it would be. Her house stood as an annexe or afterthought to her brother's palace but was hardly less commodious for that. To my eye it seemed a perfect haven of comfort and cleanliness. His lordship, I was informed, was abroad upon a mission for Eliza in Scotland (was Bobby Spend-All really to be entrusted with so hazardous an embassy to so prickly a country?) but would return shortly to take part in the Queen's

·X·V·I·

While I was breakfasting next morning Bunnage arrived with his
harvest caravan. In the hubbub of reception (so many goodly
items to be counted, weighed and stored) I was able to slip away
to Gray's Inn where I had decided my enquiry must begin. I
hoped to get news there of an acquaintance of my earlier days
who had since become a serjeant-at-law. I was directed to his inn
in Chancery Lane but he was gone to Westminster. His clerk, a
spruce old man with the bright face of a choleric cherub and a
white halo of hair, assured me he would return to his chambers
for dinner and I might wait if I pleased.

Clearly it pleased Mr Jeremy Wagstaff to have someone to
gossip to. Having announced himself at my eternal service and lit
us both a pipe he regaled me with news of the courts. Or rather
the dearth of it. His laments were profuse. Thanks to the
universal malady there were now more suits to be tried than there
were judges to hear them or serjeants to plead them. Almost all
of both sorts had retreated to the shires. The court lists were
endless while the court houses were empty. Nor could any decent
citizen be found for jury service since most people nowadays
feared to gather together in one close place. And who could blame
them? In all his years he'd known nothing like it. What would
the country come to, he wondered, with the law held thus in
suspension? When I could get a word in edgewise I suggested
that with fewer people in London to do each other mischief –
save by infection – the rule of law might with inpunity be lifted a

little? He shook his head at my frivolity, began to repudiate such a notion but then stopped in mid-sentence.

'Don't I know you?' he said, squinting his eye at me, and cocking his head to one side like a chaffinch.

'How can I say?'

'You wouldn't have been a scribe, would you, sir? At one time. I was once of Gray's Inn and seem to remember a young fellow much like you? Name of Kyd? Tom Kyd? His father, Francis – mm, name of Francis – he was a scrivener too. Over at Lincoln's Inn. You wouldn't be his lad, would you? By any chance?' And he cocked his head the other way, eyeing me again.

I wasn't sure if I was glad to be recognised or not. To delay a direct reply I said, 'We're all who we are by chance, Mr Wagstaff.' But at once I regretted my sententiousness. The stink of it hung over us like a philosopher's fart. To dispel it I admitted I was indeed Francis Kyd's son. Though I doubted he would ever own me again. 'We've had our disagreements,' I added with a would-be careless laugh which rang about as true as a tin sixpence on a fake marble floor.

Wagstaff blew out his cheeks in satisfaction. 'I thought as much, sir. Tom Kyd. Yes. I've never yet forgot a face. Though yours took its time a-coming to me. But there's a sound reason for that, I reckon.'

'What reason?'

'No. Allow me, Mr Kyd. Let my old head make its own way to market.' He tapped his temple. 'I tell you it's fuller of folk than an egg of meat. The older I get the more faces I remember and names to go with 'em I recall. I don't know why. Most would be better forgot. At this rate I'll soon qualify as Clerk of Chambers to the Recording Angel.' He laughed agreeably with himself.

'I'm sure you'd acquit yourself admirably in that responsible position, Mr Wagstaff.'

'Maybe, sir. Maybe. But am I right in saying I heard you went to serve a great lord and became a famous poet?'

'I wouldn't say famous. My plays were always better known than I was.'

He nodded, grunted, patted his paunch as if digesting the

wisdom of my bitterness. 'Well, that's the way of it, Mr Kyd. For every known poet there's always a compost of others – like fallen leaves.'

An elegiac caesura slid between us to make a silver silence.

I said, 'I daresay you're a bit of a poet yourself on the quiet, Mr Wagstaff?'

He shook his head but a moistness in his left eye contradicted him. 'No, sir, no. I know my place. And it's nowhere near Parnassus. Time was I tried my hand but the girl died and after her no verses came, bidden or unbidden.' He wiped his eye with a crimson handkerchief.

After a suitable moment pondering the transient way of the world, I said, 'What else have you heard about me, Mr Wagstaff?' And despite myself I felt my gut tighten as I waited for his answer so much did I need yet fear it. For here, I reckoned, was the town's knowledge and opinion of me held upon deposit; here was my broken reputation, inscribed upon tablets, and stored within Wagstaff's wide-awake old brain.

Small wonder he hesitated. 'Well, Mr Kyd. I've heard several things. And to deal straight with you – not all to your credit, I'm sorry to say.'

I drew breath, expelled it. 'Go on. It's better to know the truth than not.'

'So they say, so they say.'

'Well?'

'Well, sir – it's said – but not by me, mind – it's said you were a friend of papist spies. And of one in special. A poet much like yourself, sir. A theatre man. By the name of Marlowe. A quarrelsome young rascal who got himself killed in a drabhouse down at Tilbury some six months back.'

What a two-faced hobgoblin gossip is! So much here was as false as it was true. 'Is that all you've heard?'

'No. There's more yet.'

'What?'

'That you were arrested for penning libels against the Huguen-ots come over from France and settled here. But before you could be brought to trial for inciting public riot, sir, you dropped stone dead of the plague in Newgate. And that, begging your pardon, Mr Kyd, is why it took me so long to put a name to you. You being, as I thought, as rotted in your grave as a walnut in pickle.'

I smiled at his melancholy simile while wondering how to comb out the truth from such a tangled fleece.

'Would you accept from me, Mr Wagstaff, that not everything you've heard is necessarily true?'

'Of course I would, my boy. Of course. Haven't I been told you were dead and yet here you are before me? Large as life and twice as natural?' And he nudged at my knee with his pipe-stem to show he meant no offence.

I took none. Instead I explained the truth as I knew it while omitting any mention of Chelsea. I pointed out in particular that, yes, Christofer had been my friend but no, he'd never been so far as I knew a Roman spy. Nor was he overly quarrelsome. On two occasions when he'd been caught up in brawls he'd been, to my certain knowledge, the innocent party. Words could run away with him, I agreed, but that was all. And he'd died at Deptford not Tilbury. And in a house of good not ill repute. What was worse, I said, was that it was more than likely he was killed deliberately. As a matter of policy. Oh, and I'd been imprisoned in the Clink not at Newgate from where I'd been rescued by a great and noble lady whose identity I was not at liberty to divulge.

'I guessed there might be more to it than meets the eye, Mr Kyd. We live in a wicked world. Why in the very month you speak of – last May again – a young fellow in Lincoln's Inn was arrested for harbouring a priest of the old persuasion. The priest – by the name of Harrington, William Harrington, denies the charge but his friend, name of Donne, Henry Donne, faced with the rack, betrayed him. Declared Harrington had said mass and heard confessions in his chamber. Even blown a trumpet out of the window as a secret signal to summon those young gentlemen as wanted to be shriven.'

Wagstaff laughed. I smiled as best I could which wasn't much since the parallels with my recent past ran too close for comfort. I said I could well believe his story. It was only too dreadfully true of these dreadful times.

'Young Donne's died since in Newgate.'

'Of the plague?'

'Mm. What else holds fashion, sir? You were luckier in the Clink from the sound of it.'

'I didn't think so at the time, believe me. But maybe. And Harrington? What's happened to him?'

'He's awaiting trial. But I doubt it'll be heard until next year. As I say the lists are long.'

'What sort of man is he?'

'A Yorkshire Jesuit, Mr Kyd. Some say they're the worst, worse even than your Lancashire sort. Educated abroad of course. In France. At Rheims, I heard. If you ask me he'll refuse trial by jury when it comes to it. Most of 'em do – so their blood won't be on too many of their persecutors' heads. Considerate fellows really – your Roman martyrs.'

'Do I detect in you a certain sympathy for the old faith, Mr Wagstaff?'

He grinned – a pert chorister's grin. Suddenly I could see him singing as a boy in Lord Wolsey's time. 'I always say a Christian's a Christian, Mr Kyd, whether in Canterbury or Rome. And that's a sight more than can be said of your Jew or heathen, God blast 'em all.'

The bounds of Mr Wagstaff's Christian tolerance being thus beaten and proclaimed I said, 'In the catalogue of your memory do you hold any cognisance of a man called Ingram Frizer?'

Was it my imagination or did the air grow thicker, stiller? The old man frowned – that I do know. But whether to concentrate the better upon this unusual name or to condemn it I cannot say because we were interrupted by a bellow from outside. A shout of 'Jeremy, you old tosser, what's for din-dins?' blasted us like a broadside from a well-cannoned Spanish galliass.

This explosion heralded the entrance of my old acquaintance Charles Rigby. If I had changed so had he. It took us twenty seconds at least to recognise each other. Which was hardly surprising since he saw before him a well-dressed cripple whom he'd thought dead while to my eyes he'd become what I've just compared him with: a heavily charged warship in human form, propelled by oar and sail, beef and wind. Thus opposed we sized each other up alert for combat until we'd read each other's colours and found ourselves old friends upon Time's swelling sea.

'Tom! You sly bastard!' As ever as the world had been born on the wrong side of Charles's cheerful estimation.

'Charles, my old cocker!' Like me Charles had been born within the sound of Bow Bells.

We embraced powerfully; our reunion presided over, clucked over, by the ever-indulgent Jeremy. Charles forgave the old man the lack of any dinner prepared and bore me off to the buttery bar where we absorbed three dozen choice Whitstable oysters the size of tennis balls spiced with chopped shallots in red vinegar, mopped round with hot bread and chased down with a gallon of double ale. Only after that, belching where we stood, did I digress from our mutual reminiscences into the true purpose of my visit.

I said (choosing my words) 'My dear Charles, I'm sure you've gleaned something of my situation – and I don't doubt you've heard even more upon your own account during my enforced absence from London – your clerk most certainly has but be that as it may – and if I repeat myself you have only yourself to blame for feasting me so handsomely – but my point is I need your help.'

'You have it. What?'

'I'm in search of someone called Ingram Frizer. Have you ever heard of such a man?'

'Frizer? No. Can't say I have. Unusual name, though.'

'I believe he's a murderer. He killed the friend I spoke of at dinner.'

'Deliberately?'

'The inquest said in self-defence.'

'But you doubt that?'

'Yes. I do.'

'Was Frizer brought to trial? He should've been. For man-slaughter. Mind you nowadays – well, such niceties aren't always observed, are they?'

'In this case they were.'

'Oh? Really? Eliza Regina playing it straight for once? You astonish me.'

'Only to bend the law the better.'

'How?'

'By granting Frizer a pardon. Here. In Chancery.'

Charles laughed. 'Oh, dear. Oh, dear. And from this puddle of horsepiss you deduce what? That Frizer works for Her Majesty? Perchance?'

I grinned, nodded. 'What do you think, Charles?'

'I'd say there was a certain logic to your thinking, Tom, yes, mm, yes.'

'Good. I'm glad you agree.'

'Any idea how Frizer ranks in the Queen's service?'

'None. But my guess is not very highly.'

'Reliable workhorse? Deserving and getting protection from his superiors? At least when it suits them?'

'I think so.'

'Quite. You wouldn't know the date he was tried, would you?'

'It was last June. The twenty-eighth, I was told.'

'Excellent!' He clapped me on the back. 'That's all we need to know! Alpha and omega! Off we trot! Records will have the rest so let's go along, shall we?'

Charles took me by the arm and marched me out of the buttery. A few doors to our left down Chancery Lane stood a building designed to impress: three spreading storeys of reguarly tarred timbers, wide jetted windows and plaster as white as any laundered linen. Here were kept the rolls, patents, grants and records of the great court of Chancery; here were England's doings written out on lambskin. Didn't I know? My script had sometimes found its place here.

As we approached the jutting entrance two severely dressed men who might have been lawyers, if not well-heeled puritans, bustled out. The one I didn't know but the other I did. Robert Poley.

Thanks be to God he didn't even glance in my direction so engrossed was he in the jovial converse of his companion. The two of them hurried away from us, down the lane, on a rolling wave of laughter. Seeing and hearing them I had such an apprehension of a world of rottenness I wanted to be quit of it. That man going away from me so cheerfully had watched my Christofer die! That man had seen me hang on Top's pillar day after day! And shown no pity! How could such a cormorant wax so sleek?

'Are you all right, Tom?'

I'd stopped in my tracks. Small wonder Charles had queried what had struck me. I drew breath, pretended I was indeed all right. 'Yes, yes. I'm sorry. I thought I saw someone I knew.'

'But you didn't?'

'No.' I don't think I've ever told a truer lie. What did I know of Poley? What can anyone save Satan know of such men as he?

'In we go,' said Charles, ushering me up the steps.

Charles made our requirements known to the counter clerk who instructed another to accompany us up to the third floor. The building smelt like an old, forsaken wasps' nest: dusty, nose-ticklingly dry. But it was far from empty. Every room we passed, and each landing, was either lined with shelving or entirely filled by book-stacks reared up from floor to ceiling. The aisles between were narrow, allowing just enough room for the more sinuous sort of lawyer – before success has gone to his stomach. Curiously the higher we climbed the more I felt I wasn't above ground at all. Rather this was a catacomb. Laid to rest upon these ordered shelves were the mortified remains of a million arguments, passionate pleadings, remorseless judgments. Some were bound books, others enclosed in boxes, yet more enrolled in parchment and tied with ribbon that had once been red but now was pale as time itself.

It soon became apparent that each stack concerned itself with the cases heard in a particular court. However by dint of much squeezing along the aisles (Charles suffered considerably) we came at last to the correct stack and to the place where the rolls recording the cases heard in Chancery upon the twenty-eighth of June in this year of disgrace were to be found. Except they weren't. The place was empty. Not one roll for that day remained. All had gone. Our clerk expressed himself amazed and agitated. This was highly unusual, not to say quite contrary to the rules of the house which were absolute. No documents could be removed. Not upon any account. By anyone. They could only be perused in the presence of a clerk whose duty was to ensure that all such rolls, parchments or files were returned to their exact positions in the stacks. He must report this at once and would we kindly accompany him downstairs since it was also a rule that no person might be left unsupervised among the rolls.

We followed him down. And waited while the counter clerk left his post to investigate the loss. When he returned he knew no more than we did. He apologised to Charles and assured him he would immediately report the disappearance of the rolls to the Lord Chancellor's office. He hoped we'd not been too inconvenienced although clearly we had and that in all his ten years of service he had never known such a thing. He saw us to the door, sweating profusely, afraid for his future.

Out in the street again Charles asked me if I had any further thoughts to impart to him? I had but I didn't voice them. Instead I said it was a pity we had no way of knowing when the roll had been taken, let alone by whom. It was odd, too, because Frizer's trial and pardon had been intended, I assumed, to put a fair face on an ugly crime. And as such Eliza would surely wish it to remain firmly in place, on public record? Machiavelli's pupils did not care for their expensive falsehoods going astray, did they?

Charles agreed and assured me he would make what enquiries he could.

As we walked along I said, half-laughing, 'Come to think of it I'm the person who should have taken that document. I can't think of anyone else who would benefit from reading it.'

'Unless there's someone who wishes you *not* to see it?'

'I'd forgotten I was talking to a lawyer.'

'In which case it may not have been stolen at all. Merely deliberately mislaid. Put on another shelf or in some other pigeon hole.'

I thought of Robert Poley. Had he feared I might call to look through the court records? Could he have heard that I'd left Sussex? If so, from whom? A servant in Lycia's household?

Perhaps. But such an informer would not, could not know of my intentions. They were a secret between myself and Lycia.

I said, 'I expect the record clerks are frantically searching even now.'

'I'm sure. Their livelihoods are at stake. But, Tom, you still haven't told me what you really hoped to find in the trial transcript.'

'Oh, many things. Not least a description of how Christofer died. Also – what a man called Nick Skeres had to say for himself. He was present. As was a senior intelligencer by the name of Poley. Were any others there? But most of all I wanted information about Frizer. His usual abode. The name of his protector if he has one other than Poley, that is. I think he may have. Anything that can bring me to him.'

'You intend to avenge your friend's death?'

'Most decidedly.'

'You'll challenge this man Frizer to a duel?'

'If necessary. But it isn't only satisfaction for Christofer that I want. Oh, no. I want names, too. The names of those above Frizer who conspired against him and me.'

'I see. You hope to force them out of him?'

'I do, Charles. And I shall.'

'Well, I wish you luck. But if he's what you think he is – a hired assassin – might he not prove, well, rather more agile than yourself? After all, it's plain you've suffered certain injuries, Tom. To see you bring an oyster to your mouth is to marvel at the triumph of gluttony over dexterity.'

We laughed. I earnestly demonstrated my rapier's ingenious grip – making a few passes in the air. He nodded admiringly but I could tell he was unconvinced. And I, remembering my awkward victory over that less than sturdy beggar on the road to Coulsdon, I was obliged to admit I would need not only old Mother Fortune on my side but Providence as well.

We'd reached Charles's inn. I declined his invitation to come up for more refreshment. My head had cleared and I had no inclination to cloud it again with beer or wine. Knowing Charles either or both would flow uninterruptedly till supper and beyond.

I doubted we would part before we heard St Clement's clock chime midnight. I thanked him and he promised to keep me informed if he heard anything pertinent to my quest: as well he might within the whispering corridors or gossipy backstairs of the Inns of Court.

As I made my way towards the Strand an instinctive itch at my back convinced me I was followed. Although the streets were nothing like as busy as they should've been there was still enough human traffic (almost all with mouths and noses muffled so the people passing seemed more like shifting Saracens than brass-faced Cockneys) to enable a practised villain to dog my steps as if upon a proper errand. I stopped several times, turning sharply, hoping to give my apprehension an identity. But whoever it was eluded my eye either by crossing the street or turning down an alley. I went on, indignation kindling inside me. Eventually it burst into flame and I stopped and turned again. This time I was sure I saw someone dart into Temple archway. I made after him but by the time I'd got there and hopped down the path to the church there was no one to be seen. Had my quarry hidden in the church itself? I went in. But found only an encircling gloom and the granite memorials of crusading knights as dead as the world of honour they had fought for.

The sudden exercise had incited my beer-swollen bladder to bursting point. I hurried out of the church in real fear I might defile it and was obliged to relieve myself precipitately into an open drain beside the porch. Old soldiers say a man is never so vulnerable as when he's at easement so it's hardly surprising I was startled into drenching my boots when someone tapped me on the shoulder. Was this my Ishmael or some pious usher or busybody porter come to remonstrate with me? But no, it was none of these. It was Jeremy Wagstaff. Red-faced. Puffed. And at my service.

'Have you been following me?' I demanded.

'No, sir. I saw you from across the street. Saw you dash in at the arch here. You looked in a fierce hurry, Mr Kyd. So I came after.'

'I had a sense of someone dogging me – keeping just out of

sight. I tried turning about several times but couldn't spot him. Then I thought I saw him dodge in here.'

'Well, that wasn't me, sir. I've only just come down the lane. So either you were mistaken to else the villain knew his business.'

'I fear it was the latter, Jeremy.'

'Mr Charles sent me after you, sir.'

'Did he indeed?' I said, fully relieved at last in every sense and tying my points. 'Why?'

'On account of my saying I knew something of that man you were asking about, sir, before he came in.'

'Frizer?'

'Yes. I kept thinking while you were at dinner. And just as I was about to give up it came back to me. As is often the way of it. There was a gentleman of that name – well, I say he was a gentleman but I don't know for sure, gentlemen are six a penny these days – anyway I heard there was such a one, name of Frizer, served Mr Secretary Walsingham – him as was the Queen's spymaster.'

'Served in what capacity, Jeremy?'

'I couldn't say, sir. No more than I can recall who told me. I reckon the knowledge just came out of the air at me. But I'm pretty sure I heard tell that when old Sir Francis died three years back Frizer was passed on, inherited if you like, by young Thomas Walsingham. Who made him his chamberman.'

I stood riven by sky bolts. I was a tree put to heaven's torch. I blazed from head to foot. I said, 'So Francis *does* equal Frizer??'

Understandably Jeremy didn't understand. How could he? I'd told him nothing of Scadbury, nothing of Nick Skeres, let alone of Master Francis, Corin's pet satyr, insolent runner, killer shark.

And now, now it would seem – no, not seemed, it was, it was, it was! – yes, it was confirmed. Frizer who was Francis was my lover's murderer. He'd killed Christoferus and gone free. But left his earring on Chancton Down. Surely? Surely? Ripped from his ear by Nick Skeres. In which case . . .

So many thoughts battered me I could hardly speak. But as best I could I gabbled my thanks at Jeremy telling him, my words falling over each other like a litter of piglets, that his information had opened a dozen doors in my past, in my present and doubtless in my immediate future, too. I was eternally grateful to him.

I pressed a shilling into his hand (the good old boy protested it was too much) and begged him to depart at once. I was a marked man, I said. Why even my shadow might be watching us. A shadow with a torn ear, perhaps?'

Jeremy puffed away. I was glad to see him go. If Frizer had shown no mercy to Mary's nephew I doubted he would hesitate to destroy an equally harmless Jeremy Wagstaff.

Once the old man was safely gone I resumed my way towards the Strand. This time I made sure I had no shadow. I stopped countless times, took three false turnings, doubled back twice and, apart from almost challenging a muffled-up baker's boy, arrived back at Lycia's apartments without incident or hurt. From this I could only assume that whoever had followed me had either relinquished his pursuit for reasons of his own or else I had been mistaken from the start. Neither explanation was of particular satisfaction or comfort to me.

To calm my mind I wrote to Lycia, telling her of my day's adventures and my thoughts surrounding old Jeremy's revelation. If what he'd said was true (and for me it had the clear ring of unalloyed truth) then I had surely found, I wrote, my Ishmael?

Frizer and Skeres had indeed been instructed by Heneage to keep watch over our Springtime foolery. At Deptford Frizer had murdered Christofer in Skeres' presence. Not to mention Robert Poley's. All that was certain now even if I hadn't seen the roll. Frizer for reasons as yet unknown to us had killed his state accomplice on Chancton Down but his victim had resisted and torn the telltale earring from its anchorage. The initials scratched inside it confirmed Wagstaff's report and also suggested *I.F.* and *T.W.* were not merely master and servant but loving friends. In which case Frizer must have surely relished murdering his rival in Walsingham's affections? I could imagine, I wrote, the malignant pleasure Frizer would have taken in killing Christofer.

At this point I broke off from my letter. Hadn't Charles doubted my fitness to challenge a professional assassin? And hadn't I shared his doubt? And that before I knew for certain who Frizer really was? When he was still little more than an unusual name; had not yet been proved to be that preening monster, Master Francis. How could I hope to challenge him and live? Frizer-cum-Francis-cum-Ishmael was no half-starved beggar. And yet I was bound by every oath I'd ever made to myself and Lycia to take revenge upon him. For myself and Christofer.

What was more, and worse, Frizer must be the key to the whole conspiracy against us. Only he could tell me who had ordered our destruction. But was I the man to force that intelligence from him? At the level of brute strength, no, but at the level of true justice, yes. Did I hear Lucifer laughing? What more happy sight can there be for the prince of Hell than that of right outfaced by might?

It had grown late. I decided I would examine this new dilemma in the light of morning, told Lycia as much, and concluded by saying that ink and paper were poor substitutes for her, her kisses, her eyes, her voice, her touch, her everything. I wished her good night, sweet lady, good night, good night, she was my Bel-imperia come true. With that I sealed my letter and went to bed.

·X·V·I·I·

The next morning I found my mind made up. Viz: what couldn't be cured had to be endured. I should not, would not, allow myself to be deflected from my purpose because my enemy had turned out to be my physical superior. I must allow justice the chance to supply whatever I needed beyond my own strength when the moment came. That was my fate. And to meet it I must find Frizer. And the surest way to find him was to let him find me. I would take to the streets so he, or his accomplices, might follow me if they chose. I felt sure my shadow of yesterday would prove more substantial today. Whoever he was I must take my chance and make myself his target.

Braced by this decision I put on the same clothes as I'd worn the day before (blood red velvet slashed with black set off by fresh linen) and, muffling my mouth against the pest, set out eastwards for the city.

I was aiming for my old lodgings upon the assumption that they would almost certainly be watched. I went straight down Fleet Street, passed through Temple Bar and came to Ludgate where I stopped for a moment to become a watcher myself outside Christofer's old apartment which stood beside the Apothecaries's Hall. The place was shuttered. The hall, too. As if our chemists had given up any hope of remedying the plague and fled the town. As well they might since almost every house on every side was boarded up and daubed with fresh red crosses. No one appeared to dwell here save a well-fed rat as big as any cat and three scrawny dogs noisily disputing tenure of a heap of garbage, glistening with putrefaction. The stench was profound. Upon the hill above me Paul's bell tolled in the leaden air.

I hurried away, glad to be back on the main thoroughfare of Ludgate Hill. So far no one appeared to have taken the slightest interest in me. I detected no footfall behind me persisting any longer than was congruent with business other than me or mine. I came to St Paul's and went through the west door.

There wasn't a soul within. No men of business or pleasure, no scribes ready to write you anything, no girls for hire or boys of the game, not even a deacon soliciting alms to repair the roof. The only person I encountered was a muslin-turbaned meat-porter hurrying through the transept with the roseate carcass of a calf upon his back.

Void of the usual play of people St Paul's could be seen for what it had become: a pale, protesting ghost of its former gaudy self. All the glory I had known as a boy, the glimmer of gilt and candlelight was gone, the painted glass was broken, the walls whitewashed, the chapels mere kennels. Never had the nave looked so long.

I hurried out by way of the north door, glad to be gone from such a dismal house that seemed neither of God nor Man. In West Cheap my spirits revived a little. Here was life of a sort. Some stalls and shops were open and at Poultry the cages were full of laying hens – it now being fervently thought that a diet of eggs was a sure guard against the sickness.

As I turned into Bucklersbury I looked back. Still no one followed me. I felt aggrieved. Here was I determined to bring my condition to a crisis and my enemies refused the challenge! How dared they? But now, surely, here, back at my old haunts, someone would be waiting? I drew breath, flexed my arms and shoulders and swaggered as boldly as I might down the lane, passing the shut door of the Green Man (rather a surprise, that) and turned into the stairwell that led up to my lodgings.

And at once faced sharply about in the entrance to confront anyone who might, even then, be crossing from Walbrook to accost me. But still there was no one. All was deserted. Any life that had returned here in May had since departed yet again. Once more grass and weeds grew between the cobbles. I saw darnels, thistles, mildewed Michaelmas daisies. If Ludgate had been a rubbish tip, St Paul's a morgue, Walbrook was a rank neglected garden.

I climbed the shadowed stairs to my old lodgings from which I'd been so abruptly wrenched six months before. The door was boarded up. Great clouts nailed five oak planks to the doorposts. Short of a crowbar there was no way to prise them loose. I went down again and banged upon the main door of the Green Man. After five minutes repeated knocking I got an answer. A woman's voice, sharp with distrust, asked who was there? I recognised it as Meg's, the landlord's wife.

I said, 'It's Tom, Meg. Tom Kyd.'

'For Chrissake,' came the Cockney answer. 'Where've you sprung from, mate? We thought you was dead.'

'So did I, Meg. But I'm not. So open up, will you?' The spy panel in the door slid back and Meg's dark eyes squinted out at me like spikes. 'You don't look nothin' like Tom Kyd, mister. And I should know.'

'I promise I do, Meg. Look.' And I loosened my scarf to reveal my full face.

Meg laughed cracklingly as she recognised me. 'Jesus God, look at your clothes! Who've you come as? Lord 'Orsemanure? Where'd you get all that gear?'

'Just open up, love, and I'll tell you.'

Bolts squealed and Meg let me in. I made to embrace her but she was too bent on bolting the door again. When she straightened up I was shocked by what I saw. Poor Meg looked starved and peaky beyond belief. What had become of the bold landlady whose rough wit kept the beer and laughter flowing? As for the house itself, it was stale, dull. It looked more like a puritan prayer hall than a decent city boozer.

'What happened, Meg?' I said, gazing about me at the benches upturned on every table, the beer taps shrouded with napkins, the lute gathering dust on the wall, the hatch to the kitchen closed and curtained with a spider's web.

'Jack died,' she said.

I was grieved to hear it. Jack had been a good landlord to me both as tenant and regular.

'What of?' I said, thinking I knew the answer.

'Of a quinsy, would you believe it? His throat swelled right up so he choked. An' that was it. He was gone. So quick. It was 'orrible. I tried to carry on but I couldn't get no help and besides nobody came no more on account of you know what, right?' She meant the plague which, superstitiously, was seldom referred to by that name anymore.

'What've you been living on?'

'Air. Bad air.'

'When did he die?'

'Last August. The seventeenth.'

'Was it him boarded up my lodgings?' Talking to Meg I was become a cockney again.

'Oh, yeah. Like when he heard you'd got took he got Jimmy the joiner to come an' nail it up. He said it was the least we could do. He always said you'd come back, Tom.'

'And I have.'

'Yeah.' Her voice was flat. Flat as a pancake left over from Shrovetide.

'Not much of a welcome, Meg.'

'No. It's like that these days.'

'Anyway it's good to see you again.'

'Is it?'

'Yes.'

But she hadn't really heard me. Instead she was listening to booted footsteps outside. I listened too. Once they were gone she said, 'You wasn't followed here, was you?'

'No. Why do you ask?'

'Just wondered.' But her anxious eyes and edgy tone belied her casual answer.

'No, Meg. Why?'

She was reluctant to speak. I repeated the question. Still she didn't answer. Her eyes evaded mine.

I said, 'What made you say that? Has someone been asking for me?'

She winced then nodded. 'Yeah. Day before yesterday.'

'Who?'

'Two fellows. Couple of bastards if you ask me. Jesus.'

'Did you know them?'

'I knew one all right. Not the other. No.'

'Who was he? The one you knew?'

'Charley Cockatrice.'

Meg described a notorious knife man who had for years terrorised the shopkeepers and stallholders from Grasschurch Street to the South gate of the bridge where his manor yielded to Dolly Delilah – the suburb madam. Cockatrice and his mates specialised in what was traditionally but euphemistically called 'trader insurance' or even 'property protection'. In other words if you wished to continue in business you were obliged to pay the Cockatrice a weekly sum or else find your shop or stall broken open or set on fire or you and your family marked for life by his knife. Charley's stripes were to be seen on many beggars' faces in the city. Needless to say he was honoured as a Cockney character. Gallants would come from Westminster to sup with him at his favourite hostelry – the Three Kings in East Cheap.

'How did the other man strike you?'

'Dunno really. 'Cept I did hear Charley call him *sir*.'

'What did he look like?'

'He kept his face covered. With a yellow scarf. He was well dressed. Like you.'

'Was he tall, medium, small?'

'Medium.'

'Fat, thin?'

'Neither. Stocky. But big with it. Heavy.'

'What did he sound like?'

'He didn't say much.'

'Londoner, was he?'

'Could be. He spoke, you know, like you actors do. With all of his mouth. As if everybody else was half deaf.'

I had to laugh. 'You mean he pronounced his words properly?'

'Yeah, like he was at Whitehall or somewhere.'

'Anyway what did you tell them?'

'That I reckoned you was dead. And that was when this other man said no, you wasn't.'

'Anything else?'

'No. 'Cept Charley said I was to tell him if I saw you. 'Specially if you came here. I've got to leave word at the Three Kings, Tom. Else he'll cut me, he says.'

She was panting with fear. I patted her shoulder, put my arm about her to comfort her as best I could.

'Don't worry, Meg,' I said. 'You'll be safe. You can tell them I've been here.'

'I can? You really mean that?'

'Yes. And you can also tell Charley Cockatrice if he so much as lays a finger on you I'll make sure he's hanged for it.' And without naming Lycia I told Meg of my preferment in a great lady's eyes.

'So you don't aim to live here no more?'

'No.'

'Pity. I could do with a protector.'

I kissed her cheek commiserately. Poor Meg. Then I gave her two shillings and told her to start eating properly again but meanwhile I had to go. She clung to me, begging me to stay, began to recall the old days, whined, cajoled, seized my hand to kiss it, then swore when I withdrew it but clipped me to her once more, saying, 'Stay, Tom, stay, I need a good fellow like you. And I won't tell Charley, honest.'

But when I refused again, she cursed me swearing she would betray me to the whole wide world after all. 'You wait, Tom Kyd, you wait! I'll tell the Cockatrice to get you, God blind me if I don't!'

How soon this world sours. A word can change it. A thought undo it. A kiss mend or mar it.

I decided to return to the Strand by water. I had made myself enough of a target for one morning. Especially as I had no doubt Meg would honour her word at once. She could be almost at East Cheap already.

I took a boat from Queen Hithe to Surrey Lane Steps shutting my ears to the predictable fancies of the waterman who had heard on good authority from a high-up gentleman who had sat just where I was sitting only yesterday that the Queen had been dead this twelvemonth but none had dared break the news to the public for fear of rebellion, innovation and riot. Indeed, what they'd done – would I believe it? – was preserve her sitting bolt upright in her chair looking for all the world as if she was still alive and they'd put a speaking tube right up her – oh, yes – right through her body to her mouth from arse to gob, sir, if I would pardon the expression, in order that a specially trained midget could be hidden under her jewelled skirt and by speaking up the tube – made of purest silver – answer for her. Her eyes were glass naturally, but so cleverly ensconced in their sockets and moistened with oil of rosemary that they seemed to move. This way all the world was deceived, the state preserved and the Pope defied. Dead cunning, wasn't it? Didn't I agree?

We reached Surrey Lane before he could relate in detail the process of evisceration and boning that had been required prior to packing the royal skin full of molten wax mixed with sawdust. For this I was thankful but as he sculled us into a placket (as a free slot between boats is vulgarly known among watermen) and I turned to step ashore I felt the air bristle. Just as I had at Chancton Ring. Behind me my garrulous rowman groaned. I looked back. His oars were abandoned. He was clutching his upper arm – the left one. His face was angry with pain. Between his thumb and fingers the vellum flight of a crossbow bolt protruded. And now he was swearing more violently than Meg.

I stepped to him and hurried him by his good arm, the boat rocking, to the steps where he slumped down, gasping for breath and issuing yet more curses. Already other watermen were coming to us while several more had rushed up the steps and were gone with a great hue and cry.

We comforted our man as best we could while a barber-surgeon was sent for. The bolt had gone clean through the muscle. Its steel barb was out the other side. Someone provided aqua vitae. The waterman swallowed it from the bottle, opening his throat to it as if it were mild ale not fiery spirit. As he finished he grinned and smacked his lips and devoutly wished whoever had shot him to damnation.

Just as his eyes turned to me and he was about to enquire if I knew anything pertinent to his misfortune there came a great yelling and three of his fellows returned with a crossbow held triumphantly aloft. They were dragging a man after them by the heels, so that his head banged on every step as they descended. Here was the villain, they announced. Look at the bastard. Did we know him? I peered eagerly at their prisoner. Was this my Ishmael? His face was bruised and one eye almost closed. But this was no Ingram Frizer. For a start he was weasel-thin. To continue he was bald as a coot and meanly dressed. And to conclude his ears were each entire, neither torn nor even scarred. A cut-throat he might be but not of Nicholas Skeres – of that I was certain.

I asked his name. For answer he laughed in my face. One of the watermen booted him in the ribs and advised him to speak more respectfully. He laughed again but this time kept his mouth wide open, hell's orifice agape, pointing into it with his forefinger, urgently inviting me to inspect him more closely. I did. He had no tongue. Or rather he possessed the stump of one like a docked mastiff's tail. Most had been removed long since. He could laugh, he could emit whole torrents of grunts and mewings, he could cough and belch, gesticulate and mime – but he could not speak.

I straightened up to see the barber and his apprentice arriving with two constables. One of these at once identified our prisoner as a certain Henry Cato, a sometime thief turned hired marksman who five years back had ill-advisedly informed against his then employer – an Italian known as Don Donato. Donato bought himself out of Newgate within an hour of being committed there and took his revenge upon Cato before noon. To trim the tongue of an informer or *grass* is a common practice in that brotherhood. A *grass* is so named, it is said, after the feathery heads of meadow grass that scatter their seed as the breeze blows; a pleasing, country figure for a cowardly, back-alley traitor. But who am I to talk?

While the barber attended the wounded waterman the two constables commanded a boat to take them and Cato down to Bridewell. At once a dozen boatmen offered their services gratis and the next moment Cato was forcibly embarked upon the ebbing tide. Meantime the barber had clipped the flight of the bolt with his scissors down to the shaft, allowed my oarsman another almighty draught of aqua vitae and, even as he drank it down, pulled the bolt by the barb clean out of his arm and clapped a bandage all round the flexive muscle. Only then, some five seconds after the operation, did the patient cry out – such was the barber's dexterity. I paid his fee and also left money for the waterman's recovery. I learned later the wound healed without putrefaction and my waterman was honoured with an oarsman's place upon the royal barge when Eliza proceeded to Windsor to preside at her Tilts upon Accession Day. Since when I dare suppose he's even now distressing the ears of his latest passenger with his conviction that he conveyed a stuffed yet speaking dummy from Whitehall to Windsor.

For the remainder of that, my second day in London I rested within doors reflecting on my misadventures.

Had the Cockatrice sent Cato? I doubted it. Meg could not have got to the Three Kings in time for him to hire Cato and have him in position at Surrey Lane before I got there. The distance was too far. Therefore Cato had acted for another. Who? Always the same question. Who?

Should I risk another foray? Chance my life a third time in the city? There were several places I had planned to visit – not least Whitefriars to gather news of Lord Strange and Dick Baines. Also Walsingham's house in Sidon Lane beside the Tower where I intended to discover Lady Audrey's whereabouts. I was certain she had much to answer for. I'd become more and more convinced she must have persuaded Nick Skeres by money or love or both to hunt me down in Sussex. And at the heels of that assumption came that other nagging question: had she done this with or without Walsingham's knowledge? I could not exonerate Audrey. She was rightly included in my catalogue of persecutors with cause, real or imagined, to harm me. Her secret taste for violence against herself coupled with her public delight in teasing her admirers beyond the limits of a fair lady's permitted cruelty weighed more in my remembrance than her later declared contrition. Like Meg tawdry Audrey's kindness could curdle in the instant.

Both Whitefriars and Sidon Lane were well within the Cockatrice's reach never mind who else might be instructed to shadow and destroy me. I therefore decided for the moment to take myself off to a third place of enquiry I proposed to visit: Deptford. I would go early the next morning in a covered boat sculled by two watermen not one. If this sounds like a craven stratagem it was and I make no apology for it with so many enemies ranged against me. After Cato discretion was become the better part of valour as the old proverb has it.

With this intent resolved I sat down to write to Lycia. I related all I've set down here only adding that I hoped to dream of her that night.

Instead I dreamed of Christofer. And I dreamed him dead. I had woken from sleep in our bed in Bucklersbury. Moonlight from the window shone on his sleeping face. He lay on his back. There were pennies on his eyes. He was dead. I shook him telling him not to be dead. I took the penny from his left eye, then from his right . . .

And woke screaming. Was sat bolt upright. The dream horror remained before me. I could see his face still, it refused to fade, the right eyesocket was a well of blood. No eye was there at all. Quite gone.

I jumped from bed, shuddering violently. I walked the room trying to quell my heart, measure my breath, asking myself where had this dream come from? Because now I thought of it I had never before asked myself how Christofer had died. Oh, I had assumed from a sword or dagger's thrust but never (such was my guilt) pictured to myself the manner of his murder. I'd disbelieved the inquest's story of a quarrel but refused to ask what method Frizer had employed to deprive my Christofer of breath. Was this true? Had I been informed by a dream? Then, with a shudder, I remembered Francis dispatching the monkfish. Hadn't he said the kindest cut was through the eye?

·X·V·I·I·I·

I was dressed and willing the dawn to arrive. It ignored my wishes, refusing to break for hours and when at last it came it brought with it coal-black clouds and spitting rain.

I approached the river steps with caution lest someone was keeping watch but if anyone was, he remained as circumspect as me. I took a boat for Deptford. The tarpaulin hood proved a blessing (quite apart from hiding me from surveillance) since the squalls of rain had turned to a solid downpour. The easterly wind had dropped and the waves it had whipped up no longer ran against the tide. The rain fell vertically out of the sky while the Thames was become a rain-pocked sluice ebbing swiftly out of the city.

We shot the bridge by the mid-most arch, riding the torrent with schoolboy exultation, but relieved to reach the calmer waters beyond. Even so my oarsmen hardly needed to exert themselves so quickly ran the flood. We passed the Tower in a trice, were upon the cherry orchards of Bermondsey only in what seemed a moment later, then came the lavender fields of Rotherhithe with the limekilns of the Isle of Dogs opposite and sooner than I thought was possible we'd arrived at Eliza's fabled dockyards and Deptford Strand. I disembarked at St Nicholas's steps just upstream of the church itself. I don't suppose my voyage of some seven miles had taken much more than half an hour. My watermen declared it a record. I told them I was paying them for nothing. They replied I should take my time at Deptford so the tide could turn again. That way they could take me back with as little exertion as we had come. I agreed, gave them money for refreshment and we parted in good humour.

The rain was easing so intead of going – as I had first intended – to the house where Christofer had died I turned towards St Nicholas. As I entered the churchyard I saw a canvas pavilion erected to one side of the path which led to the west door. Its shape was as elegant as anything you might see at a lord's hunting breakfast but the cloth of it was tarred, greasy with work and rain. From inside came the sound of a man singing. A voice made of grunts and muscular solemnity. I stopped to listen. The tune was predictable; the words not quite so. Certainly I hadn't heard them before. They went thus:

> There were seven foresters at Pickeram Side,
> At Pickeram they did dwell,
> And for a drop of Johnny Cock's blood
> They rode the fords of Hell.

I came to the open end of the tent and looked inside. A deep pit, a pile of dry earth, and the bald head of a gravedigger greeted me. The man threw up another spadeful and continued his ballad.

> A traveller told where Johnny Cock lay,
> Asleep aneath the hill –

I said, 'Good morning.'

The digger stopped. So did the spade in mid-swing. The head turned with emphatic slowness and my gravedigger stared up at me. Never have I seen anyone quite so bald of face: he had no beard, no eyebrows, no eyelashes – not even a hair in a nostril.

He eyed me with a slug's indifference. I nodded amicably. He grunted without commitment. Finally he spoke. With a Scotch accent so thick it was well-nigh another tongue. 'Och? I dun ken thee. Ye wouldnae seen the lad? Wee Walter? He's gane to fetch a pint o' wine a guid hour syne.'

I replied that I hadn't seen him but I dared say he wouldn't be long.

His answer was sharp, 'How'd ye ken that? He'll be touting his arse for a penny, that's what. The laddie's nae called Waterfront Wally for naught.'

I decided to disregard this aspect of the matter. I said, 'Can you direct me to the sexton's house?'

'Ye want Lucas Holt?'

'If he's the sexton, yes. Or the parson if he's here.'

'Mak' up thi mind. Which harlot's son do ye wish for? The rector's gone a-visiting, the sexton's at market.'

'Then I'll settle for your curate if you have one. What's his name?'

The gravedigger laughed brutally. 'He's nae need for a name nae more.'

'Why not?'

'Tak a look.'

And he waved me towards the church with his spade. I followed his curt direction and went in. Before the altar stood a coffin. Was this a Scotch joke? Did he mean I was to find the curate within the coffin while he dug his grave without? I supposed it was so and, despite myself, found I was smiling at the grave-digger's deep dug humour.

I went forward. Why I don't know. I could hardly expect a boxed-up corpse to show me the parish register – which, as you may imagine, was my reason for stopping at that modest house of God. There were no flowers on the coffin. Not even a sprig of rosemary. Let alone pansies. Had the curate been unloved, I wondered? It's more than possible nowadays with the people's loyalties still divided whatever the Queen's ministers may pronounce to the contrary.

To my left I heard a sob. I turned. A woman, shrouded by a black shawl, crouched huddled in the shadows. I went to her and she looked up. She was as round and wrinkled as a baked apple.

She said without preamble, 'He went to help a poor family at Rotherhithe. They'd been boarded in. Boarded up alive. On account of the pest. They were starving. My son broke the boards to pass food into them.'

'He was punished for that?'

'Yes, sir. He was.'

'By the authorities?'

'No, sir. By God Himself. The Lord struck him down. My only son dead of the pest for doing His bidding.' The woman wept again. I could say nothing to alleviate her grief except to murmur my regret at such apparent injustice. I went out to find the sexton.

The rain had now cleared completely and there was even a glow of sun on the gravedigger's workaday pavilion and the soft grey stone of St Nicholas's tower. At the tent's opening stood a man whom I took to be the sexton judging by his stout posture, sober garb and the two live cockerels fresh from market swinging by their legs in his hand.

He greeted me. And was as Kentish a man as ever I heard. 'Good day to you, sir. Scotch Jack here tells me you've been asking after me?'

'If you're the sexton, yes.'

'Lucas Holt, at your service, sir.'

He held out his hand, one of the cockerels in the other tried to crow but failed.

I took his hand and told him my name was Scrivener – an alias I had settled upon whilst waiting for the dawn. I'd decided it would be prudent to conduct my enquiries at Deptford as a certain John Scrivener.

'I've come to consult the parish register, Mr Holt.'

'In what regard, sir, may I ask? Would you be looking for a marriage, a baptism or a death?'

'A death.'

At this moment the gravedigger's boy – a pouting russet-haired cupid – returned to a roar of rabid abuse from Scotch Jack. The air reverberated. Mr Holt apologised – quite unnecessarily had he known who I really was. However I took this opportunity to move away thus obliging the sexton to come with me.

As we walked through the church to the vestry Mr Holt

confirmed that the curate had most regrettably met his death in the way his mother had related but he had been by no means unloved. Quite the opposite in fact. The truth was the cause of death had been concealed. Necessarily so because otherwise – for fear of infection – he'd have been thrown into the official plague pits at Millwall rather than buried decently here in his beloved churchyard. To save him from this fate the doctor, at the persuasion of the parson, had declared him dead of an inward canker. He begged me not to reveal this to anyone lest the crowner, as he called the coroner, came to hear of it.

I said, as casually as I could, 'How would you describe your coroner here at Deptford?'

Mr Holt blew out his cheeks as a prologue to diplomacy. 'Phouf – well, sir – to begin with, sir, he's new. Newly appointed if you understand me?'

I did. I said, 'Oh? Is that so? Since when?'

'Early October.'

'What happened? Did the previous man retire?'

'Aye, sir. And a week later he was dead. Mind you he was a good age. Sixty odd.'

'How was he regarded?'

'Very highly, sir. But of course we don't have only the one crowner here at Deptford, sir. By no means.'

'You have several?'

'Indeed, sir. Well, two if I'm to speak true. You see, sir, when the Queen's in residence at Greenwich we come within the verge and her crowner Mr Danby takes charge.'

It isn't just divinity that hedges our Queen about. A twelve-mile radius from her person defines a magic circle – a zone of peremptory powers. And since she'd been at Greenwich last May it followed that her very own coroner had held the inquest. How handy, how neat, for Mr Vice.

We had reached the vestry. Mr Holt unlocked a coffer which contained several leather bound registers.

'The death, sir, you're after?'

'It happened last May. A friend of mine. On the thirtieth day of the month.'

Mr Holt took out one of the registers and as he turned the pages I saw that this particular register had been begun at Michaelmas '92. When he reached May '93 his broad finger traced three burials on the last day of the month and five more on the first of June. And the first to be entered for that day was that of Christofer Marlowe.

Despite myself I shivered. 'That's who I'm looking for,' I said. 'Can you show me his grave?'

Another puff-out of his cheeks. 'Well, I don't know, sir. I'm not sure I can. I can't say I rightly remember where that particular gentleman was put and we've had any number of burials since. Still it may be Scotch Jack will recall the place.'

As he returned the register to the coffer his cockerel tried to crow again. He shook it and the bird twisted up to peck his hand but the straining neck couldn't reach its target. It fell back to hang headlong beside its neighbour.

'The wife stews 'em in wine with onions and mushrooms, sir,' Mr Holt said by way of superfluous explanation.

He locked the coffer and we left the vestry.

Scotch Jack took his time to remember Christofer's resting place. And while he thought his apprentice Walter seemed consumed by a desire to speak and a need to stay silent. Finally the gravedigger decided that Mr Marlowe or Marley or Morley – he reckoned he'd heard him spoken of as the last of those three but once the breath was gone what was in a name? – aye, he was by the north wall to the left of the big holly tree. And now as he minded it there'd been some debate as to whether he should be buried in hallowed ground at all –

I interrupted him. 'Debate between who?'

'Them as brought him hither.'

'Can you remember them?'

'Aye, the rector himself and twa strangers.'

'Could you describe them?'

Scotch Jack shrugged, doubted he could, but by persistent questioning I elicited possible descriptions of Robert Poley and Nick Skeres: Poley's aquiline nose, Nick's pale blue eyes. A court of law would have found them as insufficient as they were dubiously got but I didn't.

I said, 'I presume the parson had heard something to the dead man's disadvantage?'

How odd it was to speak so detachedly of Christofer. Suddenly I felt a traitor to him all over again. I found myself beginning to shake at the shame of it. But I drew breath and managed to subdue the tremor. Pretty Walter, I noted, had noticed however.

'Nay, sir, the disputation lay betwixt the strangers. They couldna decide if a blasphemer was worthy of burial within or without the wall.'

'They spoke of him as a blasphemer?'

'Aye, and an atheist too, the wee whoor's bastard.'

My doing, my fault, my Christofer traduced. Had Old Nick put in a word for him? Against a Poley intent on maintaining lies they'd wrung from me at Chelsea? Even after death? I felt I might choke. I tried to speak. My spittle was gone. And all the while Walter's eyes watched me.

Scotch Jack said, 'It was the rector settled the matter. He's aye a big soft thing. Jack, he says, dig here inside the wall. Better be wrong fro' mercy than reet out o' too much scruple. And he points to the place yonder. Gae see for thyself.'

I needed no further urging. I left my informants where they stood and went to the north side of the churchyard. I soon saw the holly tree and some moments later I was looking down at a nameless grave graced only by a makeshift cross made out of a couple of hazel wands lashed together and a bunch of five rain-stained marigolds. All about me dozens of headstones granted the bodies below them not only identity but brief biographies, too. But no stone commemorated Christofer. So this hazel cross and these marigolds must, I decided, mark his grave. But who had placed them there?

As I knelt to touch the ground above him an astonishing fragrance greeted me. It rose up from the moss and grasses. It suffused the air, imbued my nostrils. Violets? Could it be? Violets? Of all flowers? The odour of sanctity? Oh, this was impossible not to say absurd. I peered closer. No violets were to be seen anywhere near and yet the scent was undeniable. I laughed at the sweet incongruity of it. At its mystery too. How could my Christofer's grave smell of violets? Saint Christoferus? What a joke.

Something touched my hand. I jumped. Was there a ghost here in broad day? I turned. Walter crouched beside me. He slipped his hand into mine.

He said, 'I made the cross, mister.' Cupid was a Cockney.

'You crept up on me?'

He grinned but continued with his first thought. 'I dint reckon it was right – him not to have nuffink. The marigolds was me, too.'

'You're quite sure this is the place?'

'Oh, yeah. I helped dig it. It was ever so early.'

'Early?'

'In the mornin'. 'Fore it was light. Like they wanted him out of the way. You know, quick. He *was* a poet, wasn't he? I mean that *is* true, innit? Straight up true? I wasn't told no lie?'

'No. Quite true. He was a poet all right.'

'Oh, thank Christ for that. That's why I did the cross. And still leave him flowers. On account of his being a poet. I wouldn't if he wasn't. Nor would I – ' He stopped, blushed prettily, even winsomely.

'What? What else wouldn't you do?'

'What you fink, mister?'

'No, you tell me, Walter.'

'Sell me bum.'

So Scotch Jack had been right. 'Sell it for what?' I said.

'Oil of violets, of course. Can't you smell it?'

I had to laugh. 'So that's how it is. I did wonder where the smell came from.'

'D'you like it?'

'Of course.'

He fished in his pocket and brought out a small phial of blue glass. He handed it to me. 'There. I bought that this mornin'. Proceeds of a big black bugger – near split me in half he did.'

I tried to look censorious but failed. Pretty Walter smiled like the guileless infant he wasn't. I eased off the cork. The scent of violets was intense. Such a distillation of vapours couldn't have been cheap. I said as much.

'What did this cost you, Walter?'

'Who cares?' he said. 'Shake it over your mate, mister. Go on.'

I looked him in the eye for a moment and found my own sting with tears. Still holding my wicked cherub's hand I sprinkled the oil of violets over the earth above Christofer and as the phial was emptied I wept.

And all the while that gravedigger's boy held my hand. When my tears ceased and I turned to look at him he handed me a perfect lace handkerchief (filched, I'm sure) so I could wipe my face. As I returned it to him with a grateful smile he stretched up and kissed me on the mouth. It was a salute of purest sympathy.

'What's the betting you're a poet, too, mister?' he said. And with that he jumped to his feet and was gone, leaving me alone with Christofer. I patted the earth once more and rose up.

Then, looking down at the grave, I said, 'I'm getting closer, my dear. You'll be revenged, I promise. And so shall I.'

I left the churchyard by the wicket gate at the eastern end having no need or wish for further conversation with Scotch Jack or the sexton.

I went next to Eleanor Bull's establishment where I took a room in the name of John Scrivener. Not that I planned to stay at Deptford but I thought my enquiries in that house would be better pursued (and cloaked) if I posed as an ordinary client.

Widow Bull was one of the largest and stateliest women I ever saw. Her face was as broad as her neck which emerged from a wide lawn collar in the old fashion. Otherwise she was dressed entirely in black velvet but her jewels, especially the diamond and sapphire rings which encrusted her pudgy white hands, were the finest Amsterdam could supply. Gossip had it she was one of the richest women in England if you counted cash rather than land. She ruled her hotel (as she referred to it after the French fashion) like a matriarch though in truth she was childless.

Meeting her watchful eye and observing her weighty manner you could not doubt that this house was the soberest house in Deptford – if not in all England. It reeked of quiet business and solid money. It was clearly a haven for exporters and importers, bankers and brokers, shipbuilders and chandlers not to mention any number of respectable travellers. You would have been right. And wrong.

Widow Bull received me herself at her table which commanded all the comings and goings of the entrance hall and upon the main stairs. She wrote my false name in the guest book requesting me to sign or make my mark against the stated price (excessive) of the room I had taken. She then asked after my luggage and when I said I had none demanded that I pay in advance. Once this was settled she conducted me herself to my room on the first floor overlooking a dull but decent garden at the back. I had asked for a quiet room and this answered perfectly. I also noted that the garden wall was a good ten feet high and topped with iron spikes. No nearby house overlooked the garden either. Eleanor Bull's hotel seemed not merely respectable but secure as well.

She asked me if I required any other service and I ordered dinner to be brought. She said the waiter who would bring it was responsible for the clients upon that floor and could answer any further needs I might have as they arose. With the smallest smile in the world she suggested I need not hesitate to ask for whatever a gentleman might want. By day or night. Her hotel aimed to please the discerning. The only rule of the house, she said, was that guests were respectfully asked to observe a certain discretion: what a frequent and valued client – Her Majesty's Vice Chamberlain as it happened – called – 'not frightening the livestock'. With that stiletto hint and another miniature smile she wished me good day.

So Sir Thomas Heneage used the place. Hired it on behalf of his officers. Of course. What better, safer house for his agents, posing as men of business, to convene in? Especially should they wish to question or murder a suspect outside the formalities of Chelsea.

As I waited for dinner to arrive I reviewed what else I had

gleaned that morning. And was forced to conclude that everything confirmed the official report without casting any real doubt upon it. Perhaps the only new aspect of the affair was Nick Skeres' reported argument with Poley. Did this suggest Skeres had been higher in the service than I'd suspected? No mere factotum? Could he have commanded Frizer at Scadbury? Rather than the reverse? Was his apparent foolishness a front for someone shrewder? Christofer had once hinted as much and I'd disregarded his warning. But Old Nick, whatever his rank and character had been, was dead. And so beyond my reach, beyond the promise I had made on Christofer's grave that morning.

Next I tried to guess at the purpose of Heneage's agents meeting Christofer here. Had it begun as routine? Thanks to my false witness Christofer had been commanded to report daily to the Privy Council from the eighteenth of May until his death-day here. In this very room? Possibly. Certainly I intended – well, hoped – to find out which room he died in. But what had his reporting daily entailed? A visit to Whitehall? Or to Chelsea? Or anywhere else where Heneage stipulated? Had Christofer come here thinking he was simply observing that day's requirement of his bail? Was he surprised to find no privy councillor present? Just Heneage's henchmen? Or had Heneage been here all along only to be deliberately omitted from the coroner's report? Widow Bull, I felt sure, would have willingly withheld such information had so influential a client requested it. No small part of her revenues depended perhaps upon Heneage's continuing favour?

How much of that day had Christofer spent here? When had he arrived? In the morning, in the afternoon? For dinner? For supper? Before either or after the former? My head teemed with such questions like worms in an angler's box. Had Walsingham accompanied him? It was an easy ride from Scadbury. Walsingham approved the accommodation and service here. Supposing this – ?

But a discreet tap at the door checked my wriggling thoughts. I strode to it and admitted the floor waiter with a linen-covered tray. He was attended by a maid who carried a brassbound box of polished rosewood. He was sleek yet saturnine; she anxious-eyed. As she entered she stumbled a little under the weight of her burden.

The waiter wished me an obsequious good day and setting the tray to one side sharply supervised the maid as she set the table, taking napkins, cutlery, glass and china plates from the heavy, rosewood canteen. Next the tray's cloth covering was ceremoniously removed and the devilled quails with baby turnips and carrots I had ordered at Widow Bull's recommendation were revealed. They looked and proved to be delicious. The Burgundy wine was served from a glass decanter.

I was called to table by the maid who would remain to wait upon me while I ate. I gathered from the waiter's speaking look and a murmur to the effect that she was a good, clean girl from whom I might negotiate additional services, should I be so inclined after I had eaten. If so a word to him would suffice when it was time to clear the board. The girl had no authority to arrange such matters for herself. That said he withdrew.

The girl served me dutifully. She was silent, so pale as to be almost translucent, perhaps seventeen, perhaps more, and tremulously deferential. She looked half-starved which was odd. Most inn-servants eat well. In body she seemed more boy than girl. And she had the melancholy air of someone who wished she had never been born. I found her more to be pitied than desired.

I said, 'How long have you worked here, child?'

'For over a year, sir.' Her voice was little more than a suspiration.

I was glad to learn this and said so. It meant she would have been employed there when Christofer was killed.

'What's your name?' To my surprise this harmless question caused her to pant like a bird caught on a quicklime twig. 'What's the matter? Is it a secret?'

'I've forgotten it, sir.'

'Forgotten it? You can't have. No one forgets their name.'

'Well, no. I mean I know it really. But it's never used here. And I'm glad. Here I'm just called Betty.'

'Won't you tell me? I promise I won't tell anyone else.'

She shook her head. 'I'm too ashamed, sir.'

By patient persistence I gradually discovered that the girl had run away from her family at Kingston at the age of twelve when they had tried to betroth her to a wealthy cornmerchant of fifty. Since that time she had worked in many taverns but it was only upon coming to Deptford that she had been lured into whoredom. It had occurred conventionally enough. She had been seduced by Mr Clifford, the floor waiter, who was now her pimp. She hated him, herself and all the clients who abused her. She had imagined that by submitting to this degradation she would be able to save a little money but no, the waiter took it all, though to be fair to him he had to pay much of it to Widow Bull. Almost all the younger female servants were required to please the clients in this way. It was the rule of the house. As in a nunnery, I said? But that pale girl didn't or couldn't acknowledge the joke. So this respectable hotel was in reality a brothel? I added by way of explanation. She nodded.

I said, 'Can you keep a secret?'

Again she surprised me. 'I'm not allowed to, sir.'

'What do you mean?'

'I have to report everything I hear to Mr Clifford.'

'You're his eyes and ears?'

'Yes, sir.'

'And *do* you report everything you hear?'

For the first time the faintest gleam of a smile suffused her. She said, 'Well, not everything perhaps – not always.'

I had finished eating. I told her to clear the table and to call Mr Clifford. She did. When he arrived I informed him that Betty had performed her duties admirably and then, sotto voce, that I did require certain further services from her. He replied she would cost me three shillings. I agreed. He assured me she would be back in five minutes once she had returned the cutlery and glass to the sculleries. She was. She knocked and I admitted her. Her eyes were bright with reproach. Without saying it they said she had hoped better of me, that I would not be like so many other of her clients. I shut and bolted the door.

·297·

I said, keeping my voice low, 'Are there any means of listening to what is said in the rooms here?'

She nodded and indicated a series of neat holes drilled in the linenfold wainscotting on either side of the bed. They were discreetly placed within the natural shadows cast by the moulding of the wood. And – if noticed at all – might easily have been mistaken for ventilation against damp.

I said, more quietly, 'Is there nowhere here we can speak safely?'

For answer she looked at the bed. Then she said, 'Only there, sir.' I wanted to assure her I had not in truth recalled her for that purpose although it was inevitable she would assume as much. That rather I wanted information. However I could not say this without the risk of being overheard. Was Mr Clifford's ear pressed even now to an artificial orifice on the landing outside?

She said, 'Shall I draw the curtains, sir?' It was my turn to nod. She went to the bed, pulled back the counterpane to reveal crisp sheets and proud pillows. Then she drew the curtains all about it except for those at the side where she stood. That done she stood like a statue. 'What do you wish me to do now, sir? I am wholly at your disposal. Shall I undress or do you want to remove my clothes for me?' She spoke like a puppet. The tears stole from her eyes.

If I'm honest I must say that at that moment I felt a quick surge of desire for that sad, flat girl. I wanted to hold and comfort her, cradle and console her, prove to her that pity and love were possible even in these most miserable and mercenary circumstances; even in Eleanor Bull's vile house. But instead I shook my head, put my fingers to my lips and stepped forward to the bed where I sat myself down fully dressed and invited her, by signs, to sit beside me, equally dressed. I then whispered to her to draw the last curtains close.

That accomplished we sat like two children in a make-believe tent. I smiled, hoping to encourage her, to convince her of my good intentions. 'Now we can talk in safety,' I said. But I could see she was yet to believe me.

'Is that *all* you want of me, sir? To talk?'

'Yes, I assure you. That's all. Nothing else. I need answers to one or two important questions. It may be you know them. We'll see. But I promise I'll pay you, my dear. Just as if you were the most practised doxy in Deptford.'

'Oh, dear,' came her answer. I was confounded.

'I thought you'd be pleased?' I said.

'Oh, I would be, sir. If it could really be like that.'

'Why can't it?' No reply except a furious blush of shame and a half-stifled sob. 'Why not?' I repeated.

'It just can't. It isn't allowed.'

'What do you mean? Explain.' She hung her head. I spoke again, voicing what I felt. 'Oh, my dear girl – how I wish I knew your name. Your real name.'

She looked up at me closely as if seeking earnestly to know the construction of my mind. Her eyes asked, can I trust you? Mine must have said she could.

She leaned forward. 'I'm called Bridget,' she whispered. 'But don't tell a soul, please, I beg you, beg you.'

I hastened to reassure her. 'You can trust me, Bridget. I won't tell anyone. But you still haven't explained what cannot be. Why can't I pay you for nothing if I choose?'

'I will tell you, sir. In fact I must for my own safety's sake. But please, you ask your questions first. I'd prefer it that way round. At least then you won't be quite such a stranger to me.'

Still mystified I agreed to this stipulation. Told her we had a bargain I would keep her to: when I had questioned her she would explain in full the true terms of her employment in that so-called hotel. She smiled, as if partially relieved.

I said, 'Please listen carefully, Bridget. I want you to think back a few months. Five in fact. To last May. To the thirtieth of that month when something very serious happened here.'

'You mean the murder, sir?'

'Is that what you call it? Murder?'

'We all did.'

'No one thought it was an accident?'

'Oh, no, sir. It couldn't have been.'

'Why not?'

'Because of where it happened, sir. In the room above here.'

At this revelation I shivered and looked up at the bed's canopy as though my eyes might pierce the pleated damask and even penetrate the ceiling.

'Up there? Directly above us?'

'Oh, yes, sir. Room 21.' I shivered again. To my surprise she put her hand on my sleeve. 'Are you all right, sir?'

I wasn't but said I was. 'The man who died was my friend. I loved him dearly. He was a poet.'

'So everybody said.'

'His name was Christofer. Christofer Marlowe. He was twenty-nine. But in spirit still a boy. And he's the reason I asked if you could keep a secret. I don't want others to know of my enquiries concerning Christofer. Can you keep such a thing to yourself, Bridget?'

'I'll do my best, sir.'

'You can't promise?'

Once again she seemed haunted, oppressed. 'I'll try, sir. I want to because I like you. I think you're a good man. But if I can't it'll be because – ' She stopped, clutching her arms across her chest, and shuddered most pitifully. 'Well, perhaps you can imagine, sir? Can you?' she added.

'You're saying Mr Clifford will maltreat you?'

'Yes, sir. He will.'

This was said as plain fact not from self-pity. I said, 'We must do something to save you from this slavery, Bridget. But why did you say Christofer's death could not have been an accident? Happening where it did? In room 21?'

'Because that's one of the private rooms, sir.'

'The private rooms?'

'There are three in a row – all on the second floor – all next door to each other. They're only ever used by private guests.'

'And who would they be?'

'Why, the Widow Bull's people. Her important friends. They don't pay. Least not so as to be seen paying. They're far too grand for that.'

'Oh, I see. Or do I? No, I don't. How does that make Christofer's death a murder?'

'Because they said they'd quarrelled about the bill, sir. The bill for supper. But they wouldn't. You don't get given a bill in Room 21. Everything's on the house, sir – up there.' She raised her eyes. I followed her gaze and could almost imagine a bloodstain spreading across the canopy: a stain darker than the crimson damask; Christofer's precious life blood finding its way through the floorboards to come to rest in a bellying, seeping pool above our heads. 'Honestly, sir, we all laughed when we heard the story. Even Mr Clifford said pull his other leg it had morris bells on – and he never danced a decent morris in his life.'

At this mild jibe at her persecutor's expense Bridget suddenly smiled. I smiled too, pleased by this change in her. It seemed the girl might be capable of happiness after all. I too was glad. Glad to have my own rooted doubt of the official story confirmed. Had I not always said Christofer would never dispute a bill except to insist on paying it? But such friendly squabbles do not lead to murder. Now Bridget's account was even better: there wouldn't have been a bill to question in the first place. I asked her what else she'd heard and she said three of the gentlemen concerned had arrived in the morning, taken their dinner in Room 21, then strolled round and round the garden in the afternoon before returning to their room again for supper. Except by then they'd been joined by three other men.

'Three more?' I said, my heart leaping. Here was news indeed. New news. The coroner's report – if you included Christofer – had mentioned only four men. Here were six. What was more, and better still, Bridget said she'd seen them all with her own eyes because on that particular day she'd been assigned to polishing the silver in the pantry that overlooks the garden. Could she describe them? She thought she could.

I said, 'Begin with the first three you saw.'

'One was quite small. Bright as a bullfinch. Round-faced, not much beard, with high heels to his boots.' Here was no one but Christofer. I told her so. She nodded. 'Then there was a taller man with russet hair. Very richly dressed in green and brown.'

This had to be Walsingham: his predilection for forest colours was a household joke at Scadbury.

'And the third?'

'Dark curly hair. A gold earring he kept fingering when he wasn't touching his toes or boxing at the air. He was very proud of his body, I thought. It was very shapely. And very strong-looking.' Who else but Ingram Frizer, alias Master Francis? So all three had come to Deptford. But why? Presumably to meet the other three men? And why? For what purpose?

Even as I asked myself these questions I congratulated Bridget on the sharp accuracy of her descriptions. Could she do as well by the others who arrived later?

She said, 'I'll try. The first was long-nosed with very dark eyes. I think he had a canker in him.'

'Why do you say that?'

'Because he looked as if he was nursing something in his belly, sir. Something he didn't like but couldn't pretend wasn't there. His hand would keep pressing at the place. Time after time he'd snatch it away only to find it had gone back there again. And all the while he seemed to hope no one had noticed.'

I could not have painted Robert Poley more exactly myself. I told Bridget so and this further compliment won from her a sun-in-February smile.

Next she sketched Nick Skeres with two strokes. 'His eyes were like sparrows' eggs. You know, dirty blue. And his hair was the colour of old straw.'

I said, 'That man has since died. The man with the earring killed him.'

'Why, sir?'

'I don't know for sure. Not yet. But I've made many guesses. And intend to find out. Who knows – perhaps one day I'll be able to tell you? But now I need to hear about the last man. What can you remember of him?'

Here she faltered. A large man, soberly dressed. Aged fifty or so. From these broad facts I couldn't place him as certainly as the others. He might have been Sebastian Skeate, or Magog as I'd nicknamed him in my misery at Chelsea.

'Did these last three arrive together?'

'Oh, no, sir. The first two came first and the last one last bringing a letter.'

'A letter?'

'Yes, sir.'

So Poley and Skeres had been brought a letter? Perhaps by Skeate? Why not? He might well have been the postman. Especially if the missive was not to be entrusted to lesser hands.

'Who received the letter – did you see?'

'Oh, yes. They were stood right in front of my window. The man with the canker took it. It was he broke the seal. And I don't think he liked what he read, sir. Not at all. Not one bit.'

'Why? What did he do? Crumple it up? Tear it across?'

'No. He just went still. Still as a statue. But he looked, oh, so angry. Then he folded and folded the letter till I thought his knuckles would crack.'

Keeping my face effigy straight I teased her, demanding to know with all due gravity the complete contents of that letter. Bridget apologised, saying she was afraid she couldn't tell me, begging my pardon, because it hadn't been read aloud. Only when I smiled did she realise I'd been joking whereupon she smiled, too. An April smile this time.

Next I asked her to think back to the initial arrival of Christofer, Walsingham and Frizer. What impression had they made upon her – in their character, in their behaviour when first they entered the garden? She was silent for a while before saying: 'The bullfinch man, your friend, was the centre of attention, sir. The other two, whether they liked it or not – and I don't think the muscular one with the earring did – they seemed to defer to him all the time – even the tall one in green and brown who was obviously the richest of them. It was as if they were there on his behalf more than their own, really, if you see what I mean?'

'I do, Bridget. I see it exactly like that. Go on.'

'And, well, I had the feeling they were waiting, sir.'

'Waiting? For what? For the others to arrive?'

'Oh, no. For something else, I'm sure.'

'What makes you say that?'

·303·

'The muscular man kept watching the sky. And twice he licked his finger and held it up in the air.'

'To test which way the wind blew?'

'There wasn't any wind, sir.'

'You're sure?'

'Not a breath.'

'Then he must've been hoping for a wind.'

'I think so, sir.'

'They were waiting there for a wind – not for the other men?'

'I'm certain of it.'

'So when they arrived they must've been surprised?'

'Oh, yes, sir, they were.'

'Pleasantly surprised?'

'Oh, no, I wouldn't say that, sir, no. In fact I'd say they were very displeased.'

'Well, well, Bridget, I'm already in your debt. You've told me more in five minutes than I've learned in as many months.'

For here was a packet of news. From this could I not reasonably deduce that Christofer, Walsingham and Frizer had come to Deptford to take ship somewhere? Or rather that Walsingham had tried to send Christofer abroad for his own safety? And Walsingham's, too, come to that, given Heneage's visit to Scadbury? Would this not perhaps account for the mistaken rumour Lycia had heard that Christofer had taken refuge in Paris? False in fact but sprung from this seedbed of truth, from this frustrated attempt to smuggle him overseas? Because frustrated it had been. Viciously. Murderously. And by none but Frizer. Frizer who, as an agent of the Crown, must have sent word to Bob Poley who had come at once with Nick Skeres to Deptford and set in motion the events that led to Christofer's death that evening. Yes, Frizer must have betrayed his ostensible master, Walsingham, for great Eliza's greater good. Yes! Of course. All was plain. Or so I thought.

I said, 'Who among them would you say was the most displeased, Bridget?'

'Oh, the green and brown gentleman. Definitely. He was furious with the canker man. But your friend was more resigned,

I thought. He kept shrugging, trying to calm the other two down.'

'And the muscular man?'

'Oh, he went off to one side and amused himself by practising sword and dagger with the box trees.'

I could only too easily picture Frizer doing that. See him striking home to their green hearts.

'What of the man with the sparrow-egg eyes, Bridget?'

'Oh, he just seemed to agree with everything the canker man said. He stayed close beside him, nodding all the time, nod, nod, nod.'

'He didn't speak to the muscle man?'

'Only at first.'

'Did they appear at ease with each other?'

'Not especially.'

Had a rift opened between Skeres and Frizer? And since Skeres had come with Poley might it be that he'd already left Scadbury? Had been recalled to Chelsea for other duties, perhaps?

I said, 'So how did the argument resolve?'

'Well, the green and brown gentleman calmed down eventually. He seemed to agree to what the canker man said. In fact they all shook hands, clapped each other on the shoulder, and began to smile except then the last man arrived.'

'With the letter?'

'Yes.'

'And that changed everything yet again?'

'Completely. This time it was the canker man who was furious. But I've told you that, haven't I?'

'Yes, but it doesn't matter. Go on. What you say has the ring of absolute truth, Bridget. And that's been a rare commodity of late. At least in my world. Perhaps in yours, too?'

She nodded. 'For as long as I can remember, sir. Anyway the canker man muttered something out of the side of his mouth at the blue-eyed man and he glowered too. Then something was said which made the green and brown gentleman roar with laughter as did Mr Marlowe, your friend, sir. In fact the pair of them embraced, hugging each other while laughing at the others.'

'And the muscular man?'

'He just grinned to himself.'

'And did some more exercises?'

'Yes, sir. You seem to know all about him, sir?'

'Oh, I do, Bridget, I do. And a good deal about the others, too. But I didn't know anything of what you've just told me.'

'But you know what it was they were talking about?'

'No. But I can make a fair guess.'

'I did try to hear but always they were either just out of earshot or spoke so quietly or quickly I couldn't catch their words.'

'They met in quiet sort – as we might say?'

'Yes, sir. Except for the ups and downs of their moods.'

'Of course. Yes. How did they leave the garden? All together, separately, how?'

'Well, first, the man who brought the letter went away with the green and brown gentleman who looked back twice, rather anxiously I thought, at your friend. His friend too, I'd say, from the way they were together.'

'While he and the other three stayed in the garden?'

'Yes, sir. But not for long. For about ten minutes. Then they went in for supper.'

'Cheerfully, would you say?'

'Yes.'

'Even Christofer?'

'Him most of all.'

'Really? Well, Bridget, you're a wonderful witness. Now it only remains for you to tell me what you know of the murder itself.'

But to this she didn't answer me directly. Instead she said time was passing. And as she said it her previous anxiety grew again in her eyes. Mr Clifford would begin to wonder what was keeping her since he believed such assignations as this should never last longer than twenty minutes. That was enough time in which to satisfy any man if a girl knew her business, he always said. Therefore, and now her anxiety became a pitiful trembling, we must – as she put it – do it.

I repeated that there was no need. I respected her and would pay her as I had promised. She answered she dared not return to Mr Clifford without any sign of venality upon her. If she did he would abuse her himself. And I at least had spoken kindly to her.

'So I am the lesser of two evils?'

'Yes, sir,' she whispered and lifted up her skirts. Tears fell from her eyes.

'My poor Bridget,' I said.

'Please, sir. Just do it as quickly as you can.'

Never have I made sadder – or slower – sport. But eventually the shameful action was accomplished. At its end she cried out a little – like a rabbit ensnared. Finally as she buttoned her blouse – her breasts were no more than a boy's – she thanked me for making her safe from Mr Clifford's interferences.

A flood of righteous hatred rose in me. How could such a child be degraded so? By him? By me? I said, 'I shall get you away from here, Bridget.'

Her eyes came alive. 'Where to, sir?'

'To the country. You would serve a great lady – a lady in her own right – who would treat you properly, I promise.'

'Oh, sir! Would she?'

'Without question. All her servants praise her. Do you agree?' She did, nodding with a genuine liveliness. 'Very well, it will be done. But now I want you to show me the room above here. Room 21. Where Christofer died.'

'Oh, I can't, sir. That's impossible.'

'Why?'

'It's always locked. Mr Clifford keeps the keys.'

I took spent tallow from one of the candles and warmed it in my hands. Then I asked Bridget to bring me the key from the door and made an impression of it in the flattened pad of wax. 'Could you do that with the key to Room 21, do you think?' She looked doubtful. I said, 'I shall extend my stay here until tomorrow, Bridget. I hadn't intended to, but I shall. That should give you time. And if you wish I'll tell Mr Clifford I like you so much I want you to spend the night with me. Then we can go up to Room 21 when the house is asleep.'

She shook her head. 'Oh, I'd never do that, sir. Never visit the murder room.'

'Very well. I'll go alone.'

'But I'll come to you here tonight, sir.'

'Only if you wish it.'

'Oh, I do, sir. Otherwise I'll have go to go Mr Clifford.'

Agreement was made between us. I paid her the three shilling fee and handed her the ball of tallow. She promised to take an impression of the key if she could. I told her I would go into the town to make further enquiries and be back at least an hour before supper.

Before she left she said, 'Did you mean that about taking me into the country, sir?'

'From the bottom of my heart, Bridget. You deserve better than this. Why, a Muscovy serf is better treated,' I said. Whereat she smiled a full August smile and went from the room.

When I got to the pier to release my watermen from waiting they were hard at work snoring off a skinful of dinner swallowed in a dockside beerhouse more renowned for its liquor than its meat. It took them a little while to comprehend first who I was and second that I now intended to spend the night at Deptford and therefore they were free to accept another fare back to the city. But they declared themselves satisfied with my money and, besides, the tide had already turned so their return trip would be almost as easy as our coming that morning. Even as I departed I saw three likely passengers approach – a solid citizen with his capacious wife and their burly mastiff.

My next port of call was the courthouse. It was shut up but I found a janitor who for a penny piece (at Deptford everyone, it seemed, had his or her price) agreed to advise the Clerk of the Court, who lived next door, of my presence. Whom should he say I was? Once again I became John Scrivener but even as I said it I wondered if I should have invented another alias? Would a more experienced enquirer have covered his identity more securely? Three public places in Deptford now knew me by this name: the church, the hotel, the courthouse. My momentary unease was disrupted, however, by the appearance of the Court Clerk, a professionally moribund soul with quick suspicious eyes. However once I announced – not quite falsely – that I had come upon the Queen's business he agreed to open up the court's record office.

Deptford's records were not so voluminous as those of the Court of Chancery but nevertheless they were substantial, especially in matters of commerce. It took us a while to locate the coroner's report for the first of June. Or rather, as in Chancery in the matter of Frizer's pardon, the shelf where it should have resided.

Was I surprised by its absence? Yes and no. By which I mean that my initial surprise was overtaken at once by wordly resignation – as if I'd said to myself I might have known as much. Even so I was irritated. I had wanted to read the coroner's lies for myself. To read between the lines of them – to decipher that invisible text that would perhaps delineate the truth of Christofer's death in Room 21.

To this irritation some further disquiet next accrued: the record's absence was surely yet more evidence of a conspiracy compounded by a cover-up? Someone had anticipated I might search these archives and taken this precautionary action. When? Was I watched for even here? I decided to take more care when I left the courthouse than I had when coming to it.

As in Chancery the Court Clerk professed himself seriously concerned. He shouted at once for the janitor who fetched the Clerk's assistant: an earnest, harelike youth who trembled in his down-at-heel shoes. Rigorously questioned by the Clerk he stammered out an explanation. Last Tuesday, he said, when the Court Clerk had been churching his wife after her eighth born, a gentleman had come from Greenwich, richly dressed. He'd carried a gold perfume box which smelt as if Christmas was already come. This gentleman had shown him a letter with the seal of the Vice-Chamberlain of the Queen's Household upon it authorising the bearer to examine and remove any document appertaining to the coroner's business on the first day of June last. Consequently he had granted this obviously important personage access to the shelves and witnessed the removal of just one report out of six which appertained to the day in question. Aware of the exceptional nature of this proceeding he had respectfully requested that the gentleman sign for the document in the daybook. This he had done and we might inspect the entry.

The Clerk sent him down to fetch it and there, sure enough, was a note for the Tuesday before to the effect that the coroner's report relating to the death of Mr C. Morley (so it was written) had been removed upon authority by a profoundly illegible signature.

I asked the assistant clerk if he could describe this visitor? But he couldn't. He was no Bridget. He lacked any gift for instant seizure of the salient feature. All I got was a vague impression of someone approaching middle age and tending to fat. He couldn't remember the colour of the eyes but his clothes had been a rich, dull red. His hair? He kept his hat on, he said.

There being nothing further to be learned at the courthouse I bade them good afternoon and began, with renewed caution, to make my way back to the hotel. I took a roundabout route, pausing to tour the bristling dockyards where a dozen new warships were under construction. Alongside them were two *fregatas* of Spain being converted into honest English frigates after their capture off the Azores. Or so a bollard sage informed me. Eliza's fear of her Spanish brother-in-law is nowhere near abated despite the defeating of his invincible armada five years ago. Still she builds ever mightier navies to ensure we remain the offshore terror of Europe.

As I viewed the immense industry of the dockyards I felt a sharp tug at my sleeve. I whirled about, drawing my dagger with a dervish flash. And just in the nick of time recognised Walter, the gravedigger's boy, white-faced, my steel at his throat.

'Jesus Christ, mister! S'only me!'

'Walter!'

'Gawd blind me – fer a minute I fort this is it, mate, yew've copped yer lot. Strufe!'

I sheathed my dagger and apologised. 'Forgive me, Walter, but – '

'Dead nervous, ain't yer?'

'Yes! But with reason, believe me.'

'I bet. Well, right, but – um – I got sommink else to tell yer. I remembered it the minute yew'd gone.'

'What?'

It was his turn to fear conspiracy. He looked round and then nodded towards a wooden jetty that stood out over the rising tide. 'Over there? All right?' We walked out to stand fifteen feet above the water and to be overheard by no one save a pair of cormorants taking turns to fish from the same perch – a mussel-encrusted buoy furnished from a beer barrel.

'Well, Walter?'

'There was this uvver fella.'

'Someone else?' Here was news to rank with Bridget's evidence. 'Who? Are you saying he attended the burial?'

'Nah. This one comes the next day. Before I'd even put the cross up – right?'

'Did you speak to him?'

'Nah. Juss saw 'im come in at the gate.'

'Did he ask to be directed to the grave?'

'Nah. Went straight to it. So 'e must've known or bin told, right?'

'Right. Except the mound of fresh earth would've been a pretty good indication – ?'

'Never! We dug five graves that day, mister. Five. You should've seen the yard. It was like a field full of dirty great molehills.'

'So this man didn't speak to anyone? Not to you? Nor to Scotch Jack?'

'Not reelly. On 'is way aht he passed the time of day but that was it. Nuffink else.'

'What did he look like?'

'A great big purse full of money. Flat face. Square body. Heavy. Be a right sod to bury – yew'd need a coffin as broad as it was long. But it was 'is voice that got me. Like grease wiv gravel in. Never 'eard a voice like that before. Unusual. Very. Distinctive.'

I was turned to ice. I knew who this must be. Dick Baines. No one else but he. Dick Baines had come especially to visit Christofer's grave? The day after he was buried? On the second of June? So why had he told me all those months ago in Sussex he'd been in Muscovy buying furs when Christofer was killed? And even as I remembered this, Meg's description of the man who'd accompanied Charley Cockatrice to Bucklersbury came to mind. Hadn't she called him a stocky man, a heavy man with a Whitehall voice? Who'd kept his face hidden in a yellow scarf? Had this also been Baines? If so then Baines must be, if not my Ishmael then his right hand, his lieutenant, his agent. An agent hidden from view behind Poley and Heneage perhaps?

I said, 'What was this man's demeanour at the graveside, Walter? Did you happen to see?'

'Yeah. He juss stood there really. Lookin' dahn.'

'Did he seem perturbed? Saddened?'

'Nah, not 'specially. More serious sort of. Like 'e was payin' his last respects, you know? Like people do. You get a lot of that in our graveyard. It sobers 'em up. Everybody 'cept Scotch Jack, that is. He's always pissed.'

I had to smile. 'And that was all?'

'Nah. There was one uvver fing.'

'What?'

'He knelt and patted the earth like you did. And then crossed himself. After that he came away.'

So Dick Baines still adhered to the ways of the old faith? Hardly surprising in itself. Many did. Old habits die hard, they say. I doubted I should read too much into that. Unless – but I put this incipient thought aside. Or rather Walter interrupted it.

'Worf a penny, is it, mister? Wot I've tole yer?'

I laughed. 'No, Walter, it's worth sixpence.' And I gave the money to him. He clicked his tongue in delight. 'But if anyone asks you about me – be careful. Just say you see a lot of gentlemen in your line of business – all right?'

'Right, sir. An' that's true too, innit? I do see all sorts, don't I?'

'Quite. Yes. And there's nothing like telling the truth where and when you can, Walter. Now off you go while I stay here. And take care.'

'You sound dead serious, mister?'

'I am. My friend was murdered.'

'Murdered?'

'In cold blood. By men more ruthless than any dockyard ruffian. So keep your counsel.'

'Christ! I will, mister, I will. Jesus God!'

He scampered away. I remained staring out at the river. From the Isle of Dogs opposite a thin mist was rising heralding the dusk. After allowing Walter a good ten minutes to be well clear of me I set back for Widow Bull's hypocritical house.

As I approached the hotel I heard a whisper from a doorway as the muffled figure of Bridget announced herself out of shadow. She swiftly handed me the wax I'd supplied her with. It now bore the deep impression of a key. When I asked how she'd managed to acquire it despite her doubts she refused to answer, saying she dared not be absent from her duties a moment longer. And with that she was gone – a ghost more frightened of the living than the living are of ghosts.

With the precious wax in my hands I went at once in search of a locksmith and was soon directed to an alley off Market Street. The locksmith asked no questions save of a practical sort – what was the gauge of the haft, the thickness of the flag (as he called the flange)? To these I answered from what I remembered of the key to my room, only hoping my observations had been accurate and that the key of Room 21 bore a likeness, a sameness to that of mine. As I waited for the work to be done I had time to reflect upon how ill-prepared I was: how ill-fitted with the basic skills required of a keen enquirer or discreet detector. Nevertheless I encouraged myself by thinking that those violently beggared of honour (as I was) had all to win and little to lose from any knowledge however clumsily gained if that same knowledge could lead them to a just revenge.

In less than half an hour I was again on my way back to the hotel but this time through the gathered dusk. Once in my room I called for hot water to wash and supper to be brought. Again Mr Clifford took my orders. He also hoped the girl Betty had given satisfaction? I said she had while inwardly yearning to strike him to the ground and kick his teeth down his throat and his balls back inside his belly whence they should never have descended in the first place. Over and above these righteous imaginings I also told him that so pleased had I been with his Betty I required her services throughout the night. He smiled a lizard smile. That would, of course, be immediately arranged, sir, but a payment on account would be helpful. Say four shillings against a further six? I didn't argue even though the price was frankly exorbitant. Why, for ten shillings you can hire any of the most luxurious and accomplished bona robas in London for three nights in a row. Whereas poor Bridget – but it was unseemly to bargain for so piteous a child. I contained my disgust, paid Clifford and dismissed him. But as the door shut I spat into the fire. My gob sizzled.

After supper Bridget came to me just as she had after dinner. Yet less fearfully. She even smiled a little. I tried to persuade her to wait up with me and then risk guiding me to Room 21. I would, I assured her, protect her from her employers should we be discovered. But she again refused, repeating that she dared not visit the death room. And shuddered so violently I asked her why. But she would not explain and I did not press her.

Meanwhile she said she was mine again to do with as I pleased. Had I not already paid Mr Clifford good money in advance? So what was my pleasure?

'To see you sleep, child,' I said. Her whole being surrendered to happiness. Her eyes, burnished by firelight, shone. 'I'll even tell you a story to put you to sleep if you like?'

She nodded, saying she was weary beyond belief. She undressed to her shift and got into bed. I tucked in the sheets around her and, taking a chair, sat beside her pillow. Then, like a father to a daughter I told her old Mother Goose's tale of Cinderella. As ever it pleased utterly. Christofer had always insisted it was the only story in the world. As I came to the moment when Cinderella's foot slid into the slipper Bridget's eyes closed for good and she slept. I watched beside her until the dockyard clock struck midnight. But unlike Cinderella I allowed the twelve strokes to finish. Only then did I take up a candle and tread softly to the door.

I stepped out into the corridor confident of my enterprise. I had decided that if I met any of the staff I would complain of a persistent but unlikely noise as of water dripping coming from the room above mine. But I met no one on the landing nor on the stair leading to the second floor – the boards, polished to a mirror's gloss, creaked, then snapped like roast chestnuts on a fireshovel but no other sounds disturbed me.

Arriving at the door of Room 21 I found myself reluctant to reach for my new-forged key. After several deep breaths I willed myself to insert it in the lock while part of me, ever contrariwise, still hoped it wouldn't fit. But no. Fortune thought differently. It not only fitted perfectly but turned at once. As I withdrew it I touched the door. It swung silently inwards on oiled hinges. I stepped in with it. Chill air struck my face, my candle flamed back at me, wax peppered my hand, my cheek and the door slammed shut behind me.

But what was this black shape? This scraping noise? This bristling whirr more horrible than twenty crossbow bolts? Something was battering at the lattice. It was a black angel beating against glass and lead and moonlight. Then it fell and became a croaking Fury that scuttled across the floor with skin-crawling scratch of claws before spewing itself around itself in a circle – one huge wing an urgent fan, the other a twisted, useless paddle. I stared in horror at this savage thing. This wounded raven. Its wicked beak sprang from its head like a steel wedge. And when it croaked I saw its black leather tongue. Its calling was, I swear, from another world than ours.

As for the rest of the room – well, it was a void awash with virgin light as cold and clear as aqua fortis. There was no bed, no table, no chairs, no close-stool, no fire-irons, no matting, not a thing save bare boards and this spinning, scraping screaming raven with its damaged wing. It was a black vortex presaging death, nothing but death.

As my five wits returned I realised this frantic creature would soon betray me with its noise. I edged past it to the window and flung the lattice wide. Then I tore off my jerkin and, praying its thickness would protect me from that vicious beak, I attempted to envelop the raven in it. But try as I might this huge carrion bird was still strong enough to throw off its padded weight or else bear it on its back across the floor. But at my third assay I managed to contain its flailing wing and stabbing beak and manhandle the whole hideous, pulsating bundle to the opened window where I flung it at the air. Revulsed and at the point of retching I watched the raven fall away hoping to see it stunned to death upon the paving stones below. But no, it struck a bush instead! Out of which it flapped and flailed with terrible squawk-ings. It landed on the path. And proceeded to waddle along it with a sudden, smug reshufflement of its wings. Both were now retracted, folded along its back as if it had sustained no hurt at all. Had its whirling dance been a pretence? How could I say? But even as I stared down upon it that agent of night broke into a hop, thence to a skittish run, spread out its powerful wings (yes, both) and flapped away, cawing most balefully.

As I shut the window I asked myself how this thing had come to be there at all? Had I released a phantom? Or had a careless servant left the window open then shut it later while failing to notice the raven's presence in that empty room? It seemed unlikely but as an explanation I much preferred it to my previous thought and so adopted it forthwith. I drew breath again and only then realised I could hear the steady plip of liquid falling to those naked boards. I looked down in some surmise. Hadn't I already invented just such a sound as a pretext for my visit here? Was this yet another trick of this dubious house? No! Or do I mean yes? For here was blood. My blood. Blood dripping from my wrist to the floor. The raven's beak must have pierced it but in my haste I'd failed to feel the wound. Just as at football when you take a knock only to discover the bruise and ache of it after the game.

I wrapped my jerkin around the cut and looked about the room. Its emptiness mocked me. Any foolish hopes I'd had of searching among the furnishings for a sign of what had happened here were gone. All gone. Perhaps I should've known? Perhaps I should've guessed it would be so? Had not authority already taken care to remove almost all trace of Christofer? Provided an unmarked grave, emptied the archives? Surely Eliza's agents had anticipated my every move? Known I would need to view this place where they'd killed Christofer? And as a consequence stripped it bare – even of its firedogs? I could only suppose so. Now all it contained was my thudding heartbeats and some spatterings of blood – not Christofer's but mine. That seemed fitting somehow.

Two minutes later I was safely back in my own room. I exchanged my jerkin for a towel to stem the blood which still flowed from my wrist. Then I sat down beside the dying fire and finished what was left of my supper wine. As I sat there trying to think of nothing and failing, Bridget opened her eyes.

'What was that noise? I was dreaming it was thunder, then I woke and it wasn't. It was footsteps above. Was that you?'

'Yes. I was doing battle with a raven.'

Her eyes widened in wonder. 'A raven? In Room 21?'

I explained what had happened. It took her a little while to comprehend my story but when she heard I'd hurt my wrist she jumped from the bed to examine it. She at once insisted on washing and bandaging it. She did both with a deftness that surprised me creating a bandage by knotting two of my handkerchiefs together. When these were bound around my wrist she took another and twirling it into a tourniquet tied it over the others to keep them securely in place. That done she gripped the vein just above the place with her thumb, holding it there until the blood flow ceased.

While she did all this I told her my enquiries there at Deptford were now at an end. I would leave in the morning and (dropping my voice to a whisper) take her with me if she was still of a mind to break out of her bondage? She murmured she was. Then, I said, she must make her own way out of the hotel and wait for me at the harbour steps. At seven o'clock. No later. She need bring nothing with her. Everything would be supplied for her comfort when we reached our destination. She must have no fear of that. She kissed my hands in gratitude as if I were a bishop.

When eventually we got to bed she snuggled against me like the child she essentially was. Her true desire of me was, I knew, simply warmth and comfort. This I endeavoured to supply as platonically as possible but as she lay against me, with her thin back and haunches pressed against my chest and belly I felt that familiar, initially insidious, ever-insistent throb in my groin. A man at a stand has no conscience, they say. And it's true. Too true. There was I doing my honest best to be a caring guardian to this prostituted child and already my importunate body was traducing me, tempting me, teasing me into using her in the very way she feared and hated. And I as vehemently had deplored.

Determined my baser nature should not overwhelm my better one I turned away from Bridget hoping the cooler sheets on the other side would reduce my tumefaction. They did nothing of the sort. Rather the contusion so increased (I was a knight of the burning pizzle) I was inclined to end this urgency with my own hand. But even as I debated my predicament within the remnants of my brain – the most of it having descended to my lower half – Bridget turned to me in her sleep.

That did it! Now I knew I must be as strong of will as any puritan pastor. In zealous desperation I reached for the bolster behind our heads and pulled and pushed it firmly between us. Bridget at once embraced it with a sigh and slept again. After a while I slept, too – though in the interim with my fleshly dilemma thus curtailed by a roly-poly of horsehair and linen I was more inclined to stay awake and laugh.

Bridget slept like an emaciated angel; I lay on my back like a defunct pharisee. Separated thus I was again at ease. As my blood and being returned to their higher seat I was free to busy myself in dreams. And eventually I did. Would I hadn't. My brain became an ante-chamber of Hell.

I was in the room above. In the way of dreams it was also this room. It was furnished again. Exactly as this one was. Except everything was black and silver. The blackest black. The brightest silver. The raven perched on a bedpost. Its head was cocked, its eye a mirror. It was observing the occupants below. As was I. Yes, my presence was there too. Unseen, pervasive, yet me. I was floating above everything, above everyone, (the ceiling had dissolved) above the raven, above Christofer, Frizer, Poley and Skeres.

Unseen and all pervasive I may have been but I had a hundred eyes and as many screaming mouths out of which no sound came. Why was I screaming? Why was I shouting stop, stop? Because those below me held Christofer spread-eagled across the supper table. Christofer was become a human sacrifice upon a damask altar. He'd been stripped naked. He was smeared with grease and wine and – oh, God, oh heaven – Mr Francis, Mr Faun, Mr Shark, Mr-in-plain-name-Frizer was teasing Christofer's modest cock, enticing it to stand up like the perky tent-peg I'd always called it – and then – oh, was this my cruel reward for my earlier restraint? – and then, oh, Lucifer, oh Beelzebub (for only from your world do such fancies come), and then Frizer whipped out his knife and all my mouths screamed: no! no! no! But yes, oh, yes. This other world meant exactly what it did. Just as this one does. Frizer struck off that dear member. At the root. Even as the enforced seed jetted forth. Just as the Ottoman's cruel soldiery do with any Christian captive. But then – wait – one must have patience in these infernal regions – for what's to come is still sure and worse. This next is beyond Hell, beyond Topcliffe, beyond Burghley, beyond Eliza even. Because now Frizer pushed the dear, cut off part into Christofer's open mouth. He gagged Christofer with his own private flesh.

Do you retch or vomit? Or are you one who has seen worse at Smithfield or on Tower Hill? Never fear there was worse to come. Yet more for me to witness in suspensive helplessness. Truly I was my own ghost at this feast of horror. Because even as the life blood flooded out of my love's pillaged groin in a silver torrent (for each and every thing was still either black or silver or both) so that same knife was come to Christofer's eye. To his right eye. And then pierced it. Oh, summit of unkindness.

Stabbed the eye and entered to the brain. Skewered that coil of invention. Pricked that bubble of all eloquence. Dimmed that heavenly lamp.

But only now was Hell's malice ready for its masterstroke. Now came my final punishment. For Frizer looked at me and grinned. And in his grinning he wasn't Ingram Frizer only. No. He'd become me! And I was as suddenly he as he was me. And Christofer, why he was – dear God, dear Lucifer – he was our mutual prey, our shared victim. My hand was Frizer's, my knife his knife and together we, Hell's agents, we killed Christofer. All came together. I was my love's executioner. Christofer died under my hand, mine! Was this, is this, true justice?

I think it was. But at the time, at that point, I woke. But only into another dream in which the canopy above me was filling with Christofer's blood. It was dripping down upon me. What is more it was red – this nightmare showed true colours. Soon I knew the bag would burst and I and Bridget would be drowned in crimson. I woke in earnest –

'What? What is it?'

Bridget had sat bolt upright. She was shaking me as I beat with my fists upon the bolster, shouting, shuddering, fighting my dream world for breath.

'What is it?'

'I don't know. I was dreaming. I'd just killed Christofer with my own hand which was also someone else's. That was the worst part – his hand, my hand. And Christofer's blood will drown us both – we must get out – look!' I pointed to the tester above us. But of course it was no longer gravid; no longer did it belly down towards me like crimson curds in muslin. I stared at its refound normalcy and shuddered.

Bridget pulled the bolster from out between us and flung it to the floor. Then she put her arm fiercely round my neck and brought my head to rest against her shoulder. She stroked my hair and murmured words of solace to me, as if she were an ample mother and I a fractious child.

I said, 'I thought I was here to comfort you, Bridget?' But such was the force of that dreadful dream my voice was still not quite mine.

Bridget hushed me and I obeyed her command. Slowly the nightmare faded but even as it detached itself from my mind I wondered if I hadn't witnessed within it a terrible truth? Suppose like that other dream this had not been dream only but revelation too? Had Christofer indeed died like that? Held by Poley and Skeres? Mutilated by Frizer before being killed by Frizer? Was this the stinking truth of the matter and not my guilty imagining? Could I, would I, ever know? I muttered something to this effect but Bridget simply kissed my brow for answer and soon I fell asleep devoid of further feeling save contentment at her blessed, innocent nearness.

mouthed. Never had she seen such luxury, she said. She'd thought the Widow Bull's house grand but this was beyond belief. As she looked about her I sent for Mr Bunnage who on arrival brought with him three letters from Lycia. I informed him of my wish that Bridget should be taken into service in Sussex and my belief that her ladyship would be delighted with her. When would a packhorse train next be going there? Why, at dawn tomorrow, sir. And he would be in charge of it. The girl could come with him. She would be as safe as if she was his daughter.

That settled I sent for the housekeeper and commanded her to find Bridget fresh clothes to wear inside the house and to travel in next day: clothes more in keeping with her new status as a waiting woman of her ladyship. Before they left the room Bridget kissed my hand and thanked me ten times over. She had never thought, she said, that her life could change. She'd thought she was bound to die at Deptford and indeed had deliberately begun six weeks ago to starve herself to that end. I told her to eat again without fear and to return to me that afternoon at four o'clock. Whereupon she kissed my cheek and ran from the room.

I now turned to Lycia's letters. The first congratulated me on my escape from death at the hands of those beggars below Coulsdon, the second on the results of my enquiries in Chancery, especially the discovery that Francis was Frizer. Now surely, Lycia wrote, I must search him out either at Walsingham's London house or in the country at Scadbury? Already she was at her prayers for my success and safety in this next imperative. The third letter expressed her horror at my so narrow escape from the hired marksman, Cato. She agreed with my conclusion – such a man couldn't have been hired by a mere city ruffian, surely? Someone of the rank of Poley at least must have sent him. But was I a cat? She thought I might be. Already, according to her reckoning I'd used up seven lives. Two upon the Downs from two crossbolts, a third when the cottage was fired and poor little Martin murdered, the fourth when she had rescued me from prison, the fifth at Topcliffe's hands either at Chelsea or upon the public scaffold, the sixth this last attempt by Cato and the seventh that day long ago I'd told her of – that day at the theatre when the soldiers shot a woman and her suckling child instead of me. She begged me as I loved her not to squander my last remaining pair of lives. Take care, Tom, take care, I implore you, she wrote.

As I read and reread Lycia's letters, so kind, so full of encouragement I felt a detachment I disliked grow within me. The fault was mine not hers. She wrote from another world. A world which although it had its dangers, illusions and, I doubted not, its share of viciousness too, was even so a world apart from Deptford. The truth was my savage experiences in that place had divorced me from Sussex and Lycia – or so it seemed. Oh, I cried aloud in the silence of my room, oh, Lycia, if only you were here so I might tell it, tell it all to your face.

But since she wasn't I seized pen and paper and wrote furiously instead, omitting nothing, not the puniest of detail, not the most fleeting thought. I set down everything of Widow Bull, of Walsingham in the garden, of Room 21 and of my evil dreams. Only when all was written out could I return to her last letter and read again with unforced pleasure of Sussex, of Dr Thwaite who'd cured a madman with a distillation of belladonna which had miraculously proved fatal to the frenzy not the patient. No wonder the more ignorant of the villagers accounted him a wizard. Mary, too, was well enough but subject to the morning sickness. The cottage meanwhile was being rebuilt exactly as it had been before and she had paid for the headstone that marked little Martin's grave.

Lycia concluded with such a protestation of love that I felt both warmed and weakened by it. How unworthy I was of such a being, such a goddess. Still shaken by the force of her affection I took up my pen and begged her to forgive me for the horrors I had just related to her and commended Bridget to her, imploring her for love of me to cherish the child whom I believed to possess a rare spirit and intelligence.

I left this postscript unfinished because I intended to question Bridget a little further so I might again praise her to Lycia. Knowing my mistress as I did the more I told her of Bridget the better; my lady was a glutton for information, for detail, for gossip. She relished every possible human convolution, adored news of any kind. She was of the opinion that broadsheets, news sheets, should be printed every day. Our world, she said, was far too secret; it bred corruption – look at Eliza. Oh, how Lycia loathed Eliza.

Next, as I waited for Bridget to return, I gritted my teeth and wrote to Walsingham at his house in London by the Tower. To do this, was I told myself, to grasp the nettle. My submissive – no, subservient letter was brief: an earnest request that I might have the honour to wait upon him the next day or at his lordship's earliest convenience. I had certain serious matters I wished to report to him concerning our mutual and always to be lamented friend, Christofer. I added that whatsoever he might have heard to the contrary I was no traitor to him or Christofer nor ever had been. Therefore I begged him to receive me.

Having scribbled this necessary but crawling compôte of truth and untruth I called for a messenger and ordered its delivery within the hour. The man went at once. How promptly the world dispatches itself for those with means or the appearance of them.

Bridget's arrival at four o'clock cheered me. Her presence removed the distaste left in my mouth by my note to Walsingham. She was transformed. Her hair shone, her cheeks even had a hint of colour, her eyes had hope in them while the housekeeper had found her a most fitting dress of myrtle green silk.

After admiring her, making her laugh and blush, I said, 'I'm writing to your future benefactress, Bridget. My lady Lycia. I've already told her everything that happened at Deptford – yes, everything – because Lycia's a woman who commands the whole truth from those she loves or is about to love. And, thanks be, she's good enough, strong enough and already knows enough to endure it. She's quite without equal, believe me. So you need keep no secrets from her.'

'You love her, sir?'

'With all my heart though my heart is a mean thing compared with hers.'

'No, please. Yours is a good heart, a generous heart, I know it for myself. How else am I here? Have you told her about your dream? And me beside you while you dreamt it?'

'Yes.'

'And also about me being obliged to – ?' She stopped and reddened furiously.

'Yes.'

'Won't she mind? Won't she say I'm – ?'

I interrupted her. 'No, she'll understand, Bridget, because I've told her why we were obliged to do it. But now I need to know a little more. About your family at Kingston.'

She hung her head and wept. 'That was a lie, sir.'

I was shocked, 'You haven't got any family at Kingston?'

'Oh, yes. They're there, sir, yes, but I wasn't betrothed to anyone.'

'So you didn't run away from home?'

'Oh, yes, yes I did, yes!'

'Explain, child.'

'Well, sir, my parents are strict Baptists, sir. The strictest of the strict. I came to love a boy who'd signed to sail to the Indies. My father said good riddance to him but I thought my heart would break. So I followed him.'

I smiled. 'You ran away to sea?'

'No. Only as far – as far as Deptford.' She drew breath. 'But when I got there his ship had sailed. Gone with the tide and a good west wind. I didn't dare go home. My father would've killed me. And stepped proudly to the scaffold for it proclaiming he'd fulfilled God's will on his strumpet daughter.'

'When you're nothing of the kind.'

'Oh, I am, sir! Now I am,' she said, close to tears again.

'No, Bridget, there's a difference. And you're quite guiltless. Believe me, I know. I've done worse than you – oh, yes, far worse – under duress. And I cursed myself for it until Lycia taught me otherwise.' She nodded but I could tell she hadn't quite believed me. I would have to leave the rest of her cure to Lycia. I said, 'So your story to me was only half-true?'

'Yes, sir, I'm sorry, sir. I wanted to appear better in your eyes. To have run away from an arranged marriage seemed somehow, well, more respectable, than following a carpenter's apprentice to sea.'

'Was that what he was? A carpenter?'

'Yes, sir. His face was all freckles.'

'He had ginger hair?'

She nodded. 'And crooked teeth.' She was half-laughing, half-crying.

'And you loved him?'

'Oh, yes. I worshipped him.'

'Well, who knows you may find him again?'

'It would take a miracle for that.'

'Then believe in miracles, Bridget, like the good Christian you are. But what happened next? Did a kind, solicitous, well-dressed citizen called Mr Clifford offer to help you in your predicament?'

'How did you guess that, sir?'

'It wasn't very difficult, my dear. The world's wickedness is almost invariably the same. Nothing is more predictable than wrong-doing. Clifford took you to the hotel?'

'Yes. And Widow Bull looked me over and said I would do.'

'As what?'

'As a kitchen maid to start with. That was how I came to be in the pantry when your friend was in the garden. Mr Clifford became my master. I had to share his bed. I'd been a virgin till then.' Once more she hung her head but then added in a mumble, 'A little later I was promoted chambermaid and like the other girls – he had three others – I had to serve any of the guests on his floor.'

'Such as me?'

She didn't reply. I took her hand and pressed it. I thanked her for telling me her history and assured her again that she would be safe and do well in Sussex. Her slavery was past, she need never see Deptford again. I thanked her too for her comforting of me (she wasn't the only one in need of help) after my nightmare and told her that without her I should never have discovered certain vital facts concerning Christofer's death. She'd aided me more than she could know. I promised to see her off in the morning and asked her to write to me from Sussex. Could she write with her own hand? Yes, she could. I patted it and kissed it. Told her like a proud father that I was proud of her. She laughed and hugged me. Here was another kind of happiness new to me.

The next morning I rode with Bridget, Mr Bunnage and the packhorse train as far as Herne Hill. How I longed to continue the journey with them. To come again to Lycia. My purpose in accompanying Bridget that far was to ensure that she should in no way be subject to public inspection by the Surrey sheriff's doctors.

But how arbitrary is authority! The road block was gone, the cordon sanitaire quite vanished, the corrals for the waiting refugees removed. The plague could now be carried into Surrey and beyond without any hindrance at all. I wondered at this change only to be informed by a constable on his way to the pound with a couple of stray goats that the sheriff had ordered the ending of the medical inspections. Why? He grinned at the question. Where had I been all my life, he enquired? The service had been suspended because it didn't pay enough, did it? The poor had no money, right? While the perfumed filthy rich rode past nose in air, didn't they? Without contributing a penny. Was he right or right or right again, eh? I laughed at his suburban cynicism and agreed he was.

On Fox Hill I said farewell to Bridget promising her she would hear from me by way of my daily letters to Lycia. And with this I gave her the one I'd written the day before and since completed with a fuller and further commendation to her ladyship. As she had cared for me, I'd written, so must she care for this new waif of fortune. I watched Bridget go, only turning my horse's head when the last bend in the road obscured any further wave of her hand.

Riding back to London I decided to call in at the Rose. As with my letter to Walsingham this was another grasping of another nettle. How would Mr Henslowe receive me? I could scarcely hope for the prodigal's welcome however much I'd urged Bridget to keep her faith in miracles. Henslowe would have undoubtedly heard of my part in Christofer's fate and passed the news to Alleyn still out on tour. Because of me the company had lost its most successful poet. And Ned Alleyn, an author of leading roles beyond compare. Where now would he find his Tamburlaines, his Fausts, his Mortimers? Let alone such slinking Machiavellis as the Duke of Guise or that jolly Jew of Malta – every death another naughty laugh – Barabas?

But the least I could do, I told myself, was to try to explain. To tell Henslowe how in the midst of my reworking of *God Speed the Plough* I'd been snatched away to Chelsea. He might listen or he might not. But I knew I had to risk it. Some kind of accord had to be made with my lost paradise – the theatre of the Rose.

Henslowe was cordial enough. Indeed after wincing at my crippledness he went so far as to offer me a glass of muscat wine and a cinnamon cake. What's more he heard me out. And nodded diplomatically when I begged him to relate my history to Ned and the rest of the company. When I said I was determined to seek out my enemy he told me what I'd told myself: that I had turned into my very own kind of mad hero. He reckoned Seneca would be proud of me, wasn't Seneca the chap we poets were always quoting? He smiled his monkey smile and I laughed, grateful to him. Philip Henslowe had proved kinder than I'd dared to hope. I'd expected censorious sniffings at the very least if not a direct rebuff.

He told me the company was shortly to return – they were up North now at York but were determined to return for Christmas come what may. They'd hoped to be back before All Hallows but business was so good they'd stayed on. He was sorry I hadn't been able to revise *God Speed the Plough* but given the circumstances he had no doubt Ned would forgive me. Yes, he'd written to inform him of Christofer's death. It had been a bad blow but he'd suspected no foul play. Perhaps that had been naive of him but there it was – he'd believed the official report. Of course he'd been struggling to survive himself. And these days people died or disappeared daily. Look how I had. Why, he'd only heard of my own imprisonment a couple of months ago. He'd sent to Bucklersbury to enquire after my progress with the script (the which, by the way, Ned himself was now at work upon) only to be informed that my lodgings were nailed up and I was in the Clink. When he'd gone there – the prison being adjacent to the Rose and his bordello and indistinguishable from either as the old company joke used to have it – the governor had given him to understand I was now under the protection of a great lord who could not be named. A great lord's sister, I answered. He knew Lady Lycia, he said, well, leastways he knew her by sight and had heard a lot about her. She was said to be a mantis woman, was she not? A what, I said? One not unlike a tropic insect which devours those that breed with it, he replied. I told him he'd heard fools' talk and closed the subject.

He took no offence. And had in his turn news for me. The days of Lord Strange were, he reckoned, truly numbered now. The continuance of the company under his patronage was in grave doubt. So much so – but this was entirely between ourselves – that Ned had already written to other interested parties to sound them out. No, he'd rather not name names – I knew how delicate, even fragile such things were in the theatre, didn't I? A word in the wrong place and you'd have offended Sussex for instance, infuriated Nottingham for example and gladdened the heart of Southampton who never intended to back you in the first place having his own fish to fry. Thus without telling me Henslowe had named those lords most likely to replace Ferdinando.

Lord Strange – or rather Derby as he now was – had got iller and iller, he said, ever since September when he'd come into the title. He had now returned to London. The word came only yesterday. And with it an enquiry concerning me: did Henslowe know of my wherabouts?

'His lordship asked after me?'

'He did, Mr Kyd, yes. In no uncertain terms. His note said he understood from a mutual friend – of yours and his, he meant – that you'd now come out of the country and were once again in the city.'

A chill ran through me. This information must have come from Baines. I said, 'Was the note in his lordship's own hand?'

'Unmistakably so. I recognised every shake of it. It's astonishing he can write at all really given the palpitations he endures.'

'I don't suppose he said why he wanted to see me?'

'No, but he called you his friend. And said the matter was urgent as he wasn't long for this world. So why don't you go, Mr Kyd? From the sound of it you could hear something to your advantage?'

I thanked Henslowe and rode along to the horseferry in division of mind. Should I answer Ferdinando's call? And if I did, should I go at once? Or wait? Or ought I to ignore it altogether?

Was it a trap as Baines's letter had surely been? I'd ignored that initial invitation upon Lycia's advice so why not this one upon my own? And did his enquiry of Henslowe really mean he didn't know I was a guest of Bobby Radcliffe's sister in the Strand? Surely Baines must know this? Great houses are like colanders – they leak information at every aperture. Discarded by Lycia though Baines might be I was certain he remained on good terms with her brother and his household. He was that kind of man.

Once more I was at sea, bobbing like a cork on a swell of unknowing. Had Baines persuaded Ferdinando to initiate enquiries for me? Or had his lordship acted on his own behalf? Or – new consideration consequent to this – was Baines still in favour at Whitefriars? Or not? Perhaps my speculations about him were beside the point? Suppose between the writing of his letter to me in Sussex and Ferdinando's note to Henslowe, Dick Baines had fallen from yet another's grace? First from Lycia's, now Ferdinando's?

Consumed by these thoughts I entered my room to find my messenger to Walsingham waiting. He had an answer for me. I thanked him. He left. This is what I read: 'Mr Kyd: my master has instructed me to reply to your request. He can perceive no useful purpose in an interview. To him you are and will ever remain a common informer and a treacherous friend. If you value your life do not communicate again. Lady Audrey is of a like opinion. Keep clear.'

The note was signed with a dashed-off, arrogant F. I presumed it stood for Frizer. But did Walsingham now consider himself an equal with royalty? Was I forbidden on pain of death to come within twelve miles of his person? As Raleigh had been by Eliza on marrying Miss Throckmorton? I laughed but angrily.

But then again, as with Ferdinando's enquiry, whose words were these? Walsingham's or Frizer's? Had Frizer, as his secretary, intercepted my message and answered it without consulting his employer? Were these Walsingham's true feelings towards me or was this Ingram Frizer's fashioning of the event to suit his loyalty to Eliza's state? Again I shivered. I knew myself to be a marked man. But marked down by whom, by what? Public interest or private hatred?

This rebuff from whomsoever it came did nevertheless serve its turn. At least upon the meagre principle that it's a truly ill wind which blows no one any good. It had the effect of making me determined to risk answering Ferdinando's call. If I must stay clear of Walsingham then I would pursue my quest in this other quarter.

·X·X·

The following day I went to Whitefriars. To that ancient house which for five years had meant more to me than my own home ever had. England dwelt there. Old England, that is. The England that was before our royal vixen's royal father destroyed it utterly, razing the best of it to the ground and making beggars of half his subjects.

To enter these London lodgings of the Stanleys was to discover a world of stone and luxury. Here were no universal modern comforts – only occasional old ones. No new-fangled wainscotting – just dim and draught-billowed Arras cloths dating from God knows when; no bright rush-mattings – simply footworn stone; few chairs with backs save for their lordships and their favourites – rather a ready supply of benches such as any follower of St Benedict, or any grammar schoolboy come to that, would have found familiar. If this sounds bleak it wasn't. Because everywhere there was polished brass, and gold, and soft buffed silver, and painted glass and fires spiked with dried thyme or lavender burning in every hearth even in summer (my former patron felt the cold tremendously) and the best and brightest wax candles flaming before polished scones or Italian mirrors and frankincense drifting out of the chapel at every canonical hour, while the liveries of the staff would have graced even the Queen's eternal darling – Robert Devereux himself.

The old ways held sway everywhere. Even as far as the privies. Ferdinando – and me, too, once I'd overcome my plebian prudery – would join his servants at the communal bench and evacuate himself most companionably. A ten-yard length of scrubbed ashboard with sixteen convenient holes set within it, each with its own pot lid answered the needs of the highest to the lowest – the last four apertures being of various smaller sizes for the children of the house. The buckets beneath were emptied thrice daily into the Thames. As a result the house smelt fresher than most whilst always retaining a heady residue of humanity, prayer and something lost.

Don't mistake me. I'm no Pope's man though I've sometimes wished I were. Or rather I wish – here's the break in England's heart – I wish we'd never had cause to part from Rome. But such regrets are childish. We had cause like it or not. Besides it's not for us to call back yesterday even if it may occasionally be visited.

As I approached the main door the worn arch of it lifted my heart. Seeing it again tears sprang to my eyes. The ghost of the silly poet in me was once more charmed, seduced, impressed. But when it opened and I had been admitted my old world effusions were tempered by my present reception. I'd assumed – what a fantastical builder of imaginary futures I am – that I'd be welcomed with an all-embracing pleasure and find myself led straightaway, superseding all other petitioners, to his lordship's presence. No. I was made to wait.

I was deposited, charmingly, smoothly, in an anteroom I knew from past experience to be the repository of other men's messengers, tailors, grocers, charcoal merchants beseeching payment. Not that any such were present. Placed there by a steward new to me I was left in a perfect hiatus with only a blazing fire and an old rheumaticky dog for company. After a moment the dog heaved itself to its feet and stalked, stiff-legged from the room.

Minutes passed, then an hour. I was brought a tradesman's dinner of cheese and pickles, good beer. With it came the old dog again whose name I now remembered – Plautus. He helped eat the cheese and was happy to wash it down with beer poured into the empty pickle dish. As he finished his burp of gratitude was timed to perfection. Plautus had always been a gentleman.

Later I heard voices at the door. Recognising both I looked up expectantly but no one entered. The first was the dry rasp of

Father Ignatius and the second belonged to Dick Baines – those unctuous yet hearty tones could only be his. I strode to the door and pulling it open was confronted by Father Ignatius. Beyond him I glimpsed Dick's broad back turning a corner of the corridor. I wanted to push past and go after him but Iggy blocked my exit.

'Thomas,' he said with his ever-politic smile. 'I'd heard you'd arrived. His lordship will be pleased.'

'Was that Dick Baines, father?'

'Of course. No other. He's a constant visitor. But for his company and encouragement his lordship would have died long ago. Or so we all believe' Another tensile smirk. 'He'll be with him now. Dick reads to him. Or else they play at dice or cards. Occasionally at chequers. Not chess. Alas, his lordship cannot concentrate long enough for chess. How did you hear he desired to see you? Or did you divine it in your water? With your poet's intuition?' Father Iggy had long ago put this world and most of its inhabitants into inverted commas the better to emphasise the ineffable superiority of the next – to which he, for one, was self-evidently bound.

I said, 'Neither. I just heard he'd been enquiring for me.'

'From whom did you hear?'

Trust Iggy to require the name of my informant. 'Does it matter?' I answered, bristling.

'No, not especially. One can discover it easily enough if necessary. I don't suppose it is. His lordship sent far and wide for news of you. I advised him *not* to see you, by the way.' Honeyed laugh. 'I only tell you this so you know where you stand, of course.'

I drew breath, loathing the man as ever. 'Why? Why did you advise him against seeing me?'

'I believe enough damage has been done, Thomas. More than enough.'

'Who by? Me? Is that what you mean?' By now I was boiling.

'If you insist – yes.'

He stood his ground. I was tempted to spit at his feet. Instead I said, 'Did you stop my letters?'

'What letters?'

'The letters I wrote from prison last June. I wrote three to his lordship. Three!'

'Did you indeed? Then I'm more than surprised I didn't see them, Thomas.'

Could I believe him? I doubted it. I said, 'I shall ask his lordship when I see him.'

'Do. He can't wait to embrace you again.'

'Really? Then why have I already kicked my heels in here for two hours? Or did you fail to advise him of my arrival? For some reason?'

'Not at all. Word was sent at once. I expect he's needed to compose himself before this emotional occasion, this precious reunion. Have you been fed?' He spoke as if I were a horse.

'Beer and cheese.'

'You feel slighted? Put about? Disobliged?'

I shrugged. I was damned if I was going to admit pique to Father Ignatius. I said untruthfully, 'I'm inured to discomfort, father.'

'Is that so? Then you're well on your way to leading a holier life, Thomas. But it would seem our new steward – he's from Stoneyhurst by the way, devout as they come of course but with little or nothing between his faithful ears – it seems he must have mistook your state.' He paused to look me up and down. 'I should've thought your clothes would have alerted him to your importance. Whom do you serve nowadays, dare I ask?'

I held his ironic eye. 'Myself.' I answered.

Iggy laughed. 'Then you are unique, Thomas! A non-pareil! Unparalleled! I know of no one, no one in this world certainly, who serves himself. Not even His Holiness the Pope. Or rather least of all his Holiness. How do you do it?'

'Easily. I've become an atheist.'

His face darkened and for an instant I detected something genuine in him. He said, 'Oh, have a care, Thomas, I beg you. That's no joke – not in this world or the next. No laughing matter at all. But come along, we can't have you resenting your welcome here whatever I may feel about your visit. I'll take you through to somewhere more comfortable. And less draughty. I'm sure you'll remember it.'

I followed him upstairs to his lorship's library where I had often spent many hours fair-copying Ferdinando's verses. He had a subtler mind than Walsingham, was far better read, but his talent for prosody was not much better. Some of his satires had an edge but his elegies sank under the weight of their own sincerity. His wit rarely survived the journey from brain to page. However I remain grateful to Ferdinando Stanley since by copying his efforts I convinced myself I could do better. And so became a poet myself.

Another generous fire burned in the library but now there was a Turkey rug before it and another on the table. The padded chairs had backs and this time I had the company not of old Plautus but of Monsignor his lordship's privileged puss-cat – an enormous grey-blue Persian that was almost as much a cushion as a creature.

I waited for the rest of the afternoon until five o'clock. During this while I reflected upon Dick Baines. The day before I'd wondered if he was out of favour. Now I was assured he wasn't. In fact it appeared he had ingratiated himself even further with Ferdy, as he always called him. Why? Out of unadulterate human kindness? Possibly – though according to Lycia, Dick had never done anything for nothing. But what advantages were there in a dying patron? More than a few, surely? A deed of gift wrested from a wasting brain? A remunerative codicil to the will? Yes, both were possible. Or did Dick's devotion to the latest Earl of Derby also have an eye to the future? Was he hoping Ferdy's successor would look upon him with equal favour? After all, to be banker, broker, adviser to a succession of Stanleys is no small matter. Could his letter to me have been part of this strategy? Had he urged this reunion upon Ferdy? Was I a pawn on his career's chessboard? Had Dick superseded Iggy in his lordship's confidence and was my visit proof of it? Hence Father Ignatius's double-edged welcome and this continuing delay?

As these thoughts chased themselves like cloud shadows across water meadows I suddenly wondered if I was about to be visited, there and then, by Dick Baines? The thought was a jolt. What would I do? How should I behave? What ought I to say? How much did he know? Should I beard him at once? Ask him where was his hand in all of this? Why, for instance, had he gone to Deptford to stand at Christofer's unmarked grave? And how had he known it was his? Had he really been surprised to hear Poley was an agent of Eliza? Or was he too of the service, though unseen? Come to that what had he really been doing in France all those years ago? Apart from buying wine for the Cecils, as Lycia had said? What, for pity's sake, *was* his part in my butchered life and Christofer's? Was he the end of all my searchings? Of heart and mind and God knows where? Did I dare ask: are you, are you my Ishmael?

Put thus my desperate questions seemed childishly awkward and far too easily refutable. Dick could and would, I was sure, turn them all aside or stand them on their heads. He'd smile and smile and be a villain. Or not. Even so I made up my mind to ask them, to blurt them out however crassly, however naively (why pretend I was a politician when I wasn't?) if Dick Baines called in upon me.

He didn't. As so often life begged my questions. And with every passing minute I told myself to take matters into my own hands. Why shouldn't I rush out from there and burst in upon them both? Take Ferdinando and Dick by storm? Force them to hear me! Force Dick to declare himself in another's presence!

So urged one half of me – my good angel perhaps? – while the other counselled caution, or was it cowardice? I felt as though I was balanced on the knife edge of myself. And then the clock struck five. Five o'clock! Five in the afternoon! An hour to me as devilish as midnight. That time. That dreadful hour when at Chelsea I swore to tell my inquisitors anything they wanted, anything. This clock, that clock did it! I would go! I'd confront them both! I strode at once towards the door even as the bell for compline joined the chiming of the hours. But before I could wrench it open there was a knock and the earnest new steward appeared.

He looked as startled as I did. The pair of us in mid-movement: he entering, me exiting. On stage we'd have got a laugh.

He shook himself like a flummoxed pullet and said, 'His lordship will see you now, sir.'

'And about time,' I said. 'Is Mr Baines still with him?'

'Oh, no, sir. He never stays for compline.

'I'm to join his lordship at prayer?'

'That is his wish, sir. If you would be so good. This way, sir.'

I followed him without much gladness. I wanted earthly answers, information, facts, not beseechings of a heavenly power. He led me through to an interior balcony which overlooked the chapel. Within this shuttered prayer box screened from view by pierced wooden panels brought over from Spain lay Ferdinando Stanley. The air about him was heavy with incense and vibrant with prayers and responses sung by a powerful quartet of choristers stationed below while Father Ignatius and the rest of the household knelt before the altar.

I was shocked by my lord's appearance. He lay upon a litter mattressed twice over. He wore a silk gown but was blanketed by a huge heap of furs: sable, bear, wolf. Charcoal braziers were placed all round him. This private box glowed with heat but still Ferdinando shook. He looked as grey as a winter sea.

'It's so cold, isn't it?' were his first words. His question didn't admit of a denial. I nodded diplomatically while still recovering from my shock at the sight of him: the only brightness in Ferdinando was the red rimming of his eyes. The rest was dull, palpitating shriveldom. It was evident his shaking wasn't caused by exterior cold. His illness lay within. He read my thoughts. 'Dick says it isn't cold that makes me shiver, though I've always felt the cold, no, he says there's some other cause. And gives me tinctures made up especially for me by a doctor of the Grand Sophy now retired from Persia and home again in Islington. Do you know Islington, Thomas? A pretty place. I once wondered whether to build a summer house at Islington – we have some land there. Or we did. For all I know Dick may have sold it. I leave everything to him now. How good of you to come. Are you well?'

Ferdinando's appearance might have changed but the stream of his conversation hadn't. It flowed directly from him without stop or particular coherence. What unity it possessed came from its evenness of tone. And an absolute certainty of being listened to.

How could he ask after my health? Knowing what he must? I swallowed my exasperation and said, 'I believe you've been asking for me, my lord?'

'Everywhere, my dear. Oh, yes, everywhere. I've scoured the city for you. Sent messengers all over the place.'

'But not to Sussex Place?'

'You're staying with Bobby Radcliffe?'

'No, he's on an embassy to Scotland.'

'Is that so? Does he speak the language? Forgive me, we should never joke about the Scotch – such a solemn race. So vengeful. Bloody handed to a fault. I didn't know you knew Radcliffe?'

'I don't. I've met him, of course. Who hasn't in the theatre? But I'm a guest of his sister.'

'Really? Lady Lycia? How *very* interesting. And why hasn't Dick told me this? He knows her terribly well, I hear. He might have said. He knew I was frantic for my Thomas.'

Was he deliberately quoting Christofer's play? I couldn't be sure. Ferdinando's references are as slippery as trout. I said in all apparent innocence, 'Perhaps he didn't know, sir?'

'Rubbish. Of course he did. He told me ages ago she'd hauled you out of the Clink. And that you were her guest in Sussex. But not in London. He didn't tell me she'd given you the run of her London house. I was told you'd returned to your own lodgings. Really this won't do. And I shall tell him so. What's the point of Dick if he isn't the fount of all knowledge? None. None at all. he becomes a nothing – a nullity. A gossipy broker with a boil on his bottom. He's got a nasty one at the moment. It pains him dreadfully. He has to perch sideway on chairs like a nun on a horse. Fancy a man of his age getting boils. I tell him it's a sure

·342·

sign of impure thoughts. So what of dear Lycia? Such a formidable woman. Are she and Dick still intimates?'

'No, sir. He fell from favour.'

'Did he? Well, well, here's news indeed! When ? When? He's never said. Don't tell me you've supplanted him? Did you? I'm sure you did. Oh, my dear boy, it's so good to see you. You perk me up no end. I feel almost alive again. If it weren't for this fearsome chill in my bones I'd be my old self. But fancy, just fancy Dick, Dick of all people, not telling me all? Withholding things from me. Such as you and Lycia being lovers. Aren't you terrified of her? I am. You haven't kissed me, have you? I think you should.'

I kissed him dutifully upon the cheek. He pouted. 'Not there, boy.' And he pursed up his bloodless lips in a parody of a kiss. I touched him briefly with mine. 'You're older,' he said. 'And whatever happened to your poor hands?'

I couldn't believe my ears. Or rather I could. This was so like, too like Ferdinando to pretend he didn't know of my misfortunes!

I bit back my anger and said, 'Hasn't Dick told you? He must have?'

To my surprise Ferdinando began to cry. 'I didn't mean to,' he said.

'Mean what?'

'To get you into trouble, Tom.'

I shivered where I sat. Suddenly that sweaty closet was icy cold. I said, 'What are you saying, sir?'

'Only – you must forgive me, promise you will – only that I gave my consent. They refer everything to me, you see. Everything.'

What could he mean? 'Your consent? Consent to what? And to whom? Who are *they*?'

He sighed impatiently at my question. 'Oh, my dear, you used not to be so slow, so dull. Father Ignatius, of course. And Dick. They're *they*. But you must never say I said so. You won't, will you? Promise?' His eyes, big as a child's and full of sudden doubt and fear beseeched me. 'I didn't want to give it, Tom. Not one bit. I was most reluctant, believe you me.'

'But you did? Even so?'

'Don't sound so hard, please. They said it was all for the best. For the greater good. And for the cause as well. But I stuck out. I kept saying it did seem such a shame. And I'd been rather fond of you really. Whereupon they said if I felt like that I could always ask you back, couldn't I? Afterwards. Reinstate you. That way I could easily make amends, they said, why not? And, well, I inclined to agree. So that's what I want to do, my dear. Yes. Oh, so much. To have you back. Here with me. To be my companion. To read to me. To amuse me. You're much more my sort of person than Dick. I'll reward you. Do say yes.'

I could hardly think for horror. Let alone reply. Was this palsied thing under its mound of furs human? Eventually I managed to say, 'I want this stated plainly without equivocation, sir. Have you just told me you gave your permission for Dick and Father Ignatius to betray me to Eliza's agents?'

He giggled. 'But of course, my dear. Yes.'

'Why?'

'Because they said I had to.'

'You said for the cause. What cause? Rome's? Are you active for Rome?'

Ferdinando croaked with laughter. I was reminded of the raven in Room 21 at Deptford. His tongue looked almost as black. 'But of course, my dear! One is ever loyal. It's in the blood but I wouldn't say I was really active – I mean, just look at me!' More laughter. Had his malady ruined his brain as well as his body, I wondered? It was difficult to say – given his former genius for non sequitors. 'No, I'm not at all active,' he continued. 'I don't so much work for the cause – heaven forbid – as emblazon it. Yes! That's it. Yes. Not to put too fine a point upon it we Stanleys do – well – rather stand for something, don't you know? Our family's faith has never altered. And as such we tend to be referred to. Even deferred to. People look to us to give a lead. But that's all I do. I tell Father Ignatius I'm a touchstone. He agrees. I leave it to him to do all the – you know – the arrangements, the day-to-day planning, that sort of thing. He loves it. He adores to rule the roost does Iggy.'

I said, 'Does he rule Dick, too?'

He pulled me closer and whispered conspiratorially in my ear. As if this were a game. 'Between ourselves, my dear, they quarrel all the time. Oh, yes. It's bicker, bicker, bicker. But in the end it's Iggy who's in charge. He's the one responsible. It's he who must report back, you see.'

I'd demanded clarity. Now it seemed I'd got it. Well – up to a point. If Father Ignatius commanded Ferdinando and Dick then together they constituted a closet triumvirate for Rome. With Dick as chief executant, Ferdy as figurehead and profound exchequer and Iggy as guardian of the faith, spiritual leader and temporal strategist. But if as I suspected Baines had the ear and trust of Heneage (and even higher who knew?) then another question had to be asked: to whom or what was Dick more loyal? Eliza or Rome? Where was his bias? Was he a spy for Eliza at Whitefriars or a spy for Rome at Whitehall? Either (in which case which?) or both? Such double men aren't easily dissected. To say they deceive one side the better to serve another is not always true. Often they hardly know themselves. They drink and please their fancies. In the end they can only be loyal to the games they play. And their own doubtful survival.

I said, 'Why did they choose me?'

'So you could betray Christofer, of course. Dick wasn't after you, Tom. Not as such. Nor was Iggy. You weren't their quarry. Christofer was. He was so much better known than you. That's why I was on your side. I've always cared for you, my dear. Far more than for Christofer. It seemed so unfair on you and I said so.'

'They *knew* I'd betray Christofer?'

'Oh, yes, it was a foregone conclusion, they said. Everybody confesses everything at Chelsea apparently. Though Dick tells me you held out rather – somewhat to his surprise. He thought you'd break at once. But you were made of sterner stuff, he said.'

My eyes burned with fury. My breath was lost. I could have throttled Ferdinando where he lay. Somehow I controlled myself. Somehow I breathed again. I said, 'Why did they want Christofer?'

'Oh, to have him put on trial and executed, of course, as an atheist.'

'How would that help Rome?'

'Just what I asked, my dear.'

'And what was the answer?'

'Dick needed a success. He'd come under suspicion at Court. And of course the rumours as to his loyalty were largely correct. So naturally he needed to improve his standing with the Cecils and Heneage. Not to mention Eliza who'd become excessively crabby last Spring. Something had to be done to keep Dick in place. So what better, what could be more spectacular, than for him to be the loyal instrument, the keenest of keen intelligencers, who brings our naughtiest poet to book? Rather a coup if you'll forgive the pun. Heneage, too, was champing at the bit for a major scandal. And Dick was only too anxious to oblige. He even thought it might get him his knighthood.' Another giggle.

'And how exactly did Dick set about doing all this?'

'Easily. Through one of our people already in the field, as we say.'

'Where?' But I could answer the question before I'd finished asking it. 'At Scadbury in Kent? With Walsingham?'

'How did you guess, dear boy?'

'I didn't, did I? I was there. With Christofer.'

'Oh, of course! How stupid of me. Of course you were. Well, according to Dick everything just fell into place. It was almost uncanny, he said. As if it had been preordained. Which in a way it was, I suppose. The man in question – a rather unsettling creature by the name of Frizer – had first been put there by Eliza to keep an eye on Walsingham. But meanwhile Dick, clever Dick, had won Frizer over to *us*, d'you see? I'm sure you remember Frizer?'

'Yes, he was known as Master Francis. I loathed him.'

'Me too. A most difficult, dislikeable man. Excessively physical. Dick tells me he buggered Walsingham senseless before you and Christofer arrived. And was so jealous of your friend he needed no urging to steal that manuscript of that ridiculous lecture – but you know all about this, don't you, dear boy? Silly me. I'm so sorry – I keep forgetting just how much you must know and how pertinent you were to Dick's plan.'

'It was Dick ordered Frizer to steal the manuscript?'

'Oh, no. Nothing so crude as that. Give the man some credit. Dick advised Heneage to instruct Frizer to purloin it, didn't he? Thus getting our enemies to do our work for us. That's the beauty of penetrating the other side's body politic, isn't it? It enables one to employ a certain finesse.'

Again Ferdinando giggled. Did his sick brain imagine I'd be pleased by his revelations. I said, 'But what went wrong?'

'Wrong? I don't understand? What do you mean – wrong?'

'Well, Dick's complot didn't end as you'd all envisaged, did it?'

He bristled. 'Don't you try to implicate me, Tom. I told you I stand at one remove.'

I nearly bit my toungue not saying what I thought: that he was up to his neck in it quite as much as Baines, quite as much as Father Ignatius. Instead I said, 'Dick's plan seems to have failed. Christofer wasn't tried in public, was he? Just murdered in private.'

'Oh, I see. Yes. Quite right, my dear. Yes. And *that*, between you, me and the bedpost, is why Dick and Iggy bicker so. The whole affair has rather soured Dick, I'm afraid. Which is why he's no longer such good company and I need you, you, dear Tom, to replace him.'

'But you still haven't said why the plan failed. Why?'

'I do wish you wouldn't sound so hard.'

'Why?'

He sighed at my insistence. 'You used not to be so brusque, Tom. I always said you were the most civilised of poets. Now you aren't, it seems.'

'Tell me! What happened?'

'Rome spoke.'

'It did?'

'Mm. Iggy got the message. Rome annulled the whole business at the very last moment. They said there was to be no public trial and no public execution. The Vatican feared Eliza would put

Marlowe on show as a Roman spy, you see. Present his blasphemies and atheism as masks for his supposed intelligence work for the Pope!'

'Use him to discredit your cause yet further?'

'Quite. Rome wasn't having *that*. Oh, no. But they didn't seem to care what happened to Dick as a result. So, of course, he and Iggy quarrelled like mad. It was all rather awful really. Everything had gone so smoothly up till then. But Dick – quite rightly in my view – wanted to know how on earth he was supposed to put this change of plan to Heneage without casting huge suspicion upon himself? After all, the whole affair had been thought up to do precisely the opposite – to make Dick look as white as an annunciation lily.'

Closing my mind to his description of an operation that had included my tortures as smooth I said, 'So what did Dick do?'

Ferdinando hesitated. His eyes filled with a kind of coy, flirtatious doubt. 'I do rather wonder if I ought to tell you, my dear. Given your attitude. I'm not asking you to feel grateful – how could I? – but I do feel – well, I am trying to make amends to you, Tom. Sincerely I am.'

That did it! That half-baked, self-deceiving apology did it! The carbuncle that was me burst. I took that shrivelled lord by the shoulders and shook him till he cried. His head flopped back and forth like a rag doll's while I cursed him, hissing, screaming in bursts, 'God damn you! God blast you! Hell roast you! How dare you pretend to love me! How dare you say you want me back? You didn't last June! Am I to be grateful because you spoke for me so feebly you were overruled? Am I to forgive you? Live as your kept companion to salve your rotten conscience? I'd rather die! But now you listen you! You listen! You tell me everything or I'll shake you to death. To death here and now. I'll snap the breath out of your windpipe. Like this!'

And I flung him back then forward more violently than ever. His head jerked crazily and colour flooded his face. A sickening puce. His breath stopped. I thought I'd already killed him. I pushed him back against the cushions, propping him there. Was he dead? No. His eyes were opening. They took a while to focus.

I waited. Eventually he spoke in a whisper as dry as sand shaken upon paper.

'Oh, Thomas, you're right. I deserve it. I know you can't forgive me but one always lives in hope, doesn't one? So foolish. I'll tell you everything, I promise.'

I took control of myself again. I said, 'Very well. What did Dick do next? When he got the counter command from Rome?'

Ferdinando sighed, shook his head, raised a feeble hand to finger his throat. For a moment I thought I'd have to shake him again but to my relief he spoke. He said, 'Dick risked his life.'

'How?'

'Well, it's rather complicated really. But please, promise you won't be cross again, will you? Though I do understand how bitter you must feel.'

'Good. I do feel bitter. Yes.'

'Your voice used to be so warm.'

'Go on.'

'Well, Walsingham decided to get Christofer abroad. He persuaded him he had to break his bail and take a boat to France.'

'Only the wind failed?'

He was startled. 'How do you know that?'

'I've no need to tell you, have I? Go on.'

'Well, anyway they went to Deptford with Frizer who naturally sent word to his superiors at Chelsea – '

'Yes. Two agents came down. One of them's dead now but the other's still alive – Robert Poley. Do you know him?'

'No. Nor do I wish to.'

'Very wise of you. What then?'

'Well, Frizer also got a message to Dick warning him of what he'd had to do. After all, Frizer's life would've been forfeit if Walsingham had got Christofer to France, wouldn't it?'

'I daresay. So – forewarned thus what did Dick do?'

Another hesitation. His eyes avoided mine. I reached forward, placing my hands on his emaciated shoulders. He shuddered, murmured, 'No, no. I'll tell you, Tom, I will.' And suddenly I saw myself as no better than Poley or Topcliffe. To shake this withered leaf into speech was as easy for me as enforcing my confession had been to them. I almost choked on the bile of my own revulsion. To be no better than these! To be reduced to their methods! But even so I didn't remove my hands from Ferdinando's shoulders until he began to speak again – in earnest.

He said in a deathly whisper, 'Dick had a letter sent as if from Heneage ordering Christofer's death then and there. That very day. At Deptford. It was to be after supper. And the cause of death was to be reported as an accident incurred during an argument about the supper bill. That said they could employ whatever means they wished – a knife, a broken neck, a fatal fall.'

'Dick forged this letter?'

'Good heavens no. Just Heneage's seal. He got an apprentice scribe to write it – the poor lad met with a mortifying accident the next day – and then attached the seal. Dick prides himself on his collection of seal rings.' I wondered if he had Ferdinando's. He saw my look and nodded. 'Oh, yes, he's always getting mine copied. But there again Iggy always tells me so I get another one designed. It's become quite a game for us. Such a tease. He knows that I know that he knows sort of thing.' He looked at me imploring a smile for this small pleasantry. I found I hadn't got one.

I said, 'And when Heneage discovered the deception?'

Oh, he blew up. Like gunpowder in a fireship. Bits went everywhere. There was a tremendous pother. And *three* internal enquiries, would you believe? He was so piqued, you see. He'd set his heart on a show trial. It was to crown his career. Get him the Secretaryship in substance not in shadow. You know Burghley's never officially appointed him? So devious – that man. But despite all Dick's survived – well, just. I won't say he's whiter than white anymore – a cloud does hang somewhat over and above his head. But there's no proof and no link. Even so he can't forgive Iggy. He thinks Iggy should've stood up to the Vatican, told them a dedicated and experienced man such as he safely lodged in the heart of the English service was worth any number of show trials of paltry poets. One does see his point. It had taken Dick years to get where he was, poor fellow. Come what may he's a spent force now – and his life's work come to nothing and through no fault of his own.'

I stared at Ferdinando Stanley. As much as I despised him and was disgusted by his lordly frivolity of mind, part of me could still pity him and also wonder now if his illness – this grey palsy – was entirely natural? I thought that if I ever saw Dr Thwaite again I'd ask him if such a condition might owe as much to the hand of man as of God? In other words were those tinctures Dick's distinguished doctor prescribed quite what they seemed? Or were they bringing Ferdinando to an inexorable but premature end?

My good angel suggested I advise him of this possibility but I regret to say my bad angel thought otherwise and I held my tongue.

Instead I said, 'Have you told me everything?'

'So stern, Thomas. Yes, yes. I have.' My doubt must have disturbed him because he hurriedly added that on second thoughts there was one other thing. Just one last thing. What was that? 'Well, I do think – unlikely as it may seem – that Dick did rather care for your friend Christofer.'

'What makes you say that?' What pain was this in my heart?

'Oh – any number of things. I may be wrong but I don't think so. I'm rather good at matters sentimental or so I flatter myself. He often said – and with genuine regret – what good friends they'd been. Years back, of course. In France. Dick was over there buying wine for Burghley but also keeping a weather eye on various students – mostly of the poorer sort placed there at the privy purse's expense. Secretary Walsingham was a terror, apparently. Dead set on getting value for money. Anyway Dick rather fell for Christofer.'

'They became true friends?'

'So Dick always said.'

'Loving friends?'

'I've no idea. Does it matter? It was all so long ago. '86, was it?' Such insouciant vagueness! I saw I'd underestimated my former patron. He too could administer secret poison. This was his revenge. I might assault him, shake him like a puppet, but he in his turn, tit for tat, could and would distress my mind, stir jealousies I'd never dreamed of. And appear gracious, too, even as he did it. Even as he slipped the envenomed point between my ribs.

I said, 'I must go.'

He tried to prevent me. He begged, he whined, he promised me anything I wished for if only I would stay. He conjured up visions of us working together, preparing a slim volume of his verses – to be published privately, of course. He would reaffirm his patronage of his theatre company – I would write plays again, even act again if I chose. What did it matter if I had a stiff knee and crippled hands? There were plenty of parts for handsome cripples – I could play Vulcan, Richard of Gloucester, the Sheriff of Nottingham.

'Please, my dear. Forgive and forget. I do blame myself and I'll make it up to you. Let some good come out of evil, I beg you.'

I left him blathering – this quasi-Ishmael – in that stinking box as Father Ignatius called upon God to lighten our darkness.

·X·X·I·

Two days later Lycia's father died and her brother returned to London. Two hours after his magnificent arrival I found myself *persona non grata* at Sussex Place. His steward informed me that his lordship had been advised to be rid of me. When I asked by whom I was told that was no concern of mine. When I pointed out I was a guest of Lady Lycia the steward smiled indulgently and said the entire house now belonged to the new earl and it was he who decided who stayed and who did not. I answered I would protest to Lady Lycia. He seriously advised me to do nothing of the sort and to take myself off before dusk. Otherwise his lordship would not hesitate to have me forcibly ejected. When I begged for an interview with Bobby Spend-All I was told that was out of the question; his lordship did not meet unsound men.

I went. What else could I do? I supposed Ferdinando, piqued by my refusal to return to him, had poisoned Sussex against me. Or perhaps Dick Baines had? I couldn't tell and, suddenly – it was an unfamiliar feeling – I didn't care. I would go where I chose. To my own place whatever the danger. Yes, I would return to Bucklersbury where I would be beholden to no one. I would be my own man again. And if that meant I was a dead one, thanks to Charley Cockatrice, then so be it.

On this surge of angry impetuosity I took a boat for the city. When I got there with my trunk and a grumbling porter I found the Green Man more shut up than ever and the staircase up to my lodgings covered with dry onion skins which drifted like feathers about my feet. As I reached my door I became aware of an insidious smell. I'd known the place stink of everything from tobacco to pickled herrings to dirty dishcloths but never like this. It was if anything more unpleasant than nightsoil. It had something of burnt cabbage mixed with cat's piss about it.

And what new horror was this? From beneath my now unboarded door ran a stream of blood – or was it? It seemed so in the encroaching dusklight. I stepped back, the sole of my left shoe sticking to the floor. Who had unbarred my door? I'd warned the porter I'd need his assistance to regain entry but the door way looked as it always had except for several bright, splintery scars on the doorposts where a hammer had clawed out the planks and nails.

Not knowing what I might find within I paid off my porter. He left laconically wishing me joy of my return and saying there was no place like home he always said.

I peered again at the substance oozing out from my lodgings. It certainly looked like blood; thick, stale gut blood. I took out my old key and inserted it in the lock. It wouldn't turn. I fiddled, eased it this way, that way. Had I lost the knack? Had it rusted? No, the key when I withdrew it bore a trace of oil. Finally I had to admit what I already knew: the lock had been changed. If I wished to gain entry – did I? – my bravado was somewhat diminished – then I would have to put my shoulder to the door.

I did. Once, twice, thrice. But apart from jarring my shoulder I couldn't budge it. But my thudding against the door had aroused certain sounds. Urgent squeakings and scrabblings as of mice – or rats. I shuddered at the thought – I'm no hero when it comes to such creatures – but nevertheless put my shoulder to it a fourth time. And fell into a world of rotting onions and scurrying vermin.

My lodgings had become a pickling house. And a neglected one at that. What furnishings I'd had (and my books, God help me!) were gone and in their place were sacks of onions all decaying. Beside them stood two barrels of vinegar and boxes full of empty jars. Whoever had established this enterprise had since abandoned it leaving a heap of peeled onions suppurating in a bowl. The stench was overpowering. I flung open the windows and by such daylight as was left I saw the source of what I'd thought was blood and which I'd trod in. It stemmed from the lower sacks which had collapsed under the weight of the onions above them and turned to pulp. They must have been packed while wet or drenched with rain on their way here.

But who could have done this. Meg perhaps? Given the use of my lodgings by Charley Cockatrice? It seemed likely. He might have offered her this stock of onions extorted from those market men who owed him money. Many did. Or else he'd had them stolen in a storm. Had she imagined she might scratch a living by pickling them? Poor Meg.

But whatever the explanation I was still enraged and at once proceeded to hurl the offending merchandise out into the street. I flung everything I could from the windows. The dusk rained onions. The jars shattered on the cobbles. I heaved the barrels out, too. They burst on impact and the sharp scent of spewed vinegar was a blessed antidote to the sickly stench of rotten onion. Is there a worse smell in the world? It clogs up your nostrils, turns your stomach and soils your throat. It's a stench as viscous as the pulpy ooze it comes from.

As I worked like a madman to clear the place a voice said, 'Looks like we've got a ripe one 'ere, mate, dunnit?'

I turned fast. To see two men in the doorway. With the porter behind them. The two men were soberly dressed – you might've mistaken them for church wardens except for their knives. Small, neat knives – not much longer than an oyster knife – such as all true cockney villains favour: the neat emblems of serious malefaction. They're know as chivs or chivvies.

I said, 'Who sent you? Charley Cockatrice?'

'Nah. We was passin'. But he won't like it.' Grin. 'Yer chucking his stuff aht into the street.' Another thin grin meaning he meant it. Meanly.

Recking nothing I said, 'Then go and tell him.'

For reply they laughed out of anticipated pleasure – these lads love their work – and advanced towards me. 'We'll tell him after – all right?'

I told them to be gone if they valued their lives but my grand boast held little conviction. What a fool I'd been to return to the Cockatrice's den. Would I never learn what was good for me? I drew my sword and our mismatch began. To say I was lucky is to understate. I didn't deserve to win. But by sheer luck my first wild stroke confounded their cat-footed expertise. The furious slash of my sword in the half-light caught my immediate opponent across his voluble gullet.

He stopped in absolute disbelief, rocking on his feet that were now stuck like mine in the onion juice. It was as comical as it was deadly. That putridity, it seemed, had for an instant given me equality with two human torpedos. I thanked my stars. But then as that one fell his companion was upon me. A wild animal far quicker than I. No vegetable ooze could hold this weaving, ducking, feinting alley cat – his little knife ever upward, pointed at my groin, my heart, my throat, my eye. A wild animal, did I say? An alley cat? Well, yes. But better description still: street viper, half my age.

I still don't know how I escaped that knife. I only thank God I did. Here was self defence in earnest. With a pickled onion for my ultimate saviour. My foot – within our desperate contest – knocked over a jar I thought was empty. It wasn't. It spilt out spiced vinegar and fragrant onions across the general rot. And my adversary, striking upward at my throat stepped on one of these peeled onions, one so round, so hard, so like a schoolboy's marble that he missed not just his footing but all his sinuous composure. To say I was upon him in the instant would not be true, however. In violent reality we all need time to comprehend the violence done – either by ourselves or by others set against us. No, rather I gazed at him while he fell backwards hitting the base of his skull on the edge of a box. The shock bemused him. He shook his head. He tried to scramble to his feet but now I'd not only seen but recognised my chance. I lunged straight at him. He ducked. My sword skewered him through the cheek. My dagger struck his belly. I couldn't believe it. I almost laughed. I had him twice transfixed. His knife fell from his hand in sheer surprise. I wrenched out both blades. He stared blank-eyed at me then stepped towards the door in a jigging parody of his former nimbleness. I let him go. And heard him cry out as he stumbled on the stairs. There was a thudding followed by a manifold silence.

Somehow I got myself away from there, shouldering my trunk for myself. I would employ no more porters. Evidently the last one had sold the news of my return to my opponents. And now having killed them I would be the more marked. Not by the Cockatrice alone but by the city sheriffs, too. I would be safer on Bankside within the Liberty of the Clink. Who knew – perhaps Dolly Delilah might provide me with a pair of bully boys of my own? But first I would need Philip Henslowe's help. At Queen Hythe I crossed over, trying not to think of my old lodgings and the shambles they'd become.

Henslowe let me stay in his whorehouse. It had been closed now for almost the whole of the year. Its once-bright sign of two rabbits dancing was peeled and faded. Inside the place was musty but I was welcome to make myself at home there at no charge, he said. Philip Henslowe is frequently maligned (many call him money-grubbing) but to me he was yet again kindly even generous.

But is there anywhere more melancholy than an empty brothel? The very fabric of the place seemed imbued with lust's regrets. Scut House (as it was locally known) breathed a wordless sadness. The public rooms had a kind of cushioned amplitude but the private chambers above were mere cubicles – wooden stalls for human livestock. The first night I spent there a wind got up and the entire edifice creaked and groaned as if rocked by the couplings of a thousand desperate ghosts.

Staying there alone filled me with foreboding. I seemed to lose all resolve. I did nothing. Repeatedly I told myself such lassitude was dangerous. Did I not know everything? What stood between me and my revenge? Do it! Execute it! Search out Frizer and somehow destroy him! Then Baines! Why hesitate? They – beyond dispute – were my two Ishmaels. So hunt them down or stoop like an eagle from heaven upon them.

So I urged myself. And still I made no move. Except to write to Lycia telling her everything that had passed since sending

Bridget to her. Three days later I got her post-haste reply. She admonished me roundly, soundly. I knew what I must do, she said. And her advice was my advice. So do it. But not only did she confirm what I should do but told me how to do it. And sent the means for it, too. Yes, Lycia's messenger brought more money. Fifty marks no less to take me in princely style to the Queen's tournament upon Accession Day. Walsingham would attend with Frizer. And Dick too. Lycia would look for me there. At Windsor. God speed me. Post scriptum: the girl Bridget was a sweet thing and she had written to Bobby telling him he was a fool to turn me out.

·X·X·I·I·

Ten days later I rode out to Windsor taking with me Dolly Delilah's most experienced bodyguard – a tiny Irish cut-throat known only as Squire Bantam. He wore my livery (newly invented) and we both rode the best hired horses his mistress could provide. And mine pay for.

Windsor was jam-packed. The decision to hold the Tilts there rather than at Whitehall together with the already established increase in the town's population thanks to London's pestilence ensured there was not a room to be had unless you were Eliza's guest at the castle. Or could afford to set up your own pavilion in her park.

I and my squire (I felt like some daft Spanish grandee riding out to reclaim the world) were obliged to put up outside the town in a straggling, pelting village without even a beerhouse to its name. But the cottage room we hired was just about clean, the fleas were honest enough and at least the milk was fresh even if the bread wasn't. Squire Bantam however remained unimpressed by such country conveniences. Had he not told me as we rode out from Southwark he regarded anywhere beyond the sound of St Saviour's bell as not worth (I quote him) a Sligo tory's turd?

The next day we joined the crowds flocking to the great lawn below the castle where the tilt yard was set up in imitation of that at Whitehall. A square of closely mown grass was flanked on three sides with tiers of benches placed upon scaffolding. The fourth side was left open to allow entrance for Eliza and her household. Her canopied throne stood by itself before the barrier.

Hedged about by wire screens to protect her from splintered lances – and other more purposed attempts against her person and her life. Nevertheless she had the closest view of her combatants while those courtiers privileged to sit immediately behind her could see, thanks to throne, canopy and screens, hardly anything. It was better to be less favoured and so occupy one of the enclosures for the common sort which stood at the four corners of this purposeful chivalric cockpit.

The meadows beyond were dotted with the pavilions and tents of the tilters. Here their mounts stood to be groomed to glossy perfection before being caparisoned as richly as their riders. One great shire horse was being transformed – by pasteboard garniture into an elephant. Another into a hippopotamus. While alongside stood decorated chariots awaiting their noble occupants. I discovered the Sussex pavilion but saw no sign of Bobby Spend-All nor of Lycia. I admired the Earl of Cumberland's fashioned in the form of a canvas castle. And even Walsingham, I learned, had been entered in the list.

The standing enclosures were already full and most of the tiered benches taken. England was hastening to this mock battlefield as to a theatre. The which, in some sense, it was. For tilting has its etiquettes, its pretensions to significance, its desire to please the highest and impress the lowest just as the playhouses have. To do it also costs the earth. Our nobility, ever in quest of monopolies and preferment, annually bankrupt themselves to flatter Eliza: to wear her glove on an armoured bicep; to present themselves as heroes or penitents or monsters to amuse her; to outvie each other not only at the Tilt itself but in knightly show beforehand.

And so it was, yet again, at Windsor, for this the thirty-fourth tournament of our blessed demi-virgin's reign. At precisely noon when all were gathered a fanfare resounded from the castle startling a flight of royal swans off the river and into the sun-bright November air. It is of course received wisdom that wherever the Queen goes great Sol accompanies her to do her homage. Some wags insist he shines out at her arse but this I cannot, alas, confirm. But certainly He shone that day. Next as the trumpeting continued we turned as one to behold our mighty monarch's approach.

She came in this order: first a vanguard of expendable baronets, new-made knights and lesser bishops (such as would be dubbed cannon-fodder were this a true field of battle), then those dukes, marquesses, earls and viscounts who by reason of age or infirmity or plain horse-sense were not to be tilting that day, all richly dressed and carrying their caps under their left arm. After these marched a company of the Queen's arquebusiers (renowned for their sharp shooting) followed by the Knights of the Garter, some armoured for the Tilt, but not Henry Percy whom I suddenly spotted among them – he looked studiously out of place but was accoutred less carelessly than when I'd last encountered him at Scadbury. Behind this noble order came John Cantuar himself, then the Lord High Chancellor carrying the royal seals in a velvet purse and flanked by two Gentlemen of the Wardrobe, one bearing the sceptre, the other Eliza's naked sword of state. An innovation this. She used to show it sheathed. The blade flashed in the November sun.

Then came the Queen herself. Borne along in what I can only describe as an ornamental wheelbarrow. Though this wasn't immediately apparent. At first you would have been forgiven for believing Our Supreme Goddess was carried aloft in a bejewelled litter upon the upholstered shoulders of four of her current favourites – one of whom I noted with bilious disquiet was none other than Heneage. But a closer look revealed two liveried grooms shoving hard from behind while upholding the handles of this royal pushcart upon which both the litter and its majestical occupant rested. Its wheels were concealed by a black valance. The four nobles merely carried the featherweight, fluttery canopy. By such artifice two sweating men of no account did the work of four of great account who needed only to pretend to a light but loyal perspiration.

Now at last – well, this last at least – I arrive at Eliza's person. To this sixty-year-old she who embodies – or so we are advised from every Sunday pulpit – all that's best within us and among us. Who is England now and always. Whose wisdom is infinite, whose breath is sweet despite the blackness of her rotted teeth, whose youth is – by decree – eternal. Her learning's beyond compare, too. She speaks fourteen foreign tongues – it's rumoured she can even say 'enjoy your meal' in Anthropophagus. She is also, naturally, routinely, a profound theologian, subtle politician, rigorous mathematician, inspired lutenist, fearless huntress, mellifluous soprano with perfect pitch and platonic mistress of all the world.

Her visage is an unwrinkled mask. Of porcelain, it appears. It is said her *maquillage* each morning takes three hours and is supervised by Mr Hilliard himself. Her bare breasts plumped up by whalebone from below are invariably netted by jewelled filigree as befits a virgin and a prince. Had she any hair to speak of it would be dyed red and she could wear it flowing to her maiden shoulders if she chose. But as she is almost bald she sports any number of ingenious wigs instead, dressed in any number of ways for every occasion. They come complete with various crowns and circlets, brooches and pretty veilings. For that day she wore a thrice-tiered pyramid of false hair and tiaras which in form and stature appeared, oddly, I thought, to emulate, even imitate, her detested rival's triple crown. Some say we become our enemies and that is why we hate them. Has Eliza turned a mirror-Pope? Not in faith but in pride?

Her dress left me speechless. As it was meant to do. Here was the commonwealth cut up. And made into a quilt of taffeta roses all of purest white edged with pearls and centred by rubies. From head to foot, from cuff to shoulder, she was covered in artificial roses. And drenched in real rosewater, too. The innocent perfume enveloped her, belied her, drifting out from her triumphal wheelbarrow to tease the nostrils of her cheering subjects. Her ruffs and cuffs were diamond sunbursts upon golden gossamer while the diaphanous canopy above her head (a four-cornered ark of stretched silk also bedecked with taffeta roses) was finialed with shivering ostrich plumes whiter than the driven snow.

After Her Majesty came a host of her ladies-in-waiting, some thirty or so. And among them Lycia. My heart jumped. How magnificent my lady looked. Older than those beside her, and so composed of expression, so dark-eyed, many would account her as I did a sibyl. She wore densely jewelled black. She jetted jet. I watched her in awe and love. She passed on without seeing me. But behind her was Lady Audrey. My heart did nothing. I simply stared. Her eye caught mine. I held it. She looked away with a quick turn of her head. She was gone and I was glad.

Next in the cavalcade marched a band of the royal Halberdiers who as the Queen reached the tilting square suddenly blared out a triumphal fanfare bright with trumpets and dark with drums. At this the whole multitude rose to cheer Eliza to the heavens. It was as though the earth had quaked to emit thunder from below. And then, so well-managed are these occasions of our state, at this general shout, upon the wave of this provoked acclaim for our precious tyrant, her knights appeared. What a procession they made!

At their head rode Cumberland, the Queen's perennial champion, in his customary role as the Knight of Pendragon Castle. All our nobility aspire to the Arthurian ideal, of course. Inside every money-grubbing lordling there's a Sir Galahad itching to get out. Pendragon's motto: *Hasta quando* – cryptic Latin meaning 'I'll wield my spear for my Queen until the sun, moon and earth are in eclipse', was as extravagantly accoutred as ever. His black armour blazed golden suns, his blue surcoat rivalled heaven, the Queen's glove was in his hat. For some reason, never explained, he was accompanied by a bevy of sailor lads who, stripped to the waist, tumbled and somersaulted all about him in a dazzling display of irrelevant gymnastics. They got an enormous cheer.

Cumberland with his jolly boys was followed by all that is finest, fittest – and richest among Britain's best. Every gentle jack of them parading and pretending, as in a masque, to be other than they really were. All mounted, all disguised, all armoured from gorget to greave (every suit built at Greenwich fattens the royal purse) and all bearing their shields ablaze with loyal emblems to present to their one and only lady.

Almost at once I spotted Sussex. Mind you he was far from inconspicuous. Fully armed in silver-gilt he was nevertheless bareheaded. He carried his golden helmet proudly as his saddle bow. As well he might. It was worth displaying – a stupendous feat of craftmanship had created a yellow metal plume some two feet high studded with topaz and amethyst and backed by peacock feathers. His motto alarmed me. It read for all to see: *Amando Fidando Troppo Sam Rovinato.* Which is as much as to say 'Ruin awaits those who are too faithful and too loving.' Was he reflecting upon his armourer's bill or was this a warning to those who served him? Suddenly I was glad to be no friend of Lycia's brother.

Next I saw Walsingham. He was presenting himself as an Unknown Gentleman in hope of a Knighthood, which, I felt, was fitting. My feelings towards him remained divided. I couldn't say I liked him but he had loved Christofer enough to try to save him from Heneage – probably at some risk to himself. On the other hand he employed Frizer but had failed, it seemed, to have noticed his secretary's other loyalty. Or had he? And protected him nonetheless? Walsingham would be weak enough for that, I reckoned. But even as he passed I dismissed him from my mind. He was welcome to his little world. And his mistress.

The Earl of Essex was, of course, quite unmistakable. As vulgar as ever. What a swaggerer that man is! Give him a paunch and a red nose and he would be a pot-house hero, a tap-room captain. His armour even outdid Sussex and he, like Cumberland, wore the Queen's glove – but on his sleeve. Some say they're lovers. I doubt it. Both she and he adore themselves so much that like magnets come together they would surely serve only to repel each other?

Rather to my amaze the Earl of Southampton now appeared. I'd never thought of him at the Tilts. He came as a Melancholy Knight made lunatic by love, I think. Certainly he kept rolling his eyes about and his armour was most artistically rusty. He seemed to have forgotten to put on shoes and his motto read: *Amo Ergo Sum* which hardly needs translation, I daresay. Southampton it was who stole the heart of our company's most promising apprentice: that deceptively mild young man from Stratford. A clever actor looking older than his years and thus able to play anyone. Very good at rustics of various kinds and excellent as befuddled aldermen. He even played the ghost in my Hamlet but got so many laughs we had to recast him as the gadfly gentleman at the end. He sincerely admired Christofer. And wrote rather well in imitation of him. The last I heard he was found dead of the plague. If that proves true (I pray it doesn't) then we shall have lost a useful actor and a promising poet.

But now Eliza had reached her throne whereupon once seated in glory and in gracious receipt of her knights' homage – every single one of them upon his knee with her ladies, her household and soldiery in their turn deployed upon either side – then the trumpets rang out again and the crowds cheered anew. So brave, so beautiful was the sight before me and such was the concerted force of this enthusiasm all about me that I found I was on my feet and cheering, too. Me! Cheering Eliza! Me! Tom Kyd – Top's man! Cripple, malcontent, sometime poet! I had hurled my hat into the air along with a thousand others to dance in the breeze with the banners and the flags. What *had* possessed me? And – fool that I was – I was flooded with a sudden happiness, glad with an absurd sense of a burden gone – thrown away with my hat (I never saw it again), joyous to have cast off suspicion and fear, contempt and anger, and relieved, oh, so blessedly relieved to forego my mad lust for revenge, and suddenly, like a simpleton, simply cheer my Queen. Shout myself hoarse for Eliza, England and my very soul. Yes, my soul cried out: Oh Gloriana, great Justicer, protect us all, your loyal children! And if we err then chastise us, oh, chastise for the greater good of you, your lords and commons! Of us all, of – oh, this brave new world – this England! Only your hand can safely steer our ship of state! Hurrah, hurrah, hurrah! God save the Queen!

Then I saw Frizer. As in my nightmare so in broad day his eye caught mine and he grinned. He was stood below me looking back and up at me, his head turned. My basilisk! And yes, I was made stone in mid-cheer. All my ridiculous bliss was gone. Hot truth returned. Hate drenched me. And I must have clasped Squire Bantam's shoulder with more strength than I thought I possessed because he cried out in protest. Even so I was already pushing my way out of this terrace of humanity, shoving and barging without apology, oblivious to honest outrage so hellbent was I to reach this subordinate Ishmael, Dick Baines's hired knife.

As I descended so unceremoniously I saw Frizer move away. Not from cowardice – of that I was sure – but out of circumspection and for advantage. To draw me to a convenient place where his superior strength could overcome me without others' interference. Some private place where he could dispose of me as cruelly as he had Christofer, as he had Martin, as he had Skeres. Was he my quarry or was I his? No matter. I had no choice. I must kill this assassin or die in the attempt.

There was a tug at my sleeve and I realised Squire Bantam had kept close. He said, 'Is he your man, sir?' Bantam having lived in Bear Lane all his life sounded more Irish than the Irish. I assured him I would never mistake Ingram Frizer. 'Would he be leading us on?' he enquired.

I almost laughed. I said, 'Of course.'

'And will he be having his pals join him?'

'I doubt it. He thinks himself the equal of many men.'

'So I see, sir. A most arrogant sprog. It'll be a pleasure to save his throat the cost of another drink.'

He grinned. I didn't. My tiny squire evidently had more confidence than me. Frizer meanwhile had walked rapidly towards a string of tents close to the river. We followed as eagerly as he hoped we would. The world of chivalry, of compliment, of proffered allegiance to a prince as supposedly honourable as those knights who flattered her, was left behind. Echoes of it, of cheers, of trumpets and brave speeches, came to us on the wind. But now beyond the tiltyard and the pavilions that serviced its elaborate artifice there was a muddy bank greased by geese and six wind-pollarded aspens weeping gold into the river. Here Frizer stopped to face us. I noticed his torn ear lobe with satisfaction at another question answered.

Frizer said, 'Mr Kyd – I was advised to expect you.' His sense of theatre appeared well-developed if banal.

'I'm sure you were.' So Ferdinando had betrayed me to Baines who'd warned Frizer. 'I daresay your master ordered you to keep watch for me?'

'You mean Mr Walsingham?'

'No, I don't mean Walsingham. Nor Heneage. No.' Did he blink? I couldn't tell. A minor shiver might have ruffled his oiled surface but that was all. And was it my imagination too that he looked older than when I'd known him only as Francis? Was the gristle of him sterner while the prauncer had dwindled – at least a little?

'Who then?' he said.

'Dick Baines, I suggest. Am I right?'

For answer he drew both sword and dagger – faster than I thought possible. Fortunately for me Squire Bantam's response was as swift. The knife in his hand left it before my weapons were even drawn. It found its mark in Frizer's neck, immediately above the neat ruff and below his Adam's apple. His eyes blinked with the shock, his mouth opened but no sound came, his dagger fell from his hand and he clasped his throat, sinking to his knees.

Bantam said, 'We may go, sir. He won't survive that.'

But Bantam didn't know Frizer in his entirety. Frizer wrested the knife from his throat and hurled it straight at me. It hit me in the chest. I stepped back believing myself wounded. But then as quickly realised the knife had fallen to the ground – was at my feet – and the blow I'd felt had come not from its point but from the hilt. Exultation filled me. I was Fortune's heir at last.

I strode forward. Frizer struggled to his feet. For the first time I saw doubt in his eyes. He raised his sword but there was no strength in his arm, nor in his legs. He teetered like a drunk. I swept his sword aside and was about to strike him when he slipped on the greasy bank, fell sideways and then, gurgling most dreadfully he half-crawled, half-slid towards the water like a giant slug trailing vermilion slime.

I let him go. Bantam joined me to observe his end. Frizer launched himself into the water as if he hoped to become a pantomime shark again or a sporting swimmer teasing Walsingham's latest guests. He floated out into the river, kicking fiercely with his heels but not using his arms at all – just as he had done in the May masque. But now the victim was himself and the water's redness was supplied by him not by paint powder.

I can't pretend pity stirred in me. It didn't. I watched Frizer with an absolute indifference. His kicking became feebler. Soon it stopped. Then he turned over on his back and floated briefly like a dead fish – a human pike. He tried to raise an arm but whether in defiance or as a last ironic salute I couldn't say. After that he floated away.

Bantam said, 'God rest his soul.' I didn't. Nor do I wish I had. I wanted nothing less than damnation for Christofer's murderer the more especially if my nightmare at Deptford had held a mirror to the truth. With this thought I suddenly regretted I had let him go. Why hadn't I held the man at my mercy? Surely I could've forced him to confirm what he had done in every particular? I cursed myself even as Frizer's body was lost.

But there it was. Or rather wasn't. I'd missed my chance and Frizer was gone. And I was alive.

I said, 'I owe you my life, Squire Bantam.'

'Think nothing of it, sir.'

'Oh, I shall. Nor shall I forget. But for you I should've been quite outmatched.'

'Oh, I wouldn't say that.'

'I would. But I confess that when you said it would be a pleasure to spare him the price of another drink – well, forgive me, but I didn't believe you.'

'You're among many, sir. Most look at me and say what harm can there be in that manikin? Which suits me, I can tell you.'

'I've never seen a knife thrown like that before.'

'Have you not, sir? Well, if you lack the size you must make do with art. But I can tell you, sir, when I had a wife I'd stand her up against a door and throw my knives to stick close about her until I had etched her shapely shape in steel so that when she walked away without a hair out of place folk gasped to see it and me not a one for bragging, sir, I swear it.'

I laughed. 'Well, I'm eternally grateful to you, Squire Bantam. And to Dolly Delilah for recommending you to be my bodyguard. I shall tell her you fulfilled your duties impeccably.'

I had no stomach for any further spectacle that day and so, to

Bantam's disappointment, I proposed we made our return to London then and there. I had no means of discovering if Baines was at the Tilts and even if he was I doubted I would find him in such a gathering. Frizer had been ordered to keep watch for me as the crowd assembled and then do with me as he chose but now with everyone in place to look for Baines would be like scanning a cliff face full of nesting seagulls to find one particular bird.

As Squire Bantam pleaded for us to stay a little – did I not relish the sight of our lords and masters knocking each other's expensive blocks off for everything but the honour of it? – I noticed a manservant approach. He wore the Sussex livery. He removed his cap and enquired if I was not Mr Thomas Kyd? For a second I wondered whether it was wise to acknowledge myself since the new earl had made only too plain – and too recently – his absolute distrust of me. My reserve prompted him to say that he had come to me on behalf of Lady Lycia who wished to speak to me. I was astonished. Having seen her in attendance on the Queen I'd assumed it would be impossible to meet her face to face. I certainly could not have approached her. Nor had I expected her to seek me out. I asked him where should I attend her? For reply he turned on his heel inviting us to follow him.

He led us to a silk pavilion rich with carpet and comfort. I was asked to leave Squire Bantam outside before being conducted within. As my eyes grew used to the dimness I saw first Lycia and then Lady Audrey. At the sight of Lycia I melted, at the sight of Audrey I froze.

Lycia said, 'Lady Audrey has asked me to arrange this interview, Tom, while Mr Walsingham is busy at the barriers.'

I gathered myself together and kissed their hands as politely as I could. Lycia invited me to sit. I obeyed. To look from Lycia to Audrey was to experience real pain. To see the genuine and the false so juxtaposed, seated thus side by side, as if one was the equal of the other – how could Lycia bear to do it?

But Lycia interrupted my speculation. She said, 'Lady Audrey wished to explain certain matters to you, my dear. She prays that you will hear her. Will you?'

'Of course, And all the more especially since you wish it, madam.'

'Then I shall leave you together.'

'Oh, no!' exclaimed Lady Audrey. 'Please stay, Lycia. I want you to hear it, too.'

Lycia nodded and stayed. I looked from her to Audrey, who looked down at her lap.

She said, 'I sent Nick Skeres to kill you, Tom. And it's been on my conscience ever since. Can you forgive me? Can you? Will you?'

I said, 'Easily. Since he didn't succeed.' She sobbed and hung her head. I continued, hardly recognising my voice – or rather the levelness of its tone. 'You were jealous, I daresay?' She nodded. 'Never mind that I was a cripple? More dead than alive? And that much of my condition was due to Nick himself – since he helped steal the papers that brought me to torture and disgrace?'

'I only wished to say how sorry I was, Tom. And that the minute I sent him I regretted it. So much so I confessed what I'd done to Walsingham. I had to. I couldn't live with myself. And he sent Mr Francis down to Sussex to prevent Nick from doing what I'd ordered him to do.'

I nodded. 'And he did. I found Nick's body. His throat was cut from ear to ear. But not, mind you, before he'd tried to shoot me dead. I was saved by pure chance. A buzzing fly preserved my life – the life you wanted ended.'

'I didn't! Please! I changed my mind, Tom! Haven't I said? Please forgive me, please.'

'I have already. For what that's worth.'

'Why are you so hard? You used not to be so hard!'

'Ask yourself, Audrey. And by the way. I've just killed Master Francis as you call him. Or rather my companion did – for me. He's floating downriver even now.'

'You've killed Francis?'

'His real name was Frizer. He was also in the service of the Queen. Oh, *and* the Pope as well. A handy-dandy sort of henchman. A man for all treasons. He killed Christofer, too. And a tiny boy called Martin – my lady's cowman's son.'

'Is this true?' she gasped at Lycia. Lycia nodded. 'Oh, God, why didn't Walsingham tell me?'

'It may be he didn't know quite all of it. Or if he did, concealed it. I doubt it even matters now.'

'He was terribly sad at Christofer's death. But now he says he's shut it out of his mind. He says we must think afresh, forget the past, and I agree, I want to, too, and that's why I begged Lycia to arrange this meeting, Tom. And I'm glad you can forgive me even if you don't sound as though you do.' And again she burst into a storm of weeping.

Lycia said, 'Try to be kinder – can't you?'

'Get rid of her. I've seen enough of her,' I answered, not caring if Audrey heard me which she didn't so busy was she with her own grief.

To my considerable surprise Lycia rose obediently, said something gentle to Lady Audrey who smiled tearfully and allowed herself to be drawn meekly from the pavilion, even curtsying to me as she went.

When Lycia returned she kissed me on the mouth and said, 'Oh, my dear, how glad I am to see you, how very glad. You look older.'

'So did Ingram Frizer.'

'How are your hands?'

'Serviceable. Look.' I held out my hands to show her. 'But I'm not sure I could've beaten Frizer by myself. As it was I wasn't tested thanks to Squire Bantam.'

And I told her of Bantam's wicked expertise with a knife and Frizer's death.

'You'd best be gone from here, Tom,' she said. 'Audrey will be bound to tell Walsingham and he may call for you and your squire's arrest for murder of his secretary.'

I agreed regretfully. I said, 'It seems I'm doomed to be apart from you, madam?'

'No, my dear. You may return to me soon.'

'Despite your brother?'

'Yes. Since our father died I've inherited the house in Sussex while losing my apartments in London. But Bobby has no jurisdiction over anyone I entertain in Sussex. We can both say boo to that particular goose.' She laughed. 'Or should I say gander?'

'When shall I return?'

'At Christmas, I suggest. But first – '

I stopped her mouth with a kiss. And when we were done I said, 'Tell me of Mary.'

'Mary wishes to marry, Tom. To make herself respectable. She's found a decent man, a widower, who'll accept her and your child. Though I've told her I will take the child if she agrees to be wet nurse.'

'You don't sound so certain as before?'

'No, I'm not. You made me see how cruel I would be if I seized your baby from Mary against her will.' Tears stood in her eyes. 'Oh, Tom, if I could conceive I would demand you serve me here and now. I wouldn't care how crudely.'

We embraced again. I kissed her eyes. And promised to come to her at Christmas. 'And now – what of Bridget?'

She laughed. 'That child! Oh, Tom! What a transformation! From a frightened mouse to a trusting squirrel in a fortnight. I like her more each day. But I'm jealous of her.'

'I told her you could never be jealous.'

'Then you don't know me, Tom.'

'I do! You're far too wise for such pettiness. Just because poor Bridget was forced to – '

'Oh, I don't mean your lying with her. That was a sad nothing. I mean your caring for her. It's love one is jealous of. Not jigging in bed. When Bridget speaks of you her eyes shine. Her whole being glows. She becomes softer, rounder even. That's why I'm jealous.'

'Rounder? She's a stick.'

'She's gaining weight like a baby. You won't recognise her.' She laughed and hugged me. 'But I shall keep my eye on you and Bridget at Christmas. Oh, yes. I don't trust you, Thomas. Not with women. Not now I know you.'

'I love Bridget most paternally.'

'You won't when you see her again. Of that I'm sure. Besides didn't you tell me in your letter how you had to fight against your desires that night at Deptford? Just before your dream? That terrible dream? Oh, my Tom, if that vision was true then Frizer deserved to die not just three times over but many, many more. But now, now you must go. Yes. At once. We can't have you arrested here. Besides you've got your final Ishmael to find. Your final revenge to make. Your final release to enjoy. And when you come to me, oh, Tom, my dearest, what sport we'll make.' Again we embraced but this time as our kiss broke off she said, 'You'll find him at my brother's house. At Sussex Place.'

'Dick's there?'

'Yes, I thought he would be here but he declined, I heard. He's busy brokering several business ventures for Bobby. Ferdinando Stanley's theatre company among them, by the way.'

'I'm sure. Do you ever see Dick now?'

'Never! I told you what he did.'

'He's still banished from your presence – as I am from your brother's?'

'Yes. And he always will be. But you must, must go, Tom. I don't want you to but you must. And you must ride straightaway to the Strand. Catch Dick there while Bobby's here. We stay tonight at the castle. So go and God bless you, keep you and bring you to me at Christmas.'

She returned another kiss and then almost pushed me out of the tent. I left rejoicing at my reunion with her, on fire to do her bidding.

·X·X·I·I·I·

In this spirit of knightly endeavour I rode back to London to confront my last enemy. But when I got to Sussex Place my squire's enquiry for Baines was met with outright denial. He wasn't there. He had left an hour before. No, his destination was quite unknown nor had he said if or when he would return, good night.

It was already dusk. And I was at a stop. Had we been belied? It was likely enough but reason told me otherwise. After all, hadn't I sent in Squire Bantam on my behalf precisely because I was the one person certain to be refused the truth? Whereas he would most likely to be told it? As for Lycia's assurance that Baines would be there, well, even she could not prevent a chance departure, could she?

Bantam was of the opposite opinion however. And suggested we withdraw to a quiet corner where we could observe both the main gate and the alley that ran beside the house down to the river. Reluctantly I agreed. We found a noissome but shadowed spot, where half-hidden by a massive brick buttress, we kept watch.

As we waited lights appeared within the house and cressets and lanterns were lit without. A mist from the river crept up the alley and seeped around us, staining the cobbles with an oily wetness. An hour passed. I grew impatient but my squire admonished me, telling me that in such a mallarky as this, sir, it was of the essence to cultivate the patience of the blessed martyrs. Despite the dampness, the chill and the stink around us I had to smile.

Bantam breathed the wisdom of the city's streets. I'd always thought I had, too. In fact I'd prided myself on my Cockney canniness. But compared with him I was a maladroit amateur. Bantam was the shrewdest, daintiest villain I had ever met and I was profoundly glad he was for me not against me.

And then, some twenty minutes later, our patience or rather his, was rewarded.

A side gate in the alley opened and out rode a bulky figure on a big-boned silver roan. Bantam nudged me in trimph. The shadowy rider came up the alley and turned to his right going eastward down the Strand to Temple Bar. We followed at once. He heard our horses and looked back. Torches before a tavern's door confirmed my quarry's identity. Without thinking I called out his name. For answer Baines kicked his horse to a trot. Bantam cursed me. We too broke into a trot. I apologised for so stupidly announcing our presence. Bantam was unassuaged. He'd got no fancy for a three-horse race on greasy cobbles, he said, teeth-gritted. Our pace increased. Baines looked back again. This time I did not call out. His pace increased.

Once beyond the Bar Baines kicked his roan to a canter. Once again Bantam cursed. But we cantered after. Thanks to me and aided by the eastward incline of Fleet Street down to Ludgate, our progress was become a race. Just as Bantam feared. What's more our horses' hooves struck unevenly, sparking sometimes on cobbles, clogged sometimes by refuse. The danger of a fall increased but now my blood was up and I cared no more for Bantam's complaints nor my own neck. I called out to Baines again. He broke into a gallop. So did I. And as I rode I shouted over and over, 'Ishmael! Ishmael!'

I had, I suppose, gone a little mad. Bantam was left behind. Baines was urging his horse through Ludgate's lately rebuilt arch, its new paint and gilding emblazoned by twelve massive cressets burning like bonfires in the misted air, and I was after him. His roan hit Ludgate Hill at the gallop and so did I. Baines's horse was strong. Only as we came up to Paul's churchyard did his pace slacken but then so did mine. I almost laughed at the equine irony of it. Both hunter and hunted were at the mercy of their innocent mounts. But as the hill levelled out Baines turned right into an alley going down towards St Andrew's by the river.

I followed. The alley led to small court hemmed about by tenements, mostly derelict or boarded up. Baines was nowhere to be seen. But his horse was. It stood, unhitched, blown, glad to stand.

A dozen unbarred doorways, rotting stairs, dark passages invited my choice. But would Baines take refuge in a tenement? I thought not. He might lose himself on foot in such a slum but only to shake me off and reach somewhere else. Had he already doubled back towards Whitefriars and the safety of Ferdinando's house?

As I pondered this Bantam came up beside me. It needed no word from me to pronounce my dilemma. It was obvious at once. Bantam (may God bless him with increase) did not reproach me.

He said instead, 'What a shame it is a good horse can't talk. Or can he?'

And he hopped lightly down and walked across to Baines's silver roan. Gently he took the discarded reins and hitched them lightly to a horse ring set in the wall of the most substantial building in that shabby courtyard. It had a solid Italianate air. As he did so he murmured sweet Irish nothings to the roan, telling him what a fine, intelligent beast he was. And what a galloper. The best this side of the Curragh. The roan seemed to appreciate Bantam's blarney and even pricked his ears and turned his head to nod towards the doorway beside which he'd been tethered.

By coincidence at that moment a faint glow appeared at an upper window. No more than a single candle's worth set well back but enough to betray a presence within. Bantam returned to me.

'He's inside there, the good gelding says.'

'He told you so himself, did he?'

'Surely he did, sir. He has the softest mouth, the most velvet nostrils and they breathed volumes to me.'

I laughed and pointed up at the window. I said, 'Even as you communed with your informer that light appeared.'

'Didn't I say he was an eloquent animal? Shall I try the door, sir?'

'It'll be locked. Or else barred inside.'

'I'll take a look.'

Bantam examined the solid, nail-studded door with an expert's respect and announced cheerfully it was indeed both locked and barred. The lock, he said, he could deal with at once and did so, taking what looked like a barber-surgeon's wallet from inside his shirt. Out of it he selected a thin steel probe with a retractable hook at the end of it.

'You could do your crocheting with this, sir, if you had a mind. I've often darned my stockings with it.'

He bent to the lock, inserting the probe, turning it this way, then that, before gradually withdrawing it a fraction at a time before turning it again, and then again. After a minute or so a faint click followed by a sharper clunk was heard and Bantam pronounced the lock turned. He pushed gently at it and sure enough the door moved a little until it came up against the bar within.

Before I could ask what was next to be done Bantam had stepped back and was eyeing the heavy stone facade of the building. There were no windows on the ground floor. Or rather there had once been two from the look of it but both had long since been sealed with stone that matched the existent fabric. What was this place? It had the look of a bondhouse. The three windows on the upper floor were heavily barred but this did not deter Bantam. Rather he kicked off his boots to reveal stockings that had never ever, notwithstanding his previous boast, been darned. He asked me politely to guard his boots. I assured him I would – with my life if necessary.

Bantam scaled that facade as though he were an ape upon a rock face. He sprang from the mounting block by the main door to the sill of the first false window. Thence he scrambled to its pediment and then, finding toeholds where I could see none, he reached the true window above. Once upon that sill he paused for a while working intently at the window's catch. As it swung inwards he waved cheerfully to me. And proceeded to prove himself not only a monkey but also an eel. Whoever had measured that window's bars for their security had not accounted for my ingenious squire. Bantam was as malleable as a gipsy's boy. I swear he could even elongate his skull at will. Having insinuated himself between those bars he saluted me again and was gone into darkness.

I dismounted and took guard where I could watch both the door and that other window above me to the right. The candle glow stayed dim but steady. I waited a long time with my feet rooted to the cold ground while my mind raced: what kept Bantam? What was he seeing? Couldn't he find his way to the door to unbar it? Were there others there? Was he apprehended? Were they questioning him even now? Were they – ?

The door was opening. My self-questioning ceased. My squire stood grinning, beckoning to me. I came to him.

He whispered, 'There's all sorts here, sir. Bears and wolves and leopards and stripped cats the size of heifers. Not to mention fox and ermine, ocelot and sable – oh, superb sables, sir.'

I said, 'What are you babbling about?'

'His furs, sir, his furs! The place is stuffed full of 'em. There's a pelt for every kind of beast that ever was in here. And altogether worth the King of Spain's ransom, I'll be bound.'

So this was the building's purpose. To house Dick's wealth. His merchandise. The furs he bought in Muscovy.

Bantam said, 'He's packing.'

'Packing?'

'Two trunks. Looks like he's poised for flight, sir.'

'Then we must clip his wings.'

'A pleasure, sir. May I lead the way.'

'You may, Bantam. But this time I'd be grateful if you'd leave this matter's conclusion to me.'

'If you say so, sir. He's far more your match than that other fellow was at Windsor. You may not be too nimble on your feet, sir, but your man up there carries an awful lot of weight. Too much, I'd say. So with your knee and his belly I'd give you even odds, sir. But I'll stand by. Just in case, sir. Would that be right, sir?'

'Yes, it would. Thank you.'

'This way, sir. And may me and Holy Mary guard you.'

We entered a pitch-black world of softness. My feeling hands brushed against every kind of fur – deep pelts, short pelts – all hung up upon cables like so much washing. Sables smoothed my cheeks, ermine melted at my grasp, trim leopard tickled my nostrils. Claws and nails scraped the back of my hands and then, blundering through this obscurity, I found I'd run my head into an entire tiger's maw. Its great teeth combed my hair for me. If it hadn't been so dark I would've laughed. As it was I swore in alarm and my squire hushed me fiercely.

We reached the stairs. Bantam drew me to their left-hand side, hissing in my ear that they creaked less upon that quarter. Once again I thanked my stars for providing such a squire and forward scout. We crept upwards feeling and counting our way to the top. Typically Bantam had noted the number of them: thirteen.

Once upon the landing the candlelight spilling from the room to our right and tuneless whistling within it made our path clear and further stealth superfluous.

I charged forward hoping my tread sounded like the thud of doom in my Ishmael's ears. I flung the door open and confronted Dick's capacious backside bent over a travelling trunk. He'd been deaf to me. But without thought I at once took aim with my boot and kicked that mighty rump as hard as I could. At my back Bantam laughed in delight.

'Mother of God, sir, what a target!'

I laughed, too. In the instant I had turned my desperate revenge to farce. How Christofer would've relished the scene, its absurdity, its gross lack of grace.

Baines didn't. He sprawled like a harpooned whale across the open trunk, fighting for breath, fighting for mobility pushing and heaving himself up and round to face me.

I waited. Saying nothing. Eventually he got himself upright, still breathing stertoriously and tenderly fingering his coccyx.

He looked at me as if to say: how could you? Still I waited for him to speak first. I was damned if I would open this final interview.

'Oh, cherry-pie,' he said at last. 'You gave me quite a jolt.' His voice was as thickly honeyed as ever.

I said, 'I know the truth, Dick.'

He laughed. 'Then you're a lucky man, old son. Not many do. What truth?'

'Ferdinando's truth.'

'Really? I shouldn't believe everything you hear from him. His mind's not what it was, poor soul. It wanders rather.'

'It doesn't. His testimony agrees with other enquiries I've made.'

'Is that so? Mm. I did hear you'd been burrowing about somewhere.'

'Did you hire Charley Cockatrice to kill me?'

'Never heard of him.'

'Nor of Henry Cato?'

'No. Can't oblige. Sorry.'

I knew he was lying but I let the questions pass. I'd more important matters to uncover, 'Ferdinando tells me you truly cared for Christofer? I've also heard that you went down to Deptford to view his grave? Although you told me and Lady Lycia you were in Muscovy at the time.'

'Did I?'

'You don't deny you went to Deptford?'

He shrugged. 'Does it matter, dear heart?'

I felt my temper kindle. 'Yes, it does matter! It matters a lot to me! If not to you.'

'Why so?' His broad face was bland as butter, the eyes hard as nailheads.

His blunt question wrong-footed me. I stammered. 'Because – because it confirms what Ferdinando told me – I need to know, Dick – did you really care for Christofer?'

He laughed in my face. 'Oh, I see. Oh, dear, oh, dear. You're as bad as he is, Tom. Such sentimental sausages – the pair of you. Do sit down, old son. Why don't you? Please. This childish catechism is hardly helpful, is it? To either of us. Take a pew.'

For answer I drew my sword. Dick sighed. I brought the point of it to rest against his belly. He held my eye and then took the blade between fastidious finger and thumb and set it to one side. I felt Bantam tense beside me. My hackles rose, too.

'You sit. I'll stand,' I said.

'I'll need a cushion. That is if you have no objection?'

'Take one.'

He did and placed it on a chair before lowering himself into it with an expressive groan. 'Oh, my dear fellow – it's so good to see you again. I say that despite the bruise on my bottom. Not to mention a boil I had lanced yesterday – thank God you missed that or I should've been in real trouble.' Grunt. Shift. 'Now – shall I talk or will you? I ask because I don't for a moment doubt you've discovered many totally fascinating, possibly pertinent matters concerning me, your good self and your dear defunct friend. Indeed it's only fair to say I know damn well you have since I've made it my business to – well, how shall I say? – to monitor your various doings since your return to town.' Out-breath. Smile. Wink. 'So who's it to be, old fruit? You to reveal all or me? Mind you, with due respect, I would modestly suggest that anything you know I know but what I know you may not. If you understand me? But the choice is yours, of course. You hold all the cards, as it were.'

I decided to let him speak. Whether from weakness or maturity I can't say – but I didn't sheathe my sword.

He said, 'You're right, Tom, It did indeed harrow my soul to supply Christofer's death warrant. We'd been such close friends in France even if we had grown apart after. But there it is. Or rather was. I was in a cleft stick, I had no choice as Ferdy told you only last week, did he not?'

'You've discussed my interview with him?'

'Not especially. There was no need. I'd had it transcribed.'

I was nonplussed. 'Transcribed?'

He grinned. 'But of course, sweetheart, what would you expect? Knowing what I knew? That Ferdy wished to replace me with you? Besides that nasty little prayer box of his – so fetid, especially with him in it – is a positive echo chamber. All you need is a couple of shorthand clerks behind those screens and you're home and dry. The text of your reunion was on my desk here the very next day with a copy to Father Ignatius. I've got it somewhere if you'd like to cast an eye over it?'

I stared at him and then shook my head, partly in denial, partly in stupefaction at such offhand expertise. He and Bantam shared much professional common ground. Once again I was the amateur outsider.

I said, 'But not all of what I was told is to be believed?'

Dick shrugged. 'No. Or rather let's say Ferdy exaggerates. From time to time. For example, I don't bicker with Iggy. Why bother? We're on the same side. He gets his orders, too. However – yes – by and large Ferdy's version accords with certain realities. Though they're ancient history now. But to return to the meat of it. Yes, I was obliged to order Christofer's death – thanks to the Vatican it was him or me – and, as I say, it hurt, it really did. What a sweet boy he'd been, back in '86. So young, so eager. Like a puppy. I'd been sent to keep an eye on him, of course, at Rheims. Oddly enough I replaced a fellow of the same name as myself who'd made rather a mare's nest of his mission to poison the college's water supply. Funny old world but thus it goes.' He grinned then slipped the knife in. 'Christofer was a virgin then, of course.'

'But he rejected you? And you've nursed a hate for him ever since? And used me to destroy him?'

For the first time I saw a flicker of doubt, of fear even, in those steel-bright eyes.

'Quite the reverse, old son. I introduced him to any number of mysteries – physical, spiritual, political.'

Was he lying? How could I tell? And if I questioned him further wouldn't he just lie again? And again? Did he even know himself any longer what was true and what was not? And, as he said, did it really matter anymore if he'd seduced Christofer or Christofer (as I thought) had rejected him? Who cared if Dick had loved or hated Christofer? Did I? No. If I was honest I didn't. I'd gone beyond both. All I wanted was the bill of my suffering paid. The reckoning made. The cause of it – dead. Baines dead. My Ishmael dead.

I said, with a glance at Bantam, 'We killed Ingram Frizer this morning.'

Dick roared with delight. 'Excellent,' he said. 'Well done! Saved me the trouble. I tell you, Tom, I've been seriously exercised in my mind about that character. He'd become a real liability. Especially when we got him the Queen's pardon. Such a cocky sod. Where? Where did you dispose of him, may I ask?'

'At Windsor.'

'You're quite sure you made a proper job of it? Frizer's tremendously resourceful. And fearfully strong.'

'I've no doubt of it.'

'Let's hope posterity bears you out Thomas. So you've been at the tilts? Fun, were they? I usually go but this year I had rather more pressing concerns. As you can see I'm on the point of going abroad again. On behalf of Bob Devereux, no less.' He indicated the two trunks – one packed and locked, the other open and almost full. Mostly of documents. 'Business, of course. Lading bills, letters of credit, all the usual stuff. I sometimes say I don't deal in goods I deal in paper.' He laughed but with less conviction.

I said, 'Who removed the rolls from Chancery, Dick?'

'Haven't a notion, sweetheart. But Poley would've organised it. I warned him you were poking about, looking for trouble, advised him for the sake of the service to cover our tracks, muddy the waters etcetera. I daresay it was Poley hired those other people you mentioned – Charley Someone and Henry Who? He often farms out minor mischiefs.'

'Did you go to Deptford again?'

'Again?'

'Recently. To remove the coroner's report? The assistant clerk there described someone very like you, Dick. A gentleman from Whitehall, he said.'

'Ah, well, we have plenty of those, have we not? And some very like me, I daresay, but, no, no, dear heart, I haven't been near the place, no. Holds too many painful memories for me.'

Had his effrontery no limit? I said, 'Did you mean Christofer to be killed at Widow Bull's house?'

He laughed. 'Oh, no. Absolutely not. No, the whole thing was a pig's breakfast. The plan was to convince Christofer he was off the hook despite the evidence against him. Yours, dear boy, plus a few choice additions from me. For reasons of state we were giving him chance to skip bail. Just as his pal Walsingham had intended. That's why Bob Poley ordered supper. To add conviction to our story – Christofer must have a decent meal before setting sail blah-blah. But, here's the rub, just as it was time to go, your clever friend smelt a rat. Saw through our plan. Refused to budge. Kicked up an awful row. Well, what could our fellows do but do it, there and then? Instead of – as planned – in some nameless alley at the back of the docks? So, a mess, a cock-up. Entailing endless fuss with constables, the coroner, the sexton, the parson, not to mention fixing up an official pardon for Frizer – not easy believe you me. And all the while yours truly under a most tremendous cloud. Heneage enquiring here, there and everywhere. However that's all nightsoil under the bridge, is it not?'

'No,' I said. 'It isn't. How did Christofer die? Did they tell you?'

'Oh, yes. I had a full report from both sides of the fence, as it were. Yes. Frizer struck him through the right eye. He died at once. Textbook stuff. He didn't suffer apparently.'

So that part of my dreaming was true. I said. 'Frizer didn't do anything else to him?'

'Sorry, sausage, I don't follow? Any what else?'

I told Dick of my dream at Deptford; of how Frizer had mutilated Christofer and mocked him, obscenely.

Dick shrugged. He said, 'Know nothing of that, old son. If you ask me you must've dreamt that up for yourself. Pulled it out from your own guilty conscience possibly?' Big grin. 'How much do you want?'

The same old Dick. The babble followed by the key point. I let the room grow still. And asked him to repeat his question. He said it again, adding that he was prepared to put up a substantial sum, in return for my withdrawal from the premises, or if I preferred, our safe conduct of him with his trunks to Billing's Gate where a boat for Italy awaited him.

'You're off to Rome?'

'Home at last,' he replied.

I said, 'I'm here to kill you, Dick.'

'I know. Five thousand marks suit you? Instead?'

Bantam whistled through his teeth at hearing such a sum. I said, 'You consider your life's worth that, Dick?'

He grinned and doubled it. 'Ten thousand, dear boy.' This time Bantam was lost for expression of any kind at all. I too said nothing. 'Fifteen?' Silence. 'With the stock here thrown in? The furs down below must be worth almost as much again. This is wealth beyond avarice, Tom. What do you say? Make you equal with the highest in the land. With Lady Lycia even.'

His eyes probed mine, seeking weakness in me. But as I returned his gaze I saw Christofer dying as in my dream. True or not, no money in the world could pay for that nightmare. I said, 'You're life's not worth a brass farthing Dick.'

At that moment Bantam cocked his head, muttered something and left the room. As I drew my dagger to join my sword Dick rose carefully from the chair, seizing the cushion in one hand. He had no other weapon.

He said, 'You wouldn't kill a defenceless man, Tom, would you? Not you – a poet?'

I answered I would and I did. I struck him clean through the stomach with my sword and straight to the heart with my dagger. He looked at me in dismay, with an infinite reproach. His mouth moved.

He said, 'Oh, dear. Who put you up to this, sweetheart? Not Pandora, I hope?'

And with that he fell forward crying like a child mumbling disjointed misery out of which I picked such words as 'please' and 'unfair' and 'why' and 'me' and 'pity'.

I watched Dick Baines die – the blood in me as cold as the steel I'd killed him with.

But then I heard Bantam calling urgently to me to snuff the

candle and as I pinched it out I became aware of torches in the courtyard below. And the horror dawned. This was why Baines had indulged me so, insisted upon sitting and explaining. What a fool I was! Of course! He'd been playing for time. And now that help he'd sent for had arrived. Too late for him but not too late to decimate me. And Bantam.

I rushed for the stairs colliding with my squire on the landing.

He said, 'There's three of 'em, sir. One's leading off our horses now. D'you hear?' I listened and heard the innocent clip-clop of freedom departing. 'There's no other way out from here – just the front door. And they know it. They're waiting there!'

'Do we rush at them?'

'Yes and no, sir. With your permission I'll go first.'

'Please do,' I said, without any irony at all.

'We keep close. Then when we're ready, I'll touch your arm. Out I go – with you following after in the instant.'

We crept creaklessly down the stairs and, as we descended, became aware of torchlight from the open doorway filtering in along the hanging skins. We kept to the left-hand, shadowed side feeling our way through furred darkness. When we neared the door Bantam stopped. We took breath. Then he touched my arm, I froze as bidden, and he sprang out.

But who was this? What had Bantam become? A whirling dervish? A bear's pelt flew about his head like an absurd, thick flag that got hurled to one side even as he parried a swordthrust from his right. I charged through to find my squire engaged with someone unknown to me (how many nameless killers can Eliza command?) while the other man flung off the great bear's skin he'd been enveloped by to reveal himself as Poley. He lunged at me, I lunged back. Bob Poley lost his footing and fell. I ran. I wanted no more revenge. I was full of it and sick of it. Behind me came footsteps. I hobbled faster, found an alley that twisted down the hill. I took it, hopping, skipping, hoping. I slipped, stumbled sideways. Someone was upon me. I tried to rise. Felt suddenly too tired. Fell back, not caring who it might be. It was Bantam, helping me to my feet, dusting me down like a fallen child, assuring me that all was well. Both men had fled.

But we must hurry. Only then did I feel the blood seeping from my side.

In the limbo days that followed I had more than enough time to dwell upon Dick's last words to me. They had discomforted me quite as much as the wound in my side. How had Baines come to know my private name for Lycia? That name she'd laughed at when I'd confessed it to her? How had he known of Pandora? I shrank from accepting the only explanation. That my lady had told him. Because if that were so – I hated to think it – then Lycia had lied to me when she said she'd cast off Dick Baines for ever.

That thought and its inevitable concomitants tormented me as I lay on my narrow bed in Scut House loyally tended by Bantam and visited daily by Dolly Delilah. Even Henslowe called in from time to time. Poley's thrust had been deep but not of itself fatal. He'd skewered the muscle above my left hip but missed any vital parts. The wound however festered, refused to heal cleanly and I was feverish for days that became weeks until at last Dolly brought in a barber who was, she assured me, a dab-hand abortionist for her girls. This backstreet adept cauterised my wound with a kill or cure brutality that left me agonised, then senseless despite the brandy I'd swallowed beforehand and the belt I'd had to bite on during his proceeding. But once conscious I realised I was saved. The fever evaporated within a week and after another my appetite returned and shortly after that I was able to sit up in bed, then try out my wobbly legs, and finally contemplate a future once again.

I wrote to Lycia explaining my strange victory over Ishmael but I made no mention of Dick Baines's knowledge of my covert name for her. That, I'd decided, would have to wait until I stood before her face to face, hand to hand, lip to lip. I regretted I was still too feeble to travel to Sussex for Christmas but I hoped to be there for Epiphany.

Her replies were kind and loving. She, too, was impatient to see me but knew I would set out just as soon as I was able.

Meanwhile I should know I was her dearest knight, her champion without equal, and I must look forward to a hero's welcome. Epiphany would be not only the Feast of the Kings but also her feast of *her* king! Had I not achieved what she'd always wanted, my release from shame and doubt?

From shame, perhaps. But from doubt? I wasn't sure. Pandora? Pandora? Why, why had Baines said it? Not without purpose – of that I was certain. He'd intended to sow a fertile suspicion. And he'd succeeded. Already it had grown in the darkness of my mind: how could, why should my Lycia lie to me? Why?

But as my health returned I told myself I'd been guilty of an invalid's exaggerated fancies. I put them from me and refreshed my brain by making active preparations for my journey. I planned to set out on New Year's day – a new year, a new life.

Henslowe called on Christmas Eve to inform me the plague ban was lifted and the Rose could re-open. As would Scut House. Ned Alleyn and the company had returned, though now, as he had long suspected, their patron was to be the new earl of Sussex – Bobby Spend-All. Did I know him? I didn't answer that. But Henslowe didn't notice. He went straight on saying I was welcome to attend the opening play – or any other come to that – free of charge, of course. On the twenty seventh. That was the date set. The opening play was going to be none other than the one I'd been working on when – but here he checked himself and dared to say I wouldn't want to go over that old ground again, would I?

I agreed I wouldn't but thanked him for his kind offer. The truth was, I said, that I no longer had much appetite for the theatre. He nodded judiciously as if I had suddenly become as mature as him.

Workmen moved into Scut House to refurbish it. The first snow fell. By my chosen date of departure I was not only well enough to go but also glad to, such was the noise of the builders and decorators Henslowe was employing to work through the holiday season for double their usual money.

Bantam declared himself heartbroken at my going but when I suggested he come with me he declined, invoking his detestation of everything rustic. I promised to enquire for him whenever I returned to London. But I knew in my bones I never would return. I also told him I owed him my life twice if not three times over but when I tried to reward him he turned the tables on me by producing one of Baines's trunks. He'd been back for it that same night, he said, and had won himself part of that fortune Baines had offered me. Would I care to share it with him? There was plenty of it? Was I fool to say no? Perhaps. But I did.

At Billing's Gate I took a merchant coaster bound first for Faversham, then Hastings and Shoreham Harbour which was a morning's ride from my destination.

As we slid down the Thames (I averted my eyes from Deptford) the snow began to fall in earnest. Soon we moved as in a white and grey cocoon. There was no sense of progress at all until we reached Faversham. Setting out from there still the snow fell and again we seemed not to be sailing anywhere until we put in at Hastings. It was the oddest sensation. Like a dream you can't quite savour even as you dream it.

But as we approached Shoreham the snow ceased, the sky began to clear, light returned and with it life and movement. I'd woken from that winter dream.

I left my baggage at the Blue Anchor and hired a horse to carry me home.

By the time I reached the house the first stars were shining in a frost bright sky and there were lights at every window. As I rode nearer I could hear laughter, chatter and the sound of several lutes and mandolins. I saw people moving within. My heart seemed to open like a rose and forgetting all doubt I rode to the door, feeling like the king Lycia had told me I was.

As I swung down from my horse the steward came to welcome me most warmly. He ushered me in and the first person I saw I scarcely recognised. I stopped in mid-step as she recognised me.

She cried out, 'Oh, it's you! You!' And she ran into my arms. Bridget, new-made, shining with delight, plump as a turtle dove.

I said, 'Oh, Bridget, you're quite changed.'

'No I'm not,' she said. 'I'm the same as I was before you knew me – only better.' I laughed, she laughed, we hugged each other again and again. Finally she said, 'And now I shall take you to your lady. To Lady Lycia. She can't wait to see you, Tom.'

And seizing my hand she led me through to the great hall.

·E·P·I·L·O·G·U·S·

It is said the truth makes us free. It doesn't. I told Tom the truth and the truth has imprisoned me. I wish I'd lied but at the time I believed he of all men deserved the truth. But why couldn't he accept me as I was? Imperfect, human? And forgive me? Instead of making me his idol only to hurl me to the ground? Leaving me smashed to smithereens?

His return was joyful. We lived in bliss for weeks. But as the Feast of Annunciation drew near a melancholy seemed to creep into his bosom and dwell there. He took to spending too much time alone. He even finished his translation of *Cornèlie* but only I think to avoid me. I questioned my favourite waiting lady, Bridget, who was as a daughter to him, but she swore she knew nothing. Like a fool I trusted her.

One morning when he awoke beside me but did not reach out his hand to caress my breast or belly I turned to him and asked him what the matter was. He regarded me for a long time before he answered. When he spoke he called me not his Lycia but Pandora, his former, unfitting name for me. Puzzled I asked him why? Why had he called me that? Pandora was forgotten, surely? He said no and that I knew why he'd named me thus. I didn't. I said, explain, please explain. I wish I hadn't. For then it was I learned how Dick had poisoned Tom against me with his latest breath.

Hurt beyond hurt by this betrayal I tried to cure the wound with the absolute truth. I admitted to Tom I had written three times to Dick after I'd cast him off but only in Tom's necessary defence. Not because I wished to. Dick had kept urging me to persuade Tom to return to Lord Strange's service and had even hinted that if I didn't he might make public my private opinions of Eliza. To hold Dick off and to allay his suspicions of my intentions I'd painted a false picture of Tom so he should have no idea of the true recovery he was making. I had written that my pet poet was still an invalid, frail, full of odd fancies, such as naming me Pandora. That, I told him, was how Dick had come to know that name, as part of a cloak for the dagger truth that Tom was become my present lover and my future avenger.

On hearing this confession Tom rose from my bed and standing stark before me reviled me most dreadfully. He accused me of exploiting him witchlike for my own purposes. I didn't deny it. For it was in some sense true. I had wished to punish Dick. But I did say I'd served his turn, too, hadn't I? He replied that I must have known Baines was his Ishmael all along? I said I'd suspected he was but had not known for certain. Did I deny I'd used him as my private instrument? I didn't. But again protested I'd done it for his sake, too. His, his, his and only then mine. Couldn't he forgive me? His answer was he'd been doubly deceived, doubly abused, was no one in the world straight-dealing, trustworthy, honest, pure? I said I was or at least I tried to be. That I had never deceived him save by that omission. I begged him to forgive me.

He wouldn't listen. He went from my room, my house, my life. I lay abed the entire morning, weeping. When in the end I called for Bridget to help me dress I was informed she had departed, too.

I don't know where they've gone. Some days I wish I knew, some days I don't. Half of me longs for a letter, half of me dreads one. I live in fearful hope. Which is no life at all. I have only myself to blame. But meanwhile I wish Tom well and Bridget, too. At least I think I do. I pray I do. I want to be generous, forgiving. Oh, God, grant I may be. Let them both fare well in this deceiving world.